Praise for Neil Lancaster:

'One of my favourite reads of the year'
Matt Nixson, *Daily Express*

'The best police procedural I've read in years'
Jane Casey

'Grabbed me from the first page'
Ian Rankin

'Great storytelling with a whiplash
smart hero and heroine'
Daily Mail

'Absolutely blown away by how good this is'
Marion Todd

'A cracking good story'
Gytha Lodge

'The strongest start to a series I've seen in years'
Tony Kent

Praise for Neil Lancaster:

'This is a page-turner you won't want to miss!'
Denzil Meyrick

'A thriller writer set to blow up the bestseller lists'
C. L. Taylor

'Rock hard cop stuff, from a writer who's done it for real. Absolutely terrific'
Paul Finch

'The best police procedural money can buy'
Imran Mahmood

'If you like *Line of Duty*, you must snap this up'
Cass Green

'A genuinely thrilling adventure'
Scottish Sun

'A powerful and gripping story … DS Max Craigie is a fantastic creation'
Howard Linskey

Neil Lancaster is the No.1 digital bestselling author of both the Tom Novak and Max Craigie series. His latest novel, *Dead Man's Grave*, was longlisted for the 2021 William McIlvanney Prize for Best Scottish Crime Book of the Year. He served as a military policeman and worked for the Metropolitan Police as a detective, investigating serious crimes in the capital and beyond. As a covert policing specialist, he used a variety of tactics to obtain evidence against murderers, human traffickers, drug dealers and fraudsters.

He now lives in the Scottish Highlands, writes crime and thriller novels and works as a broadcaster and commentator on true crime documentaries. He is a key expert on two Sky Crime TV series, *Meet, Marry, Murder* and *Made for Murder.*

@neillancaster66

@NeilLancasterCrime

www.neillancastercrime.co.uk

Also by Neil Lancaster

The Max Craigie Novels
Dead Man's Grave

The Tom Novak Novels
Going Dark
Going Rogue
Going Back

NEIL LANCASTER

THE BLOOD TIDE

ONE PLACE. MANY STORIES

This novel is entirely a work of fiction. The names, characters and incidents portrayed in it are the work of the author's imagination. Any resemblance to actual persons, living or dead, events or localities is entirely coincidental.

HQ
An imprint of HarperCollins*Publishers* Ltd
1 London Bridge Street
London SE1 9GF

www.harpercollins.co.uk

HarperCollins*Publishers*
1st Floor, Watermarque Building, Ringsend Road
Dublin 4, Ireland

This edition 2022

1
First published in Great Britain by
HQ, an imprint of HarperCollins*Publishers* Ltd 2022

ISBN: 9780008518462 (HB)
ISBN: 9780008527747 (TPB)

MIX
Paper from
responsible sources
FSC™ C007454

This book is produced from independently certified FSC™ paper to ensure responsible forest management.

For more information visit: www.harpercollins.co.uk/green

This book is set in 10.7/15.5 pt. Sabon by Type-it AS, Trondheim

Printed and Bound in the UK using 100% Renewable Electricity at CPI Group (UK) Ltd, Croydon, CR0 4YY

For my boys.
Alec, Richard and Ollie.
I'm so proud of you all.

1

THE RIB CHUGGED steadily, its engine low, as it nosed into Loch Torridon. The slack tide and absence of tricky currents allowed the boat to cut soundlessly through the water towards the small beach by the road. Jimmy McLeish had left his Toyota pick-up parked there, trailer still attached, as he often did when he went out fishing or picking up his creels. It wouldn't cause any comment or curiosity, so he should have been relaxed. He was anything but relaxed, though, because this cargo wasn't the usual fish or lobster. This was a whole different ballgame.

The night was dark and moonless, with the inky darkness that you get only in the Highlands, far away from light pollution. If it hadn't been for Jimmy's night vision goggles, he would never have been able to navigate his way in past the rocks. Lights tonight would be a mistake, however, because of what lay in a black bag between his feet. The night was his ally.

Jimmy scanned the scene before him, the ghostly green tinge from the goggles bathing the landscape in an unnatural glow. A few specks of light were visible to the west, where a handful of dwellings dotted the tiny clachans of Fasag and Torridon, but beyond that there was just deep, impenetrable blackness. This was his neighbourhood. This wild, beautiful coastline was his home.

He took a deep breath and edged the small craft towards the shore of the sea loch, aiming for the tiny single-track road that ran parallel with the edge of the frigid water. He scanned the shore and let out a sigh of relief when he saw the shape of his pick-up truck, a silhouette against the craggy rock that bordered the road. Another vehicle was parked right behind it, as expected. Three brief flashes of a torch indicated he was good to go. That was the agreed signal, so Macca, Scally's right-hand man, was there waiting for him. Jimmy gently increased the engine power, and the small rib picked up speed towards the truck.

His task was childishly simple, so he really shouldn't have been this nervous. He reached into his jacket and pulled out his battered hip-flask. His hands shook as he unscrewed the cap and took a hefty nip of the peaty whisky, enjoying the warmth as it slid down his throat.

The torch flashed again, three times, as he killed the engine and nosed the boat to the shore, close enough to his launch trailer. There was a soft bump as the rib came to a halt on the stony sand and he flipped up the goggles on their harness. The sudden silence was absolute. He looked at the shore but saw nothing in the blackness. There was no one there.

He waited, nestling his goggles down to scan the area, the scenery once again bathed in the soft green light. The beads of sweat on his forehead made the rubber eyepiece feel greasy and slick. He had seen the flashes from the shore, he was certain of it, so where the hell was Macca? He jumped off the small boat into the shallows and pulled the rib ashore, feeling the gravelly surface grip the keel. He quickly jammed a stake into the ground and lashed a line to it.

He looked again at the new vehicle, which was as dark and foreboding as the landscape surrounding them. As he adjusted the intensifying properties of the goggles, hoping to see something, the landscape gradually lightened. His eyes followed the loch's shore towards Torridon, where his wife would be sitting at home in front of the fire. More than ever, he regretted the blazing row that they'd had before he left. As always it was about money, or the lack of it. He'd stormed out, giving her no indication of where he was going or what he was doing. He hoped that enough cash to pay the outstanding bills and maybe get a nice meal would soften her up. Part of him wished that he could be with her, right now, rather than here in the inky blackness, waiting for the distinctly intimidating Macca. Not for the first time, he wondered if he had made a terrible mistake.

Suddenly a blinding burst of torchlight shone directly on him, immediately overwhelming the image-intensifying properties of the goggles. He gasped and pulled them away from his face. Stars danced in front of his eyes from the sudden assault on his senses. He blinked rapidly, rubbed his eyes, but the flare remained.

When he opened them, he was once again flooded with bright light from a head torch worn by a huge man. This wasn't the short, stocky Macca.

'Jesus, you almost bloody blinded me,' Jimmy said. 'Who the hell are you? I was expecting Macca.'

'I'm Davie, and this is Callum. Scally sent us. You got the bag?' The man was tall and muscular, with a pale face and dark hair. His accent was pure Glasgow and there was something about it that Jimmy didn't like. The torchlight only partially lit the man's face giving it a ghostly, unpleasant quality. Jimmy's thoughts flashed briefly to the times his brother would scare him by holding a torch underneath his face. He felt a prickle of fear begin to grip at his gut. This didn't feel right.

'Aye, it's here. You got my money?'

'Of course we have, but we need to see the package first,' said Davie, with a smirk.

'But Scally said cash on delivery,' Jimmy said, his voice faltering, unsure where this was going.

'Cash on delivery? You hear this? Mannie here wants paying before we've even seen in the bag.'

The man called Callum stepped forward. He was a full head shorter than Davie and much slimmer, although it was hard to see him properly, the only light sources being Davie's head torch and what looked like a penlight in Callum's hand. 'Oh dear, my friend, is this your first time?' Callum said. 'Nobody gets paid before we check the bag, right? Do be a sport and pass it over then we need to get your rib out of the water, pronto. I know this is a little bit of a backwater, but the local constabulary may venture here. Come on, chop-chop.'

Callum had a surprisingly light, cultured accent that sounded like it came from southern England. Despite the man's light timbre, his voice was laced with sarcasm, and even by the flickering light, Jimmy could see the half-smile, his teeth shining white. The hairs on the back of Jimmy's neck began to prickle. They seemed to be seasoned professionals, but unlike any criminals Jimmy had encountered before. He suddenly felt very exposed.

'Aye well,' Jimmy said, 'give us a hand getting the rib hooked up, but we'll leave the bag where it is until we're out of the water.'

'Fair enough. Give Davie your keys and he'll reverse your truck.'

Jimmy tossed his keys at the big man who caught them and walked away up the beach.

Jimmy eased the wheeled launch ramp into the water and within a few minutes had the rib secured. Davie was soon reversing the pick-up, with trailer attached, onto the beach. Jimmy used the winch to pull the boat and launch trailer onto the back of the vehicle. He then spent a few moments securing the rib with straps, until it was tightly fastened and ready to go.

'Now, old bean. I believe you have something for us?' said Callum. 'Much as we trust you, we'd like to see it before we hand over your fee.'

Jimmy reached into the rib and dragged over the heavy waterproof canoe bag. He heaved it with a grunt onto the stony sand at the side of the truck. Davie quickly unbuckled the bag and reached inside. His head torch lit up the interior with a bright blaze of white light.

'Tiger stamped,' said Davie, a trace of pleasure in his voice.

'Capital. Sling it in the back of the truck then, Jimmy,' said Callum.

With a growing sense of unease, Jimmy did as he was asked, carefully securing the canoe bag, then hefted it onto his shoulder. Callum's torch illuminated the back of the truck. It was bathed in bright white light. Jimmy heaved the bag into the load-bed and it landed with a thump, but didn't lie flat.

'Shift it, man. It needs to be out of sight,' said Callum in an oddly simpering voice, which managed to combine insincerity and sarcasm in equal measure.

Jimmy suddenly felt cold. He swallowed, reached in and dragged the bag away from a long object that was stopping it from lying flat. The bright torch beam fell on a pale face. Jimmy let out a yelp. A dead body stared up at him with sightless eyes. There was a red-rimmed hole, deep and black, in the centre of its forehead. Even in Jimmy's blind panic, he recognised Macca, Scally's right-hand man. His heart raced and bile rose in his throat. He was about to be ripped off, or worse.

He turned to stare at Davie and Callum as terror thundered towards him like an express truck. They both gazed back, with unpleasant, yet amused looks on their faces. Davie stepped forward. The head torch beam flooded into Jimmy's eyes, blinding him.

2

THE MORNING SUN peered over the horizon and sent shafts of light across the sweeping Glasgow skyline. PC Hamish Beattie yawned as he drove his marked police car from what he hoped was the final call of the night. An argument in the street in Erskine between two drunken nightclubbers had been simple enough to sort out, a stiff word and an empty threat was all that was required to see both men staggering off home.

Being single crewed had its disadvantages, but he enjoyed working on his own, beholden to no one. Hamish's twenty-eight years of experience meant that he rarely needed to reach for his radio for backup, instead relying on his powers of persuasion to sort problems. He always thought that if he ended up in a roll-around with a prisoner, he had failed. Hamish wasn't big and he was certainly no fighter, but he was a good negotiator, a peacemaker and he hardly ever needed to go beyond his persuasive abilities.

After a long and frustrating night, racing from call to call, sorting out Glaswegian problems, Hamish couldn't wait to get home to his bed. He had four days off and he planned to start work on some DIY. He squinted into the low sun as he crossed onto Erskine Bridge, the modern two-lane structure that spanned the River Clyde. Light danced on the water's flat surface below. He flipped down the sun-visor with a yawn, as he drove along the smooth tarmac, hoping that there was nothing else to do back at Clydebank Police Station. His sergeant was a flyer, and even if he arrived ten minutes too early, he would come up with some bullshit task for him to do. 'Cleared your property record? Have you finished that misper report?' This was why Hamish always tried to arrive bang on end-of-shift time. A man of his service wasn't working for free, that was for sure.

Hamish blinked and rubbed his eyes. Unease began to rise in his gut. Something was wrong. He couldn't work it out at first, his sleep-deprived brain failing to interpret what he was seeing. A silhouette stood against the barriers to his nearside, next to the edge. This early on a Sunday morning, the bridge was usually devoid of pedestrians, but it wasn't abnormal to see people stopping to take in the view.

This, however, was not a pedestrian. He or she was on the wrong side of the barrier, perched on the ledge, both arms leaning back with nothing separating them from the drop below. Hamish let out an exasperated sigh, thoughts of cotton sheets and a cosy duvet disappearing fast.

A jumper. Another bloody jumper. It wouldn't be the first that Hamish had dealt with, and as sure as the sun rises in the east, it wouldn't be the last. Fifteen people had leaped to their deaths from the bridge last year, and many more had threatened to do so.

'Charlie seven nine, we've a jumper, wrong side of the barrier. Erskine Bridge, eastbound side of the carriageway. I'm going in to engage. Back up, please,' he said into the radio clipped to his chest.

'Charlie seven nine, all received. Units being despatched now.'

He pulled his car over to the side of the carriageway and put on the hazard lights and blue strobes. The man didn't turn to look at Hamish as he closed the door to his car and steadily climbed the crash-barrier onto the footway. He always found that a calm and collected approach worked best on folk like this.

'You okay, pal?' said Hamish, in a soft voice. He could now see the figure was a man, wearing a rumpled suit and scuffed shoes.

The man didn't speak but shifted slightly to look at Hamish. He shook his head, almost imperceptibly, before turning back to stare down at the glinting river below. It was a long way down, one hundred and twenty-five feet, Hamish recalled, from the last inquest he had attended for one of these. The man was quite young, perhaps early thirties, with neat hair and a slight build. Hamish reckoned if he could get close enough, he could drag him over the barrier, but first he had to get the man to acknowledge his presence.

'Pal, look at me again, yeah? I'm Hamish, and I want to help you. However bad shit is, this isn't the way. There'll be a better option.'

The man turned, fixing Hamish with eyes that were brimming with tears. His face was pasty-white and his mouth trembled. He was a picture of deep, unremitting fear. Not sadness, not depression. Just naked fear.

'You've no idea. I've no option,' he said in a light, almost cultured accent.

'There's always another option. Talk to me, yeah? What's your name?' said Hamish, advancing towards the man.

'Stay there, I'm going to jump, I promise you, I'm not bluffing. Just don't try and grab me,' said the man, his eyes wide.

'Whoa, I'm staying here, okay?' Hamish sat on the crash barrier, making himself as unthreatening as possible. 'What's your name?' he added, gently.

'Murdo Smith,' he said quietly, his eyes fixated on the water again, his voice soft, and full of sadness.

'Where're you from, Murdo?'

'West End,' he said, not looking at Hamish.

'On your own?' said Hamish, trying to turn the conversation to others. He had found in the past that suicidal people needed to be reminded of who they were potentially leaving behind.

'No. I'm married, with a wee boy,' he said, turning to look at Hamish, the tears brimming again, sorrow etched across his fine features.

'What's his name?' asked Hamish.

'Murdo as well, poor wee man. Daft family tradition landed him with a shite name.' He shook his head and cast his eyes downwards.

'There's another way, there always is. Wee Murdo needs you, so does your other half. You understand that, right?' Hamish said.

The faint wail of a siren reached them, splitting the silence. Murdo flinched, and a hunted look spread across his face.

Hamish reached for his radio, and whispered into the mic, 'All units, silent approach. Hold off until I call you in, or you'll send him over.' Bloody amateurs, he thought.

'It's nothing,' Hamish said, 'only cops going somewhere else. You're all good, pal, it's just me and you. Come on, come back over the barrier, you're making me nervous.'

Murdo turned again, hypnotised by the sparkling water below. 'You've no idea, no clue at all. It's because of my family I have to do this. If I don't, they'll never be safe, and I'd never live with myself if anything happened to them. He said that it would be better and that this would solve everything, but he lied. He bloody lied, and now there's no way back.' He shook as he spoke.

'Why is your family at risk? Mate, we can help you. Who is going to hurt your family?'

'You don't understand. I mean, how could you fucking understand? Cops can't help. Despite his educated posh-boy persona he's an evil bastard. He'd kill anyone if he felt it would advance his cause or protect him. He'd kill my family without a second thought. He even sent me a picture of the wee man in his school uniform.' He swallowed, choking back tears.

'We can protect you,' said Hamish, wondering if it was true.

Murdo laughed without mirth. 'This bastard owns the cops, the NCA and customs. I'm finished, but I can save my family by doing this. Just a fall and then it's all over, and they can be safe. I thought I could handle it, you know? But then he killed that poor mannie at Torridon. I've been such a bloody idiot. I've no choice.' His look of despair turned to one of determination, his jaw set tight and his eyes closing.

'No. Don't do it. There's another way. Talk to me, tell me about this guy. We are the cops, man, we can protect you.' Despite Hamish's intention to stay calm and reassuring, he felt panic rise in his chest. This bloke was going to do it, he was sure. He made a quick calculation in his head, but he wasn't close enough to rush and grab him. He'd be gone before he'd laid a hand on him, and no way he wanted that on his conscience.

'I'm sorry. I'm so sorry that you have to witness this.'

'No,' shouted Hamish, pushing himself forward, his arms reaching out to grab hold of the man.

He was too late.

Murdo extended his arms, crucifix style, and leaned forward, his body rigid. He swung out into the abyss like a felled tree. Hamish reached the railing a fraction too late, just as Murdo disappeared. He didn't look down. He had seen someone fall once before and didn't want to do so again. It was another memory he could live without.

Hamish returned to the barrier, his heart beating wildly, his breath ripped from him. He sat there for a moment, sadness washing over him.

He reached for his radio. 'Charlie seven nine, he's jumped. Can I have a supervisor, please?'

The radio exploded into life and the wail of sirens began again, drowning out the responses. Hamish thought of Murdo's family and everything left behind. His thoughts turned to that wee boy who would be growing up without his father. The hopelessness and fear in his face, his final words. Murdo had been terrified. But of what? Or, of who? And murder? A murder at Torridon? He'd need to write this up properly. There would be an inquest, and there would be questions.

It was suicide, that was clear. Murdo had jumped, but someone, somewhere, had scared him enough for suicide to be his only option.

To Hamish's mind, that made it murder.

3

HAMISH SAT IN the back of a police car, parked on the Erskine Bridge. The road was closed in both directions and the only other vehicles nearby were the CSI van, the duty inspector's car and an unmarked Astra, which had brought three investigators from the Police Investigations Review Commission. The suicide was being treated as a death during police contact, so everyone wanted a piece of it. Hamish wasn't nervous; he had done nothing wrong, as the CCTV on the bridge would prove. Still, the wheels of bureaucracy had to be allowed to turn.

His mind was whirling with shock, sadness and bone-wearying fatigue. He couldn't shake Murdo's expression just before he propelled himself from the ledge and into the void. There was something deeply troubling about it. A young man, with so much life ahead of him, and a family at home, being driven to throw himself from a bridge.

Hamish knew that this incident would join the many other terrible sights he had seen during his career, the legacy of which would inevitably return one day to haunt him. But not today. Today there was a job to do, and right now, it was giving a full explanation to the investigator from the commissioner's office, who was sitting next to him in the car, clipboard on his lap.

He was a middle-aged man, with grey hair, a lined face and a blue windcheater that bore the letters PIRC on the front and rear. The other two much younger investigators were self-importantly wandering around the bridge, trying to give the impression that they knew what they were doing.

'I'm Lenny Farquharson, the lead PIRC investigator. Now just so you know, pal, I'm ex-job myself, and no one's looking to criticise you or blame you in any way, okay?'

'Okay,' said Hamish, stifling a yawn. It wasn't a surprise that he was an ex-cop. Many PIRC investigators were, despite the assurances that things were changing and the drive to recruit and train investigators in-house. No one likes cops investigating cops, and the public didn't trust it.

'It's all on CCTV, and we can see that you never got near him, so no one can say anything negative, unless your last word was, "Jump".' The investigator smiled.

'I've made notes of his last words whilst I was waiting for everyone to arrive. He seemed shit scared of someone. Saying he had no choice and the like, how someone forced him to do it. Things like that.'

'Did you get his name?'

'Murdo Smith, said he was married with a kid and lived in West End,' said Hamish.

'Can I see your notebook?'

Hamish handed the small leather-bound notebook across to Lenny, who looked at it with a blank face, silently reading the notes.

'Okay, pal. You sure you're confident in the accuracy of these?'

'Pretty much,' said Hamish.

'Good to see someone recording things properly. So many don't, you know? Why don't I run you back to the station, you can make your statement, then get away? Probably best if I see it before you go off, mind, or the fiscal is bound to have questions.'

'That'd be great, especially as early turn have already pinched my car, but what about the body?'

'No sign of it yet. Coast guard and the Dive and Marine unit are out with a couple of our people and divers will be going down soon. It could take a while with the currents, so best get you home. No way he survived. You know that, right?'

'Aye, of course, I've dealt with a couple of these before. There were fifteen last year.'

'Tragic. Part of our job is to make recommendations, and more than once we've talked about barrier improvements, and the like.'

Hamish was surprised to feel the swell of emotion in his chest at the senseless loss of life. Death was familiar for all cops. Some hit home, others didn't. Hamish had a feeling that this one would fall into the former category.

Back at the station, Hamish spent an hour carefully typing up his witness statement, giving as much detail as he could. He knew from experience that doing this bit correctly now could make his life much easier when this hit the inquest. The fiscal was legendarily unforgiving of cops who didn't do their jobs properly.

His mind flashed back to the mention of a murder at Torridon. Could it be true, and what if it was? He'd heard nothing about it, but Murdo had sounded so convincing.

On impulse he logged into the incident records for Torridon. It was such a quiet area, where almost nothing ever happened, but he wanted to be sure. The only incident he could see was a missing person report. A local man called Jimmy McLeish had disappeared a few days ago. It had been classified as low risk only, as he often went away with no warning. But his car or boat hadn't been seen either, so it all seemed a little strange. The police hadn't even visited his wife yet, which didn't surprise Hamish, resources being what they were.

A wave of exhaustion washed over him, so he took a note of the incident number on a scrap of paper and logged off.

Once he was satisfied with his statement, he found Lenny in the front office, tapping away at a laptop. He looked up as Hamish entered the room. 'All done?'

'Aye. Do you want a signed copy now?'

'When are you back on duty?'

'Four days off.'

'Best let me check it first, need to get it right first time or the fiscal will go bloody mental. The Erskine Bridge is a damned nightmare, and this will get loads of attention. Can you log on here, in case there's any changes needed before you head off?'

Hamish sighed and logged onto the desktop terminal next to Lenny. He navigated to the statement, pushed his chair back from the desk and nodded to Lenny who balanced his spectacles on his nose and began to read.

'Looks fine to me,' he said after a moment. 'How sure are you about what Murdo said? It could become really important.'

'Pretty solid. Ninety per cent, I'd say.'

'Can you include a paragraph saying words to that effect?

Other than that, it looks good enough. Email it to me and get yourself away.'

'How about a signed copy?' Hamish looked at his watch, desperation for his bed beginning to bite hard.

Lenny sighed, and shook his head slightly. 'We normally insist on signed copies before we let you go.'

'Aye, I guess,' Hamish yawned.

Lenny's hard features softened a little. 'Look, get it sorted when you're back and then pop it in the post. My email address is on the card.' Lenny handed over a PIRC-branded business card.

'How about getting the copy to the inquiry team here?'

'Leave that with me, I'll be speaking to whoever's going to pick it up before I leave, anyway. I'll make sure they get one.'

'Great, thanks.' Hamish entered the email address from the card and there was a whoosh as the email was sent.

'No worries, I'm not so old that I don't remember what it's like being on night duty.'

'Appreciated,' Hamish yawned and looked at his watch. His eyebrows rose when he saw it was nearly 11 a.m. He should have been off duty four hours ago.

'One thing, have you copied your notebook? I'll need it for the report.'

'It's in my correspondence tray, I can get it and do it now,' he said, stifling a further yawn.

'Include it with the statement when you send the hard copy. It'll wait. You look knackered.'

'Thanks,' said Hamish, grateful not to have to mess about. He hesitated for a moment, his mind turning to the missing person report. 'One thing.' He paused.

'Aye?' said Lenny, looking up from his laptop.

'There was a missing person report a few days ago. Guy disappeared in Torridon. May be worth a look, after what Murdo said.'

'Aye, good point. I've already flagged it. Now get yourself away to your bed, pal.'

Hamish was soon in the locker room, his uniform stowed away in an orderly fashion, as was customary. A sudden feeling of sadness washed over him as he wondered if Murdo's wife had been told her husband was dead. Then Murdo's final words suddenly came back to Hamish in a flash. *This bastard owns the cops, the NCA and customs.*

Hamish had believed Murdo's despair. Something wasn't right. Who could scare a man so much that suicide was his only option? This wasn't a death borne out of depression. This came from sheer, unmitigated terror.

On impulse, Hamish reached for his phone and dialled. He knew someone who may have some insight here. He couldn't let Murdo's death pass without at least telling someone he trusted.

A soft Highland-accented voice answered, 'Max Craigie.'

'Max, it's Hamish.'

'Hamish, how you doing, pal?'

'I'm good, man, a bit knackered. You enjoy the sailing the other day?'

'It was fun, but I realise I've lots to learn. Need to do it again, but I'm assuming this isn't the reason for your call.'

'It's not, no. I'm just back from a suicide on the Erskine Bridge early this morning right at the end of my final night shift. I'm a bit worried about it. Are you on the road trip you said you were going on?'

'Aye, I'm just in my tent now at Gairloch, but I'm heading home today.'

Hamish let out a sigh and then paused for a heartbeat. 'There was something he said to me. You're in anti-corruption, right?'

'Aye, kind of,' said Max.

'Well, the guy, bloke called Murdo Smith, was telling me that he was being forced to jump to protect his family. Talked about being scared of someone, mentioned the NCA and customs, shit like that. He also said that someone had been killed up north at a loch.'

'Any reports of that?'

'Only thing I can find is a missing fisherman at Torridon. As you're in the area, may be worth a ride past. No one's spoken to his wife, yet – in fact, no one appears to have done bugger all on it, beyond classification.'

'Well, it's under an hour away, so I guess I could swing by. What are the details?'

'I can text you the log number. Sorry, I'm off the computer now.'

'It's fine, I'll get someone to dig them out. You okay, pal?'

'Aye, I'm good, but something about him made me believe it.'

'Okay, I'll have a poke about. Were PIRC there?'

'Yeah, bloke called Lenny was the lead investigator.'

'I'll have a wee nosy and see if there are any red flags. Have you written it all up?'

'Aye. All in my notebook and I did a statement, which the PIRC have.'

'Cool, what's your rota like for the next few days?' said Max.

'I'm off for four days, thank God.'

'Anything planned?'

'Loads of DIY. I'm laying a new deck. House needs sorting, ever since Jenny left,' said Hamish, trying to keep his voice even.

'You okay?'

'Ach, it's fine, my fault and that. I'm all right, internet dating will keep me busy.' He tried a laugh.

'Well, they say there's someone for everyone, Hamish, even an ugly bugger like you,' said Max.

'You always were a charmer. I may take the dinghy out in the next couple of days, if you fancy a wee sail on Bardowie?'

'I'd love to. Let me see how I'm fixed and I'll give you a shout,' said Max.

Hamish had a small sailing dinghy that he kept at a club just outside the city. They'd only been out on it a few days ago, and it had been fun.

'I'm not going far, give me a call.' Hamish stifled a yawn once more.

Max laughed. 'Go to bed, you sound knackered.'

Hamish hung up, feeling suddenly reassured. Max Craigie was one of the best. They had worked in the Met together, a long time ago, only for Max to eventually follow him north some years later. If there was anything untoward, he'd find it.

Hamish stretched extravagantly and scratched at his scalp. He shut his locker, and headed off, thoughts moving to his bed, even if it was an empty bed.

4

DS MAX CRAIGIE sat back and thought about the call. Hamish had sounded worried, and he wasn't generally one to overthink policing. On the dinghy a few days ago, he had been the absolute picture of calm, but clearly the suicide was concerning him. Max looked at his watch, realising it was probably time to get moving anyway. He'd promised Katie that he'd be home today after a couple of days on a steady route, tracing the north coast 500 on his motorcycle, a big KTM 1300cc Adventure. He'd been lucky with the weather so far, but the rain beating a tattoo on his small tent was a sign that things were about to change. The west coast had decided he'd had enough of the sun, and the more typical driving rain was about to make its presence felt.

He pulled on his Gore-Tex trousers and jacket, struggling to get the bulky kit on in the cramped space, but thankful that yesterday's stunning evening hadn't persuaded him to leave his kit hanging on the bike outside.

Max unzipped the tent and wind whipped across his face, carrying harsh rain straight off the Atlantic. He gazed across the rolling grassland and down to the sweeping Gairloch Beach and the choppy sea beyond.

Only a Highland scene could change so much in just a few hours. Yesterday the white sand and iridescent blue of the ocean could have been a tropical paradise, not the far north of Scotland. Now the slate-grey sea was speckled with foam and the wind sent white-topped waves crashing into the rocks below. Bruise-coloured clouds swirled closer by the second, full of rain and foreboding.

Max took a deep breath, narrowing his eyes against the wind and rain. He loved Scottish weather, however it arrived and in whatever form. As he looked out, he could just see the dark smudge of the Isle of Skye in the distance, a menacing shadow against the clouds.

It was going to be a howler of a day, that was for sure. Or was it? You could never really tell.

Max quickly packed away his sleeping bag and pop-up tent and stowed them in the panniers. He decided against boiling a kettle. Thankfully beyond a sleeping bag and his tent, everything was already secure in the weather-proof luggage on the bike. He'd stop later for breakfast.

He picked out his phone and dialled.

'Maxie-dude,' said DC Janie Calder.

Max sighed. 'Don't ever call me that.'

'I thought you were hitting the tourist trail? Blimey, it sounds windy there.'

'You at work?'

'Well, kind of. I'm at home on the laptop, researching that new thing Ross has a bee in his bonnet about.'

'Great, can you look up something for me? Suicide on the Erskine Bridge last night.'

There was a tapping in the background, and Max shifted

position to try to angle the phone away from the strengthening wind.

'Okay, I have the incident report up now. I can't see much, it's restricted. Seems PIRC are investigating owing to the presence of PC Hamish Beattie. Name of deceased is withheld at the moment, presumably until the next of kin is informed. Investigation is ongoing.'

'Is that it?'

'Aye. Not unusual, though, is it? It's pretty standard when it's a death in custody or during contact. Christ, it's blowing a hoolie there.'

'Fair enough. Can you also look up a misper report, somewhere near Torridon, in the last few days?'

'You know you're on leave, right?'

'I know, Hamish is a pal, though, and I said I'd take a look. He's a bit shook up.'

The keys tapped again. 'Aye, a couple of days ago, fisherman called Jimmy McLeish went missing. Him and his wife had a blazer of a row. He stormed out taking his pick-up and boat with him and she hasn't heard from him since. Seems like it's a tempestuous relationship and this isn't the first time he's pissed off. No one allocated and she's been advised to call back if he doesn't show.'

Max stared at the distant hills for a second. Rain churned up the water in the distance, a black wall of cloud thundering towards him across the sea. It wasn't unusual in cases like this for there to be a limited investigation, particularly in the far-flung and remote reaches of Scotland where manpower was stripped bare. Something didn't feel right, though. Storming out with his boat?

'Can you screenshot the relevant pages and send them over? I have my work phone with me.'

'Why am I not surprised? It's a wonder you don't have your laptop. You're job pissed, you are.'

'I prefer the term dedicated. Where does the wife live?'

'In Torridon, tiny wee place right next to the loch.'

'I'm leaving now, I'll get the details when I get there. It's pissing down here.'

'Typical west coast. Ride carefully.'

Max put his phone back in his pocket and zipped it up, squinting as the rain began to drive in, whipped into a frenzy by the westerly wind. He pulled his helmet and gloves on, climbed on the bike and pressed the ignition switch. The big engine roared as he rode off. He negotiated the tussocky grass towards the empty road, accelerating as he hit the smooth tarmac.

Forty-five minutes later he eased into the tiny clachan of Torridon, right on the edge of the huge expanse of the loch that gave the place its name. The rain had been replaced by brilliant sunshine that reflected off the water's surface. Max pulled over and checked his phone, finding the name and address that Janie had emailed him, and quickly scanning the misper report.

The place wasn't difficult to find as Janie had dropped a pin in a map and soon Max was pulling up outside a tiny, whitewashed cottage set back from the small road. He removed his helmet and surveyed the immaculate garden, the clean windows shining in the sunlight.

Max took a breath of the salty air and squinted at the

stunning scenery in front of the house. Max and Katie had explored this area not that long after she had joined him in Scotland. The loch stretched on for miles out to the sea beyond. Framed by the Torridon Hills, the Munros of Liathach, Beinn Alligin and Beinn Eighe, it was a landscape of extremes: beauty but also isolation.

Max dismounted his bike and walked up the path to the cottage, knocking on the door. It was opened by a bird-like woman of about forty, with a deep swathe of auburn hair, and an easy smile. There was no mistaking the worry that was etched on her face, however.

'Mrs McLeish?' said Max, smiling.

'Aye?'

He showed his warrant card. 'DS Max Craigie from Police Scotland. Can I take a moment of your time?'

'Of course, I was wondering when someone would turn up. Come inside or you'll be eaten alive, the midges are bad today,' she said, stepping back and opening the door wide.

Max stepped into the tidy cottage and followed her to a tiny kitchen, ducking as he crossed the threshold. A single earthenware mug lay on a scrubbed wooden table next to a plate with a half-eaten slice of toast on it. The place positively gleamed, as if every surface had been polished.

'Have I interrupted your breakfast?' asked Max.

'No, it's fine. I've no appetite, anyway. Can I make you some coffee?'

'Aye, that'd be grand, thank you,' said Max.

'Is there any news? I'm worried sick,' she said as she switched on an ancient-looking but spotless kettle and spooned fresh coffee into a cafetière.

'No, none. I was wondering if you could tell me exactly what happened, Mrs McLeish.'

'Please call me Leah. Well, there's not so much to tell. We've been having a few problems, like. Money, mostly. The fishing has been bad since Brexit, and there isn't the market for his catches, especially as the tourist season is drawing to a close. Well, it all came to a head a couple of days ago and we had a bad row. The rent is overdue, and we need oil for the heating. He just left in his truck with his rib hooked up to the trailer and didn't say where he was going. I've not seen him since.'

She poured boiling water onto the ground coffee, depressed the filter and then transferred dark, aromatic coffee into a thick, earthenware mug and handed it to Max.

'Lovely, thanks.' He took a sip. 'Great coffee. Anything unusual on the run-up to this?'

'No.' But she wouldn't meet his eye.

Max watched her face as she stared out of the window in silence. Her knuckles were white on the kitchen top. The only sound was the wind against the stone walls of the cottage.

'Leah?' Max said eventually.

She sighed, and tears brimmed beneath her blue eyes. She paused to wipe them away. 'He's got a bit odd recently.'

'How so?'

'Whispered phone calls that he thought I didn't know about, using a different phone. He has his usual Samsung, but he also has a shite Nokia. I thought it was an affair, which caused a big row, but I don't think it's that. He was also seen with a stranger.'

'A local?'

She shook her head, vehemently. 'Definitely not. This is

a small, close community. A friend saw him with a mannie in the Kinlochewe Hotel chatting in a corner. Our pal thought it looked dodgy, but you know what small communities are like.'

'Did they describe him?'

'Aye, stocky, shaven-headed bugger. Expensively dressed and definitely not a local.'

'How could they be so sure?'

'Because he had a Liverpool accent and a flash car outside. A Range Rover.'

Max paused to digest this for a moment.

'Has Jimmy ever been involved in anything illegal as far as you know?'

Leah let out a deep sigh. 'Jimmy is a good man. He's kind and hard-working, but when times are tough, he'll do what he has to in order to keep food on the table.'

'Such as?'

'I don't know. I honestly don't, but he's a local, and he knows these waters better than anyone ...' She didn't finish the sentence, but tears brimmed again.

'Anything you can tell me could help,' said Max.

'Once or twice in the past, he'd disappear for a few days with his rib, not saying why or where he'd been and then suddenly all our bills would get paid. I'd get a present and he'd be home with champagne and steak. I didn't ask how or why, and he didn't offer to explain.' The tears fell, and she reached for a tissue from a box on the side.

'What do you think he was doing? All we want to do is find him.'

'I don't know, but he's a man with a fast boat. He's got skills that people would want to use. I just paid the bloody bills with what he came home with, whether it was lobsters or something else. I didn't ask, and he didn't tell.' She paused and dabbed at her tears again. Max watched her, knowing that there was something else. He continued to look straight into her eyes, as a tense silence filled the room. Max remained impassive, showing no discomfort. She wanted to talk, he could tell. He leaned back in his chair, completely comfortable. Humans are social creatures, and silence is alien in a situation such as this. She'd break it first, he knew.

She looked away and rubbed her cheek. A classic tell.

'There was one thing.' She paused, as if considering what to say next.

Max held her gaze.

'I checked his phone once,' she said. 'The Nokia, I mean. He left it on his bedside table, popped out to collect some milk. There was just one message on there. He's lazy with pin codes and I knew it would just be all zeros.' She paused again.

'Go on,' Max said.

'I remember it, word for word. It was from someone called Macca. It just said, "Ten k for one trip, and there'll be plenty more after. But try and fuck us and shit will be bad for you."'

Max only stayed another fifteen minutes, and Leah McLeish really didn't have much more to offer beyond a general feeling of foreboding. There was certainly nothing with which to launch a murder inquiry.

Max climbed back on his motorcycle. He was about to put his helmet on when he paused and reached for his phone again. He dialled.

'Max?' Janie answered, her voice barely discernible against thumping, fast-paced music.

'What the hell's that noise?'

'Hold up,' she said, and the music stopped.

'That's shite, even for you. What is it?'

'Chase and Status.'

'Is that jazz?'

Janie laughed. 'It's drum and bass, Grandpa.'

'Whatever, I'm just away from Leah McLeish. Sounds like Jimmy was up to his ears in something.' Max told Janie about the contents of the text message.

'Right.'

'It's strange, but not enough to launch a murder inquiry. Is the incident log still restricted for the jumper?'

Max heard tapping keys. 'Yep. Still ongoing, recovery is underway, but no details of the deceased or anything significant. If PIRC are on scene, they'll want to get all relatives informed and won't derestrict it for a while yet. What's your plan?'

'Head home, I guess.'

'You in tomorrow?'

'Yes. How's Ross been?'

'Not as sweary and objectionable as usual, actually,' Janie said.

'That's a little concerning, what's happened?'

'No idea, but he was quite nice to me yesterday, made me a tea.'

'Must be something to do with his Mrs Right. I'll head home and start looking into this in the morning. Something feels wrong.'

'I don't like it when you say that. It normally means bad shit is going to happen.'

'It may be nothing. Speak tomorrow,' said Max, hanging up.

He sat on his bike, taking in the view, as ominous-looking clouds rolled in from the west, eating up the sky. It was going to be a wet four-hour journey back to Culross.

Max pulled on his helmet and pressed the ignition button. The big engine roared into life. He tweaked the throttle and pulled away.

His concerns soon melted away along with the Highland scenery as he accelerated, revelling in the power of his motorcycle. Riding his bike was like therapy, the adrenaline chasing away the darkness. Max smiled underneath his helmet as a stag bolted alongside him, sprinting towards the distant hills. All thoughts of suicides and a missing fisherman evaporated. They could wait until tomorrow.

5

MAX SPRINTED THE last five hundred metres up the rough track towards his semi-detached farmhouse, panting heavily, his breath clouding in the early morning chill. Nutmeg, his small, shaggy cockapoo jogged alongside him, her tongue lolling, as he began to ease off his pace and passed through the open gate.

He paused, wiped the sweat from his shaved scalp and walked into the house.

'Yuk, you're stinking, look at the state of you,' said Katie, his wife. She was sitting at the breakfast bar, smartly dressed in a business suit, her glasses halfway down her nose. The newspaper was open in front of her, and she had a mug of steaming coffee in her hand.

'You love me like this, treacle,' said Max in a faux cockney accent, moving towards her, puckering his mouth in an exaggerated kiss.

'Don't even think about it, not until you've showered. Coffee? There's a fresh pot.'

'You're a darling, I knew there was a reason I married you,' he said, laughing as he moved to the sink and filled a pint glass with water. He downed the water in a couple of gulps and accepted the coffee cup from Katie with a smile.

'You going to Tulliallan today?' she asked, referring to the police college and HQ building in Kincardine, twenty minutes away. Max had a small, decrepit office there that he shared with his colleagues, DI Ross Fraser and DC Janie Calder. They only occasionally visited it, preferring to work from home and meet away from the sprawling police complex. Their role was such as to make staying in the shadows preferable.

'Not if I can help it. I've a bit to do on the laptop here first, and then I'll maybe go out, depending on what I find.'

'And what do you think you'll find?'

'Who knows? There was a suicide on the Erskine yesterday that an old pal isn't happy about,' said Max, taking another mouthful of coffee.

'I saw it in the paper. Is anyone ever happy about a suicide?'

'Obviously not, but Hamish didn't like something about it. No evidence, just need a little poke about.'

'Well, lotsa luck. Now, I can't stand here gassing. I'm a very busy woman, and some of us have work to do.' Katie finished her coffee with a gulp, then leaned over and kissed Max lightly on the cheek, screwing up her nose as she did. 'Phew, you stink. Go and get a shower. I'm off to work, have a good day.' Her eyes twinkled as she smiled.

And with that she was gone, leaving a pleasant floral smell in her wake.

Max watched her slim form, topped by tousled, dirty blonde hair, head out of the kitchen, into the lounge and through the patio doors. A second later her car slowly passed the window, its tyres crunching the gravel drive as she headed off into Glasgow where she worked as a paralegal in a solicitor's office.

Max was so glad to have Katie back. It had been a difficult

time during their trial separation, but they were giving it a go, and so far, things were great. Katie loved the farmhouse, Scotland and more importantly seemed to love him, again. And Nutmeg, of course; everyone loved Nutmeg.

Max picked up the paper that his wife had left behind. The suicide hadn't even made the front page. UNNAMED MAN PLUNGED TO HIS DEATH AT NOTORIOUS SUICIDE BRIDGE. Max read the report, which had scant details only, simply mentioning that the thirty-one-year-old victim was a married father, and that his body had been recovered by divers. An anodyne statement had been made by the local chief superintendent, asking for witnesses and reaffirming that there were no suspicious circumstances. Max's brow furrowed. It seemed a little quick to be making announcements like that. This was, in police parlance, an unexplained death and there would need to be an inquest.

Max drained his coffee and headed for the shower. He had work to do.

Max sat on his sofa, munching a slice of toast, a fresh coffee resting on the table in front of him. He opened his police-issue laptop and scrolled to the incident database and the log for the suicide on the bridge. He looked at the events that began with Hamish's initial message, through to Murdo Smith's body being recovered by the dive team. It all seemed fairly innocuous and there were no immediate red flags. Max noted that the PIRC had been informed by the duty officer early on, as was standard. This was a death during police contact, and a referral was mandatory. Max scribbled the name and contact number of the lead investigator, Lenny Farquharson.

It looked like the inquiry would be locally managed and merely supervised by PIRC. This was useful, because although the chief constable had given Max's small team unrestricted access to all Police Scotland databases, these didn't include the PIRC files. The nature of their remit meant they needed to see everything. The Policing Standards Reassurance Team, as they were called, was something of a misnomer. It was just the three of them, and their remit was wide-ranging. To identify and tackle corruption that others couldn't.

Max kept scrolling.

It all seemed to have been cleared up, and the report to the fiscal prepared by the officer in charge, a DS Charlie Finn. This again struck Max as being a little pre-emptive, bearing in mind the short time frame. He moved to the person concerned screen and took a screenshot, before looking at the details. The further he read, the more interested he became.

Name: Murdo Smith
Age: 31
Address: 46 Westhaughton Road, Glasgow
Next of Kin: Leanne Smith
Occupation: Intelligence Officer, National Crime Agency

Max jolted a little at the sight of Murdo Smith's occupation.

An intelligence officer with the NCA.

Hamish's words came back to Max.

'Scared of someone, mentioned the NCA and customs, shit like that. He also said that someone had been killed up north at a loch.'

Max took a long pull of his coffee, and screwed his face at

the cold, bitter liquid. He stared at the screen, his mind turning over the possibilities, and what, if anything, he could do.

An NCA officer who committed suicide after making allegations about bent cops and murder. A missing fisherman who was clearly up to his neck in something bad.

He had known Hamish for years; he wasn't given to hyperbole, and he certainly wasn't a conspiracy theorist. He was an experienced, hard-bitten street cop who rarely took anything at face value. He lived by the ABC of policing. Accept nothing, believe no one, confirm everything.

And yet Max recalled his words verbatim.

'Something about him made me believe it.'

6

TAM HARDIE STRETCHED across the top of his rough blanket on the narrow bunk in his cell at HMP Edinburgh, popularly referred to as Saughton jail. He tried to block out the pounding cacophony of music blaring from the nearby cells. The sweet-and-sickly stench of spice, a synthetic cannabis, managed to overpower everything, even the air freshener blocks he had positioned in his cell.

He sighed as he stared at the chipped paintwork on the brick walls, and the cracked glass of the small window that was the only source of natural light. His mind returned, briefly, to the palatial home he had shared with his wife and kids before he had been locked up. Hardie yawned as he stared at, but didn't really see, the television in the corner of his cell.

He had settled into the prison regime well enough, his reputation making sure that he was treated with the utmost respect by both staff and inmates. No one was liable to give the leader of the most dangerous and notorious Scottish gang any grief. Not if they wanted to hold onto their bollocks, anyway.

One little bastard had tried it on when he had first entered the jail. A 'napalm', a pan full of boiling water laced with sugar, to make it stick to the skin, had soon announced that Tam

Hardie was not to be pissed about with. The little shit hadn't grassed, as Tam knew he wouldn't. For Hardie, his time inside would be nothing like most other inmates'. No one would try to get the upper hand with him and he'd never be short of what most fellow cons considered 'luxuries' from the canteen. Big fucking deal, he thought. He could drown in Pot Noodles, juice, crisps and toiletries, but he was still in this hell-hole and nothing would make his time more palatable.

Hardie had his reputation, that was a given, but he had precious little else. He reached over to his bedside cabinet and picked up the latest letter from his wife to scan its contents for probably the fourth or fifth time. They were doing okay in the villa in North Cyprus, and the kids were settled in an international school. They'd planned for this eventuality, and as soon as the extent of his problems emerged, they'd all gone, fortunately out of reach of UK law enforcement.

Hardie scratched at the scar tissue on his cheek, feeling the rough bristles around the puckered skin, the legacy of a violent encounter with Max bloody Craigie. He felt a rising tide of loathing in his gut at the thought of the man responsible for putting him in here. He had considered organising a hit on him, but the lack of cash had precluded a professional job, especially since a serving cop always meant a much higher price. He also had to admit that he really wanted to look the bastard in the eye when he killed him.

His mind turned back to the events of a few months ago and the stupid blood feud that had cost him everything. His desire to avenge the deaths of his family members, caused by the Leitch family, had blinded him, and made him make all the mistakes that had led to his incarceration. He reminded himself that revenge was a dish best served cold, and he could wait.

His cell door rattled, jerking him from his reverie. Gifford, one of the screws he had onside, appeared. Hardie looked at the man with distaste. He was a weasel, but easy to control.

'Visitor, Mr Hardie,' he said, his eyes lowered.

'What? It's not visiting time and I'm expecting no one,' Hardie said.

'Two gentlemen to see you in health care. I'm assured that you'll be interested to meet them,' said Gifford, his voice catching in his throat.

'Health care? I'm not sick, what the fuck is going on?'

'Maybe just come along. If you want to leave, you can at any time, and I'll bring you back.'

Hardie mused for a moment before standing. Whatever it was, it would be a distraction from the twenty-three-hour bang-up that staff shortages had inflicted on them recently.

'Come on then.'

They strode along the landing, his new Nike Air trainers squeaking on the shiny floor. The smell of the polish competed with the ever-present stink of male body odour. Each cell door's wicket was open with only a square of thick Perspex separating them from the corridor. Most cells had a face looking out, hearing the footsteps. A few inmates nodded at Hardie, but the majority averted their eyes as he walked past.

They went through several sets of locked, chipped steel gates, and into the health care block, which Hardie had visited only once before.

'Who am I meeting?' he asked, his voice firm.

'I don't know their names, but I'm assured this is all in

order and that the nature of the visit is not going to attract the attention of other inmates,' said Gifford.

'If anyone thinks I'm gonna be a grass, then they can get tae fuck and you can get me back to my pad right now.'

'I don't think that's being suggested, and I'm fairly sure it's in your interests to at least listen to them. Bang on the door if you want out.'

Gifford unlocked the heavy door with a key on a long chain attached to his belt and pushed it open.

Two men in their thirties were sitting at the desk which was normally occupied by the prison doctor. They appraised him with amused half-smiles. One was huge, muscular and tough-looking with dark, closely cropped hair. The other smaller, slighter and wiry. He was expensively dressed with wavy hair brushed back and bouffant. They didn't look like they belonged together. Hardie was reminded of a celebrity actor with his impossibly huge minder.

'Mr Hardie, so pleased to meet you. I'm Callum and my good friend here is Davie. Do come in and have a seat, won't you?' the smaller man said, in a cultured English accent.

'I'm not talking to cops,' said Hardie.

'We're not cops, Tam, of that I can assure you. But we are people who can make things happen.'

'Like how?'

'In ways you couldn't possibly imagine, pal,' the big man said in a gruff Glasgow brogue. 'Now sit down, we need to talk. Shut the door, Gifford.' He didn't take his eyes away from Tam's and they were hard and dark, like pebbles.

Gifford meekly pulled the door shut and they were alone.

There was a long pause, as Hardie surveyed each man

in turn. He had spent a lifetime in the company of crooks, thieves, drug dealers, murderers and worse, but he couldn't figure these two out. They looked dangerous, but smart, not like typical villains.

Hardie eventually took his seat and leaned back. 'I'm waiting,' he said, calmly folding his hands in his lap.

'How long have you been here?' Callum asked.

'Seven months, but I'm sure you know this,' Hardie said.

'So, a mere twenty-nine years left to serve then?' Callum smirked.

'What's your point?' said Hardie, his scant store of patience evaporating.

'I think we may be able to help each other out a little. Let's put our cards on the table, shall we?' A wide grin stretched across his face, and he ran a hand through his thick thatch of hair. Posh boys' hair, thought Hardie, the bugger thinks he's Hugh Grant.

'Go on.'

'As I understand it, you are, shall I put it bluntly, broke. For all your late father's abilities, his money-laundering skills were a little, shall we say, analogue in a digital world?'

Hardie sat back and appraised the man.

'All your properties, businesses and cash are restrained by Police Scotland. I'm told they have a team of money-laundering experts and forensic accountants all over it. As I see it, you have zero chance of getting even a red cent of it back – am I right?'

Hardie's eyes narrowed. Whoever these bastards were, they were well informed. 'Aye, that's about the size of it.'

'Glad we understand each other. So, you can't enjoy money right now, beyond a few little canteen luxuries. Your wife and two kids are residing in a rather nice villa in North Cyprus, although it's not up to the standards of your old place. I guess the absence of an extradition treaty with the UK made it attractive. Just being careful, eh, in case some of the assets in your wife's name come back to, what's the crude expression? Bite her on the arse?'

'Spot on,' said Davie.

'Can't be easy for you. Not to provide properly for your family.'

'If I had any tits, pal, you'd be getting on them, right about now,' said Hardie, his face darkening as he fought the urge to smash the smug prick's face through the solid table.

'Now, now, dear boy, no need to get fractious. We may be in a position to help. You, of course, had a well-functioning merchandise distribution network that we would like to avail ourselves of, in return for a generous share of the profits.' Callum's mouth widened into a white-toothed smile. Hardie noticed innocent little dimples on both of his cheeks. Callum lifted his small hands in an apparent show of conciliation. To some, this would have been charming, but Hardie could read men well, and he recognised the disparity between the warmth of the smile and the coldness in those hard eyes. Hardie glanced at Callum's smooth, delicate-looking palms, and shivered. The nails looked like they'd been recently manicured. The man reminded Hardie of a pretty snake he'd once seen in his garden, sizing up a mouse. Despite his diminutive size, Callum's eyes showed not even a trace of fear. For the first time in a long while, Hardie felt a touch of unease. The man had a strange presence, he had to admit.

Hardie glanced between the two men, then shook his

head. 'Maybe you aren't as well informed as you think, boys. Scousers have moved in since I've been here. They've sewn up Glasgow and Edinburgh and they're county-lining to all the far north areas. I've no money, so no product. Without the product, I can't muscle in on Scally. If I was outside, I could sort this in ten minutes.'

'That's about right,' said Davie. 'A crew from Manchester tried to establish the trade route, but Scally had more clout. We heard Scally supplied them with some product that magically disappeared. I understand he's a little pissed off about that,' chuckled Callum.

'Look, can you get to the fucking point? All this is very interesting, and I did hear that Scally sorted the Mancs out, but right now, I couldn't give a shit, okay? If you can get me out of here, then I can sort this once and for all, but if not, and I'm fairly sure you can't—'

'You're right, we can't help with that, but we can offer a lifeline in other areas. Scally's network is being, shall we say, "disrupted",' said Davie.

'Disrupted by who?'

Rather than answer, Callum reached into his pocket and pulled out an A4 sheet of paper which he handed across the desk. Hardie picked it up and stared at the image. It had been taken in the dark, but the flash had illuminated two faces, both pale and ghost-like. Each had a neat bullet hole in the centre of their foreheads. He recognised one of them. Macca, Scally's right-hand man. Although Hardie had been out of the game for six months, his people on the outside had kept him in the loop.

'Your work?' said Hardie, looking straight into Callum's eyes.

'Possibly, old boy. I'm sure Scally is upset at losing his merchandise, but with the very specific intelligence we have access to we can destroy his supply routes. He has a number of deliveries arriving along the west coast, and we'll be there to remove the merchandise from his people. Easy as taking candy from a Scouse baby. We already have ten kilos of high-grade cocaine, ready to go. All we need is access to your distribution network.'

'What's in it for me? I'm still in jail.'

'You are, but your wife and children aren't, and your brothers received much lighter sentences than you. They'll be out in three years or thereabouts, and the Hardie empire can carry on into the next generation. With the money that our partnership will bring, who knows, there may even be enough to make life far more comfortable all round. With cash comes opportunity, if you understand me, Mr Hardie. We are here offering opportunities.'

'You got a plan for that?'

'Possibly, but it will be expensive. Very, very expensive, so we need to move fast. These importations are going to be happening soon, so we need someone to distribute. I mean, it's not like we're going to sell it, is it?' said Callum, his face impassive.

Hardie gave each man a full thirty-second stare. Direct, eye to eye. He saw something of himself in both.

A smile stretched across Hardie's face. 'You're on. Fifty-fifty split.'

'Fifty-fifty? You're not paying for the product. It's basically money for nothing for you and your organisation.'

'Are you paying for the product?'

'Fair point, well made, of course. Neither are we,' Callum chuckled, and it was an unpleasant sound.

Callum placed a tiny mobile phone on the table, the likes of which Hardie had not seen before, together with a charging cable. 'Fifty-fifty it is, then.'

'Is that a safe phone?' asked Hardie, nodding at the compact handset.

'Yes. It's encrypted,' Callum said. 'You'll be able to make calls and send messages, which can't be intercepted. Well, technically they can, but they'd be scrambled. It has no other functions beyond calls and messages, which self-delete after five minutes of sending or receipt. Use the secure message facility on them, and only call us if you have to. Can you keep it hidden?'

'I don't generally get searched, and if I do, it'll be Gifford, and he knows which side his bread is buttered.'

'Perfect. We'll be in touch,' said Callum.

There was a pause as the three exchanged stares. The refrigerator in the corner of the room hummed.

'You know who I am, right?' said Hardie.

'Of course,' said Davie.

'Then you know what I'm capable of, even from inside this shite-hole.'

'Of course, it's why we've approached you.'

'Well then, you know that if you cross me, or try and fuck me, I'll have the skin removed from both of your bodies whilst you're still alive,' Hardie said, showing his teeth in a wolfish grin.

'As if, old boy, as if,' said Callum, returning the smile.

'Then you're on.'

7

'THAT WAS EASIER than expected,' said Davie to Callum as they walked through the reception area, passing the duty screws who eyeballed them on their way to the exit turnstile. Gifford led them towards the small bank of lockers where their mobile phones and other valuables had been secured.

'He's desperate. All his cash and assets are restrained, and he has no chance of getting them back. Anyway, let's get out of here. This place reminds me of my boarding school days,' Callum said, wrinkling his nose.

'How the hell you ended up doing what we do is a mystery to me,' said Davie.

'Opportunities abound, old man, especially for someone with my qualifications,' Callum smiled.

They both produced small keys and unlocked their security lockers. Reaching inside they pulled out identical Android smart phones. Callum withdrew a business card and handed it to Gifford. He looked down at the single printed phone number on it and nodded, meekly.

'Call me if anything comes up, okay?'

'Yes, sir,' said Gifford, tucking the card into his pocket.

8

MAX STARED AT his screen, Nutmeg snoring next to him, her woolly head resting on his lap. He had an uncomfortable feeling in his stomach. An NCA intelligence officer, making pre-suicide allegations. He picked up his phone and scrolled through to a contact and dialled.

'Norma Kirk.' A soft Highland accent.

'Norma, it's Max Craigie.'

'Max, you old bastard,' she cried cheerfully.

'How you doing? Not seen you for ages,' Max replied, a smile stretching across his face. Norma was a civilian intelligence analyst he had been to school with on the Black Isle, many years ago. They'd dated for a few months as youngsters before Max joined the army, but soon realised that they were better suited as friends. She'd joined the police with Northern Constabulary, which was merged into Police Scotland in 2013, then joined the NCA as an analyst. They'd stayed in touch loosely over the years, occasionally meeting up when Max travelled back to see his aunt, but as is often the case, they hadn't spoken for almost a year.

'Aye, too bloody long, man. Too long. Elspeth told me you'd moved to Scotland when I was last back on the Black Isle, and you only reach out now? You're a twat, you always were,' she said. Norma was lovely and kind, and a skilled analyst, but she was no flake. She had survived and flourished in law enforcement because she was bold and confident and gave as good as she got.

'Been busy, you know. How's the NCA, better than Police Scotland?'

'Not sure I'd say that. Different shite, but they're happy for me to stay in Glasgow, whereas Police Scotland couldn't guarantee where I'd end up. You settling back in okay and not missing the cockneys too much?'

'Nah, I'm okay. How's Andy and the weans?' said Max, asking about her husband and twin boys.

'He's cool, DI now working in central. Andy junior and Lewis are driving me up the bloody wall. It's all about Minecraft and twattish YouTubers. I tell you, it's hell being a smart go-getting professional like me whilst looking after three males. I dream of a dry toilet floor. Thank Christ my ma is close by, or I'd sink.'

'Well, you were daft enough to have kids.'

'Cheeky bastard. How's the missus?'

'She's good, settling in nicely in Culross.'

'No kids?'

'No chance, at least not yet.'

'We'll see, Katie is the maternal type. You need to look after her, she's far too good for you. You okay?'

'Aye, mostly, but I take it you heard about the drama?'

'I heard. You know what the rumour mill is like. Sounded a nasty business. I know you were always anti-establishment, even at school, but bringing down every bent senior officer in Scotland?'

'Well, you know. Shit happens,' said Max.

'Aye, unlucky bastard you are. A right bloody Jonah Lomu, or something like that,' she said, chuckling.

'Jonah, as in Jonah and the whale. Jonah Lomu was a giant New Zealand rugby player, not an Old Testament character.' Max laughed. Norma was massively clever but liked to play ditzy. The skewed reference to unlucky Jonah and the whale was typical. Max could just imagine her crooked grin and deep hazel eyes that always shone with amusement, even if she wasn't actually smiling.

'Whatever, Poindexter. When did you become a Bible-basher?'

'Right, I am a busy man. Did you hear about one of your firm committing suicide on the Erskine Bridge?'

'Aye, Murdo Smith. I knew him slightly. Really sad. He seemed a nice enough guy, married with a kid.'

'What do you know about him?'

'Intelligence officer with a good reputation who had been working extensively on developing intelligence on the large-scale importation of cocaine. He had been an acknowledged expert on the supply routes into the UK, particularly how they were shifting post Brexit.'

'Right, was he working on that recently?'

'Not recently, I think he'd been doing something else. He'd identified the coastline of western Scotland as being almost impossible to police, and enormously vulnerable to small craft coming into the numerous inlets, sea lochs and small beaches in deserted areas. UK Border Force have only one cutter to patrol the entire coast, and he'd written a paper highlighting the vulnerabilities. It'd been getting some management attention up until six months ago, but things had seemingly gone quiet.'

'Any red flags?' asked Max, his voice level.

'Meaning?'

'I'm doing a little research for anti-corruption and he made a few comments to the cop before jumping.'

'Such as?' Norma's voice was laced with suspicion.

'Mostly garbled nonsense. I'm just interested.'

'I know that he was broke. Rumour flying around that he got dragged in by the management because he'd been taken to civil court for non-payment of council tax. Ended up with a decree against him, and the bosses didn't like it, what with the sensitive area he was working in.'

'Sensitive?'

'He was working on a covert job – no idea what, but I suspect it was telephone-intercept led. They don't like anyone with a question mark hanging over them being fed live updates from the line room.'

Max paused. So Murdo had been in debt, with access to the most sensitive of raw intelligence data. Telephone intercept data, which was only given to top-level security-cleared staff. These were big red flags.

'Who else was he working with?'

'Well, he was feeding evidence to a number of different teams, trafficking, drugs and money laundering.'

'Anyone of concern?'

'Not that I know of. What's this all about?' Norma's voice lowered.

'Ach, it's probably nothing,' said Max, his tone light.

'Hmm. Nice bullshit,' said Norma.

'Only poking about, I promise. I just don't like the circumstances of the death. It's probably nothing.'

'Murdo seemed a nice guy. Are you thinking this was more than suicide?'

'I can't say.'

There was a long pause before Norma spoke again. 'If there's something amiss, make sure you find it, okay?'

'I promise. We'll meet for a beer soon, yeah?'

'Sure thing. Like it only took you a year or so of being up here to call me,' said Norma, the smile having returned to her voice.

'Soon, I promise.' He hung up, making a mental note to be true to his word.

Max scrolled through his phone once more and selected Hamish's number. He wanted to get a little more from him, and he really wanted to know exactly what Murdo had said before he jumped.

The phone rang and rang before diverting to the answer machine. Max dialled again, with the same result. He looked at his watch, it was almost 11 a.m. Hamish was probably hard at work in his garden laying his deck. He always had been a DIY nut, and it was one project after another. Hamish's place was only twenty minutes away. Max stood, grabbed his car keys and tickled Nutmeg's ears as she stared adoringly at him.

Max dialled, but instead of calling Hamish, he typed in Janie's number. 'Max, are you skiving, or are you going to do any work this week?' her warm voice echoed down the line.

'You in the office?'

'Not yet, in fact I'm still in my bed,' she said, stifling a yawn.

'Well, get yourself sorted. Do you have a car?'

'No, it was in for a service, but it's done and it's back at Tulliallan.'

'Tell you what, I'll go and fetch it and pick you up in an hour or so. We need to pay a call, and I don't want to go on my own.'

'I'm flattered, what's it about?'

'The suicide on the Erskine. Did you hear anything else?'

'No, I was busy on other stuff. What's happened?'

'I'll tell you when I see you.'

'Right on, Skipper.'

'Janie?'

'Aye?'

'Call me Skipper again and I'll volunteer you for house-to-house duty for the next year,' said Max.

'Whatever, see you in a bit.' Janie rang off.

'I'm off out, girl. Go and see John and Lynne,' he said. Nutmeg cocked her head at the sound of their neighbours' names. This was always the way. Nutmeg knew, when Max went out, she visited the next-door-neighbours' place and hung about with their dogs. Obediently, she turned and trotted off through the open French doors.

9

JANIE LIVED ON the first floor of an old tenement building in Stockbridge, an upmarket suburb to the north of Edinburgh city centre. The street was leafy, and the shops all very artisanal and desirable, as were the cars parked in front of her building.

Max jogged up the staircase and rapped on the door. Thumping music was audible from within.

After a moment, the music stopped and the door swung open. Janie stood in a dressing gown, her hair still damp. She was young, with short, tidy hair and an outwardly shy persona. She and Max had been thrown together during a very difficult case a few months ago and had become close friends and colleagues. She was smart, able and brave, and there was no one Max trusted more.

'You were quick. Come in whilst I get dressed.'

'I took my bike to get the car. Hurry up, there's policing to do, and I understand that Edinburgh's noise pollution team are on their way,' said Max, following her into the flat.

'Ha, ha, very funny,' said Janie.

'What were you listening to?'

Janie looked at him with a frown. 'Seriously?'

Max nodded, keeping a straight face.

'Very early Tangerine Dream, one of the forerunners of kosmische Musik, slightly more commonly, and a little offensively, known as Krautrock. Classic stuff that came out of West Germany in the sixties and seventies. You want to listen to some on the drive? I'll tell Ross that you're a fan,' said Janie, an amused look on her face.

'No thanks, pal. Your neighbours must absolutely loathe you.'

'They think I'm a little weird.'

'Well, Mandarin Dream won't help. Hurry up.'

'It's Tangerine Dream, my sarcastic friend. Coffee in the pot on the breakfast bar, give me five.' She pressed a remote, and some soft music filled the room. She disappeared out of sight down a small corridor.

An L-shaped sofa sat in the middle of the minimalist living space beside a glass coffee table. A complex-looking hi-fi system sat on a polished wooden unit. There was not a cable or wire in sight anywhere. There was no TV that Max could see.

The kitchen was sleek, and the granite surfaces of the breakfast bar shone like mirrors. Even the dishcloth had been folded and possibly ironed. A cup sat next to the expensive-looking drip machine, and Max poured some of the aromatic coffee into it. A tiny amount dripped onto the gleaming surface. Max sipped at the strong, rich coffee and nodded appreciatively.

'Nice place,' Max called into the other room. There was no clutter. 'So, when do you get to move your stuff in?' He wandered over to a floor-to-ceiling bookshelf that was packed with a variety of titles. Arthur Conan Doyle rubbed shoulders with Dostoevsky, Marlowe, Keats and a large selection of history books. One shelf was given over to crime novels, all beautifully arranged and lined up in size order. On the next shelf down was a row of creased romance novels. Varied taste, thought Max.

Next to the bookshelf were records – what to Max looked like thousands and thousands of records, both twelve- and seven-inch vinyls; the word eclectic didn't do it justice. It struck Max how little he knew about his friend and colleague.

Curiously, there were no family photographs. The white-painted walls were all adorned with old film posters. A saxophone sat on a steel stand at the side of the room. Max picked it up, feeling its weight, admiring the craftsmanship of the polished metalwork and tubes. He was raising it to his lips when he heard Janie behind him.

'That cost me a month's wages, please be careful with it,' she said, her voice tight.

'Sorry,' he said, putting it back. He tried not to smile, but his mouth formed a kind of grimace.

'Sod off. I just like things tidy.'

'Don't look where I spilled my coffee, then.'

Janie's eyes automatically flicked across to the coffee machine, and Max laughed.

'I'm cool,' she said, but her smile was forced.

'Give us a tune then?'

'What?'

'On the sax.'

'No bloody chance.'

'Are you any good?'

'I'm okay, but I don't play to other people.'

Max chuckled. 'Come on, we need to get going.'

'Okay, you go down, I'll meet you in the car,' she said.

Max grinned. 'You're going to clean all the things I've just touched, aren't you?'

'No,' she said, not looking at him.

'I bet you are.'

'Sergeant, will you kindly piss off out of my flat and I'll see you in the car?'

Max and Janie pulled up outside Hamish Beattie's small cottage. It was situated at the top of a farm track on the outskirts of Bearsden, a commuter town north-west of Glasgow. It looked new, and had clearly been recently whitewashed, the paint shining bright against the green of the surrounding conifers.

'Nice place,' said Janie.

'Hamish built the cottage years ago, with the help of local tradesmen. He bought the plot from a farmer and did loads of the work himself. He's bloody obsessed by it all, never stops banging on about rendering, or soffits and fascias.'

It was a beautiful, if chilly day and the trees that surrounded the cottage were beginning to shake off their winter beige.

'Nice wee place, although too remote for me,' said Janie.

'If Hamish seems a bit sad at the moment, it's because his wife moved out. Come on, let's go and see him.'

Hamish's elderly Ford sat in front of the cottage, but the curtains were all shut, both downstairs and upstairs.

They got out of the car, an anonymous Volvo that Max had been given by the fleet manager when their small team had been formed. It had a beefy engine, covert blue lights and sirens for passing through traffic. The budget was one of the advantages to being on a small team, reporting direct to the chief. Since there were only three of them, whatever resources they needed they got.

Max banged on the front door, but there was no movement. The curtains remained still and the whole house seemed to be enveloped by a deep, cloying silence. Max squatted and peeped through the letter box, seeing only the internal porch door.

He looked at Janie, who just shrugged. A cloud moved in front of the weak sun, and the temperature dropped. Janie shivered.

Max's eyes narrowed as he took in the scene. The only sound was the cry of a nearby crow sitting on a conifer branch. He took his phone and dialled Hamish's number, listening as the ring tones hummed. He removed the phone from his ear, but could hear nothing, no distant ringing, no music, no TV.

They walked around the perimeter of the house. It was surrounded by a well-kept garden, with a large lawn to the rear, and tended vegetable plots ready for early spring sowing. Concern began to prick at him, his senses heightened. Combat indicators, they called them during his time in Afghanistan: feelings that, in reality were grounded in observable facts.

'I don't like this,' said Janie.

At the back of the cottage, decking slats were piled neatly beside a newly formed frame, ready to accept the timbers. A circular saw sat on a workbench and a DeWalt nail gun lay on its side. A radio sat silent, plugged into an extension cable that snaked through the cat-flap into the kitchen. Max peered through the glazed kitchen door at Hamish's tidy farmhouse-style kitchen. A carton of milk sat on the work surface alongside a solitary mug, a kettle and a pack of teabags.

Max tried the door, but it was unmoving. He looked up at

the drawn curtains along the upper floor. None of this made sense. Hamish had clearly been working in the garden and was midway through making tea. Max bent down and pushed the cat-flap open with a knuckle, sniffing the air.

'You do realise that sniffing people's homes is a bit weird, right?' said Janie.

'Doesn't smell right,' Max said, frowning.

'Gone for a walk?' said Janie.

'I doubt it.'

Janie looked through the window. 'I'd say you're right. His keys are still in the door.'

Max banged on the door again, shouting, 'Hamish?'

He pulled out his phone and dialled Hamish's number, listening through the open cat-flap. A frantic buzzing came from the kitchen work surface, as a phone began to dance across the laminate surface.

'We need to get in there,' Janie said.

Max rattled the door, his stomach beginning to tighten.

Janie went to the decking. She picked up a length of plastic packing straps that had been securing the decking slats together. Within a few seconds she had fashioned a flexible hook. She reached through the cat-flap and passed the loop over the bunch of keys and tugged sharply. The keys fell to the floor.

'Nice,' said Max.

'It's from working with you and your cockney burglar techniques.'

Within seconds Max was inside the spotless kitchen, sniffing the air once more.

It was faint, but unmistakable. Every cop knew this smell. It started off faint, a mere suggestion of something, just like Max was detecting now. His stomach tightened, his heart began to pound. Max knew. He knew right away.

Death.

The faint essence that would soon become a vile, putrid stench.

Janie's nose wrinkled. She looked at Max, alarm in her eyes.

Hamish was dead.

10

MAX REACHED FOR the handle, pulled the door open and slowly stepped into the hall, his senses heightened and alert, his heart racing at what he was about to find.

Hamish hung from a line of blue nylon cord, his feet just a few inches from the laminate flooring. His face was bloated and brick-red, his tongue blue, swollen and lolling. His hands dangled limply by his sides, and the floor was wet with urine. The small hallway reeked of recent death.

'Oh shit,' said Janie, almost as a sigh.

Max's heart sank with overwhelming sadness at the sight of his friend. He reached for Hamish's neck, feeling for a pulse. But he had seen death up close on multiple occasions and he knew that the life had been ripped from Hamish's body by the blue cord, tightly bound around his neck, biting into the flesh.

There was no pulse detectable, as expected.

Max closed his eyes, his head swimming with emotion.

'I'll call it in,' said Janie, reaching for her phone.

Max zoned out, looking at Hamish, not hearing Janie's voice as she called the emergency operator.

He moved past Hamish's swinging body and looked up

at the blue nylon cord. It had been secured in an untidy knot around the bottom of a banister rail on the landing above.

'Units are being despatched. Let's wait outside,' said Janie.

'Have they restricted the message?'

'I told them to.'

Janie went to leave, but Max took hold of her arm.

She turned to face him and frowned.

'What's wrong with this scene?' he said.

'Him doing this during a break in DIY,' Janie said. 'That isn't typical.'

Max's eyes went to the knotted, rudimentary noose around Hamish's neck. It had been pulled tightly against the back of his skull.

Something itched at his subconscious. The picture wasn't right. The scene didn't make sense.

Hamish was sad after his marriage failed, and he had just witnessed a suicide, but was it enough to push him to this?

Then it hit Max like a bolt out of the blue, as he looked again at the knotted ropes.

'The knots.'

Janie stared at the mess of blue cord attached to the banister rail.

Max knew it then and there.

Hamish had been murdered.

11

MAX AND JANIE were sitting outside the front of the house when the first car arrived, its blue lights strobing.

The door opened and a young-looking inspector got out, fixing her hat on her head as she walked up the drive, clutching a clipboard.

'DS Craigie?' she said in an English accent, her sharp eyes quizzical. This was not the type of call any officer wanted to attend.

'Yes, ma'am,' said Max.

'DI Harrison. What do we have?'

Max told her.

'You're not happy about the circumstances?'

'Not at all. It stinks. Hamish was a pal, but I was coming to see him on business after he witnessed a suicide on the Erskine a couple of days ago. I don't think he did this himself,' Max said bluntly, his sadness rapidly beginning to simmer into anger.

'Reasons?' she said, opening her folder. Whilst young, she seemed in control and efficient.

'The knots. He was a meticulous man, and he was a sailor. No way did Hamish tie those shite triple-granny knots, even in the depths of despair. He certainly wasn't suicidal when I spoke to him the other day,' said Max. He had no doubt that muscle memory would have compelled Hamish to secure that rope to the rail with a bowline, whatever mental state he was in.

'Is that it?' the inspector said, looking up from her folder.

'No. He was also in the middle of a DIY project in the garden, and midway through making a cup of tea. Hardly the mindset of a suicidal man. I just don't see it. We need a full forensic team down here. This is a murder.'

'Any note?'

'Not that I can see, but I haven't looked hard.'

'I'll get everyone here. Do I need to view the scene personally before briefing the on-call DI?'

'Not unless you want to, ma'am. I am happy to brief the SIO, but I accept it's your call. I'd recommend staying out until the CSI get here and we can do it properly,' said Max. Some duty officers, particularly the older ones, would get a little possessive about personally viewing the body, particularly when a subordinate was advising against it.

Harrison nodded. 'Then I don't need to. We'll wait for the cavalry to come; let's leave the scene as intact as we can.' She turned to the uniformed officers and instructed them to start getting the scene tape up and begin a log. There was a further hushed exchange between her and the first officer on the scene, both looked at Max as they spoke.

'DS Craigie?' the duty officer said, her voice faltering.

'Yes?'

'We have just received a call from a Mrs Jenny Beattie into the control room.'

Max's stomach lurched at the sound of Hamish's wife's

name. They had met once, a couple of years ago. 'Hamish's wife?'

'Yes, she received a text message from Hamish that was sent ninety minutes ago. He was apologising to her, and saying he was going to end it all. It was a suicide message.'

12

THE STOVE SPAT and crackled as Davie Hamilton jammed the white forensic oversuits, masks and nitrile gloves into the burning embers. The flames surged, engulfing the flimsy paper garments. Blue gloves shrivelled and melted and began to curl. Slick, oily smoke rose and ascended the flue. Within seconds, the evidence had shrunk to nothing, the flames had died, and the fire was once more a bed of glowing coals and wood. His hand trembled, just a fraction, as he closed the glass-panelled door of the iron stove that was nestled inside the huge open inglenook.

Davie sat back in the armchair and looked around the large lounge, feeling a pang of jealousy at the spacious interior: the vast leather sofa, what looked like a Persian rug, and the weird and wonderful artwork on the beamed walls. Compared to his small tenement flat in Glasgow, this place was a bloody palace. Callum was clearly making plenty of money, which, he had to admit, was probably the driving force for their association. Maybe soon Davie might be able to afford somewhere like this.

He looked into the corner of the room where a large open globe drinks cabinet sat with rows of bottles of differing types peeping over the lip. He felt the tremble begin to rise up his arms from his hands as he looked at the bottles, which seemed to sparkle in the late-morning sun.

'Tea?' said Callum.

'Nothing stronger available?' said Davie, feeling the familiar longing beginning to gnaw at him. It often happened like this. After something major or notable, his regular cravings for alcohol began to bubble. He was in control of it most of the time, limiting his consumption to late afternoons onwards, but after recent events the urge was stronger than normal.

'Oh, Davie, it's not yet afternoon, really?' he said, almost pityingly, in his shitty posh voice that almost made Davie want to wipe the smug, sanctimonious grin off his face. He knew he wouldn't act on the urge, though. For all his affected, fey posturing, Callum Mackintosh wasn't to be pissed about with.

'A successful little venture surely deserves a wee dram, right? All loose ends tied,' he said.

'Tied being more than a little metaphorical.'

'He was a skinny wee gadgie. It was too easy. Surely that deserves a wee snifter.'

Callum looked at his watch, and sighed theatrically. 'All right, tea with a small celebratory dram. I have a very fine single malt in the drinks cabinet.' He picked up his phone and composed a quick message.

'You got a butler, as well?' said Davie, attempting to lighten the atmosphere. He was suddenly feeling much calmer and more relaxed.

Callum said nothing, but his baleful look told its own story. He sighed again, before standing and walking over to the globe. He selected a bottle and poured two very small measures into heavy-looking glasses. He looked over to Davie, his head shaking in disapproval.

A mix of embarrassment and anger began to rise in Davie's chest at his supposed friend's superior attitude.

At that moment, a beautiful blonde woman walked into the room, carrying a tray bearing an earthenware teapot and two mugs.

'Thank you, darling,' said Callum, smiling widely at her. She was dressed in an expensive-looking tracksuit. Not for the first time, jealousy clutched at Davie as he looked at Callum's wife. It was a stark reminder of the things that he didn't have waiting for him at home, his wife having departed years ago, probably as a result of his drinking.

'Bit early for the scotch, isn't it?' she said in a cut-glass accent that wouldn't have been out of place in a smart London art gallery.

'Davie was insistent, darling, you know what he's like. We're celebrating a success.' Callum smiled, and patted her shapely thigh as she set the tray down on the coffee table.

'Morning, Davie,' she said, smiling brilliantly, showing straight white teeth. She tossed her hair.

'Morning, Allegra. Looking beautiful, as always,' Davie said, grinning.

'Stop flirting with my wife. Thanks, darling, now run along. We have business to discuss.'

'Charming, I'm off anyway. Pilates.' She gave them a dazzling smile and was gone, leaving a waft of expensive perfume in her wake.

'Don't know how you hold onto her,' said Davie.

'My charm and good looks, of course. That and lots of money.'

Callum poured the tea, added a splash of milk and handed it to Davie, together with the glass.

'It's a very old Glenfiddich. Cost a bloody fortune,' Callum said as they chinked glasses and downed the peaty liquid.

Davie felt all the muscles in his body relax and a sudden relief come over him as the raw spirit washed over his tonsils and carved a warm path down his throat. The relief was almost immediately replaced with the familiar sensations of regret, and longing for more. He took a deep breath to compose himself. 'It's good whisky. So, what's next?'

'One second, old man. I think a little livener is in order.' Callum pulled out a twist of paper which he unwrapped. He picked out a decent pinch of white powder and dumped it on a small mirror on the table. He chopped at it for a few seconds with a credit card, lowered his head and hoovered up the cocaine with a rolled banknote. 'Beautiful,' he sniffed, his eyes brimming.

'Any of that for me?' said Davie, his eyebrows raised.

'Just the whisky, old son. I know what you're like when you mix, and we've work to do.' He tucked the packet and banknote away and mopped up the cocaine residue with a wet finger. He rubbed it on his gums, his teeth bared in a snarl.

The big Glaswegian swallowed his anger and waited.

Callum sighed. 'Now, Hardie is arranging an introduction to someone who will take the merchandise and begin to re-establish the network. Scally has another importation imminent, somewhere west coast again, but the exact location hasn't been discussed.' His words were faster now, his pupils larger. Energy shone from his handsome face.

'Just how imminent?' Davie said.

'Hopefully finding out very soon. Our contact is monitoring phones as we speak. He needs to replenish urgently. You know how these things go; supply gets short, prices go up, junkies start looking elsewhere for their fixes. Scally's customer base will soon start to suffer.'

'So, we're just waiting?'

'Well, to a degree, but maybe there's something we can do.'

'I take it you have an idea?' said Davie.

'Well, we have hot info that Scally is sending a consignment north towards Fraserburgh today,' said Callum.

'Interesting. Anything specific?' said Davie.

'I had initially discounted it as a little small time, but it may serve a dual purpose. A guy called Stevie is driving it up at some point today.'

'You know when and where?'

'No, but I have the vehicle's make, model and registration. It's a false-plated BMW. Scally was lax enough to tell Stevie over the phone where and when to find the car, with the merchandise already secreted in the spare tyre.'

'Let's get busy.'

'Leave it to me,' Callum said, picking up his phone, then simultaneously sipping his tea and dialling.

After a short pause, he spoke, a broad smile on his handsome face. 'Ashraf, old chap, it's Callum. I'm after a favour.'

13

MAX WAS SITTING in an anonymous MIT Vauxhall next to a tired-looking senior detective. He watched the hive of activity as MIT officers and forensic teams worked away at Hamish's house.

The clouds had continued to creep across the sky and now the cottage was enveloped in a gloomy, weak light. The trees sat inert in the still air. A wave of sadness washed over Max as he watched the scene before him and tried to organise his thoughts.

A full forensic team had been called and two vans packed with equipment were parked outside. Scene tape stretched across the drive and a uniformed officer stood with a pre-formatted log, recording everyone who entered or left the premises. A photographer snapped a few shots, moved around the back and documented the common path of approach, where all officers would enter or leave the scene.

It had been set to follow Max's route into the building through the back door to minimise any contamination of the scene. A fingerprint officer was dusting clouds of aluminium powder along the surfaces of the front door with a soft brush.

The remoteness of the cottage made it easy to secure, there

being no neighbours in the immediate vicinity. However, it also meant there were no witnesses to give any insight as to what had happened that morning.

The atmosphere amongst the officers was not as it would usually be at an incident such as this. The tasks were carried out efficiently, as one would expect, but this was different. This was one of their own.

The SIO sat next to Max, whilst Janie was in their car on the phone. DI Ewan Lewis was middle-aged, wiry with short steel-grey hair, and a slightly hangdog expression behind wire-framed spectacles. He was a time-served, experienced and well-respected detective with a long history in homicide investigations. Max had worked with him on a number of occasions when his old team, Serious Organised Crime, had supported a murder inquiry. He listened intently whilst Max told him what had happened, starting with the call from Hamish a couple of days ago.

'This is probably my last major investigation before I retire, and it's one of our own. I didn't know Hamish personally, but his reputation was solid,' the DI said, sadly.

'Aye,' was all that Max could think to say.

'Okay, I've seen the scene myself, and the CSIs are now in with the pathologist, but can you tell me again why you don't think this is suicide? The facts presented so far really don't indicate that it's anything else.' He looked at Max with his sad brown eyes.

'General circumstances. The knots are shite triple-grannies, when Hamish was a sailor with his own dinghy. He was a meticulous guy, so I can't see any circumstances where he would be as slack as that. It would be his instinct to secure anything to a fixed point with a bowline, and let's be realistic, if you were going to kill yourself, you'd want the most reliable knots, right?'

'Even when suicidal?'

'I don't think he was, but yes, even when suicidal. It's more effort to tie those crap knots than to tie a sailing knot. He could do it one-handed with his eyes shut. I also don't like that his decision to kill himself came midway through cutting planks for his deck and making a cuppa,' said Max, his hackles beginning to rise.

'I can see all this, but it isn't evidence of murder. Particularly when he sent his wife a suicidal text. She also said that he was struggling with their separation,' said Lewis, his voice soft.

'Not what he told me. He was starting to date again. Come on, you can't like this. Any bastard could have sent that text.'

'The phone was locked.'

'Aye, with a fingerprint. They could have used his finger to unlock the phone once he was dead.'

'There are no finger marks on the phone.'

'And you don't see that as strange?' said Max.

Ewan let out a sigh. 'Aye, but I have to go on the evidence. There's nothing obvious on the body and no bugger saw anything, did they? No evidence of him being tied, no obvious injuries, the house is immaculate. How could someone string Hamish up, against his will and leave no trace. No injuries, no disarray, nothing?'

'Why did he lock himself in and draw the curtains?'

'I don't know. Maybe he didn't want to be disturbed? Who knows what a man in crisis would do?' asked Lewis, his voice rising a little.

'The knots. The knots make no sense.'

'Look, I get your concerns, but right now, the evidence points to suicide,' said Lewis.

'Even after what Hamish told me about the jumper on the Erskine?'

'Aye, about that,' said Lewis with a frown.

'What?' said Max, an uncomfortable feeling rising in his belly.

'There's no record of the conversation that you say Hamish told you about. No mention of Torridon, or Murdo Smith talking about any individual.'

'What about the statement to PIRC?'

'Nothing. Just that he gave his name, said it was all over, and jumped.'

'What?' shouted Max.

'I've seen the statement. The PIRC emailed it to me. Hamish must have been mistaken.'

What felt like a cold hand began to grip Max. He opened his mouth to argue, to tell the DI what Hamish had told him, but something made him stop.

'What about his notebook?'

'I've not seen it yet, I've only just got here, but we'll look at it.'

It hit Max with a sudden force. A cover-up. Another bloody cover-up. Someone had killed Hamish, and it was likely that they had also caused Murdo Smith to kill himself. Max swallowed.

'Right, well, I'm sure you guys have this in hand. Am I good to go?'

DI Lewis looked at Max for a long moment. He let out

a sigh. 'Aye. You get yourself off, make the statement and get it to me as soon as you can, okay?'

'Thanks. I'll get it right to you,' said Max. As he turned to go, Lewis called after him.

'Max?'

'Aye?'

'We have this, you know. My guys will look into this properly, and if there's anything wrong, we'll find it. You trust me, right?'

'I trust you.' Max nodded and made off, getting into his Vauxhall. Janie was sitting in the driver's seat. She turned off the music.

'Have you told Ross?' Max asked.

'Yeah.'

'What's he saying?'

'Mostly unrepeatable swearing, but he wants us in the office, pronto.'

'Beyond the swearing?'

'He doesn't like it either. Come on, let's get to Tulliallan,' said Janie, starting the engine and moving off.

14

STEVIE O'HALLORAN PULLED the ageing BMW off the A9 into the huge car park at the large retail centre, his bladder almost fit to burst, probably because of the three cans of Coke he'd downed in an attempt to chase away the previous night's hangover. His girl had given him a load of grief about it all this morning, particularly when he announced he was off for a bit on business. He'd have to buy her some perfume, or something to make it up to her. He was sick of these bloody runs, but Scally had hinted that he'd be moved off soon, maybe to Liverpool. Scally was a mean bastard at times, but he did reward hard work and loyalty.

Stevie parked at the far end of the car park in between two camper vans, close enough for a quick exit, but far enough away to be anonymous.

He pulled out his burner phone and dialled Scally's number. He wanted a call when he stopped and another when he got going again, such was the level of mistrust. It was strange, bearing in mind that they had known each other for years and years, but this was business. Big, expensive, dangerous business.

'Stevie?' a brash, rapid Scouse voice crackled in his ear.

'I've stopped, just a piss and a sarnie and I am on the way again, yeah?'

'Fuck's sake, mate, be quick. I don't want you there for more than five minutes.'

'I've been in this car bloody ages. If I stop at the side of the road, it's in full sight of everyone, and there are plenty of bizzies around.'

'Well, talk to no one, and be quick. Call me when you're on your way.' He hung up.

Stevie got out of the car, locked it and jogged towards the bustling low-rise building that looked like it mainly stocked overly expensive Scottish food and drink and tweed clothing. All very touristy and easy to blend into.

He walked straight to the plush bathrooms and, with a great deal of relief, used the urinals. After quickly washing his hands with the posh soap, he dashed to the large, bustling cafeteria for an organic falafel sandwich, root vegetable crisps and a tin of expensive-looking elderflower. Stevie would have preferred a full fat Coke and a corned beef and pickle on sliced white, but beggars couldn't be choosers. He barged to the front of the queue, ignoring the angry looks from the genteel customers. Paying the ridiculous price, he jogged back out to the car park, totally focused on getting on the road and keeping the volatile Scally happy.

He approached his car and fished for the keys, pressing the fob to activate the central locking. Just as he was reaching for the door, he became aware of a presence behind him. As he turned, his stomach churned. His keys dropped to the floor. The sound of them hitting the ground seemed strangely loud. In the silence that followed, Stevie could hear his heart trying to escape from his chest. A huge shadow fell over him. A massive bear of a man loomed, his teeth bared in a vicious smile. Stevie's heart lurched.

Just as Stevie was about to run, a cultured English voice emanated from behind him. 'Stevie, old chap. Don't do anything daft.'

Stevie turned to see a much smaller man who had appeared, as if from nowhere, by the BMW's door. A hand was extended, holding open a leather wallet. Stevie's eyes focused on it and took in the silver crest, the letters NCA. His heart sank, and his bowels almost turned to water. The NCA? Britain's FBI. Shit, things were about to get very bad.

'National Crime Agency, Stevie, I'm Grade 3 investigator, Callum Mackintosh and we're going to search you and the car. Do you understand?'

Before he could say, or do anything, he felt a massive hand close around his wrist, squeezing tightly. He dropped his bag of food and let out a yelp as his arm was wrenched around his back. With childish ease, Stevie was soon handcuffed and thrown against the car. The detention had been as swift as it was efficient.

He was quickly searched. His burner phone, an old Samsung, and his own iPhone were confiscated.

'What's the PIN for these?'

'Fuck you,' was all Stevie said. No way was he giving these bastards anything.

Callum snorted with laughter and produced a small metallic box from his rucksack. He slotted what looked like an SD card into the side of it.

'PIN?' he repeated, simply.

'Kiss my arse,' Stevie spat.

'Davie, if you wouldn't mind?' he said, smiling.

Within a moment, Stevie had been lifted off the car and slammed face down against the bonnet. The cuffs bit into his wrists, as the massive agent held him down and yanked up his hands. He braced himself for excruciating pain, but all he felt was his thumb being pressed against something smooth. The phones, Stevie thought. They were unlocking the bloody phones.

Callum said nothing, but within a moment he had produced a small lead and plugged it into the lightning port on the phone. Stevie's heart sank, they were downloading everything. The burner was not much of a worry, only having a few calls and messages from Scally, who himself had been using a burner, but his own phone was more of a problem. That had all sorts of calls, messages and things on it. He lived his bloody life on that phone. Scally had warned him not to take anything other than the burner, but he had tucked it in his pocket anyway. His girlfriend would give him hell if he was out of contact for a couple of days, and he couldn't face the moaning. If Scally found out, he'd go bloody mental, but right now, that was a minor concern. Within a few minutes the process had been repeated with the other phone, and both were then tucked back into his pockets.

Stevie was hoisted off the car and onto the ground. He lay with his face against the tarmac and watched as the boot to the BMW flipped open and Mackintosh scrabbled around in the spare-wheel compartment, a folding multi-tool in his hand. He sliced into the tyre, and Stevie sighed. He was going to jail. His first thought was that Scally was going to be fucking fuming. His second thought was how the hell had they known that the coke was in the tyre?

'Oh dear, Stevie,' said Mackintosh, holding up one of the half-kilo bricks of tightly wrapped cocaine.

'I didn't know it was there,' he protested.

'Of course you didn't. You're nicked me old China, as they say in London,' Callum said in an affected cockney accent. His smile was not a reassuring sight.

Five kilos, thought Stevie. With his previous, he was probably looking at a ten-to-fifteen-year stretch.

'Where were you taking it?' said the big brute.

'No fucking comment,' said Stevie. Scally had people everywhere and he was no snitch. 'Snitches get stitches' was Stevie's mantra.

'No comment? Oh, that's not so wise,' said Callum.

'Not wise at all,' parroted the gorilla.

'No. Fucking. Comment,' said Stevie through gritted teeth.

'Your choice. Davie, call the local uniforms for a van and secure Stevie in our vehicle whilst I finish up searching. You're off to jail. We don't care if you snitch on Scally or not. His time is drawing to a close,' said Callum.

'I don't give a toss,' Stevie spat. What the hell was going on? Stevie knew he had to find a way of getting word to Scally. He had no idea if they'd been watching, or how they'd linked him. All he knew was that Scally couldn't suspect that he had grassed or cooperated. There's nothing he wouldn't do to another human if he felt he had been disrespected. He'd seen too many of his victims over all their years of association. Removed fingers, burns with blowtorches, pulled nails, waterboarding.

Stevie was saying nothing.

*

Stevie sat on the bench at the police station, waiting for the custody officer to book him in. He had been through this process many times, but he'd not been caught for years. He found himself surprised at how sanguine he felt. Jail wasn't so bad, and he was due his time. He imagined this was what it would feel like to pay tax.

The two NCA clowns suddenly strolled into the custody office, bold as brass, as if they owned the place, full of arrogance and entitlement. He hadn't seen them since being picked up by the two taciturn local officers who had driven him the thirty minutes to the custody centre.

The custody officer, a weary middled-aged, bespectacled man looked at the two agents with something approaching disdain. 'What's the evidence of arrest?'

Callum spoke, almost as if he was performing Shakespeare, or something.

'Sergeant, myself and my colleague were in this region on an unrelated matter when we noticed this gentleman driving a BMW. His manner of driving was such that I performed a vehicle check which showed that there were some issues and it seemed likely that it was bearing false plates. We spoke to the gentleman at House of Bruar, and as a result of his answers to our questions, we performed a search of the vehicle. Secreted within the spare tyre is a quantity of white powder, packaged in a manner which suggested it could be cocaine. He was found with two mobile phones, and we believe he was heading north, feeding the coastal villages in a county lines operation. He was then arrested for possession with intent to supply a controlled drug, Sergeant.'

'Why possession with intent, rather than simple possession?' the sergeant asked, an eyebrow raised.

'Quantity, Sergeant.'

'How much?'

'Not been weighed yet, but I suspect about half a kilo?'

Stevie blinked. He stopped listening and time seemed to slow down. Half a key? He had been told there was five in that tyre. As his shock settled, he started to put it all together. He had been nicked by bent bizzies. The thieving bastards had pinched four and a half kilos of coke, and what had happened to his phones? Wiped? His initial feeling was one of fury, but this soon subsided, as he considered how it would affect him personally. Stevie had been around drug dealers for years. Loads of his pals had been locked up for moving coke and heroin, and he knew that being under five kilos made a huge difference in sentencing. If his lawyer could convince the court that he was just a courier, a guilty plea with under a key would bring the sentence right down. A slow smile stretched over Stevie's face. He reckoned he was looking at under five years, out in less than three. Stevie had enough experience to realise that these bent cops had done him a massive favour. It was still a shit situation, but things were looking up. He had just dodged a five-key charge, which, with his record, would mean a solid seven years in some shite-hole Scottish jail.

Stevie stared at his feet as he considered his options, only hearing a background hubbub of conversation.

A voice sliced through his reverie.

'What?' said Stevie, looking up at the custody sergeant.

'You've heard the officer's evidence, do you have anything to say in response? I have to note it on the record.' He fixed Stevie with a penetrating, and slightly irritated stare.

'Nothing. Nothing at all. Can I make a phone call?'

The custody sergeant glanced at the NCA officers, his eyebrows raised.

'No problem for us. This chap is small time,' the smaller one said.

Stevie couldn't believe it. He was sure they'd be holding him incommunicado. Why the hell weren't they looking further, doing house searches and things like that? Then he smiled to himself, realising exactly who he was dealing with. The corrupt bastards just wanted away with the nicked coke.

Stevie picked up the phone that was secured to the wall opposite the custody desk and read the number out to the custody sergeant.

'Who is it?' he asked.

'My girlfriend, Kelly,' Stevie replied. Kelly was a good girl who knew the score, and she would be straight onto Scally. Stevie's experience of police stations was enough to know that this call wouldn't be recorded, being the phone that detainees used to speak to their solicitors before they arrived at the police station. It was illegal to record privileged calls, but he couldn't say too much. The bastards were only a few feet away.

'Kel?' he said in a whisper.

'Stevie? Where the hell have you been? I've been worried sick.' Kelly's rapid Scouse accent boomed in his ear.

'I can't say much, but I've been nicked and I'm at the custody centre outside Perth.'

'What? You bastard, you said you were doing a driving job. What you been nicked for?'

'Drugs, babe. Can you make the call, you know who to, yeah? I got nicked with a half, not what I had. Tell him that

I'll be getting charged, and that I'll call him as soon as I get to a clean phone.'

Kelly would know exactly what to do. Scally would look after her once he got jailed. She sighed deeply. 'I'll make the call. I love you, you daft bastard.'

15

MAX, ROSS AND Janie sat in their small, dingy office in the forgotten reaches of Tulliallan police college, all clutching mugs of dark tea.

The office was down a dark corridor, tucked away where few people ever ventured, which suited them just fine. It was only big enough for a handful of people and was sparsely furnished with chipped, laminated desks and a few rickety chairs, none of which could be described as ergonomic.

Once Max had briefed them with the whole story, there was a long silence as the three colleagues stared at the table in front of them.

'This is a fucking bollocks situation,' was how Ross broke the silence. It was a fairly typical observation from the detective inspector, who despite appearances was actually a highly capable police officer. For once, he had turned up at work this morning looking quite smart. His shirt was crisp and pressed, his suit had clearly been to the cleaners and his shoes were polished. Ross was their boss, as the senior rank, but no one really took much notice of the chain of command, particularly when there was just the three of them.

'It's not great,' said Max.

'Am I going to the chief with this?' asked Ross, opening his A4 folder and scrawling in it, pausing to scratch at his paunch. A button had come undone, revealing the hairy white flesh of his prodigious belly.

The three of them were a small team with an unbreakable bond of trust. If they needed specific skills or manpower, they would call it in on a case-by-case basis. But because of the secrecy of their investigations, they kept it to just the three of them and reported direct to Chief Constable Chris Macdonald.

'At some point, but maybe we need a bit more of a dig first. We don't know exactly what we have yet,' said Max.

'So, your main concern about Hamish Beattie's apparent suicide is the knots?' said Ross.

'Bit more than that,' said Janie, sipping her tea.

'I'd say a lot more. There's Jimmy McLeish, the missing Caithness fisherman, Hamish's absent notes, Murdo's final words, DIY, knots. Need I go on?'

'No, I guess not,' said Ross.

'The investigation is leaning towards the theory that Hamish had been to several suicides in his time, and this one along with his break-up tipped him over the edge,' said Janie.

'I'm not buying that. He seemed positive, he wanted us to go sailing,' said Max.

'Well, a day trapped on a boat with you could drive anyone to suicide,' said Ross. When no one responded, he winced. 'Sorry, mouth ran away with me, there.'

'Detective Inspector,' said Janie, shaking her head.

'It's why I'm still a DI after all these bloody years,' he said.

'Any witnesses prior to his death?' asked Janie.

'Hamish lived in a cottage at the end of a track, no neighbours, not overlooked, no witnesses.'

'Convenient,' said Janie.

'Suggestions?' said Ross.

'I think brief the chief. Give him the heads-up on this. If I'm right, then this is massive. We have the last words of an NCA agent alleging corruption, the officer he speaks to before he dies is now dead, and all records of their conversation vanish. Front to back, that stinks, particularly when you add in a missing fisherman.'

'I'll give him the heads-up that we're developing this as a possible. We have no actual hard evidence, do we, beyond your knots, which, whilst persuasive, could easily be explained by mental state, right?' He nodded.

'Agreed, it's not conclusive, but it is enough for us to work on. Janie, can you start looking into the bridge-jumper suicide investigation at Clydebank, the OIC is a DS Charlie Finn, but PIRC are supervising. Maybe, Ross, if you get the guvnor to say he wants a thematic overview of it, or some such nonsense, we can get access to everything. You know the drill, learning lessons and the like. What with the excessive suicides on the bridge, that's totally plausible, right?'

'I'm sure I can do that – great suggestion,' said Ross, without sarcasm.

'Pardon?' said Max.

'Pardon what?' said Ross, looking confused.

'You're being both polite and encouraging. What's going on?' said Max.

'Yeah, I'm scared,' added Janie.

'Nothing, I'm just feeling happy to be in charge of our

small, yet efficient team,' Ross said, nodding. He stood and stretched, did up his button and tucked his shirt back into his trousers.

'You're being really weird,' said Max.

'All's well with the world, if we discount poor Hamish. Dinner with Mrs Fraser this evening at her favourite restaurant and I'm feeling that we're entering a purple patch in our work. Sheesh, can't a man be happy without getting grief?' He smiled, seraphically.

Janie gave Max a look.

Ross sighed. 'There's no pleasing you lot. I'll call the chief's staff officer now,' he continued, 'see if he has a window. I'll also keep a close brief on the alleged suicide of Hamish Beattie. As you two were pals it's best you keep out of it. I know Ewan Lewis well. He's as straight as they come,' Ross added, reaching for his phone.

'What are you going to do?' Janie asked Max.

He didn't answer. He was looking at his phone, distracted as he thought about Hamish. He absent-mindedly scrolled to the contact listed as BF. Bruce Ferguson, the mysterious former special forces operative, and current head of security to a Russian telecoms oligarch. The brother of a Caithness man murdered by Tam Hardie in a centuries-old blood feud. A man with seemingly infinite resources at his fingertips who had managed to intercept phone calls within minutes and help uncover the entire conspiracy. Should he call him?

'Max, are you away with the fucking fairies?' said Ross, phone clamped to his ear.

'Sorry, daydreaming. I'm going to look into the PIRC investigator.'

'No, not you, I need to speak to the boss, urgently,' said Ross, averting his eyes from Max and talking into the handset.

'How about Murdo Smith? You want me to look into his background?' said Janie, looking at Ross and shaking her head. He was still remonstrating with whoever was on the other end of the line.

Max's thoughts turned to Norma. 'No, leave that to me, I'll have a poke about.'

Ross loudly slammed his phone back on the desk. 'Staff officer is such a prick, I can't think why the chief employs him. You'd think he was the fucking chief.' Ross's face was beginning to return to a more normal shade of beetroot red.

'I see your good mood lasted then. What's up?' said Max, a hint of a smile on his face.

'Tried to tell me that the chief has "no windows in his diary", the snidey bugger. I told him I was coming down to his office, and I'd make him a new window where the sun don't shine if he didn't pass on my message,' said Ross, a vein in his temple beginning to pulsate.

'Okay, pal, see if you can find your chakra again,' said Max.

Ross took a deep, cleansing breath. His phone vibrated and he looked down at it. A smile slowly spread across his features. 'There you go, sometimes being a bastard does work. He's messaged him, and the chief wants to see us in an hour.'

'Really?'

'Aye. He says he has been worried about the NCA. Very worried.'

16

'WELL, THAT WAS rather simple,' said Callum as they left the police station and returned to their car. Davie glanced at his colleague, who wore a smug, satisfied expression. His face was set and pensive, with a look that Davie recognised. Callum was planning something, and it made Davie both excited and nervous.

'I think that Stevie knew the writing was on the wall. He was hardly going to start shouting, "But I had five kilos in that tyre, la," was he?' said Davie, badly emulating a Liverpool accent as they got in the car. He settled into the thick leather seats of the NCA BMW estate. He adjusted the rear-view mirror and snapped his seatbelt in place.

'No. He's old school. He's gone from facing twelve years to no more than three, meaning out in eighteen months. His statement for the interview made that clear, claiming that he was merely a courier and that he didn't know what was in the tyre.' Callum lounged in the seat as if it were a comfortable armchair. He reached into his pocket and pulled out a packet of cigarettes, put one in his mouth, and lit it, inhaling the smoke with deep pleasure, before letting it wisp out of his nostrils.

'Jesus, do you have to?' said Davie, lowering the window, wrinkling his nose.

Callum said nothing, his face impassive.

Davie opened his mouth to say more, but then closed it again. Arguing never did any good, in any case.

Callum took another drag. 'I guarantee he'll plead guilty, old man. Well worth the effort,' he said, the smoke billowing out as he spoke.

'He'd be mad not to. How have the management taken our brilliant instinct-based efforts?' said Davie, wafting the smoke away. He fucking hated Callum sometimes. He thought of no one but himself, ever, but he was resourceful and it paid to keep him onside. Davie let Callum think he was stupid, but he was just biding his time. They were going to make a load of money, and once that was done, Davie was off, and Callum could go fuck himself. Maybe Davie would take Callum's wife and move to Spain.

'I've just spoken to the witch, Louise Ellis, and she is utterly delighted with our initiative and instinct and the reputational boost this gives NCA in Scotland. We've struck a blow against an evil trade, old boy, and the police area commander is delighted,' Callum said.

'The witch isn't too bad.'

'She's a moron. Promoted that buffoon over me. Fuck her.'

'So, what next, back to Glasgow?'

'Perhaps not. I've been looking at the sneaky download of Stevie's phone. He hasn't been very careful with his security procedures. A chap in Fraserburgh is expecting this consignment for distribution in the old fishing village and others nearby. They have a terrible drug problem, you know. Shocking state of affairs.'

'So?'

'It seems that another Liverpudlian called Shorty is managing their operation in Fraserburgh and beyond. He's only a couple of hours away. Ellis isn't expecting us for a while so we may as well use the time wisely. I think Scally needs to realise that his network is shrinking, and he should limit himself to Liverpool. Now's the time for us to turn up the pressure.'

'I like your thinking. How will we locate our friend Shorty?'

'Oh, I'm sure I'll come up with something, you know me.'

Callum pulled out his phone and dialled. It connected to the Bluetooth, and after a moment, a soft Indian accent rang out through the car's speakers.

'Hello?'

'Ashraf, it's me, I need you to run a few phones. The first is a dealer in the north, the second is a dealer's wife. I need cell sites, and call data for both for yesterday and today. On the wife's number, run the first one she calls after she got a call from a police station earlier today. All clear?' Callum read both numbers out.

'No problem, I'll email it to you. Which address?' said Ashraf, a slight tremble in his voice.

Callum read out an email address that went to his encrypted burner phone. Nothing on any phone could be attributed to him. Ashraf had a real talent for being able to access communications data without alerting the necessary authorities.

'Okay, give me an hour. I need to do a few workarounds so it doesn't attract any attention, but I'll get the data to you.'

'Excellent, thanks. Call me when it's ready.' Callum hung up.

'Nice,' said Davie.

'Personal phones off from now. We don't want any trace of our presence north of here, and let's put the other plates on the car. ANPR cameras are a bugger going north.' Callum reached into his pocket and pulled out a small glass vial, tipped a little powder on his thumb and sniffed.

Davie let out a sigh and stared at the window.

'What's got into you this morning? You're partial yourself,' said Callum, his voice hard.

'Aye, man, but at a club on a night out, not in a cop shop car park.'

'Don't worry, no one can see us, everything's going according to plan. You're not having doubts, are you? Starting to bottle it?' Callum fixed Davie with a cold stare.

Davie held his gaze.

After a few seconds, Callum sniffed, swallowed. 'Come on, let's get moving,' he said, with a smile. He lowered the window and tossed out his smouldering cigarette.

Davie gritted his teeth and kept his mouth shut. He put the car in gear and moved off.

17

IT WAS JUST an hour after the summons before Ross, Max and Janie were all sitting on comfortable chairs in the chief's spacious office, at Tulliallan police college. He had sat wordlessly and listened intently as Ross explained the circumstances to him in his typically clear, concise manner.

Once he'd finished, Chief Constable Chris Macdonald leaned back in his chair. There was a long silence before he spoke. 'What a mess. I want this to be priority number one for you.' Chris Macdonald shook his head, a mix of sadness and anger clear in his handsome features.

A silence enveloped the room for a full thirty seconds before Macdonald spoke again. 'Options?'

Max chipped in, 'We keep this tight, boss. The three of us look into it carefully and steadily. Usual things. Who had the opportunity? What was the motive? Why did Murdo feel his only option was to throw himself off a bridge? What happened to Hamish's records? And why was his statement entirely at odds with what he told me?'

'As I understand it, Hamish was a most thorough officer. If Murdo had said what Hamish told you, then he would've recorded it,' said Macdonald.

'Somehow, someone got to that statement, sir. What do we know about the inquiry into the suicide?' said Janie.

'I have the full report from the OIC at Clydebank, which I'll share with you. It seems clear cut. Hamish's statement says the man jumped, and he said very little. The CCTV is unequivocal. From Police Scotland's point of view, this is a simple suicide. One thing is notable, however.' The chief glanced at his computer screen for a moment, before looking at each of them in turn. 'Hamish's pocketbook hasn't been found, not in his locker, not in his correspondence tray and not at his house.'

Ross swore. 'Don't suppose there's any chance he lost it?' he said.

'Hamish was the most meticulous officer I have ever worked with. His notebook was a thing of beauty. He recorded everything in painstaking detail,' said Max.

'So where is it?' asked Janie.

'If we knew that, we'd be halfway there,' said Macdonald.

'Boss, can you come up with something that gets us full access to the inquiry into Murdo Smith? I've seen what's on the computer, but I'd like to see what else is out there, and maybe have a chat with the OIC,' said Janie.

'That's simple to sort. I think if I order my Policing Standards Reassurance Team to carry out a fact-finding exercise into suicides on the Erskine Bridge, with an objective of making safety recommendations to the local authority, that should be good enough.'

'We could also do with a genuine reason to be asking about the disappearance of Jimmy McLeish at Torridon,' said Janie.

'I'll order a review into mispers and have this one added to the list of a number of others I want considering,' said Macdonald.

'Let's call them "thematic reviews",' said Max with a half-smile.

'Good idea,' Macdonald agreed.

'I'll look into Hamish's suicide. I know the SIO, he's a good guy, but I need a similar cover story,' said Ross.

Macdonald paused for a moment. 'Consider it done. Whatever resources or authorities you need, you will get.' Macdonald's jaw was tight, and emotion shone from his eyes.

'We're on it,' said Ross.

'Good. What's first?'

'The PIRC lead investigator Lenny Farquharson is key,' said Max. 'Someone got to Hamish's statement and to his notebook. Lenny Farquharson was the last person to see Hamish alive. He had the opportunity, and if he's connected, he had the motive.'

'Lenny Farquharson?' Macdonald said, a look of distaste on his face.

'I'm assuming you know him.'

'Years ago, but yes. He was a DS in Lothian and Borders at that time, although I think he got promoted at some point afterwards.'

'Friend of yours?' said Ross.

'No. I never trusted him. Far too cavalier,' said Macdonald.

'Well, I think he has questions to answer,' said Max.

'You going to speak to him?'

'I think I have a better idea,' said Max.

18

A SCOWL STRETCHED ACROSS Scally's meaty features as he sat back in his leather chair. He was in a box room in his modest house in a fairly dull suburb of Wavertree, but he liked to call it his study, even if it was a little pretentious. The lines on his forehead deepened as he listened to the ring tone. Fifteen fucking keys. He shuddered at how much money he had lost. Fortunately, things had been so good recently, despite a few mishaps, that he had huge cash reserves, and a new shipment arriving soon.

'Scally?' a Scouse accent said.

'Shorty, change of plan. Nothing's coming up today: supply difficulty,' he said.

'Ah bloody hell, man. I need it bad. The junkies are clucking up here.'

'I'll get some more sent up pronto. That daft twat Stevie got himself nicked in Perth. How much do you need?'

'As much as you can get me. These shite little fishing towns can't get enough of the stuff. I'm clearing half a key a night with the junkie dealers between here, Peterhead and the outskirts of Aberdeen.'

Scally should have been pleased. His operation was tight;

his men travelled north through Scotland, taking over junkie houses and getting one of them to sell the stuff in exchange for a couple of rocks a night. Shorty had built up a nice little network.

'I can get you a key tonight, mate, but that's it until the new shipment comes in. Macca's fucking vanishing act and that daft twat Stevie have put me right out. Raise the prices for a bit, keep things ticking over.'

'That'll only do me three days, max. When's the next delivery due?'

'Soon, I'll sort it. You got enough for tonight?'

'Only just,' said Shorty.

'I'll get Tug to travel up to you from Inverness with a key. Be stingy with the rocks you make from it.'

'Fair dos,' said Shorty, so called as he was only a shade over five foot five. He was a good man, and he ran his crack houses well. No one messed about with Shorty, despite his diminutive size.

Scally hung up and rubbed his temples, a headache beginning to announce its presence with a dull throb.

The door suddenly exploded in and the small, stocky form of Kyle, his youngest son burst into the room clad in a red Liverpool FC shirt, clutching a football.

'Dad, come on. You said you were gonna play footie with us,' he said, his face split with an excited grin that showed missing front teeth.

'In a bit, la. Just doing some business. Where's your brother?'

'Gone out to the green. Come on, I wanna play,' he said, throwing the ball at Scally who caught it.

'Soon, mate, promise,' he said grinning and ruffling his son's dirty blonde hair.

Laura, Scally's wife, appeared at the door. 'Come on, Kyle, leave your dad alone, go play in the garden, yeah?' A compact, slim woman with peroxide blonde hair, and twinkling blue eyes, she looked at him and grinned in her usual crooked fashion. It was her smile that had first attracted him to her all those years ago.

'Hurry up, Dad,' said Kyle as he sprinted out of the door.

'Thanks, love, I won't be long, just sorting some nonsense out,' said Scally to his wife.

'I hope that's finding Macca. Julie has been on at me constantly. Where the bloody hell is he?'

'No idea. Bugger's just vanished, I've everyone out looking for him.'

'People don't just disappear.'

'I know, I know, but what can I do? He went north on a job and never returned. Probably on another bird. You know what he's like.'

Laura scowled at her husband. They'd been together for many years, and she knew exactly who he was and what he did, but she didn't interfere, just accepted the risks and took the money that kept a roof over their heads.

'There's a house up for sale,' she said. 'Lovely place over the water on the Wirral. Can I book us to look at it?'

'Wirral? You serious, I'm no woollyback,' said Scally. He wasn't one of those bastards who didn't live in the city.

'We can't stay here forever, love. Kids need room to breathe, and if you're out doing your thing all the time, I need a better place to live,' she said, her face sharp.

Scally let out a sigh and held her gaze for a moment. 'Okay, book it up and I'll be there.' He managed a smile, knowing she was right. He loved this house, but it was too small, and he was moving up in the world. Maybe the time had come for him to get somewhere better. If it would keep Laura happy, then it would be worth it.

'Right, I'll get onto the agent,' she said, her mouth softening into a grin as she turned to leave the room.

Scally shook his head, picked up his phone and dialled.

'Tug?'

'You okay, mate?'

'Yeah, listen, I need you to get up to Fraserburgh. Give Shorty a call and arrange to get a key to him double urgent.'

'Shit, mate. What's happened?'

'Stevie got lifted. Shorty needs a key, now.'

'Jesus, how?'

'I dunno, his lady gave me a call. I don't know anything else, just get the key up there. If we don't supply the gear, some other bugger will, and I don't want to have to deal with that.'

'Okay, I'm on my way.'

Scally hung up. He was worried, and Scally wasn't a man to worry easily. As well as losing a lump of product he had Macca's missus going mad, giving him grief, but all he could tell her was the truth. That he had no bloody idea where he was. The gear had been delivered, that much he knew for sure. Something was going on. No way would Macca rip him off, they'd known each other for years and he trusted him like a brother.

And now Stevie and the five keys. He opened a drawer in the coffee table, pulled out an old, battered-looking Samsung phone and dialled. He had no choice, he would have to make contact.

He quickly composed a message. *I need to talk. Urgent.*

He didn't have to wait too long. His phone buzzed and he answered it.

'This better be fucking important.'

'It is.'

'You need to be quick. It's difficult to speak,' said the voice in a hoarse whisper.

'We may have a problem,' Scally hesitated, surprised to feel a little nervous.

'Jesus, what? You sure you're up to this? I need someone who doesn't make mistakes. It's not like there aren't other people I could use.'

'One of my lads got lifted somewhere near Perth with five. I'm worried someone's looking too closely at us. It doesn't feel like bizzies.'

There was a pause on the other end of the line.

'This could cause big problems.'

'I need to know what's going on. You have access to people who can find out.'

'Somehow, you've been compromised. Check your security systems right away and make sure everyone's phones are secure. They could be listening. No more talk anywhere about business on phones until this is addressed. That clear?'

'Crystal,' Scally confirmed.

'Message me the details. No more phone calls.' There was a click as the call ended.

Scally quickly composed a message on his secure Wickr app, inputting all the details. The app beeped as the message sent. Ten seconds later, it disappeared completely, totally erased from the phone as the encrypted message flew through the ether to its recipient. Satisfied, Scally opened the back of the phone. He pulled out the SIM card, bent it in half between his stubby fingers, and then tossed it in the bin.

Scally picked up his other phone and composed a new group message on Wickr, confident that the encryption would make it unreadable. They'd been lax, he had to admit. That stopped now.

Ditch all phones and SIM. Possible compromise. Contact me on Wickr with new numbers. Nothing on open calls or text.

19

MAX'S PHONE RANG on the Volvo's dash.

'Yeah?'

'It's Ross. Lenny's about to be called by his boss. We're being patched in, ready?' Ross's voice boomed over the car's speakers.

'Aye, go for it. Turn the volume down a bit, Janie.'

There was a tinny trill of a dial tone.

'Hello?'

'Lenny, it's David, are you at home?'

'Aye, just having my dinner.'

'Good, you're on call, right?'

'Aye, but please don't say it's something big. I'm knackered, man.'

'Nothing big, but I need you to go and meet someone urgently in Glasgow.'

'What, now? Can't it wait?'

'No, it can't. Someone calling themself "Chas" says he has information about corruption at a managerial level in Police Scotland. From how he speaks, I'd say he's a cop, and apparently he's credible. He won't go to a police station. Says it needs to be tonight, or he'll go to the press. We can't afford that, so get yourself to him.'

'What's he alleging?'

'Not entirely clear, but he's suggesting it's about procurement corruption at the highest levels. Friends being awarded massive contracts with no oversight. He seems to have a lot of detail and he says he has proof. You know we've been worried about this for a while, and this could break it all open.'

'Aye, okay, where is he?'

'I'll send you the details. He's nervous but get yourself there. He says he'll wait for another hour, and then he's leaving and won't return.'

'Okay, I'm going now.'

'Good man.'

The phone clicked as the call ended.

'You get that?' asked Ross.

'Sure did. It's going to get busy. Are you monitoring the channel?'

'Course I am.' The line went dead.

'All units stand by. Subject is about to leave the premises,' said Max into the mic.

'Alpha one from Alpha five, subject one is out of the premises and to the Mercedes. Door opening, and he's in, in, in. Door shut. He's pausing, and is on the phone, so far?'

The voice of a surveillance officer was muffled as he spoke into his collar from the back of nearby van. He was watching Lenny Farquharson leave his smart detached house at the far end of a quiet cul-de-sac in a middle-class suburb of Kirkcaldy. The van was safely out of sight in an adjacent street, the live image being relayed by a GSM-enabled camera that had been secreted earlier that day in a lamppost. Unknown cars, particularly those with occupants, are always noticed, so it paid to stay well out of the way.

'So far,' came the retort from the team leader, acknowledging that his message had been received. The vagaries of the surveillance glossary, designed over the years, allowed operators to relay the maximum information in the shortest amount of time, in an unambiguous fashion.

'Engine on, headlights on, and he's manoeuvring. And he's off, off, off. Leaves the drive and is back along the cul-de-sac towards Dunniker golf club and to your plot location, Alpha three. Be ready to take eyeball.'

'Alpha three, yes, Dunniker. Confirming I have the eyeball, and subject is west on Dunniker Way, speed thirty, one vehicle for cover.'

'Worked a treat that cover story,' said Janie.

Max chuckled. 'Well, seeing as Farquharson is on call as the senior PIRC investigator, and, when a disgruntled police officer is offering top-level intelligence, what's the PIRC to do? Ignore him? Who ya gonna call?'

'Policebusters,' Janie said.

'They have to send a senior investigator, which should keep him out of our way for long enough.'

'What will they do with the complaint?' said Janie.

'Decide he's a nut job when after an hour or so he starts talking about 5G masts controlling minds, and that the lizards are really in control.'

'Who's the complainant?'

'An undercover officer from London. He plays a madman very well, in fact, when I last worked with him, he genuinely was an utter space cadet.'

'Aren't all trained UCOs?'

'I'm a trained UCO,' said Max.

'Case rested, m'lud,' Janie said.

The surveillance team sprang into life, twelve officers in eight vehicles, with the sole intention of covertly staying behind the PIRC investigator as he travelled to meet the undercover officer posing as a complainant.

The best team available had been briefed by Max. They were more than capable, having been hand-picked for their individual skills, and, more importantly, thoroughly vetted to ensure their trustworthiness.

Max's phone buzzed in his pocket. It was the surveillance team leader, Cath.

'Max, you're good to go, mobile team is with him and we have four officers waiting back here to cover your entry and egress. Close neighbours are currently in a restaurant in Cowdenbeath. They've only just arrived, so you have plenty of time. The house is in darkness with thick curtains drawn and no light coming from inside. No visible alarm set that we know of and none registered with police or the local authority.'

'Thanks. Switch to channel two and any further comms with me on there.' Max jammed his earpiece in, looked at Janie. 'Ready?'

'Like a coiled spring, but once again you have me farting around in the evening when I should be in my comfy breeks watching the telly.'

'Barney?' Max spoke to the small, wiry man in the back of the car who had an unlit hand-rolled cigarette behind his ear. Despite not being allowed to smoke anywhere anymore, Barney almost always had a roll-up behind his ear, or possibly tucked in his mouth, ready to be lit at the next opportunity.

'Got my box of tricks and ready to rock and roll,' he said, buttoning up his worn-looking cardigan.

'How long to defeat the locks?'

'Difficult to say. I've only had the briefest of looks at the front door when I did the dummy leaflet drop earlier. It's a simple enough mortice but the rear might be easier. I suggest I try the back first, better for cover.' He had a broad Yorkshire accent and an easy-going manner. Barney was a technical wizard. Anything mechanical was his speciality. He was an electronic surveillance expert and a trained locksmith, having previously worked for the security services before being forced to retire at the age of sixty. No one knew how old he really was now, but he acted as a 'technical attack consultant', mostly because he enjoyed it, as far as Max could see.

'Are we clear?' Max said into his covert mic.

'All clear to proceed,' Cath's voice crackled in Max's ear.

'Okay, mate. Go for it,' Max said to Barney, who was jamming an earpiece into his ear.

'Two minutes,' he said, removing his roll-up with a grin that revealed surprisingly white, even teeth. 'Hold this, love.' He proffered the battered cigarette to Janie, who took it with a wrinkled nose. Barney quietly opened the rear door, easing it shut silently, slipped his rucksack on his back and then walked along the pavement adjacent to the building. He stepped over the waist-high fence and disappeared into Farquharson's rear garden.

'Why on earth did he hand me this?' said Janie, setting it down in the centre console.

Max chuckled.

'All quiet at the rear,' Barney said in a whisper. *'Approaching*

the back door. It's gonna be a piece of cake. One-lever mortice. Give me two minutes.'

'Received. Cath, our man is in the garden, eyes on, everyone,' Max said into his mic.

Barney didn't need two minutes. He didn't even need a minute. Forty seconds after entering the garden, the radio crackled once again.

'Lock defeated. Come up.'

'Bloody hell,' said Janie.

'Despite looking like your favourite uncle at Christmas, he's as sharp as a razor blade. Worth his weight in gold,' said Max.

'So I can see. Are we ready?' Janie released her seatbelt.

'I think so, unless you need to give the car a quick hoover first?'

'Come on,' said Janie, opening the door.

They both followed in Barney's wake and soon joined him in the gloomy back garden. A light drizzle had begun to fall in a fine mist that hung in the air like fog. There wasn't a breath of wind, and the deep night seemed to envelop them in an eerie silence.

'Glad he doesn't have motion sensitive cameras or a light,' whispered Janie.

'He has lights, but I've jammed them,' said Barney, waving a small hand-held device, similar to a walkie talkie. 'This'll jam his Wi-Fi router too and any wireless cameras, just in case we've missed anything.'

'Such digital expertise from a man from the analogue age?' said Max.

'Sod off. We're clear, no alarm system registered on the IR or radio frequencies. No alarm tape, either. Let's get in there,' said Barney.

'Think we need night vision goggles?'

'There's light coming from inside. He must have thick curtains, because there's nothing visible from the front. No overlooking neighbours, so I'd say good to go with just torches.'

'Are we sure there's no one in?' said Janie.

'Aye, I used my special thermal imaging camera to scan all the rooms. Got this fancy new micro drone and managed to fly it down the chimney,' said Barney.

'Very funny, Grandpa,' said Janie.

'Less of the "Grandpa", please. Anyway, if someone's home, you'll have to batter them. We heard no one on the probe, mind,' said Barney with a smile in his voice in the darkness.

'Okay, one room at a time,' said Max. 'Nice and slow. We won't be able to leave anything out of place.'

Janie and Barnie nodded, and all three pulled balaclavas over their faces. As confident as they were that no cameras were running, you could never discount old-fashioned wired CCTV recording direct to a disk or hard drive. It wouldn't do to have their faces captured. They all put on plastic overshoes and snapped nitrile gloves into place. Nothing from outside could enter the house.

Max walked ahead, clutching a small, low-light Sony handycam which he panned around the dimly lit, untidy kitchen, recording the positions of everything. There was a marble-topped breakfast bar heaped with dirty plates and takeaway boxes. Four sleek bar stools were misaligned under the overhang. LED lights in the plinths and under the eye-level units lit the room. All the appliances were sleek and modern but covered in a layer of grime. The whole space spoke of someone who had given up caring about hygiene.

'Start searching in here, I'll check and record upstairs,' said Max. 'We'll start the rest when I get back down.'

Barney and Janie knew the routine. Slow and careful. Every time you move something, you mentally mark its position so you replace it correctly. A misplaced teacup could be the thing that gives you away. The video of the property would be used for a final check, to make sure everything was as they found it.

Within three minutes Max returned, tucking the camera into his pocket.

'Anything in here?' he said in a low voice.

'Nothing, house is bogging,' said Janie.

'Gone downhill since the wife left him. He's rattling round in a nice house whilst she's off with a younger man.'

'Poor wee mannie, must be *so* hard for him,' said Janie.

'Let's move on. Living room, Barney, I want ears in the kitchen and hall, okay?'

'There's a hard-wired smoke alarm up there, so it's a piece of cake. Simple GSM listener will do the trick.' Barney reached into his bag, pulled out a small piece of electrical circuitry. He climbed up onto one of the bar stools, a small screwdriver in his hand. Within a few seconds he had the cover off and had disassembled the inner workings of the alarm. The electrical flex powering the unit snaked through a rough hole in the ceiling. Barney tucked a small, cylindrical unit in the plasterboard with it, leaving just a thin wire with a tiny microphone at the end. Seconds later, the invisible unit was wired into the power supply. He snapped the cover back on, produced a small receiver from his pocket and jammed on a set of headphones.

'Just going to release the jammer to test. Safe as houses.' He fiddled with the jammer and replaced it in his pocket.

Jumping down from the stool, he spoke softly, 'One, two, three. Test, test, test.' A thumbs-up to Max told him everything he needed to know. The GSM listening bug would use mobile phone technology to send the signal wherever it was needed.

They moved into a dark lounge, dimly lit by a couple of low lamps. A large TV with an expensive-looking soundbar underneath dominated the room, a leather recliner positioned directly in front of it. On a scratched coffee table sat a laptop. There was no other furniture in the room.

'Mrs Farquharson took the bloody lot,' said Janie. 'Sensible lady. He's revolting. Look at the bloody state of this.' She grimaced. A layer of dust coated every surface and the place stank of stale cigarette smoke. An overloaded ashtray lay on the coffee table alongside an empty whisky bottle and a half-full crystal glass.

'I want eyes and ears in here, particularly if we can get a view on where he sits and uses his computer.'

'Couple of options,' said Barney, looking around with a professional eye.

Suddenly an urgent crackling erupted in Max's ear. It was Cath. *'Max, be aware, we have a car in the cul-de-sac, not neighbours and not subject one, as they are under control. Mazda MX5, looks like a blonde female driving. She is towards your location now.'* Cath's voice had an edge to it.

'Shit,' said Janie.

'Okay, it could be nothing. We know where everyone is. Let's just sit tight, she can't see us from outside through these curtains.'

Cath's voice burst in their ears again. '*Vehicle slowing, and it's on the drive, female getting out of the car. Shit, she's coming to the door. Possible compromise, prepare to evacuate, prepare to evacuate. Team standby, standby.*'

20

MAX, JANIE AND Barney stared at each other, faces impassive, a heavy silence enveloping the room. The only sounds were their controlled breathing which seemed deafening in the depressing space. An old plastic wall clock ticked loudly in a corner. The sudden crackling in their earpieces made them all start.

'She's approaching the door, arm out and she's pressing the bell. I'm getting images of this. If I'm honest, not sure what we have here. She's actually wearing thigh-high boots.' Cath managed to sound impressed and concerned at the same time.

The doorbell chimes echoed around the house as they crouched on the lounge floor. This was serious. What if she had a bloody key?

The chimes pealed once more, the sound cutting through the oppressive air.

'Lenny, Lenny?' a heavily accented eastern European voice came through the door. 'Lenny, it's Beata, come on, I'm fuck freeze here.' Her voice was punctuated by another angry stab at the doorbell. 'Lenny, baby, come on. Don't leave girl stand on door.'

Her fist pounding against the wood sounded like a series of mini explosions. The keychain rattled with each impact.

'Beware, guys, she's making for the back of the house,' Cath called, urgently.

'The door? Barney, lock it, quick,' said Max.

'Chill, dudes. Key's in the door,' Barney said, ambling into the kitchen. He disappeared from sight for a moment, only to return seconds later. He smiled and sat down on the floor, cross-legged and out of sight from the rear of the house.

Thirty seconds later there was a frantic rattling of the back door, the keys jangling, noisily. 'Lenny, Lenny, why you ignore? Why you not answer your fuck phone? I come all way here to see you. You think I have no other client?' It was clear that Beata was not to be trifled with.

Max stifled a chuckle and was thankful they'd decided Farquharson should meet the 'complainant' in the bowels of an underground car park. It was just another way to stop him from receiving calls.

As suddenly as it had started, the banging stopped and silence descended.

There was a hard slam from the front drive, and the sound of an engine revving.

'That's her back in the car, reversing, and off the way she came. She doesn't look happy,' said Cath in Max's ear.

'Subject one is going to have an angry voicemail when his reception returns.'

'She's left the cul-de-sac. You're clear to proceed, but I'd get a move on, in case his signal comes back,' said Cath.

All three breathed a simultaneous sigh of relief.

'The dirty wee shite is using escorts,' said Janie.

Max grinned. 'Keep searching whilst Barney does his thing.'

'Wish I could have a fag,' said Barney, scratching his chin.

They scoured the living room, which didn't take long, as it was almost devoid of furniture. Max pulled open a single drawer in the small coffee table. It was jammed with takeaway menus and old pens, but as Max began to sift carefully through them, his hand brushed against something solid. He slid it out and set it on top of the menus. It was a sleek smartphone, of a type he hadn't seen before. He pressed the power button at the side, and the screen lit up, showing only three applications. The brand-name flashed across the home screen. Cryptnet.

'Janie, you ever seen one of these?'

She squatted next to Max and peered at the handset. 'Not exactly, but if I was guessing, it's the replacement for Encrochat which the NCA shut down a while back. A fully encrypted phone. Unbreakable encryption and all messages self-delete once read, both sent and received. Cameras and microphones are disabled, so no listening in. Also deletes all call data. Cost a bloody fortune, mate. Why has a PIRC investigator got this?'

'I think we know why. Barney, can you do anything with it?'

'Not here. In fact, probably not at all. It's way out of my league, requires a top-level forensics approach in a proper lab, and it's not like we can take it, is it?'

Janie looked at the phone. 'A pal of mine was a bit of an expert on these. He said that there'll be a next generation of Encrochat, but this is the first I've heard of a successor. We'll get nothing, not without custom-designed malware. Try that and we run the risk of getting rumbled.'

Max pulled out his handycam and took a short piece of video footage of the phone, turning it over in his gloved hand.

'What if we could get its number? Would that help?' said Barney innocently.

Janie and Max stared at him. 'Well,' Janie said, 'they still use GSM, so we could track it using cell sites. And you could also see the numbers he called and who called him. The calls and messages can't be intercepted, but it'd definitely be useful.'

'Tell you what, you two continue searching the rest of the place, and I'll see what I can do,' said Barney.

'Barney?' said Max.

'Ask no questions, hear no lies, but if I could potentially capture the IMSI number, you'd owe me a bottle, right?' said Barney, referring to the International Mobile Subscriber Identity number that all mobile phones required in order to make calls.

'Well, that'd get us the phone number, but how? Do you have some secret, slightly illegal kit from your spook days with MI5?'

Barney tapped the side of his nose and winked.

Janie had walked over to the drawers and was peering inside. 'We don't need it. The phone's box is here and the IMSI and IMEI is stamped on a sticker on the back,' she said, chuckling.

Max took some images of the box, making sure the numbers were recorded.

'Bugger,' Barney said, a little crestfallen at the missed opportunity.

'Nice try, though. Lucky us youngsters are here to solve your tech problems.'

'Piss off.'

Cath's voice sparked in their earpieces.

'Team at the restaurant with the neighbours say they're finishing. Could be only twenty minutes away.'

'Right, let's wrap it up. Barney, priority is eyes and ears in here, and if we can, ears upstairs. I'm assuming there'll be a smoke alarm up there. Janie, let's get going. I want to be out of here in ten minutes.'

21

TUG SAT IN his car in a desolate car park next to the equally desolate Boyndlie community hall. It was immediately off the A98, a few miles away from Fraserburgh, on the Scottish north-east coast.

The community hall was a 1970s nightmare, crouched in a scabby-surfaced concrete wasteland, next to several overflowing bottle-recycling bins.

Tug surveyed the place with disdain. He really missed Liverpool and the buzz of a big, lively city with its thriving night clubs, pubs and bars. He hadn't minded being sent north but, Christ, it was dull.

He looked south along the single carriageway, the main road between Inverness and Fraserburgh. You could see approaching headlights for over a mile in each direction. There were no street lights, only one empty house nearby and hardly any passing traffic. Sitting here in the pitch dark with his lights out, he was all but invisible. If a cop car passed, he would just claim to be a tired traveller taking forty winks.

His phone, an ancient Nokia, buzzed on the seat next to him. A message from Shorty. *Three minutes.* It was a serious pain having to do this, tonight of all nights, especially as they had been forced to ditch phones after Scally's call. He was thankful that he still had the drug line that the junkies called for their fixes. They'd never ditch that phone, scratched and primitive though it looked. It was worth far too much money.

He was itching to get back to Inverness, to sort out this daft junkie bird, Moira, whose house he was using to deal the rocks. He really needed to be on top of her, or she would smoke the whole bloody lot before the evening was out.

He saw a pair of lights round a bend in the distance, bang on time, as always. Shorty was a good guy, despite the moaning.

Tug stepped out of his anonymous Vauxhall as Shorty pulled up, nose to nose, directly in front of him in his equally anonymous Peugeot. Scally didn't believe in flash motors, apart for himself, obviously; his view was that a flash car got you noticed.

'You're a pain in the arse for making me come up here, la,' said Tug as he stepped forward to bump fists with Shorty.

'Not my fault that daft bastard Stevie got collared. I'm almost out, mate, been selling so well. The Jock junkies are mad for it,' said Shorty.

'Any idea what happened to Stevie and Macca?' asked Tug, burping loudly.

'Only what Scally said. Nicked in Perth, or somewhere equally shite and got remanded in custody. He can't have got to a phone yet, so it's all a bit sketchy.'

'How about Macca?'

'No idea. Bugger vanished with a big heap of gear.'

'Not nicked it, has he?'

'Nah, no chance. He's Scally's oldest mate, but Scally's going fucking doolally,' said Shorty.

'Shit. I want back to Liverpool, and it's only keeping the product flying in these shite-holes that'll get us moved and some other poor bastard switched in.'

Suddenly their attention was drawn to the sound of an approaching car, coming from the south. It began to slow as it neared the village hall.

'Who's that?' said Tug as the BMW estate came into view. It slowed even more and began to turn into the car park.

'No idea, mate. You carrying?'

'Am I fuck. No need up here, mate. All soft bastards,' said Tug, his eyes narrowing as the BMW slowed, its tyres crunching on the broken concrete.

'Where's the gear?' said Shorty, quietly.

'Under the end recycling bin. We're clear, mate, even if it is. I've jump leads in the car. If it's bizzies, we say I came to give you a jump start.'

The BMW stopped and the front passenger door opened, bathing the emerging passenger in a pale light. A slim, well-dressed man, with floppy, public-schoolboy hair, and a wide smile.

'Excuse me, gentlemen, but it seems we are lost. Can you direct us to Fraserburgh?' he asked in a cultured English accent.

22

'STRAIGHT UP THE road, mate,' said Tug, pointing north, eyeing the man with a degree of suspicion. There was something about him that didn't fit, and he couldn't put his finger on it.

'Excellent, thank you so much.' The man turned to go but then paused, his head tilted. 'Your accents don't sound local,' he said.

The other door swung open, and a huge brute of a man unfurled himself from the driver's seat, stretching his back as he did so. 'Shite, my back is fucking killing me after that drive. Do these mannies know the way?' His accent was broad, glottal Glaswegian.

'It seems they do,' said the smaller man.

'Aye well, we've told you. Now fuck off like, we're busy,' said Shorty, his voice tight.

There was a long silence, only punctuated by the breeze disturbing the trees that surrounded the waste ground.

'I don't think so, old boy,' the posh boy said finally, a slow grin stretching across his face as his hand moved towards his waistband.

In a flash, Shorty and Tug found themselves looking at a dark handgun with a long silencer attached. The barrel pointed unerringly at Shorty who stood closest.

'Now, we know you have a quantity of a product with you. We'd like to take it off your hands,' said Callum, projecting utter confidence.

'You don't know who you're fucking with, boys,' said Tug. He had been in many confrontations in his time with addicts and other dealers, but this was different. There was something about this man and his silenced weapon, his ironed shirt.

'Okay, now here's the thing. We know you have it, and we're going to relieve you of it. What you have isn't worth the pain I'll inflict on you if you don't cooperate. Am I making myself clear?' Callum said, glancing at the big man as if to check that he was making sense.

'Now listen to me, you fucking posh—' Tug was cut off mid-sentence by the muffled bark and jerk of the gun. What felt like a sledgehammer crashed into his kneecap. He puffed out a breath of air and collapsed to the ground like a felled tree. His screams tore through the night. It felt as though a white-hot poker had been suddenly jammed into his cartilage, and he let out another wail of agony.

The bigger man produced a pistol which he levelled calmly at Shorty. A smile stretched across his massive face. 'Don't even think about it, wee man, or I'll put one in your gut.'

Shorty's hands instinctively shot upwards, and he nodded.

'Shhhh,' Callum whispered, standing over Tug, the pistol levelled at his head. 'There, there, dear boy, quiet now,' he said, as Tug writhed in agony, gripping his destroyed limb. He bit down on his tongue and his moans quietened to a whimper.

'That's better. Peace and quiet. It's lovely, don't you think, particularly on a night like this? I'm going to count to three. If you fail to tell me where the product is, I'll put a bullet into your other knee, or maybe your shoulder. Now, where shall I put it? Knee?' He moved the pistol to Tug's undamaged limb. 'Or shoulder?' The pistol shifted again. 'Oh, I know, testicles? Not nice, but then, old chap, I'm not very nice. Now. One. Two ...' he counted, his jaw tight and the tendons in his neck protruding like steel cables.

'Under the recycling bin,' Tug gasped, his breath escaping in a low hiss. A trail of saliva ran from his mouth, mixing with bits of gravel on the ground.

'Davie?' Callum said to the big man, who lowered his pistol and made towards the recycling bins. Callum shifted his aim across to Shorty. 'I wouldn't even consider it. I'm a very good shot.'

'Got it,' said Davie, pulling out a carrier bag from underneath the bin. A brief look inside and he gave a nod.

'Let us go. We'll say fuck all, la,' said Tug. But he knew. They both knew.

'I'm sure you wouldn't, poor thing,' said Callum, nodding at Davie who raised his pistol, and put a bullet in the back of Shorty's head. He fell like a stone, dead before he hit the floor.

Tug said nothing, his eyes filling with tears. Deep racking sobs shook his body. He writhed on the ground, looking up as Callum levelled the pistol at his head with an amused expression. The pistol bucked again, the bullet smashed into Tug's forehead, bouncing around inside his cranium and destroying his brain.

23

MAX WAS TIRED when he pulled up outside his cottage just before 10 p.m. It had been a long and stressful few days. He was still sad about Hamish, but this was being tempered by his desire to get to the bottom of how he died, and more importantly, who killed him. First, he wanted to rest and see Katie and Nutmeg. Since Katie moved back in a few months ago, their time together had become more important. For the first time in years some normality had descended in his life and he wanted more of it. He was starting to realise that his dedication to work was toxic and that things needed to change. One last job, then maybe look for something nine to five.

As he walked into the house from the chilly evening air, Nutmeg exploded out of her deep sleep on Katie's lap, leaping into his arms and slobbering at his face with delight.

'Settle down, girl, settle,' he said as he deposited her on the scrubbed oak floor.

'Hey, stranger,' said Katie wearily, but with warm eyes, a glass of red wine at her side. 'Wine?' she asked as Max stooped to kiss her.

'Maybe a cranberry juice,' said Max.

'Top me up, whilst you're there,' she said, handing over her glass.

'I bet you've been waiting for me to come home, just for that top-up.'

'I don't like to disturb Nutmeg. She was fast asleep,' she laughed. When Max returned, they chinked glasses and both took sips of their drinks. Max was still avoiding alcohol and finding that life was better without it. He had fewer bad dreams, and the darkness that sometimes nipped at his mind was easier to deal with when he stuck to cranberry juice. He also genuinely liked the drink's dry, cold taste.

'Busy day?' asked Max.

'Very. Too much to do, not enough staff. You know the drill. How about you?'

'Yeah, just a bit.' Max didn't expand. He rarely talked about work, preferring to leave it behind.

His thoughts turned to the listening devices currently secreted at Farquharson's house, but he resisted the urge to switch on his laptop and watch the feed. Janie would be monitoring it until Farquharson hit the sack himself.

'Any food left?' asked Max.

'Some stew in the slow-cooker and a bit of crusty bread. You're lucky I didn't give it to Nutty,' Katie said without any anger or frustration. Despite the problems they had experienced in their marriage, leading to a trial separation a while ago, she understood that Max didn't have a normal job.

'Looks lovely,' he said as he spooned some of the rich stew into a bowl and tore off a hunk of slightly stale bread. Sitting back down, he began to eat. It was, predictably, delicious. Katie was marvellous in the kitchen, and the rural life had sparked a new-found love of cooking with local, seasonal ingredients.

Max's phone buzzed in his pocket. Looking at the display, he sighed, knowing that it would be work. He answered it.

'Janie?' he said through a mouthful of stew.

'Looked at the feeds from the probes?'

'No, I've just got home.'

'Best look. I'll send you a clip of what he just said. He made a call on the encrypted phone, no idea who to, but the requests have gone in to trace the number.'

Max stood and went to his laptop on the breakfast bar. His heart sank as he booted it up and clicked the email already waiting from Janie.

'What's this?'

'First is a link to early details of a shooting in Fraserburgh. Two drug dealers have just been shot dead in a layby on the outskirts of the town. They've been identified as Scouse dealers who were running the county lines, supplying Fraserburgh and Peterhead. Suspected that they worked for Lee "Scally" Dodd, a big dealer who filled the vacuum left behind by Tam Hardie. Also, one of Scally's main lieutenants went missing a wee while ago, dude called Macca, or more correctly Phillip McCartney. His wife reported him missing, saying he was on a trip in Scotland somewhere, but it's like he just vanished.'

Max's mind flared. He thought back to his meeting in Torridon. Macca, the mysterious stranger in the bar speaking to Jimmy McLeish.

'Jesus, Janie. This is it. Jimmy McLeish's wife Leah reported a sighting of him speaking to a Scouser called Macca in a bar before he went missing. That's it. That's the link.'

There was a long pause on the line before Janie spoke, her voice tight. 'Watch the clip. It's from about forty minutes ago,' she said eventually.

Max opened the video and maximised the screen. The pin-sharp image showed a seedy scene: Lenny Farquharson sitting in his chair with his feet extended and his laptop open, surfing the internet. Max could just make out the colouring of the BBC news website on his screen.

Suddenly Farquharson sat up, as if he had been electrocuted, his glass of whisky tumbling to the floor.

'Holy shit,' he said as he looked again at the open laptop, his shoulders heaving. He almost seemed to be hyperventilating. He placed the laptop on the carpet, stood up and began to pace.

'No, no, no, no. Stupid fucking bastards,' he hissed as he rubbed his scalp with his fingers, his face flushing a deep shade of red.

Suddenly, he grabbed his phone from the table and stabbed at it, his movements jerky, his hands quivering. He put the phone to his ear and waited.

'Cal, it's Len, just what the hell have you done?' he said, his voice shook. Max could see that his eyes were as wide as saucers. Max leaned forward, listening intently.

'It's all over the bloody news. BBC had it on a newsflash. What have you done?'

'. . .'

'What?' he shouted. 'Christ's sake, this is gonna bring shit-loads of attention. Why the fuck didn't you run this past me?'

There was a pause. 'They were just a couple of low-level scumbag dealers.'

'I know. Yeah, I know. How much?'

'...'

'What? Hardly worth it, is it?'

'...'

'Aye, I'm sure Scally will be going mental ... No, we won't get called out to this. No cops involved in the shooting, and unless someone alleges some malpractice, we won't get anywhere near it.'

'...'

'I hope you were careful.'

'...'

'Well, thank Christ for that, ANPR going north is brutal. What about phones?'

'...'

'That's one thing, at least. If they can put both of you in the area with your phones, then you're screwed. Jesus, this is reckless. You've already had enough of his product away. Okay, we need a meet soon. Make sure you're well clear. Right ... Okay, tomorrow. I'm not going into the office. Only use the Cryptnet phones, nothing whatsoever on any open lines, don't google anything, either.'

There was a pause. Farquharson swallowed, his head bowed.

'Aye, of course I know. But this is how cops investigate this kind of thing.' His voice was far more contrite now, his shoulders hunched.

There was a further pause as he listened.

'No, we're all clear. Murdo's suicide has been closed pending the inquest, and Hamish Beattie is being scaled back. No evidence of foul play.'

'...'

'I'm just being careful. Speak tomorrow.'

Max stared at the screen, stunned by what he had seen. A senior PIRC investigator, and an ex-detective inspector, had just been told of a double murder and a clear conspiracy to supply large quantities of drugs.

He also knew about Murdo and Hamish.

Max felt pure, naked rage begin to rise from his gut into his chest. His head swam with the intensity of it. He couldn't formulate the words, but he knew he had to say something. He placed his hands against the cool work surface to steady himself, his phone clenched in his fist so tight that his knuckles were white. He looked down at the phone still in his palm and listened to Janie's faint voice calling up to him from the handset, saying his name. His eyes went to Katie, who had swivelled towards him on the sofa, her face full of concern.

He put the phone back to his ear and swallowed. 'Janie, you still there?'

'Aye,' she said.

'Has Ross seen this?'

'Aye.'

'Who is Cal?'

'No idea, but we need to find out. Phone work is going in urgently.'

'What next?'

'Ross wants us in the office at six. We're going live on this. The surveillance team is away on another job down south, but they'll be with us late morning, early afternoon, ready to deploy.'

'Against who?'

'Farquharson, or preferably, Cal, if we can identify him. You know what this means, right?'

'Some corrupt bastards in law enforcement are knocking off drug dealers.'

'That's about the size of it,' said Janie.

There was a moment of silence on the line as the gravity of what they were dealing with sunk in. This was much bigger than they had anticipated. The question was, where would it end?

24

MAX TOSSED AND turned, unable to switch off his mind, visions of Hamish's hanging body swimming through his subconscious. If he'd just called him earlier, or maybe gone and spent time with him rather than travelling up north on his bike, would he still be alive? His thoughts whirled as if a cog had worked loose in his brain.

He must have eventually dropped off, because the dream tore him, viciously, from what little sleep he had managed to achieve. He lay there, breathing heavily, a sheen of icy sweat on his body, his thoughts dark and swirling.

He thought about the bank robber he had shot a couple of years ago during his time in the Metropolitan Police Flying Squad. He thought about the cloud of endless inquiries, inquests and investigations that had hung over him ever since.

He thought about the dream and how it came to him when things were bad. It was always the same. Tearing him back to that day in Helmand Province that would never leave him. He'd been on patrol next to their base when he'd watched his friend, Dippy, get ripped to pieces by an improvised explosive device. As the section corporal, Max had always felt partly responsible, and the dream made him relive it all in excruciating detail.

The look in Dippy's eyes as the last spark of life slipped away, replaced with a momentary flicker of confusion, then blank emptiness. Dippy's terrible injuries were Technicolor, vivid against the sand. The helplessness in his voice, as he begged Max to help him. Part of Max died alongside his friend that day, in the dirt and dust of Helmand Province.

Max stared at the ceiling through the darkness, listening to Katie's rhythmic breathing beside him, and Nutmeg's light snoring against his leg.

It had been a long time since the dream had visited him, but Max knew from bitter experience that sleep would not come now. PTSD had been diagnosed by occupational health in the Met, and later confirmed after he had transferred to Scotland.

He also knew that he needed to run. Max ran when the darkness came. Medication didn't help, and alcohol made it worse, as did counselling. Extreme physical exercise was his medication, be it weight-lifting, boxing, or circuits. Anything that made him push himself as hard as he was able. But running was catharsis. Running with Nutmeg took him away from everything.

He slid out of bed, silently, and, as quietly as he could, pulled on his shorts and a T-shirt from the drawer. Nutmeg stirred, knowing what she needed to do.

'You okay? It's only four o'clock.' Katie's soft, sleep-laced voice cut through the darkness. Max loved that voice. Soft and warm and tinged with the tones of Yorkshire.

'I can't sleep. I'll take Nutty out and then get into work,' he whispered softly.

'The dream?'

'Aye.'

'You okay, babe?'

'I'm fine, love. Go back to sleep. I'll feed Nutty after,' said Max, pulling on his running gear.

'Kiss me, then?' she asked, and Max could hear the smile in her voice.

Max leaned over the bed and kissed his wife on the mouth.

'You're lathered in sweat. You sure you're okay?'

'A run and I'll be good. See you later.'

'Love you,' said Katie, her hand brushing his cheek.

'You too,' said Max as he left the bedroom, Nutmeg at his heels.

It was pitch dark outside, the winter sun still a few hours away. Max slipped on a head torch and hoodie, to guard against the Scottish chill.

'Come on, Nutty.'

The little shaggy cockapoo stared adoringly at him, her tail thrashing, ready. Somehow, Nutmeg knew when the darkness began to bite.

So, they ran, in the pre-dawn, along the deserted country lanes of Culross. They ran hard. Hard enough to make it hurt, to make Max feel a little better.

25

MAX AND JANIE sat in the office and stared at the computer reports of the shooting, or more accurately the execution, of two suspected drug dealers in a deserted car park close to Fraserburgh. The MIT from Inverness had scrambled and were at the scene. Max wore a polo shirt and Janie a vest top. Her loose overshirt lay across the back of her chair. Both were red-faced, and Max had a sheen of sweat on his forehead.

Ross burst into the room, the door banging against the stop and reverberating with a crash. His expression was troubled, his cheeks flushed pink as usual.

'Fuck me, it's bastard roasting in here, what the hell is going on?' His Highland voice sounded even rougher than usual this morning.

'Heating's on the blink, I've reported it,' said Janie, without looking up from the screen.

'Well, open the bloody window then. Do I need to do everything in this shite-hole? Can't even get a decent bloody office,' he muttered to himself as he walked to the solitary window. He tugged at it, grunting. 'Bastard's stuck fast.'

'Aye, it's been painted that many times it may as well be nailed fast,' said Max.

Ross removed his jacket and looked at his watch. 'Christ, wasn't six early enough for you? Shite the bed again?'

'Couldn't sleep,' said Max. 'Seen the reports from Fraserburgh?'

'Of fucking course, man. Let me get a coffee first,' said Ross, limping his way to the coffee machine.

Max raised his eyebrows at Janie and stood up to follow Ross across the room. There were bags under Ross's eyes and one of his shoes had what looked like a recent scuff mark, as if he'd kicked a wall or tripped over. 'You okay?' he said.

'Not really. Situation with Mrs Fraser deteriorated a great deal last night. Slept on the fucking sofa, which isn't good for my back.'

'Sorry to hear that.'

'She'll get over it. Too many hours on this bloody job, and she was due a birthday dinner, which didn't happen. Anyway, never mind all that. What's occurring?'

'You heard anything?' Max called over to Janie.

'Aye, a pal's on the team that got scrambled. Two of Scally's men, bullets to the head, one also got kneecapped.'

'Jesus,' said Max, rubbing his temples.

There was a deep silence as Ross made coffee and they all turned it over. A double homicide. Tortured and then executed.

'Farquharson is still at home, snoring, from what I can hear,' said Janie, holding up an iPad with a long earbud snaking downwards. 'I've been listening half the bloody night.' She yawned and leaned back on her chair. Max went and sat down next to her, positioning the iPad between them and pulling out the cable. The soft hissing sound of snoring filtered from the tinny speaker. The low-light camera displayed a ghostly image of the lounge in which they had planted their covert surveillance devices.

'Does this change what we do?' said Max.

'My opinion is no,' said Ross, coming over to join them and handing out two coffees. 'We still go behind Farquharson. He'll lead us to these bastards, then we take the lot of them out across the pavement. Murder team will handle the shooting, we go after the bent cops.'

'Agreed,' said Max.

Ross sat with a grunt in his chair, which squealed in protest. He wiped sweat from his brow. 'Right, lots has been going on whilst you two lazy bastards were skulking around doing the sneaky-beaky shite. With my immense skill and contacts, I've managed to get authorisation in double-quick time. Do I get any thanks, eh? No, just you buggers playing James Bond, whilst I'm tied to a computer doing authority applications.' He took a sip of his coffee and sighed appreciatively.

'Didn't the chief say he'd authorise quickly?' asked Max.

'Aye, he did, but I had to do the work, you know,' replied Ross.

'We all know that it was done on an urgent oral basis,' said Janie, catching Max's eye. 'So you just explained it to him, recorded on audio and the chief's PA typed it all up and sent it to the surveillance commissioner, right?'

'Well, possibly, but I had to make her a cup of tea,' said Ross, yawning.

'So, you actually did sod all?' said Max.

'It's called greasing the wheels, making things happen. Facilitating. Anyway, where are we with this job, eh, Janie?'

She flashed him an irritated look and brought up the relevant screen on her laptop. 'So, let's start with Farquharson,' she said. 'He served twenty-four years in the police, first Lothian and Borders until we amalgamated. Reached DI, worked broadly in a number of roles. Left a few years ago and joined PIRC as a senior investigator.'

'Why'd he leave?' asked Max.

'Not clear, but he did miss out on a chief inspector board. It seems he made himself unpopular and there were a few doubts about him. Left in a tantrum and walked straight into his current job. He was married, two grown-up kids, but recently divorced. As I heard it, she cleaned him out financially. Wise lady. That fits with his current financial situation,' Janie said, looking up from her screen.

'Meaning?' said Ross.

'He's in mortgage arrears to the tune of twelve grand. There's a few maxed-out credit cards in his name and a very big overdraft that isn't covered by his income. His maintenance to his ex-wife is eye-watering.'

'Bloody typical, women always go for the jugular. Take Mrs Fraser, for instance, I'm always broke because of her,' said Ross.

'Mary just likes nice things,' said Max.

'Bloody expensive things, daft bint.'

'I'm going to tell her you said that,' said Max.

'Might as well. My stock is low enough as it is,' said Ross.

'That bad?' said Max.

'Aye. I think she's missing me.'

'I doubt that very much.'

'Anyway,' Janie said. 'I hate to butt in, gentlemen, but may I continue?'

'Please do,' said Ross.

'So, we need to use Farquharson to take us to "Cal", whoever he is. He's clearly responsible for shooting the dealers in Fraserburgh, and it's obvious he didn't do it alone,' Janie continued, scribbling in an A4 notebook.

'So, what do you suggest?' said Ross.

'We get the surveillance team behind Farquharson,' said Max. 'You heard him last night. He used the words "both of them", so we know there were at least two involved in the shooting. From the phone call, we know they ripped off a kilo of drugs. I think it's inevitable they plan to meet today. We witness the meet, identify "Cal" and we either follow them, to gain more evidence, or take them out on the street. The surveillance team is defensively armed, and we can get a gunship to run with a proper firearms team.'

'I think this is our best shot. Janie, any observations?' said Ross.

'We have to identify the shooters. With what Murdo said to Hamish, I think we've got someone from law enforcement shooting drug dealers, and they probably killed Macca.'

'How could you know that?' said Ross.

'Quite simple. The phone number that called in to Farquharson's encrypted phone last night. Whilst you two were in bed, I tracked it using historic cell site intelligence. It isn't often switched on, and it isn't on now, but some of the cell locations are revealing.' Janie paused to sip her coffee. 'It was near Fraserburgh last night. And, around the time Macca went missing, the phone attributed to "Cal" was cell sited on the west coast of Scotland, near where Macca's wife said he was going. Want to know something else?' said Janie.

'Go on,' said Max.

'It was near where Jimmy McLeish, our fisherman, went missing. And his mobile phone fell off the network at exactly the right time.'

'And this ties in perfectly with the misper report by Leah McLeish,' added Max.

'Jesus. I think we can guess what the cargo was. This is great work,' said Ross.

'Was that a compliment?'

'Don't get bloody used to it.'

'Murdo Smith had been heavily researching importation via sea lochs. That's no coincidence,' said Max, thinking back to his chat with Norma.

The room fell silent. Corrupt law-enforcement agents committing multiple murders and intercepting drug importations into a Scottish sea loch.

'Whoever this is, they've access to intelligence at the highest level. They not only know who's bringing in the drugs, they know where it's coming in. They knew when and where, and they were there to intercept it. That's intelligence coming in from covert and secure channels, which is tightly controlled and not widely disseminated. Someone at a senior level is at the centre of this,' said Max.

Ross nodded. 'Someone, be it a cop, NCA or customs, is wiping out Scally's network, and stealing his drugs. They're taking over. The bastards are taking over the drug supply network in Scotland and beyond, and they're one of ours.'

26

MAX PICKED UP his phone and dialled. He watched Janie and Ross, beavering away, working the intelligence and looking at the leads. Ross's sleeves were rolled up and his tie was loose, such was the heat coming from the boiling radiator. There was loads to do before they deployed, but no time to get it done.

'Max, how you doing?' Norma's voice sounded in Max's ear. 'You don't phone me for bloody ages, and then you call me, at a horribly early hour, when I can still taste toothpaste. It's uncivilised.'

'Sorry, but this is important.'

'Why am I not surprised?'

'Murdo was working on west coast importations, right?'

'Yeah, well, until he got shunted sideways. Why?'

'Who was he giving the intelligence to?'

'Drugs team in Glasgow. Not sure what happened to it all, though.'

'How many on the team?'

'A dozen or so. What's this about?'

'Who was in charge? Just trying to establish how Murdo could have made himself enemies.'

'Well, Callum Mackintosh is the grade-three posh boy, bit of a toff, sounds like a bloody English public schoolboy.'

Max's stomach lurched. Cal.

'Know much about him?'

'Always works with Davie Hamilton. Massive, rough-arsed Glaswegian. They get good results, though, only the other day they nicked a Scouse courier on the A9. Half a kilo of coke in his spare tyre. Bosses loved them for it.'

Realisation hit Max like a truck. He got to his feet, knocking his rickety old chair to the cigarette-stained carpet. This was it. This was the break. Max looked out of the dusty window, which faced a moss-covered wall. A rusted downpipe dripped water into a brown pool on the floor below. He opened his mouth to speak, but then shut it again.

Janie and Max both turned and looked at Max, eyebrows raised.

'You still there?' Norma said.

'What's the courier's name?'

'Hold up.' There was a tapping of keys. 'Steven O'Halloran. Bloke with a fair old history. Suspected member of Lee "Scally" Dodd's crew from Liverpool. They've been steadily taking over half of Scotland since Hardie got locked up.'

Max blinked. Callum was clearly at the centre of this. It was too much of a coincidence. Someone was taking all of Scally's crew out, the question was, why? Macca's disappearance, one of Scally's dealers getting locked up, and now two of his dealers being murdered in Scotland.

'Can I ask a favour? It's one I need you to keep to yourself.'

'Not sure I like the sound of this, but go on,' said Norma.

'Can you send me details of the arrest in Perth and also, if you have them, any photos of Callum and Davie?'

'I'm sure I can find some. There were some pics taken on

a team piss-up day not so long ago. I think I can lay my hands on them, but why?'

'You trust me, right?'

'Course, you daft nugget.'

'I'll tell you all about it, but we need to get to the bottom of something first.'

'Fine, but only because it's you, and I don't like Callum very much. He's a snidey so-and-so,' said Norma.

'Cheers, mate. Message them to my phone, yeah. Oh, and while you're at it, include their phone numbers.'

'You owe me a pint. In fact, you owe me several.'

'Consider it done. Thanks,' said Max, hanging up.

'Guys, we have a break here.' Max turned to Janie and Ross.

'About bloody time,' said Ross.

Max recounted the details of his conversation with Norma.

'Okay, sounds like we have something to go on, at least. Options?' said Ross.

'We need to get behind all of them, but I'm not sure we have the resources for that, without taking this wide – and that will be bound to leak. I say we stick with Farquharson, as planned. We evidence his meet with Cal, preferably on camera, and film a test call to the Encrophone. The team can then split onto Cal and Davie and track their movements. They'll have a safe house for their firearms and stolen drugs. Get that and together with the cell siting on their phones, we bring it all together.'

Ross muttered under his breath for a moment. 'I think it's a good strategy, and it bloody needs to be. I have to go to a covert Gold Group meeting with the brass in an hour. Chief is chairing it, and senior people from NCA, PIRC and customs are attending. I need to prepare some slides for a briefing, and need to sound like I'm at least vaguely competent.'

'Fat chance of that then,' said Max.

'Farquharson's still asleep, by the way,' Janie said. 'Must be all the whisky he put away last night.' She pointed at the iPad in front of her.

Max's phone vibrated on the desk. Picking it up, he saw it was a message from Norma. A picture was attached.

Cal is the poncy-looking prick on the left. Steven O'Halloran, dob 11/07/78, close associate of Scally Dodd. No fixed abode given. Arrest House of Bruar, possession W/I half a kg of high-purity cocaine. Custody no 1265 at Perth custody centre. Charged and remanded in custody. Currently at HMP Perth. Best of luck, you cheeky twat.

A photo of two men, in their late thirties, arms around each other, was displayed on the screen. Callum Mackintosh stared, his eyes glassy, a bottle of beer clutched in his hand. Foppish hair fell over his face, half concealing an arrogant, yet simpering expression. Hamilton was a brute of a man, with short hair and bulldog features, set in a scowl.

Max read out the message and showed the screen to Janie and Ross.

His phone buzzed again with another text.

Cal and Davie's phone numbers.

Two mobile phone numbers were listed.

'He is a poncy twat,' said Ross, impressed. 'Look at that hair. I like the sound of your mate too. My kind of lady. Does she want a job with us? We could do with a good analyst. Get those printed and ready for the surveillance team, and give me a copy for the meeting. Janie, start on those numbers,' said Ross.

Janie nodded and scribbled on her notepad, then she paused. 'Is it just me or is half a key too small a package for Scally's close associate? Why not use a junkie runner, or a youngster to take the risk with that amount?' She paused again, thoughtful. 'I'll look into the arrest.'

'Good call. I think it's fair to assume that Cal and Davie did a bit of "liberating" of the product. How often do you hear of NCA doing a random stop like that?' said Max.

Ross burped. 'Aye, never. Right, enough gassing, I've a meeting to go to. What's your mate the analyst's name, Max?'

'Norma Kirk, why?' said Max.

'Just asking,' said Ross, turning to his screen and settling a pair of reading glasses on his nose.

27

SCALLY STOOD IN the back room of a dingy pub, in a dank street in Everton. He looked down the cue and across the green baize of the pool table, eyeing the triangle of multicoloured balls. There were only three other people in the room: Scally's brother Spike who was as close as identical to him as it was possible to be, despite not being twins; the wordless barman, who sat behind a newspaper, pretending to pay no attention; and a large, muscled man with styled and sculpted blonde hair. The big man looked nervous. His face glistened with sweat and his hand almost trembled as he lifted his pint to his lips and took a sip.

A TV was on the wall above the bar, tuned to a channel that was showing horse racing with the sound turned down low. Spike stared up at the screen with mild interest, and yawned.

Scally struck the white ball with enormous force, scattering the triangle of balls in all directions. None sank into a pocket.

'Your turn, Cheeks,' he said, still not looking at the blond-haired man, as he scraped a little chalk on the tip of his cue.

Cheeks leaned down and lined up a shot, the cue visibly shaking as he struck the white. It glanced off a striped ball and flew into a corner pocket.

Cheeks chuckled, but the sound died on his lips.

'Oops,' Scally said, his face completely blank, as he looked for the first time at Cheeks.

Scally bent over the table and looked down the cue, eyeing up a ball that was close to the corner pocket. He struck the white hard and the blue ball rattled into the pocket. The noise was deafening in the silence of the room.

'Shot,' said Cheeks, in a broad Mancunian accent. His smile looked forced.

Scally silently moved around the table to where the white lay. He bent down and hit the white, this time too hard, sending the red ball bouncing out of the pocket and back into the white, scattering the remaining balls all over the table.

'Hard lines,' said Cheeks.

'Your shot,' said Scally.

Cheeks was just bending down to take his shot when Scally spoke.

'Tell me about the kilo you owe me, Cheeks?' He studied his fingernails.

Cheeks took his shot and stood up, leaving the cue on the table. He wiped a hand across his forehead. 'We got fucked over.'

Scally picked up the cue and leaned over the table again, lining up a shot. 'You have a grass in Manchester, la?'

'No, mate, I trust my people.'

'Where's the gear?'

'I'll get you the money, Scally.'

'I didn't ask that. I asked, where's the gear?' His voice was low and even, but it carried enormous menace. He stood up straight and stared at Cheeks, his deep-set eyes glinting.

'It got took, man.'

'By who?'

'I don't know. They just took it, held us with a fucking strap. Said they'd shoot us.'

'Took by who?' Scally's face was hard.

'Scally, I need some time. I can get it, but I need to—'

He didn't finish his sentence. In a second, Scally had reversed the cue and swung it with terrible force, the thick end colliding with Cheeks's temple. The bigger man dropped like a stone onto the sticky floor. Blood flowed from a two-inch gash, and he cried out.

'Where's my fucking money, you fucking Manc bastard?' Scally's calm tone had completely gone, replaced with an incandescent, raging fury. He unleashed a torrent of vicious kicks to the prone man's muscled torso. He smashed the cue to pieces against the man's ribs and threw them across the room.

'Scally, man. No, no.' Cheeks howled.

'Last chance. Who took the gear?' Scally growled.

Cheeks looked up from the floor, blood pouring from the wound on his face.

'It was a poncy fucker, bastard called Cal with a gorilla of a mate. They were tooled up.'

'Where were they from?' Scally whispered.

'I dunno, man. He looked like a toff, but the big bastard was a jock. I know nothing else. They just jumped us with a—' His words were halted by a further onslaught of kicks and punches from the now-raging Scally.

Cheeks curled up into the foetal position as the blows rained down on him. Spike looked on, sipping his drink calmly as if they were still playing pool. The bartender remained behind his newspaper.

Suddenly Scally stopped, leaving Cheeks moaning on the floor, the blood forming a pool on the already-filthy floor. He went to a table and picked up his half-empty glass and sat down on the cracked bar stool. He drained the drink, took out a napkin and wiped the blood off his hands.

'Same again, Alf,' he said.

Alf poured another pint of lager from the tap and set it down in front of Scally before retreating behind his newspaper.

Scally reached for a small attaché case on the floor by the stool. He pulled out a sleek-looking laptop, opened it up, and stared at the screen with intense concentration for a few moments, tapping away at the keys.

Cheeks rolled over on the floor, spat out blood. His head rested in a puddle of red liquid, one swollen eye wide with terror, staring up at Scally.

'Organisation, Cheeks,' Scally said, not looking round. 'I'm all about planning and organisation, which is why I make records, you know? Research and record, that's my motto. I can find out everything about anyone on this laptop. I mean, it's well protected. Cops could never get into it, and even if they did, it'd wipe. You see, I'm a businessman. I look after my product and my customers and I keep a close eye on profit and loss. Now, it's only a key you lost, but it's about reputation. If you can lose a key that you haven't paid for, what do others think eh, la?' He snapped the laptop shut and slotted it back into the attaché case.

Scally took an exploratory sip from his pint. 'The thing is, people are taking fucking liberties with me at the moment, and

I can't have it. People need to learn about consequences.' He swivelled on the stool and looked down at the broken man on the floor.

Cheeks moaned, turning onto his front. He tried to crawl away, then struggle to his feet, his hands slipping in the blood.

'Scally, I promise I'll—' But he didn't get to finish his sentence. Like a rocket, Scally propelled himself off his stool, his pint glass still in his hand. In a flash he covered the six feet between them. His foot lashed out in a vicious kick, straight into the side of his head. Cheeks collapsed, out cold.

Scally emptied the rest of his beer over the prone form. He reached forward, grabbed a handful of the man's hair and slammed the pint glass into his face. It shattered into a million pieces. A huge gash opened up across his face, stretching from cheekbone to mouth.

Scally looked with revulsion at the now unconscious and heavily bleeding Cheeks. He dropped the glass to the floor.

'Get us another pint, Alf,' he said, sitting down at the bar and reaching for a chipped and scuffed remote control. He pointed it at the TV and turned up the volume until it was loud and distorted. Scally looked at his watch. 'Just in time, Spike, lad. I've got a hundred on this next race.'

28

ROSS SAT AT the table, feeling a little out of his depth. He was at the inter-agency Gold Group meeting in the conference room at the Gartcosh crime campus. The sprawling glass-and-concrete monstrosity was bespoke-designed, built to house all the major law enforcement and prosecution agencies. Apparently, the aim was to improve agency collaboration. Ross remembered the description of the building he'd read in a glossy pamphlet in reception:

Conceived around a central atrium, the configuration mirrors a human chromosome.

Ross shook his head. Chromosome my arse, he thought. The place was a bloody bank, not a cop shop.

But the main reason he felt out of his depth was that, by some distance, he was the lowest-ranking person around the table. A thick silence hung in the air, as the occupants, all from different organisations, sat and eyed each other with suspicion. They all knew that something serious was happening, that it was sensitive, but they were short on details.

Ross's phone beeped a loud tone and vibrated on the table, piercing the silence. Several sets of eyes all homed in on him, each showing varying degrees of disapproval.

'Sorry,' he muttered, looking at the screen and seeing a message preview from his wife. She'd be angry, he thought. He'd caught enough of the message, all written in capitals with multiple exclamation marks, to know it wasn't conciliatory. He flicked the phone to silent mode. Coffees were being poured from a vacuum flask by one of the canteen staff. They placed a cup and saucer at Ross's elbow. His eyes were drawn to the posh-looking cellophane-wrapped biscuit that was perched on the saucer.

Chief Constable Chris Macdonald cleared his throat and smiled. 'Ladies and gents, time is of the essence and we all have coffee now, so I think we should get on. Perhaps a quick round of introductions, so that my staff officer can record for the minutes. Obviously, I'm Chris Macdonald, Chief Constable of Police Scotland. Ross?' he said, looking at his detective inspector, and the only other representative of the police in the room.

'DI Ross Fraser, Policing Standards Reassurance Team.' Ross smiled nervously, hoping that no questions about his small, shady team would be forthcoming.

A distinguished-looking woman, in a smart suit, spoke next. She had a cultured English accent. 'Louise Ellis. Director of Investigations, NCA Scotland.'

'Michael Jones, Border Force, Director of Crime and Financial Investigations,' said a slim, well-dressed man with thinning red hair, and thick-framed spectacles.

'Detective Chief Superintendent Miles Wakefield, Serious Organised Crime. How youse doing? All right, Ross? We worked together for a number of years, sir,' said a bald man in a badly fitting suit. He had a deep, booming voice and a strong Glaswegian accent.

'Fine thanks, boss,' said Ross, nodding at his old superintendent.

The last person in the room spoke. 'Leaving the best till last, I see. I'm David O'Neill, Head of Investigations, PIRC. Nice to see a few people I know from my days in the job.'

'So, thanks to you all, once again,' said Chris Macdonald. 'Unfortunately, I have asked you all here for a very difficult situation that's developing. I have to stress, this is of the highest level of confidentiality. We're all aware of events in Fraserburgh last night, so we can appreciate just how serious this is.' There was a long pause, and no one spoke.

Every pair of eyes in the room fixed on the chief constable. Ross noted that there was no agenda. No one was taking minutes, either. This was no standard gathering. He took an exploratory sip of his coffee and winced at the overly bitter taste. He picked up the biscuit and tore the wrapper off. The noise in the silence was almost deafening. Every pair of eyes in the room swivelled from the chief to Ross. Michael Jones shook his head with obvious disdain. A trace of a smile crossed Macdonald's face before he continued.

'As well as the horrific double murder, we have a very challenging situation that Ross and his team are currently investigating. So rather than steal his thunder, I'll hand you over, so he can explain all.' Macdonald turned to Ross.

Ross swallowed his biscuit, picked up a remote control and activated the hidden projector. The screen to the front of the conference table lit up, displaying the logo of Police Scotland.

Ross gave them the lot. The whole bloody wretched story. The suicide of Murdo Smith on the Erskine Bridge, Hamish Beattie's 'suicide', Farquharson. He laid it all out, the corrupt

NCA agents, Callum Mackintosh and Davie Hamilton, dead drug dealers, missing drug importers. He accompanied his words with photographs, audio and video clips of Farquharson speaking to Cal and maps showing cell site routes. He held nothing back. The room was shocked into a frigid, palpable, open-mouthed silence.

Louise Ellis was the first to speak, her voice caught in the beginnings of a tremble, before she regained her composure. 'What do you need from me? Whatever it is, you get it. I don't know Hamilton well, but I always thought Callum Mackintosh was one of my best people. I'm ashamed. Dead cops, dead drug dealers, and to think that I was singing their praises recently for arresting a drug courier on the A9.'

'Yeah, about that ...' said Ross.

Ellis stared at him blankly, the shock still settling in.

'We're fairly sure that they ripped off that drug courier because he was one of Scally's people. They were destroying his network and stocking up their own drug supplies. We think a lieutenant as trusted as Steven O'Halloran wouldn't be used to transport a half kilo. I suspect that your guys liberated the remainder of the product.'

'And how sure are you that they're responsible for the disappearance of Macca and Jimmy McLeish?' she asked, her face forlorn.

'Can't be certain, but an encrypted phone we believe he is using was cell sited in that very remote area at the time they went missing.'

'Murdo Smith was investigating sea loch importations, and Mackintosh was going to be lead on the case, until we had a sudden priority switch to trafficking. It all adds up,' said

Ellis, rubbing her face with a sigh. She reiterated, 'What do you need from me?'

'Well, obviously complete discretion, and we could do with the loan of an analyst. We're falling behind on the phones and an extra pair of hands would be useful with charting and interpreting the data. Max Craigie speaks highly of Norma Kirk, who he's worked with in the past and who he trusts implicitly.'

'She's yours. I'll have a cover story ready to go,' Ellis said without hesitation.

'Great, thanks,' said Ross.

'Can I just ask, why don't we go and arrest them right now? Like, this minute,' asked Ellis.

'We don't have enough evidence to charge as we stand. All we have is Farquharson using the name "Cal", and some cell siting on encrypted phones that they may or may not have anymore. If they're sensible, they'll have the drugs, guns and phones laid up somewhere safe. If we go in hard now, there's every chance we won't catch them with anything.' Ross outlined their plan to record the meeting between Farquharson and Cal and to use a test call into the crucial phone.

Ellis just nodded.

'Miles, early days, but anything to report on the murders in Fraserburgh?' asked Macdonald.

DCS Wakefield let out a weary sigh. He blinked and ran a hand through his hair before speaking. 'Ross has already done the heavy lifting in his briefing, but from the MIT perspective we know that a passing motorist called police late last night. Two cars, a Vauxhall and a Peugeot, were found, doors open, engines still running, outside Boyndlie. It's very early stages, and the scene is still being processed, but this was a cold-blooded execution. No signs of struggles, no shell casings, no drugs, and low-calibre weapons, as there are no exit wounds. We believe the victims, although I stress this isn't confirmed, to be a Brian "Tug" Wilson and Simon "Shorty" Lightfoot.'

'Any witnesses or leads?' asked Macdonald.

'None, as yet, but as I stressed earlier, we're only really beginning on this one. It's going to be tough, unless Ross's team give us a massive helping hand.'

'Michael, anything to add?' said Macdonald, looking at the Border Agency chief.

'Well, my intel teams had been working with NCA on west coast importations. We think they'll rise once Brexit kicks in, as increased checks at ports will up the risk to importers. I'm not sure who my team were liaising with, but this is a real concern, on all levels,' he said, flatly.

'Any intelligence about importations via Loch Torridon?' said Ross.

'Not that I can recall.'

'Nothing over the facilities?' Ross used the coded reference to telephone intercepts often used by the legacy customs investigators.

'Again, I'll have to confirm, but nothing was brought to me.'

'David, can you give us anything more on Farquharson?' asked Macdonald.

O'Neill looked shell-shocked. He gulped and wiped a sheen of sweat from his top lip. 'Lenny is a friend of mine from Lothian and Borders days. I recruited the bastard to PIRC after he failed to get promoted.' His face had begun to turn pale.

Everyone stared at him.

'What do you want me to do?' he said. 'I won't say a word to him, if this is all true. I want him stopped immediately.'

'What're his working hours today?' asked Ross.

'He's writing a report from home for a fiscal's inquest.'

'That's perfect. He's home right now, one of my officers is monitoring him, and we've a plan to get things moving,' said Ross.

'I'll do it, whatever it is,' said O'Neill, an angry line across his brow, colour beginning to return to his cheeks.

29

LENNY FARQUHARSON WAS sitting at home, with a laptop balanced on his knees, bored out of his mind and yet gripped with a gnawing anxiety. Try as he might, he couldn't get motivated enough to complete the fiscal's report, despite the fast-approaching deadline. When he found that he had written the same sentence three times over, he decided that he needed to take a break. He fingered the encrypted phone on the coffee table in front of him, willing it to ring with some news. Lenny hated waiting, he always wanted to deal with issues head on, but Callum and Davie frankly terrified him. They were so bloody ruthless that he didn't doubt for a second that they would just as easily kill him, without so much as a second thought. Maybe he was no longer useful to them. He shuddered.

He moved to the messy kitchen, flicking on the kettle, looking with a sudden pang of shame at the heaped pizza boxes, Indian takeaway cartons, and discarded beer cans. He really needed to sort himself out, stop this downward spiral. He just needed the money that Cal had promised him, then he would turn things around.

A buzzing from the living room made him jump. It was

typical that after all morning watching the bloody thing, it rang after he had left the room.

Rushing back into the lounge, he was dismayed to see that it wasn't the encrypted phone, but his PIRC-issued work phone. He swore under his breath, picked it up and saw his boss's name, David, flashing across the screen.

'Hi,' said Lenny, as brightly as he could manage.

'Lenny, are you at home?' said David without preamble, urgency in his voice.

'Yes, I'm writing that report.'

'Look, something's come up. I need you to come in and see me.' There was a long pause. 'It's about the two suicides. There's been a development that we need to discuss, urgently.'

'What kind of thing?' Lenny tried to keep his voice level. His insides churned, and he began to feel his face flush.

'I can't say over the phone. Bring everything you have connected to the case. Literally every single piece of paper, okay?'

'Sure but, can't you—'

'No can do, sorry. Get here for three.'

'But, surely—' David had hung up.

Lenny stared at the phone, his skin prickling. He stood and began to pace up and down the room, trying to control his breathing. What the hell was going on? He'd been so bloody careful. He'd just tweaked Hamish Beattie's statement to remove anything damning and lifted his notebook. Thank God he'd burned it on his log stove. He'd relayed the encounter with Hamish Beattie to Cal and Davie, as they'd been very clear that he needed to keep them informed of anything that may impact their activity, and they hadn't been happy about Murdo's final words.

Hamish's 'suicide' had come as a real shock to him when he heard about it through the police grapevine. An old pal from his police days made it clear that the inquiry team were satisfied it was a suicide, even if he wasn't. Cal and Davie had just smiled when he had broached the subject shortly afterwards.

'A tragic thing, Lenny, old chum,' Cal had said in that stupid posh-boy accent. 'Tragic that a public servant, overwhelmed with sadness, felt it necessary to take his life, but inevitable after witnessing so much horror.' The smile he had worn had been puke-making. Lenny knew, though. He knew what they'd done, and it made him sick to his stomach.

He needed to speak to them, now, and sort this fucking situation out. If he was part of this, he needed paying, and paying properly.

He picked up the encrypted phone and dialled.

'Lenny, old boy, how goes it?' Cal said.

'Is anything going on?'

'What do you mean?'

'My boss just called, and he sounded bloody serious about something. He refused to speak to me over the phone, but he wants to see me this afternoon, and it's about the two suicides. He says there's been a development.'

Callum let out a long sigh. 'What have I told you about worrying? Pestering me for no reason? Murdo's suicide was just that, CCTV even caught the poor sod jumping, and you took care of everything else. Nothing left to worry about. Beattie was in a pit of depression.' A hint of a chuckle in his voice made Lenny shudder.

'Jesus. A development, he said. A bloody development. You and Davie have been too reckless. We need to meet today. This situation is scaring the shit out of me and I'm not being paid enough to take these risks.'

Lenny held his breath for a full fifteen seconds, which felt like an hour.

'Cal?'

'Still here, old man. Okay, let's meet in an hour.'

'Where?'

'Usual place. I'm hungry.' The line went dead.

Lenny looked at the sleek, encrypted phone, his stomach clenched. He had only wanted to earn a few extra quid. Just enough to offset what the bitch was taking from him.

Now he wanted more. If he was in this deep, then he wanted his fair share.

Lenny looked at his watch. The meeting place was about half an hour away and he wanted to get there ahead of those two bastards. Paid to get the lie of the land. He didn't trust Callum or Davie as far as he could throw them. They would discard him, or worse, if he gave them the chance.

Lenny tucked his encrypted phone in his pocket, grabbed his coat and keys, and left the house.

30

CALLUM MACKINTOSH HUNG up the phone with a chuckle. 'Poor old Lenny's almost soiling himself. He could be a real liability, unless we stay on top of him. I'm going to read him the riot act and put the fear of God in him.' Callum leaned forward and hoovered a fat line of cocaine from the mirror on the table in front of him.

'What if the police are watching him? This is bloody reckless,' said Davie, shaking his head at Callum's proffered banknote.

'The plods know nothing, how could they? All loose ends tied up,' he said, massaging the bridge of his nose, his eyes damp with tears. He was starting to get pissed off with Davie. For a massive brute of a man he had no backbone.

'It's fucking unnecessary.'

'Oh, stop being an idiot,' Callum snapped. 'This is business, and Lenny is a weak link. He needs managing, so we meet him for a little spot of lunch and I make it crystal clear what will happen if he tries to back out now. Fear is our control mechanism over Lenny. You have the photo of his kids, right?'

'Aye, of course I do.'

'Then we show him that. Nothing else will need to be said, will it?'

'I don't know, Cal. I think you're going too far, getting carried away. You need to lay off that shite for a while and stop taking risks. We'll get caught. I don't want to find out how NCA get treated in prison. Do you?'

Callum felt a deep rage swell in his chest. His hand almost reached for the pistol tucked in his waistband, but he resisted the urge. He needed Davie, the big dull brute, at least for a little while longer. He took a breath and twisted his face into a smile. 'Now, now, let's keep it civil. No one's going to jail, you can hold me to that. We just need to meet Lenny, and make sure we're all on the same page. Remember who got us this far in the first place. If it wasn't for me, you'd still be arresting junkies on street corners. Just remember that next time you're having doubts. We wouldn't want to make any mistakes at this stage, would we?' His voice was controlled, his smile wide, but no part of it reached his eyes.

Davie was silent for a long moment, his face fixed tight. 'Okay, but we need to be more careful,' he said eventually.

'Of course, of course. Now have a line and let's get ready.' Callum handed over the banknote and the bag of cocaine, and his smile was all charm, once again.

31

'ALPHA SIX, SUBJECT *one is out, out, out. He's unlocking the car and he's in. Engine on and reversing off the drive. He's off, off, off away and towards the golf club. He's a loss to me and towards your plot, Alpha five,'* the voice of one of the surveillance vehicles crackled in Max's ear.

Max had watched his tablet screen beam footage from a camera hidden in a lamppost as Farquharson, totally unaware of his surroundings, left his detached property and got into his car. Max had heard every word that Farquharson had said during his conversation with Callum. It was on. They were good to go, and with a bit of luck, they could clear up this job today.

Farquharson couldn't possibly know of the full-strength team about to shadow his every move, recording and streaming live images as they did so. He also couldn't know about the small tracking device that had been attached to the underside of his car overnight, as belt-and-braces to make sure he wasn't lost. Each surveillance officer was armed with a Glock 17 for self-defence, and the whole team was being shadowed by two unmarked BMW X5s. They were crewed by six members of the Specialist Firearms Team, heavily armed with Heckler and

Koch G36 carbines, ready to make a dynamic intervention if needed. Everyone knew the risks. Farquharson was on his way to meet two corrupt NCA agents, both suspected of multiple murders.

Following ex-cops could be a challenge, but not Farquharson. Not today, in any case. He was preoccupied and focused, his body language that of a man with the weight of the world on his shoulders.

'And we're off,' said Max as Janie steered their Volvo, keeping a respectful distance from the team. Max was an experienced surveillance operative himself, but in a case like this, he was happy to leave it to a cohesive and experienced team who did this for a day job. Surveillance is an art, as well as a learned skill. It worked best with a well-functioning team, made up of the same officers, day in, day out. Familiarity built trust, and the ability to act, without thinking, knowing others had your back. Knowing that they could recognise when situations were changing just by the nuances and inflections in voices.

This team was the best, and therefore trusted to get on with the job without interference. Max and Janie would shadow them, as would the SFO gunships, and only get involved if the circumstances dictated.

Max dialled a number on his phone. It was answered immediately.

'Max, you old twat, are we underway?' said Norma. Things had moved quickly after the meeting and Norma was already with the team back in the offices at Tulliallan, ready to provide live intelligence support.

'We're moving.'

'Fuck me, the boss got shit moving double quick, right? Normally takes me days. Callum called him from the Encrophone. Cell site puts him in north Edinburgh, but I can't tie down much closer than that. He called another number straight after Lenny. Both of the NCA non-encrypted numbers I have for them were live up until recently, but went off after the encrypted call, so it looks like they're going dark. Davie was close by, and they're now hitting the same cell site. If I was guessing, I'd say they're moving north. In fact, they've just hit a cell site by Edinburgh Airport.' Norma sounded business-like and efficient.

'Airport? Any intelligence to suggest travel? Bank transactions, calls?'

'Nothing I can see, but I'm just getting up to speed on this. I know I'm shit hot, but I'm no miracle worker,' said Norma, her words punctuated by the tapping of computer keys. Norma was the best analyst that Max had worked with, and she was also an expert researcher, who could navigate her way around intelligence databases with almost superhuman speed.

'Good work, thanks. Let me know of any other movements or calls. Great to have you on the team.'

'Good to be here, even if it means working with you.'

Max hung up and updated Janie on what Norma had said.

'So, we're now DEFCON 5?' said Janie.

'Aye, we all ready?'

'Born ready.'

They tuned in to the surveillance radio channel. The team were following Farquharson, handing the 'eyeball' between themselves, always maintaining good distance and accurately describing his movements. It was like a game of chess, trying to anticipate him, in order to get a vehicle ahead and waiting, ready to take the eyeball. People being followed tend to keep an eye on their rear-view mirror; few expect a follower to be in front of them. The radio chatter was crisp, minimal, painting a full picture that Max could follow, almost as easily as if he were watching Farquharson himself.

'A92, approaching the roundabout with the M90. At the roundabout, on the roundabout and it's the first, the first, southbound, and he's committed, committed, M90 south towards Edinburgh,' the voice of the lead surveillance vehicle announced, switching into the vernacular specifically used for motorways.

The team tailed Farquharson from the M90 towards the Firth of Forth.

'We have a near-side signal and subject is leaving the M90, onto the A904, and he's heading generally towards Queensferry, still unaware, speed three-zero, one vehicle for cover.'

'Getting ready for a stop soon,' said Janie as she left the motorway, following in the wake of the team.

'Aye,' said Max, looking at the map on his tablet. His phone buzzed, a message from Norma.

Both cells moving. Now hitting Queensferry.

32

MAX LOOKED AT the tablet screen and watched a live feed of Farquharson strolling along the banks of the Firth of Forth. He was attempting to look casual, but for the first time since leaving home, his head swivelled left to right, clearly aware, checking his surroundings. He had driven along the front on Newhalls Road, parking in the shadow of the great expanse of steel that was the Forth Bridge, stretching overhead across the Firth.

He walked back on himself and crossed the road, side-stepping the tourists, and went up the drive, towards a large Victorian building, some kind of restaurant.

'He's up the drive and towards the Three Bridges Pub. It's a Harry Ramsden's chipper,' said the voice in Max's earpiece.

'The meet's going down there,' said Max, 'probably on the bench seats outside. Bloody perfect place, it's where I'd pick as a meeting place for an informant.'

'It's almost like they're cops, right? I could just do a fish and chips. Bloody starving,' said Janie.

'You're always starving, I don't know how you stay so thin,' said Max, not looking up from the screen.

'Stress of working with you. That and the fact you make me work so many bloody hours that I rarely get to eat a decent meal.'

'And he's in, takeaway side, up to the counter, and making an order. I'm following in, I'm starving, anyway,' said the surveillance officer. Max recognised Jeff's voice, someone he had worked with before. This was good tradecraft. Every surveillance officer needs a cover story, and there is no better reason to be at a large fish and chip shop than buying fish and chips. They needed an officer as close as possible, to give them the best control, and also an opportunity to overhear conversations.

'Jeff's always hungry,' said Max as he watched Jeff's stocky form follow Farquharson into the takeaway.

'Jammy git, I'll have another sweetie, then. Want one?'

'Aye.'

Janie handed a bag of boiled sweets over and Max took one and began to unwrap it.

Janie watched him, the palm of her hand held out, waiting. Max dutifully passed her the wrapper, which she deposited in a small bag attached to the ashtray, along with her own.

'I can see why you're single,' Max said.

'Who says I'm single?'

'Who'd put up with you?'

'Plenty of folk, actually.' Janie's eyes sparkled, mischievously.

There was a pause and they stared at each other before the moment was broken by the crackle of the radio.

'Drive past the chipper, we'll find somewhere to lay up east of them. The team will block all foot exits.'

'How long do we let them meet for?' said Janie as she

manoeuvred the Volvo out of their parking spot and drove it sedately past the Three Bridges.

'We need the meet to go down. We let them settle and get relaxed. Looking at the time, I'd say they'll all eat, so there's no rush. We'll give Jeff a chance to eavesdrop. There's still lots we don't know. Pull in here, behind the garage, in that small car park.'

Janie reversed the Volvo into a parking space and switched off the engine, sighing and stretching her back. 'Is this going to be a long day?' she said, her tone suggesting that she knew the answer.

'Why, you have plans?'

'What, working with you? I never make plans. Saves having to cancel them,' she said, unwrapping another boiled sweet and popping it in her mouth, and tucking the wrapper in the small bag.

'Not a nine-to-five job, this.'

'That's subject one out of the building, with his food, and he's sitting on a bench seat under the blue umbrella at the front, very much eyes about, clearly waiting for someone,' a voice crackled out of the radio.

'All received, permission to plot?' the controller asked over the net.

'Go ahead,' said Jeff. As always, the officer who had control of the subject steered the radio traffic; everyone had to seek permission to speak, even the controller.

Max only half-listened as the controller briskly and efficiently allocated locations for all the team members, to box off escape routes, known as 'plotting'. Once this was done, the net descended into silence. Now they just had to wait.

'There's Jeff with his fish supper,' said Max, looking at the screen. The footage from an officer's car parked about thirty metres away was all jumpy and at a strange angle.

'Jammy bugger, but no curry sauce – who orders chips without curry sauce?' said Janie.

'Subject one on the phone,' said Jeff.

Almost on cue Max's phone buzzed with a message from Norma.

Receiving a call from Cal's encro. All phones hitting the same cell site.

'Backup permission?' asked Max into his covert mic.

'Go ahead, Max,' said Jeff.

'He's receiving a call from subject two, and all three phones hitting the same mast. Game on,' said Max.

'Received.'

The net descended into total silence again.

'Okay, be aware, be aware. Two males on foot, possible for subjects two and three, coming from the west, close to the sea wall towards subject one. Very aware, team hold back and allow them to proceed. Towards you now,' said the female voice, calmness personified.

'Yes, I have them in sight now. Filming,' said a voice that Max recognised as Jim, another of the surveillance team.

'That's received, Jim,' said Max, staring at the screen.

'Jeff and Jim?' Janie raised an eyebrow.

'Aye, you know, Jeff and Jim.'

'Sound like a children's TV duo.'

The picture on the tablet screen swivelled about and zoomed in tight on the two men walking along the sea wall. Their size disparity confirmed them as Callum and Davie. The camera zoomed in tighter.

'Positive ID, positive ID, on subjects two and three, let them run, we need to evidence the meet and give Jeff a chance,' said Max into his mic.

'Received. Fifty metres from the Three Bridges. Now thirty. Now twenty.' Jim's voice quietened as the subjects closed. *'Now crossing the road, towards subject one. Hold up, they're stopping. Something's going on here, they're arguing. Jeff, do you still have control of subject one?'* There was urgency in Jim's delivery as he trained the camera on the two newcomers.

'Yes, yes. he's concentrating on his phone eating his chips, I have him covered,' Jeff's voice was low and even.

'Received, Jeff. I can't hear about what, but the smaller one is finger pointing at the bigger one. He's clearly angry about something. The big one has just told his mate to fuck himself, I think. It's definitely kicking off.'

'What the hell is going on?' said Janie, looking at the screen. Callum's finger was pointing at the much bigger man, his head up, his shoulders square. The bigger man was almost cowed in his presence.

There was a brief pause on the net, the tension was almost palpable. The meet needed to happen to capture the evidence and link all three but knowing that they were potentially armed heightened everyone's senses.

Max looked at the screen. Callum and Davie had stopped arguing and continued to walk, but Davie was trailing behind slightly. Max watched them cross the road, looking left and right as they did so.

'Stand by. We have a male, IC1, in jeans, hoodie and a cap, crossing, approaching them fast from behind. I think he may be with them. I can't get a view of his face. Advise?' said Jim.

Max looked at the screen. A small, wiry figure was striding up behind the NCA agents, hands in his pockets, but with a definite purpose. He was compact, and even with the hood and cap and through the fuzzy screen, you could tell that he was moving with confidence.

'Who the hell is that?' said Janie.

'I've no idea. Were we expecting a third?'

'No, no evidence of that. Where are the gunships?' Max felt a tickle at the back of his neck. His heart started to thump, and he wiped sweat from his forehead.

'They normally stay well away until called,' said Janie, concern creeping into her voice.

Max called Norma.

'Yes?' she said, all business.

'Any calls from anyone to a third party?'

'No, just what I told you about.'

'Thanks.' He hung up. Max tightened his seatbelt. Just as he was beginning to radio the team, he noticed movement on the tablet screen.

'Shit's about to happen. Move up,' said Max, his guts churning.

The wiry figure's hands left his pockets. Max saw a flash of something silver in the man's palm.

'Gun, he's got a gun. Jesus fucking Christ,' Jim's scream distorted the transmission.

Almost in slow motion, the man's arm extended. Sunlight glinted off the silver pistol as it bucked twice in quick succession. Callum and Davie fell as if their legs were no longer there. Dead before they hit the ground, their brains destroyed.

Two distinct cracks were audible a microsecond later as the

sound caught up with what they had just seen. The image from the camera suddenly disappeared as Jim dropped his camera.

'Janie, go!' screamed Max. Janie gunned the engine and roared out of the car park, turning back towards the pub.

The net was suddenly pandemonium, everyone demanding updates. Another crack was audible, even over the engine, followed quickly by a shout on the net. '*Officer down. Jim's down. Attacker has jumped on the back of a dark motorbike, heading away east towards the bridge. Ambulance required, urgently.*'

As Janie floored the Volvo, a trials motorbike roared past them, heading under the red steel of the bridge. The pillion passenger was fixing his helmet into place.

'That's them. Quick, U-turn and get behind them. What the bloody hell is going on?' yelled Max. 'Attacker on the back of a trials bike, heading east past us. We are pursuing,' he said into the radio.

Janie screeched to a halt and spun the wheel, expertly performing a swift U-turn. Within seconds, they were roaring along, under the red oxide of the bridge, the bike accelerating away.

'Heading east, Newhalls Road, getting away from us, two up. How's Jim?' shouted Max above the Volvo's powerful engine.

'*Ambulance required, Jim's been shot, but I think he's okay. Body armour caught it. Both subjects are dead, brains all over the bloody pavement. Local uniforms are on their way. Farquharson's in custody. Keep the commentary going. Gunships are making their way,*' said the surveillance controller, the stress of the situation distorting his normally calm delivery.

'Still heading along Newhalls Road, now left onto Long

Craig Road, narrow single-track, speed sixty. Parallel to the Forth,' Max barked into the radio. Something about this road was familiar. He had been here before.

'If we get close enough, ram the bastards, okay?' Max said to Janie.

Janie nodded, her face grim with concentration as she negotiated the twisting, narrow, tree-lined road. She hurtled past a slow-moving car, threading them between the trees and vehicle with only millimetres to spare. Max closed his eyes for a second, gripped the seat. He let out a yelp as she kicked up dust along the verge, jolting the Volvo back into the centre of the road, changing gear. Janie's face remained impassive. She blew a strand of hair out of her eye and shifted gears again. She was tough as nails, thought Max, and one of the best fast drivers he had ever seen.

Max brought up the map on his tablet, looking ahead on Longhalls Road. He zoomed out.

'Shit, I knew it. This road is a dead end in about another half a mile. Be ready, yeah, don't hesitate. Just ram them.'

The radio net was ablaze with everyone asking for updates and exact locations.

Suddenly, they rounded a bend and hurtled towards a fork in the road, a boat house in the middle. Left fork led to a jetty, secured with a metal gate. Right led to a footpath, secured by another gate. The bike slowed and went to the right, driving next to the gate, through a small footpath gap, just wide enough for the trials bike to negotiate. Within a second, it was through. The rider accelerated again, spraying dirt upwards. They roared off along the footpath, the pillion passenger's right hand held aloft, a gloved single middle digit pointing at

Max and Janie. They skidded to a halt beside the gate, but the bike was gone.

Max sat for a moment, his chest heaving.

'Update, update,' was the urgent demand over the radio net.

'We've lost them. We've bloody lost them,' he yelled, slamming his hand on dashboard.

'Helicopter is being scrambled, and we have units trying to get ahead of them.'

'They planned this,' Max said. 'Whoever did this knew when and where they were going to meet. They'll never catch them. I think they knew we would be following, and they didn't bloody care.'

33

IT WAS CLOSE to seven before Max, Janie and the surveillance team managed to get back to the police station to debrief. The whole team sat silently, some looking at phones, the loggist scribbling in his notebook, but most just staring at nothing.

The post-incident procedure had kicked in, with everyone involved in the incident being removed from the scene and isolated at Corstorphine Police Station in central Edinburgh. The scene in Queensferry was being managed by the local officers, and MIT.

PIRC were, in theory anyway, supposed to oversee the scene management and deal with the officers at the scene of the shooting, even if no officer had fired a shot in anger. But things were different this time. A senior PIRC officer was involved, so suspicion and mistrust hung in the room. The main emotion was one of angry confusion at how two murder suspects, under police surveillance, had been executed by professionals, under their very noses.

The motorcycle had melted away after it had evaded Max and Janie, and no one had any clue, or leads, as to where it had gone. No one had any descriptions of the suspects or the bike, other than basic build and clothing.

'How's Jim?' Max asked Bob, the team leader.

'Bruised and shocked, but he'll live. Bullet hit him right side of chest, gave him nasty blunt force trauma,' said Bob. There's a lot of nonsense about the effectiveness of body armour. TV shows have people shot and leaping to their feet and returning fire. That doesn't happen, all that kinetic energy has to go somewhere, and the vest just spreads it over a wider area. He would be sore for some time. But he was alive.

'Thank Christ he wore a vest. Did he manage to fire back?' asked Max.

'No, as soon as the suspect shot both subjects, he turned and let one go at Jim before he could get his Glock out of the holster. He then got on that bike which appeared as if by magic. Almost as if he knew we were there.' Bob gave him a pointed look.

Max said nothing.

'Someone must have known about this. It's almost like we led them there to be executed, and now we're supposed to cooperate with the PIRC?'

'You know as much as me,' said Max.

'Aye, right enough. How much longer? My guys are bloody knackered.'

'Soon. Did Farquharson say anything?' said Max.

'Not when I nicked him. I was on him in a second, and he just sat there, frozen, mid-chip, stunned, like. I'll tell you something, though. He's shitting a brick. I've never seen a man so scared. Just kept babbling and hyperventilating, saying they would come for him, and shite like he wanted immunity,' said Bob.

Max's phone buzzed in his pocket. It was Ross.

'Ross?' said Max.

'You okay, pal?'

'I'm fine.'

'Janie?'

'Janie's good. She did well. She's a demon driver.'

'How's the boy who was shot?'

'Sore, but he's not going to die.'

'Is the team okay?'

'They're pissed. They think someone tipped off the shooter, and they aren't happy about waiting for PIRC to interview them.'

'I can't say I blame them. Chief has their backs, trust me. Are PIRC investigators at the station?'

'Aye, locked away in a room looking at the paperwork. Team have given verbal accounts,' said Max.

'Well, you release them. If PIRC give you any shit, refer them to the Chief Constable of Police Scotland. We need to get together and see where we go from here. I want to speak to Farquharson myself, find out what he knows. This goes much further than we realised. Come back to Tulliallan, now,' said Ross.

'On our way,' said Max and he hung up.

'Bob, get your guys away. They must be knackered.'

'Cheers, mate. What about the PIRC clowns?'

'Leave them to me,' said Max.

Bob stood and then addressed the team, all disconsolately sprawled on chairs. 'Right, folks, that's us. Good work, go home, drive carefully. Keep your phones on.' The team began to gather their things, relieved to be going, most stifling yawns from almost two days of solid work.

Suddenly, the door to the briefing room burst open, and a harassed-looking investigator strode into the room. He wore a blue jacket emblazoned with the PIRC emblem, and his face was flushed.

'What's happening? I need to speak to these officers, again,' he said.

'Not anymore, you don't,' said Max. 'I'm sending them home.'

'I'm sorry, they have to stay until I authorise their release. We have much to discuss.'

'You can try and stop them, if you like, pal, but I wouldn't recommend it. They're tired and possibly a little grumpy.'

'This is an outrage. I'll talk to the Assistant Chief Constable.'

The team, all grinning, filed out of the room, each nodding or waving at the jittery PIRC investigator as they went.

'May I remind you that you are obliged to cooperate with the PIRC.' He looked at Max's ID on the lanyard slung around his neck. 'DS Craigie,' he said, noting Max's name in his notebook with an exaggerated flourish.

'Well, now,' Max paused and looked at the man's own ID badge, 'Malcolm, bearing in mind it was one of your own corrupt investigators that is at the centre of this, I'm going to be looking at everyone in PIRC, just to make sure they have no links. So, Malcolm, I'll be sure to see you another day.'

34

'SO, WHAT THE bloody hell happened?' asked Ross, his face flushed, his eyes tired. Max, Janie and Norma sat across from him in their small office at Tulliallan. They were all in T-shirts or shirt sleeves, with red faces, their foreheads damp with sweat.

'You heard the radio. It was a textbook surveillance operation, then both subjects got their brains removed by a nine-mill to the back of the swede,' said Max, without any attempt at humour.

'Aye, I know that. I'm asking for theories on who and why it happened?'

'Being honest, I haven't a bloody clue. But I know a man who could give us a starter for ten.'

'Aye, well, getting close to him is going to be a struggle. MIT are on the murders, and he's a suspect. From what I'm hearing, he isn't saying a thing, apart from banging on about protection and immunity,' said Ross.

'Big question is ...' said Janie, sipping her coffee.

'Go on,' said Ross.

'Why isn't he dead?'

'Fair,' answered Ross.

'Isn't that obvious?' said Max.

'Not particularly,' said Ross.

'Lenny is a corrupt, dirty bastard, but he doesn't know enough. Those two NCA agents got whacked because of what they knew. That's my theory, but there's only one way to find out. Get us access to Lenny. See what he knows about Murdo and Hamish. Hamish's family deserve answers.'

'Hamish's death is still officially a suicide, even though it has a big question mark over it. Murdo's is a stone-bonker suicide. It was even caught on camera.'

'I reckon they killed Hamish,' Norma said, looking at her terminal.

Everyone turned to face her.

'There's strong circumstantial evidence on Callum's and Davie's phones that they killed Hamish Beattie, Scally's men at Loch Torridon, and the two dealers in Fraserburgh. Put it this way, if they were alive, they'd likely be getting charged with at least four murders. Shame they're dead, really,' she said, blankly.

'A bit more clarity would be nice,' said Ross.

'Both had two phones on them when they were shot, an encro and their day-to-day phones. We can't get into the encros, but we've downloaded their personal phones. I've put them into i2 and created an analyst chart to illustrate.' She turned her monitor to face Ross, Max and Janie. Small, cartoonish figures, with phone numbers underneath, and building icons, were linked with a forest of lines.

'I don't have my glasses,' Ross grumbled. 'I've never been able to understand Anacapa charts, anyway, and I can barely work my phone. Can you distil your findings into words a dense twelve-year-old could understand?'

‘Anacapa? Get with the twenty-first century, Inspector. Right, I’ve overlayed the phone data, and cell sites from the encro phones with the personal phones, which aren’t encrypted. Bear in mind this includes historic GPS data, internet searches, photos, mapping and even the health app on Hamilton’s iPhone. I even know what music they were listening to on their road trips.’ Norma positively buzzed with enthusiasm, settling her steel-framed glasses on her nose.

‘This is clever-twelve-year-old stuff. I need dense level,’ said Ross, without sarcasm. He stood up and walked to the window. He looked out, leaning forward against the radiator. As his palms touched the metal, he yelped and leaped back. ‘Fucking shit. This radiator is bastard roasting. I’m gonna tear that building manager a new one if he doesn’t get it fixed soon.’ He grimaced at his red hands.

There were muted chuckles and suppressed giggles from the others.

‘You lot can fuck off, as well. I almost got third-degree burns, there. Carry on,’ he said, walking over and returning to his seat.

Norma sighed and took off her glasses, wiping them on her shirt. She began to use them as a pointer to work through the chart. ‘We now have GPS data from their handsets that I can add to the cell sites we had already, so I have detailed location data. They were definitely at Fraserburgh when the two dealers were shot and they were at Loch Torridon when Scally’s men went missing. I’m even more confident that they were close to Hamish Beattie’s home when he allegedly committed suicide. Callum’s personal phone was turned off, but Davie’s was just switched to flight mode, so it wasn’t on the network, or using GPS, but it still recorded internally. The installed iPhone health app showed a short burst of vigorous physical activity, at the exact time that Hamish Beattie took his own life. It's all in the chart,' said Norma, slotting her glasses back on with a triumphant flourish.

'What?' said Max. 'Say that again?'

'I used this in a trafficking case recently. iPhones have a health and fitness app that records activity levels. It can differentiate between cycling, running, walking or other intense activity. It's far more sensitive than GPS or cell site. Now his phone wasn't on the network, but it was recording activity on the health app.'

'Shit,' Ross said.

'This is strong evidence that Davie killed Hamish,' said Max.

'It was enough to convict in the trafficking case, and do you want to know something else?' said Norma, her eyes twinkling.

'Go on,' said Max.

'I've cross-referenced with Murdo's phone data that you sent to me, Ross. Data from these phones puts them at the same cell sites immediately before he threw himself off the Erskine Bridge. Obviously, that's not conclusive, but it adds to the whole picture. They had the opportunity to do whatever they did to make Murdo jump.'

'Jesus,' said Max. 'We've a mountain of evidence against two dead men. Question is, what did they know that got them killed?'

'Revenge?' said Janie. 'They killed four of Scally's men and were clearly trying to destroy his Scottish network.'

'I think it's bigger than that. I don't see how, for a second, Scally would know that two corrupt NCA officers were destroying his network,' said Max.

'How about them ripping off the drugs from the dealer they arrested and took to Perth? Scally would know about that by now,' said Ross.

'But how could he connect it with the two dealers being shot, and the disappearances at Loch Torridon? There would be absolutely nothing he could know about that. Unless ...' Max paused.

'Unless what?' said Ross.

'Unless someone who knows more than any of us was telling him directly.'

'What? One of ours?' said Janie.

'Yep. One of ours.'

There was a long pause and a thick, cloying silence, and Max could almost hear the mental cogs turning.

'I want to speak to Farquharson,' said Max.

'Aye, well, leave that with me,' said Ross. 'I'm sure if the chief shouts loud enough, you can have a wee word, but I know one thing, it won't be today. Lenny's going to be getting interviewed non-bloody-stop for the rest of the day. Maybe tomorrow.'

'Who knew about the surveillance op?' asked Janie.

'Well, it was limited, but there was a whole surveillance team, plus the armed officers. They knew who they were following, but they didn't know why,' said Ross.

'Apart from them?' asked Max.

'Chief and the management board, and probably the attendees at the multi-agency meeting, you know: NCA, cuzzies, PIRC and the like.'

'So, half of Scotland, then. Shit, no wonder. Jesus, we're supposed to be a covert team.'

Ross said nothing, just rubbed his eyes with his fingers and yawned. 'Let's go home, guys. It's bastard boiling in this shitehole and we all need some rest. Mrs Fraser is at the "get the fuck out of my bedroom" stage,' Ross said, miming quotation marks with his fingers.

'You know how bad this is right?' said Max, with an edge in his voice.

'Aye, pal, I do. I may look like a tub of lard, but I've been doing this job a lot fucking longer than you. I know when we have another corrupt bastard somewhere. But right now, we don't know who the shitting fuck it is, and as far as I can see, a good night's sleep, and a decent meal with the missus, who at present bloody hates me, will probably leave us able to make better decisions tomorrow. So, kindly piss off home, and we carry on tomorrow.' Ross stared at them, his face grim.

35

THE SHARP-SUITED MAN clutched a scuffed briefcase as he walked up to the reception area of Saughton jail.

He arrived at the reinforced glass window and slid his identification under the gap, together with the letter of introduction.

'Charles Appleby, solicitor, for a legal visit with my client, Tam Hardie,' he said in a flat, accentless voice.

The uniformed officer wordlessly accepted the laminated pass, noting the photograph with only partial interest, before skimming the contents of the letter.

'Booked in by my office a few days ago,' Appleby added, with a half-smile, as the officer ran his finger down the list of expected visitors.

'Aye, we have you here, pal. In you come,' the officer said. A reinforced door slid open to the side of the window.

The solicitor stepped through into the reception area, to be met by an officer with full-sleeve tattoos who stood beside an X-ray machine, similar to the ones commonly seen at airports. The officer handed Appleby a tray. 'Keys, phone, wallet, cash, you know the drill,' he said in a bored voice.

Appleby emptied his pockets into the tray and deposited

his briefcase onto the conveyor belt. They disappeared into the X-ray machine, watched by a silver-haired officer, staring at the screen.

'Okay,' said a short, wiry officer who beckoned Appleby through the metal-detector arch.

Appleby did as he was asked, without complaint. Like many in his chosen profession, it wasn't the first time he had been inside a prison, and he was certain it wouldn't be the last.

The metal detector beeped as he passed through it, and he raised his eyes at the yawning officer.

'Stand on the red dot, please, arms to the side,' said the officer, who clutched a metal detector wand in his hand.

A moody-looking prisoner in a baggy maroon tracksuit looked with scant interest at Appleby, then returned to disconsolately pushing a mop around the reception area. More like rearranging muck than clearing it up.

The tattooed officer waved his wand over Appleby's arms, legs and sides. It beeped as it went over his midriff.

'Belt buckle. Want me to remove it?' said Appleby, unbuttoning his suit jacket to show the shiny silver.

'Nah, you're good. All the other stuff you can keep but lock your mobile into one of the wee lockers, over there, please, and then step up to the desk.'

Appleby did as he was instructed, tucking the small locker key into his trouser pocket and returning to the chest-high desk.

'Finger on the reader, please.'

Appleby placed his index finger on the glass of the finger-sized reader set into the counter top.

'Never been to this prison before, Mr Appleby?' said the officer, looking at his terminal.

'Not this one, no,' he said, smiling.

The officer handed over Appleby's ID card and letter of introduction, and said, 'Wear this at all times whilst on the prison estate and hand it back at the end of your visit when you collect your phone.'

'Follow me, please, sir,' said the tattooed officer.

They walked along a myriad of corridors, regularly passing through heavy gates, opened by the wordless officer with a key from his belt. There was an ever-present smell of floor polish and sweat. The distant hum of a hundred different types of music, and bellowing male voices, all competed to be heard.

They soon arrived at a corridor lined with several rooms, each containing a table and two chairs. The officer unlocked the closest door. 'You're our only legal visitor this morning, pal. I'll go and fetch Hardie now.'

'Thank you,' said Appleby as he sat, opened his briefcase and began to leaf through a manila file of A4 papers. The officer closed the door, and walked off, whistling cheerfully.

Within five minutes the door opened again, and the tall, elegant form of Tam Hardie entered. He was dressed in neat jeans and a polo shirt, his expression flat and blank. He clearly hadn't shaved for some time, a grey-flecked beard adorning his face. He looked at Appleby with a half-amused smile across his angular features, and twinkling, cold eyes that managed to convey humour and malice at the same time. Appleby rose to his feet, ready to greet his client.

'Ring the bell when you're done, please. I'll just be along the corridor,' the officer said, closing the door without waiting for an answer.

'Hello, Mr Hardie. Like the beard, it suits you,' said Appleby with an amused smile, extending his hand.

'I got bored of shaving, Mr Appleby,' said Hardie, shrugging.

Appleby settled into the chair. 'Well, the salt-and-pepper look is a bit George Clooney.'

'You flirting with me? I don't pay you to make compliments,' said Hardie, the corners of his mouth twitching upwards.

Appleby's face shifted, his features breaking out into a wide grin. 'You don't pay me shit, pal. Ow the fuck you doin, la?' he said in the broadest of Liverpool accents.

Hardie's face split into an even wider grin. 'Hello, Scally, ya' wee Scouse bastard.'

36

'IT WAS NICE of those NCA idiots to give you a phone, la,' said Scally.

'Wickr is a wonderful thing. Secure as you like,' said Hardie.

'I appreciate you reaching out to me, mate. Those fuckers could have kept on ripping off my gear.'

'You sure we're good to talk in here?' said Hardie.

'Yeah, they can't tape legal visits. You should see my boss ID and letter of introduction. We're safe, mate.'

'Sorry about your two boys. I saw on the news that they'd been taken out,' said Hardie.

'Casualties of business,' said Scally, his face impassive.

'Well, at least you sorted it fast.'

'The NCA bastards won't be a problem anymore,' said Scally.

'I was scunnered with the bastards that they thought I'd work with them.'

'Out of their depth, mate,' said Scally, shifting in the uncomfortable chair.

'I heard about that unfortunate incident at Queensferry. Tragic stuff, pal,' said Hardie, a broad smile on his face.

'Ah, mate, it's a jungle out there. Play with fire, you get

fucking burned. Cost me a lot of money, they have. Took two of my guys out, as well. I was willing to let them run for a while, as it's bad timing to be taking out bizzies, but we can pause and consolidate. Lucky that I was just trialling Jimmy and his rib ahead of bigger consignments. Thank Christ it wasn't one of the drops I have planned. Colombians would have gone mental.'

'Aye, they don't take kindly to losses. You ready for the merchandise? The Colombians are keen to start using the west coast as soon as possible. Ports are getting sticky, and they're only gonna get worse.'

'Yeah, mate. I've got proper people now. Ex-military lads with experience on the ribs. They're sound. So, can we talk about our agreement?'

'Simple, and as we said on the phone, you do this job, do it well and make sure I get my share, and I hand my network over to you. Lock, stock, the lot, including …' Hardie seemed to be searching for the correct words. 'Let's say, one of my late father's oak trees that he planted many years ago.'

'The contact?'

'Aye. A huge asset.'

'I can see that. How the hell did he identify them from just the name "Cal" and the fact that he was a posh bastard?'

'Connections and placement, Scally.'

'Well, the whisper about when and where they were going to be put them firmly in our sights. Who's your contact? He's fucking gold dust.'

'Who said it was a he?' Hardie grinned widely. 'Best not ask. Even my father kept a very respectful distance. You'll be kept safe from the authorities, and the contact will provide a link in with the Colombians, make sure future shipments get in without a problem. The Colombians pay direct for the services provided, so you really don't need to speak, unless it's important. I'll also give you access to my whole network in Scotland. It would take you years to get that up and running yourself.'

'What do you want in return? How much is all this gonna cost me?' said Scally.

Hardie paused, looking the Liverpudlian straight in the eye.

'Despite what those NCA idiots thought, I have plenty of money in offshore accounts, shell companies, foreign properties, gold, diamonds – all hidden where no one will find it. I don't want money. Once I get what I want, the whole lot is yours, including *the* contact. The Colombians will only do business with you if I and the contact say so. You can be in a position to receive amounts of product that you could only dream of without these introductions. After I get what I want.'

'What do you want?'

'I think you know that already.'

37

THE HOUSE IN Carstairs was an unattractive pebble-dashed monstrosity, similar to many others speedily erected years ago to deal with an urgent rise in the need for affordable housing. Two marked police cars were parked next to the Volvo, just for a bit of extra muscle.

Max, Janie and Ross stood outside the building. Two of the uniformed officers were next to them, looking up at the drawn curtains on all the upstairs windows. The other two had gone to the rear, just in case their target decided to make a break for it.

'What's this dickhead's name again?' said Ross. He looked shattered and even more dishevelled than normal this morning.

'Ashraf Patel. NCA intelligence officer,' said Max.

'And what was the link again?'

'Calls in and out of Callum's phone at the relevant times. He must know something, and it has to be worth a follow up.'

Ross nodded, and yawned again, his eyes were red-rimmed and his chin bristled with stubble. 'Any evidence he's actually in there?'

'Norma said both his phone and the burner are still hitting the same mast near here, and he isn't at work today. His car's on the drive, anyway,' said Max, pointing at a small Ford Fiesta.

'Well, come on then, let's do this,' said Ross.

'Quiet and subtle approach, I think, yeah?' said Janie as they walked up the cracked, weed-strewn path. Ross immediately strolled ahead and began to bang at the door with a clubbed fist. The house remained silent.

'You all right, Ross?' Janie said.

'Fine. Can we fucking get on with this?' muttered Ross, his eyes fixed on the unmoving door.

Max and Janie exchanged a look.

'This job …' Ross grumbled, thumping the door again with the same response. Nothing moved, no shadows inside, just silence. Looking at the house adjacent to the premises, Max noticed a few curtains start to twitch. A few spots of rain began to fall, and Ross let out a sigh.

'Pissing rain's starting, and we're farting around on the doorstep. Who does he stay with?' asked Ross.

'He has a wife and a boy, but they're over in Pakistan at the moment. And have been for a wee while. He's got plenty of money troubles, rent arrears and the like,' said Janie.

Max squatted down at the letter box and pulled the metal flap back. Peeping inside, he could see nothing, just a beige carpet and a staircase.

'Police! Fucking open up,' roared Ross, suddenly, making Janie jump.

'Detective Inspector, can we have a little decorum?'

'Decorum my bloody arse,' said Ross. 'Hoof the door in, Max. I'd do it myself, but my feet are fucked. Come on, bash the bugger in,' he added, hopping from foot to foot.

Max placed his shoulder against the simple wooden door. It was unglazed with a single Yale lock, backed up by a mortice below. He eased his weight forward, feeling the door flex a millimetre inward.

'Mortice isn't on. Hold up, no need to cause unnecessary damage,' said Max. He walked over to the bin at the end of the drive, opened it and pulled out an empty Lilt bottle.

'Here we go,' said Janie. 'Max about to show us some of his Met experience.'

'Bloody hell,' Ross said. 'Cops used to live for hoofing doors off their hinges. Younger generation have gone all fucking sensitive.' He rubbed his mis-shaven jaw.

Max pulled out a penknife from his pocket.

'He's tooled up,' said Ross.

Max ignored him and began to cut the bottle. Within a minute he had fashioned a large rectangle of clear plastic. Pressing his shoulder against the door, and feeling it flex inwards again, Max slid the plastic between the door edge and the jamb. He shuffled the plastic upwards until he felt it bite against the Yale. A quick shuffle again, and the door swung open.

'Remind me to check if the breaking lockfast place rates have gone up since you arrived up here?'

'Cockney burglar trick,' said Max. 'I got one of them to teach me how to use it. They call it "loiding".' Max entered the property, quickly pulling out his extendable baton and racking it open.

'Ashraf, it's the police. We're coming in, stay where you are,' Max shouted. As he stepped along the silent corridor, taking in the pile of mail on the floor, the stained carpet, he felt cold dread begin to run down his spine. 'Ashraf?' he shouted again, but in his heart, he was already preparing himself. He stepped across the threshold, breathing lightly, his senses alive. There was a sudden watery gurgle from an unseen pipe.

Ross followed, breathing heavily, and several officers trooped in behind him.

Max knew what they were going to find, and when he entered the living room, he smelt it immediately. Death, mixed with the familiar tang of cordite from a recently discharged firearm.

Ashraf Patel sat in a large velour armchair, slumped low, his eyes open, staring vacantly. There was a hole in the side of his head. In his hand, stretched out by his side, was a silver automatic pistol.

Max stared blankly at the dead form of the intelligence officer, his mind a turmoil of emotions.

'Jesus Christ,' said one of the uniform officers. He put a hand to his mouth and turned away. The colour drained from his face and he rushed out of the room.

'Not another one,' said Max, sorrow in his voice as he looked at the prone form of Ashraf Patel. Max touched his fingers to the man's neck, but there was nothing, no warmth. Max shuddered, the feeling of dread rising, the dark shapes beginning to push into his mind. He shook his head, trying to clear the fog. Not now.

'He's been dead a while. Hours, at least. We should have come last night,' said Max, his head spinning. Another corpse. Another young life taken, and for what? He looked at the clean entry wound, just a trickle of blood congealed around his ear.

'Not suicide, that's for sure,' said Janie.

'Agreed,' said Max.

'Why?' said Ross, stepping closer.

'No powder burns or scorching around the entry wound. No way he could have got the pistol far enough away from his temple. Ashraf was murdered,' said Janie.

'Aye, that's about the size of it,' Max's voice was low, even.

'Ah, bollocks. I'll call it in,' said Ross, walking out of the room.

'Ross—' said Max at his retreating form.

'Aye?' he turned, and their eyes met.

'We're going to see Farquharson. Today,' said Max.

38

FARQUHARSON SAT ON the bench seat in the interview room at Corstorphine Police Station, shivering. His red-rimmed eyes were wide and haunted, flicking between Max and Janie, who silently faced him across the Formica-topped table. Max stared at the PIRC investigator. A suited solicitor flanked him, legal pad open, looking at Max and Janie in turn, clearly unsure where this meeting was going.

'My client has been held for seventeen hours and been interviewed at length. He's declined to answer your questions, and will continue to do so, as is his right. I understood from the other interview team that they're seeking advice from the Procurator Fiscal and that charges and court proceedings are imminent. What is the purpose of this interview?' he said, without pomposity, merely curiosity.

'This isn't an interview,' said Max, returning the solicitor's stare, his voice low and even. An overwhelming wave of fatigue washed over him, and he stifled a yawn with his hand, his eyes staying fixed on the solicitor.

'So, why are we being recorded?'

Max slid a sheet of paper across that bore the heading THREAT TO LIFE NOTICE. He said nothing, just continued to stare at Farquharson, whose eyes had come to rest on the sheet of paper.

The solicitor reached for the document, scanning it briefly before sliding it across to Farquharson, who read it with widening eyes. He looked, frankly, terrified.

'Officer, this is highly inappropriate. My client has yet to be charged and has exercised his right to not answer any questions. You must respect this.'

'I'm not asking any questions. I have no idea what questions you've been asked, and frankly, I don't care. I'm here to say that we have very good information that your life is under threat. The individuals who are still at large killed your associates from the NCA and, we believe, will be wanting you dead too. As I see it there're two possibilities. One, you get charged, go to court and get remanded in custody. Two, you're not charged, and you're released from this police station. Now, both these situations leave you in danger, and therefore you should take all measures you personally can to protect yourself from meeting the same fate as Callum and Davie. So, sign here on the dotted line, confirming I've served this notice on you, and you've understood the ramifications.' Max slid a pen across the table, his face impassive.

'Officer, I must protest. This is sheer intimidation to get my client to talk,' the solicitor babbled, clearly rattled.

'I don't care whether he talks or not, pal. I just want Lenny here to know that Callum, Davie, and now Ashraf Patel have been murdered, so someone's clearing up everyone connected to their activities.' He turned to face Lenny. 'You're one of them, therefore you should take whatever steps you can to stay safe. I just need you to acknowledge the receipt of the threat notice in accordance with the case of R v Osman for the tape that's running, okay?' Max smiled at this point for the first time.

'Ashraf is dead?' Farquharson said, in a hoarse whisper, his eyes wide.

'Oh, I take it you didn't know?' Janie said, looking at Max.

'How did he die?' he said, his voice trembling.

'Shot in the head, at his house. I've just come from there,' said Max, without even a flicker of emotion.

'Lenny, that's enough. No more. Officers, I need to speak to my client in private,' the solicitor said.

'Oh Jesus, not Ashraf. He was a nice boy. You have to help me. I can't go to prison, I'll get killed. They have people everywhere, and I'm the only one left. I need help, please.' Tears were streaming down Farquharson's face, and he began to scratch vigorously at his scalp. His whole body shook, as if he were suddenly freezing.

'Who killed them?' asked Max, softly.

'I can't say. I just can't, they'll get to me and they'll kill me.'

'It's your decision, but once we leave this room, we're not coming back. You're on your own. You understand that?'

Lenny slumped backwards, his fingers rubbing at his scalp.

Max nodded at Janie and they both stood. 'Interview terminated...' he said, pausing as his finger moved towards the switch, turning his wrist to show his watch to announce the time. 'Right if there's nothing—' Max raised his eyebrows.

'No, wait,' said Lenny, sitting up, his hands slamming down on the table.

Max and Janie sat.

There was a thirty-second pause.

'Who killed Callum and Davie? Last chance,' said Max, his face impassive.

'Scally, or his people, anyway. Callum and Davie wanted to destroy his network so they could offload their stolen drugs,' Farquharson said, his eyes desperate.

'Lenny—' began the solicitor, his voice low and chiding, as if addressing an errant child.

'What drugs?' Janie asked, cutting off the solicitor.

'Lenny,' said the solicitor, more insistently.

'No, I want to answer,' said Lenny, not looking at the solicitor. 'The coke they ripped off. They used Ashraf to get them live intercept intelligence on drug movements, and they robbed the dealers. I didn't know they were killing, though, just thought they were taking the gear to sell.'

'What was your role?'

'Murdo Smith at the NCA got too close and was becoming a problem. They were pressurising him like crazy and had scared the bloody life out of him. I think they were threatening his family. I heard them laughing about it, once. They were evil bastards, didn't care about anyone, especially Callum. When Murdo killed himself, they called me and told me to make sure there were no loose ends. All I did was change PC Beattie's statement and lose the notebook. I didn't know anything else.'

'What about Hamish Beattie?' asked Max, his voice hardening.

'I didn't know, I promise. I had no idea they were going to kill him. I just told them what he'd told me. I assured them I'd taken care of it, that it would be fine. They seemed okay with it, but then I read about his suicide. I was devastated. You have to believe me. I'm an ex-cop, I didn't want him to die.'

'Did you challenge them about it?' asked Janie.

'Yes, I was bloody livid, but they just laughed at me. They said Hamish would have blabbed at the inquest and we would have all been sunk. I'm sorry, I should have come forward at that point.' Tears were carving trails down his cheeks.

'Okay. Other officers investigating the murders of Callum and Davie will probably need to come and speak to you, again, now that you seem to be cooperating. I just want to know one thing.'

'Okay,' said Farquharson, taking a sip of water from a Styrofoam cup, his voice a little steadier.

'How were Callum and Davie going to offload the drugs? It's not like they were going to sell them on the streets,' said Max.

'I don't know, but they had reached out to a major criminal in jail about using his network. They went to see him, and they seemed excited about it. Said how much money they were going to make. Talked about millions of pounds.'

'Who was it?'

'I don't know, I promise. They wouldn't tell me. They just used me, never trusted me. They thought I could help with police inquiries, as I have access to lots of information, and still have contacts in the force.'

'What jail was it?'

'I don't know.' Max stared into his eyes and knew that he was telling the truth. Lenny was broken now, and the only way for him to avoid a conspiracy to murder charge was complete cooperation.

'One last question,' said Max.

'Yes?'

'Why weren't you killed?'

'I've been thinking about this a lot. Luck.'

'What, just luck?'

'Aye. I didn't see Callum or Davie approaching, from my position. There was a barrel and a hedge in the way, and the line of sight was obscured. I didn't see a thing until I heard the gunshots, and then a motorbike roaring off and the next thing I knew, the cop had arrested me. I genuinely think that they didn't kill me because they didn't see me. If they'd seen me, I'd be dead,' he breathed heavily. 'If they find out where I am, I'm finished.'

'That's enough. We need to speak, now,' the solicitor said.

'Okay, think hard about what you do next. It's important. I'm switching off the tape now, so that Mr Farquharson can consult with his solicitor.'

Max quickly packaged the DVD that had been in the recording machine and Lenny signed it.

'Please help me,' Farquharson's voice was imploring.

'Lenny, no more,' his solicitor barked.

'Don't you fucking tell me what to do!' Lenny screamed, spittle flying from his mouth.

'I just ...' the solicitor said, his voice calm, clearly sensing a big, billable case slipping away from him.

'Enough bullshit. Enough lies and deception. I want to do the right thing,' Lenny said, tears running down his cheeks.

'Someone will come and see you,' said Max, gently.

'I'll tell them everything. Everything I know. The killing has to stop.'

'That was an interesting interview technique,' said Janie as they left the police station and headed for their car. The rain had stopped now, leaving the streets damp but drying in the watery sunlight. The smell of wet pavement was all around them as they walked.

'Meaning?' said Max, raising his eyebrows, innocently.

'You know, the "I don't care if you don't answer questions, mate" line. Absolute BS, especially when you hit him with the TTL notice. Nice touch, by the way, but where is this new and compelling intelligence that Lenny is about to get whacked?'

'Common sense. They took out his pals, stands to reason they'll take him out too.'

'But then again, maybe not. Callum and Davie were killed by professionals, and professionals don't tend to murder someone without being paid for it. If they had been paid for it, wouldn't they have looked a little harder for him? Maybe they didn't want to kill him, or maybe they just didn't see him,' Janie said, her brow creased in thought.

'Doesn't really matter at the end of the day. We are where we are, but he let out a nugget in there,' said Max.

'The mysterious Mr Big in prison?'

'The very same. That's a fat lead that we need to explore. We know one thing for sure, right?'

'That you have the musical taste of an old man?' said Janie, pulling the car keys out of her pocket and unlocking their Volvo.

They both got in and strapped themselves into the plush leather seats. The speakers suddenly exploded with an onslaught of complicated jazz.

'Jesus, I have no music taste?' shouted Max over the noise.

'Sorry. I was listening to it earlier. This proves you're a philistine, by the way. That's Ornette Coleman, a bloody genius.'

'A bloody racket is what it is. Turn it off.'

Janie fiddled with her phone, and the music suddenly stopped. She started to drive. 'So, what were you saying?'

'We know Ashraf provided the NCA agents with advanced intelligence on forthcoming drug movements. But Mr Big in prison must have had someone with access to intelligence at an even higher level.' Outside bruise-coloured clouds were beginning to surge towards them over the hills. Max pulled out his phone and turned it around in his palm. 'They can intercept encrypted calls, intercept our calls, or, most worryingly, they have someone at the heart of this inquiry.'

39

THE TEAM OF four, now including Norma, sat in silence in the office. They had listened to Max's update from the recent 'interview' with Farquharson, and Norma was typing it up on her computer. Her hair was tied back and she wore a tight-fitting T-shirt and skirt. Her face was flushed and red with the heat.

The pipes in the office gurgled and clanked as the ancient system continued to pump boiling hot water through the radiators.

'So, the bastard coughed, then,' said Ross, rubbing his temples as if he could massage the creases and tiredness away.

'Well, kind of. I served the TTL notice on him and pointed out what had recently happened to Ashraf, and he kind of spilled his guts. The MIT are into him now and he's singing like the proverbial canary,' said Max.

'Minor point on that. I'm assuming that you wouldn't be so daft as to serve an unauthorised TTL?' said Ross. He raised his bushy eyebrows.

Max paused, mouth half open, his eyes moving side to side.

'Before you try bullshitting me, I know it hasn't been authorised, as I have to countersign it. I know I'm getting old, but I'm not bastard senile,' said Ross, fanning himself with a clipboard.

'I was hoping you could pull it out of the bag with a retrospective authorisation, or something ...' said Max, his voice trailing off.

Ross's eyes glinted. 'Oh, aye, I bet you did. You're a bloody cowboy, Craigie.' He stared at him for a long moment then blew out a sigh. 'Leave it with me. It's hard to say there isn't a threat-to-life situation, considering he's the only one who doesn't have a bullet in his head, and I think we could argue that your intentions were honourable. Next time, call me first, eh? You've spent too much time with slapdash cockneys, pal,' said Ross, making a note.

'Can I just make sure I have this clear – as I'm still getting myself up to speed?' said Norma, squinting through her spectacles at her screen, then spinning her chair around to face the rest of the room.

'Crack on,' he said.

Norma then gave the briefest of bullet point summaries of the case, finishing with, 'Is my understanding all correct?'

'Bang on, mate. There's a reason I recruited you. These two thick buggers would never have been able to condense this shite show down to six sentences,' said Ross, wiping his forehead with a handkerchief.

'Well, if Callum and Davie were using Mr Big in prison, it makes some sense of the cell sites. I have their phones on at least one occasion very close to Saughton prison. They travelled there from their home addresses, both phones hitting the same masts throughout. The personal phones were then switched off, and back blocks on again, at exactly the same time, which we know suggests some badness is happening.'

'Hold up. Can you be sure they hit the prison – how tight is your cell siting?' asked Janie.

'As tight as it can be. I can be sure enough that's where they were going.'

'How come?'

'The handset downloads we got from the MIT. Davie used his map application to satnav to the jail at that exact time, immediately before he switched it off, and Callum had earlier made a phone call to a mobile number that intelligence checks show to be a prison officer at Saughton, also cell siting at the jail. Conclusive enough?' Norma smiled brightly, her hazel eyes sparkling.

'Do we know who the prison officer is?' asked Janie, who despite the heat was still wearing a hoodie and looked cool and unflustered.

'It's a pay-as-you-go, but he isn't careful enough with his airtime top-ups. His name is William Gifford, lives not far from the prison. He uses a credit card registered to him, which is bad tradecraft if he's bent,' said Norma, with a sigh, as if she was a bit disappointed it had been so easy.

'Excellent, although I'm taking credit for this tremendous piece of intelligence analysis, as it was my idea to recruit you,' said Ross with a chuckle.

'Credit's all yours, but my price is a nice coffee,' she said.

'Anyone have a contact within prison liaison?' said Ross.

'Aye, I've a pal who used to do it. He'll know who to speak to. What do we need?' said Janie.

'We need to know who the hell they were going to see that day, and we need to know more about Gifford,' said Max.

'On it,' said Janie, picking up her phone and dialling.

'Want to know something else?' said Norma.

'Obviously,' said Max.

'It'll cost you a Krispy Kreme.'

'You got it, go on.'

'Callum received very few calls on his encrypted phone, but he did receive an unidentified one from this number. It had never made a call before that initial visit to the prison.' She pointed to a mobile number on the screen.

'And?'

'It's cell sited at the prison, too. As sure as I can be, anyway.'

'So, they gave him a phone?' said Max.

'That's a reasonable assumption. Dirty wee bastards. God rest their corrupt, festering souls,' said Ross with a sneer.

'Did it make any other calls?' asked Max.

'Only to Callum. There's evidence of some mobile internet usage that I can't get any information on. It may be that a messaging service was being used. You know, Telegram, Wickr, or similar. I'd need the handset to be sure.'

'Fat chance of that,' grumbled Ross.

'Hashtag, just sayin',' said Norma, her palms raised, eyes flashing mischievously as she returned to the increasingly complex chart on her screen.

'What?' said Ross. He turned, his brow creased.

'Hashtag. You know, the internet? It's on the computer. There's hashtags, Twitter and Instagram,' said Norma.

'You're saying words that are meaningless to me. I may have to reassess my decision to bring you into my elite team.'

'Get with the programme. Social media is a vital investigative tool,' Norma said, turning back to her screen.

Ross shook his head. 'Instantgram, Twatter and fucking

Faceache. Load of wankers who share every minute of their tedious days.'

'Right, we're on,' said Janie, standing up. 'My pal is putting a call in to the prison intelligence officer for Saughton. Apparently, he's there now, so we should get moving,'

'Not before time, this office is doing my nut in,' said Max, wiping his brow with his sleeve.

'I quite like it – can we keep it like this?' said Janie.

'You're a goddam freak, woman, you could grow rubber in here, and you're dressed in a bloody sweatshirt,' said Ross, fanning himself with a sheaf of documents. 'Now piss off and find some bloody evidence.'

40

MAX AND JANIE'S passage into the prison was swift, as if any obstacles had been cleared prior to their arrival.

They were met at reception by a wiry, middle-aged DC, dressed in jeans and a pressed shirt, who identified himself as Pete Barr, the prison liaison officer. He had a broken nose, and sharp, enquiring eyes. His features split into a grin as he shook hands with them both. He escorted them through reception with the minimum of fuss and into a dank, windowless room. He waved them to a couple of nylon-covered armchairs that looked like they belonged in a 1970s school staffroom. Taking a seat behind his desk, he shifted aside a mound of paperwork and opened a solitary laptop in the middle of the carnage of documents.

'First things first, tea? It's just boiled.' He nodded at a kettle in the corner of the room.

'Life-saver, milk no sugar,' said Max.

'Same, thanks,' said Janie.

'So, what can I do for you?' he said as he stood and walked across the room. 'The officer seemed in the dark as to what this was about, but he had nice things to say about you, Janie.' He busied himself with some mugs.

'All lies, I'm sure,' said Janie.

'We're looking at a case connected to the two recently murdered NCA agents at Queensferry,' said Max, accepting the tea that Pete handed to him.

'I heard about that. Nasty business,' Pete said, passing another cup to Janie and taking his seat. 'What's it got to do with Saughton?'

'We think that they visited the jail a few days ago, and we'd like to know why and who they saw,' said Max.

'What type of visit, social or legal?'

'No idea, that's what we'd like to know.'

'What date?'

Max told him.

Pete tapped at his laptop. 'I'm bringing up the visitor records now. What were their names?'

Max told him.

'Nope, no record of any official visit, either legal or social. Are you sure about this?'

'Pretty much, we understand that they used satnav to get here, and their phones cell sites seem to confirm it,' said Janie.

'Hardly conclusive,' said Pete.

Max hesitated for a moment, assessing whether he should release this information. He decided that he would, his gut telling him that Pete was straight. 'We also have information that he called a member of staff here the same morning. Is it possible that an unofficial visit had been arranged?'

Pete sighed and looked at Max. 'Well, if it was a covert visit, I'm supposed to be told, certainly if it's cops visiting an informant or for another off-books reason, but I can't guarantee that it didn't happen, particularly with NCA. Can you tell me who the staff member was?'

'In confidence?'

'Of course. I work with screws day in, day out and most of them are great blokes, but there are one or two I wouldn't trust to go to the shop for a cut loaf,' he said with a look of distaste.

Max paused again, staring at Pete, wondering if he could trust this man. Telling the wrong person now could get more people killed, add to the bodies of Murdo, Hamish, Callum and Davie. Pete held his gaze, and eventually Max let out a sigh. 'William Gifford,' he said.

'Right,' was all that Pete said, but the look on his face told another story.

'You know him?' said Janie.

'Aye, a bit. Senior screw on Ratho houseblock. A little too close to some of the inmates, as far as I'm concerned. Plus, he's a bit of a creepy wee fanny.'

'Is there anything you can do to confirm?' asked Max.

'Give me a minute,' said Pete, resuming tapping the keys on his laptop.

'What time do you think the visit went down?'

Max told him.

He resumed tapping at the keys, staring intently at the screen for a few minutes, before swivelling the laptop around so that Max and Janie could see.

'This them?'

A frozen image showed Callum Mackintosh and Davie Hamilton standing in the reception area by the X-ray machine.

'That's them. Is there a record of their visit?' asked Max.

'Aye, but not as either social or legal visitors. They use

a different system to record those. They were shown as coming in for other purposes.' Pete's jaw was clenched. 'This database is used for contractors, or other visitors for training, maintenance and the like. They were booked in as visiting health care and were escorted by – guess who?'

'Gifford?'

'Boom.' Pete smiled weakly, but it didn't reach his eyes.

'Can we see what they actually did?' said Max.

'Give me a second. We use health care to book in cops for covert visits. No one questions a health care visit, and the visitors can easily be sneaked in there.' He swivelled the laptop back around and continued, tapping away, his face a picture of concentration.

'Here are the health care images,' he continued to scroll.

'As I thought,' he said eventually with a sigh. 'Gifford went to Ratho houseblock and brought an inmate across to health care. Recognise him?' He flipped the laptop around again.

Max's face remained blank but inside shock hit him like a speeding train. He swallowed as he took in the scarred face, neat hair and cruel blue eyes.

41

TAM HARDIE.

The man who had tried to kill him, and have others kill him, who removed the skin from a rival dealer's belly whilst he was still alive. The man who had held Max's elderly aunt, with a gun to her head; who had bugged his house, tapped his phones, corrupted scores of cops and killed repeatedly, mercilessly, in some warped sense of family honour.

Max looked at the image, feeling dark, pulsating rage begin to rise. He breathed steadily, forcing the feelings down inside. Not now, he thought. Now was a time for a cool head, not for this.

'We were part of the team that put Tam Hardie away, Pete,' said Janie, also staring at the screen.

'Ah right, that explains a lot. On the face of it, he's a model prisoner. Few rumours that he was responsible for napalming another inmate, but unsurprisingly, no one saw a thing, not even the poor sod who got burned. Other than that, he keeps himself to himself, plays a little pool and cards with a select few pals, and that's it. No bugger messes with him, though. Just a look from him can sort out most problems in the houseblock.'

Max remained silent. Inwardly he was trying to get hold of

his emotions, to calm the rage that was boiling in his gut. He breathed in as controlled a fashion as he could. One of the few lessons he'd found useful during his counselling had been the square-breathing technique. Gently inhale for four seconds, hold for four, then exhale for four. He closed his eyes, letting the breaths ease the kinks out of his rumpled brain.

'You okay? You look like you've seen a ghost.' Pete's voice cut through the mist in his head.

'Max?' said Janie.

Max breathed deeply again. 'What other visitors does he have?'

Pete swung the laptop around again and tapped at the keys.

'Very few. He writes to and phones his wife in North Cyprus.'

'Nothing else?'

'No. Well, nothing other than a legal visit just this morning. His brief came in for the early slot.'

'What was the solicitor's name?' asked Max, his mind refocussing.

'Charles Appleby, of Appleby, James Associates,' said Pete.

Max looked at Janie. 'That's not his solicitor's firm. He was with a fancy Edinburgh firm for the trial and appeal,' said Max.

'Well, that's what I have here,' said Pete with a frown. 'Does it matter? Maybe he changed firms, people do it, especially after failed appeals.'

'Can you get an image of the solicitor?' said Max, his excitement returning.

Pete tapped and scrolled again before turning the laptop to show Max and Janie a still of the CCTV.

Janie swore. Max punched the air. It was definitely him. No

doubt about it. Max and Janie had the man's image burned into their memories from all the briefing slides they had seen over the previous days.

Dressed in a sharp suit, he carried a briefcase. His hair was tidy and neat and he was clean shaven.

Lee 'Scally' Dodd.

42

THE WHOLE TEAM worked silently in the office. The only sounds were the soft tapping of Norma's computer keys and the gurgling, clanking radiators that filled the room with unwanted heat.

Norma was chewing with great relish, a few grains of sugar adhered to her lips, and an empty Krispy Kreme bag on her desk.

The knowledge that Hardie was at the centre of this conspiracy had shocked them all, and they knew that the situation now required a new plan of attack.

'Theories?' Ross said, suddenly.

When Max spoke, his voice was low and flat. 'It's simple. Our recently departed NCA friends approached Hardie in jail and told him they were ripping off Scally's drugs and destroying his network. They didn't fancy selling it on the streets themselves, so they figured that Hardie was a man with a network they could utilise. There's no evidence they visited him before this, and it seems they gave him a phone.'

'So why have them whacked?' asked Janie.

'Well, there are a number of possibilities. Foremost being that they're NCA, and Hardie wouldn't trust them. Also, maybe

Hardie didn't need their money. The confiscation proceedings haven't been as successful as we hoped, so I'm guessing he's got plenty stashed. I would say Hardie still has access to a much bigger supplier than Scally. All the intel is that Scally was mid-tier only, whereas Hardie was getting supplied direct from Colombia. Hardie didn't need Callum and Davie, but he was willing to use them to bring Scally onside. Look at the quantities that they ripped from Scally. A kilo here, four kilos there, and whatever was on that rib at Torridon. Whereas before Hardie got locked up, he was bringing in proper wholesale amounts, direct from the cartel in Colombia.'

'Where are you going with this?' said Ross.

'Hardie has something that Scally needs. A major supplier and access to a properly organised network throughout the UK. Scally has something that Hardie needs. Muscle on the outside and the simple fact that Scally is clever, ambitious and a good organiser. Hardie's management team were the brothers, who are all in jail. He needs a good organiser at the national level. Scally offers that. Hardie can continue to make serious money from jail.'

'So Hardie gave up Callum and Davie to bring Scally onside, so that they could form an alliance and he could be the drug kingpin again?' said Janie.

'That's how I see it,' said Max.

'But why? He's still in jail, and he'll more than likely stay there until he dies,' said Norma, looking up from her screen.

'Power,' said Max. 'He's inside, but he can still control a major drugs empire. He's still the man. He's the don, and you know what he still has access to?'

'Go on,' said Norma.

'Someone senior in law enforcement. Someone at a much higher level than Callum, Davie and Ashraf. Someone who had the inside track on our supposedly covert surveillance job on Lenny. Someone who was corrupt enough to give live, operational details on a police investigation to Hardie, or Scally. There's no other explanation.' Max spoke rapidly. His voice hard-edged, his jaw tight.

Silence descended once again.

'So, what next?' said Janie.

'We stop them. We did it once, and we can do it again,' said Ross.

'Aye, damn right. I've a plan. Is the chief still up for authorising surveillance activity?' said Max.

'Yes, definitely. Against who?' said Ross.

'We know Scally and Hardie are speaking. We know they have a channel of communication; we just need to listen in. Drug prices are massively high at the moment, because there's a coke supply problem. I'm confident a large consignment will be coming in soon to get Scally up and running. We intercept that, their cash flow dies and they're vulnerable,' said Max.

'They're on encrypted phones. We can't intercept them.'

'We won't need to. Is Barney available?'

'I'm sure he will be,' said Ross.

'Then get him here,' said Max.

43

HARDIE FELT A LITTLE nervous, as he always did before he spoke to the contact. All he really knew about the man was that he had been one of his late father's contacts, recruited many years ago, when he was very junior in his organisation.

The contact wasn't junior anymore. Not in the slightest. In fact, as well as climbing the seniority ladder, he had managed to make significant contacts in the Colombian cartel. They held him in high regard and kept him on a generous retainer. Hardie's relationship with him was one of equals.

The contact didn't like direct calls, but Hardie had little choice. He was restricted to the quiet times in prison when everyone was banged up. He checked his watch, it was almost 8 p.m., the contact would be expecting the call now. The houseblock was noisy with blaring TVs and stereos, perfect for covering their brief conversation. This wasn't something that could be done in a written message.

Hardie dialled the number from memory on the small, encrypted handset. It only rang once.

'Yes,' the voice said, sharp and curt.

'It's me.'

'Are we ready to proceed?'

'Scally has confirmed he's ready, has the capacity to deal and that his infrastructure is capable of handling a big consignment.'

'Despite losing four of his men and fifteen kilos of product?'

'He has lots of good people and he's a bloody good organiser. He just got unlucky. Scally has proved himself in taking care of them.'

'And you're willing to hand your network to him?'

'Yes, the whole thing.'

'Can I ask why?'

'I want one final payment and then I want out,' said Hardie, simply. He trusted no one, particularly the contact who would sell him out in a heartbeat if it would suit his purpose.

'Your decision. I don't particularly care, but if this goes wrong, our associates in Medellin won't be very happy, if you understand my meaning.'

'Of course.'

'Then you'll brief Scally about the operation?'

'Leave it to me. Once this one is over, Scally is yours. He has the people, the infrastructure, and with this level of product, he can flourish.'

'What's he like? Are you sure he's not too hands-on?'

'No, he's a real manager with an extensive network that can grow with the increased supply. He has people who control crack houses in the north of England and Scotland, but he's also supplying multi-kilos of product all over the country.'

'On your head be it. In fact, on both your heads be it, because if this doesn't work out, Medellin will want to take direct action against you both. Is that clear?'

'Perfectly.'

'Hardie, it took me many years working in narcotics smuggling liaison in far-flung shit holes to develop this relationship with the cartel. I'm not jeopardising my position.'

'You won't be. Scally can handle it.'

'Right, I have to go. Message me once Scally is briefed and I'll make the final arrangements. Be ready to move at a moment's notice. The consignment is close, and we want it ashore.'

'Understood.'

The phone clicked in his ear. Hardie wiped sweat from his forehead and took a deep breath. He switched the small handset off and secreted it in a training shoe, underneath the insole in a small hollowed-out space, just big enough for the phone.

Hardie flicked on the television, hopeful for the future, despite his incarceration. A decent hit of cash from this would secure the wife and kids for life, and he could step away from the game. He'd had enough of it and didn't want to run an international drug smuggling operation from behind bars.

He was just about to settle down to watch *MasterChef*, when he suddenly became aware of the heavy, acrid smell of smoke. It was far stronger than the normal stench of cigarettes and the sour, unpleasant stink of spice. This was a thick, choking smell, with a nasty, artificial undernote. Urgent shouting erupted from the landing, and a sudden squealing, high-pitched noise echoed through the building. A fire alarm. A bloody fire alarm. What the hell was going on?

Keys rattled in his door and Gifford poked his head in. 'We need to evacuate, Mr Hardie. Thompson set fire to his bloody mattress again and the fumes are getting worse. Fire brigade are on their way. All of Ratho House is forming up in the exercise yard. Shouldn't be too long,' he said.

'Thompson's a pain in the arse. Where is he?' asked Hardie.

'In seg, he'll be there for a while after this. Wrecked his bloody cell,' said Gifford.

Hardie sat up with a muffled curse and switched off the TV, throwing the remote on the bed with force. 'For fuck's sake,' he muttered as he joined the line of cons, all shuffling along the landing in the direction of the exercise yard. Hardie had been looking forward to watching the semi-final of *MasterChef*, and it wasn't like he could record it, was it?

'I'm gonna fucking chin that bastard when he gets back from seg. I was watching bloody *MasterChef*,' said Mad Dog, a huge bank robber who fell in step alongside Hardie.

'Aye, he's a sandwich short of a picnic, pal,' said Hardie as they walked towards the yard.

'Come on, gentlemen, let's keep moving. We need to clear these bloody fumes, or you'll lose brain cells from the chemicals,' shouted Gifford.

'Some of us have more to lose than others, eh?' said Mad Dog as they were let into the yard.

The hour in the yard was actually something of a bonus. They hadn't had a great deal of yard time, with staff numbers being so bad, and Hardie spent a pleasant enough hour in the fresh air, chatting to a few pals. He shivered as he walked back to his cell, trying to shake off the evening chill.

'Bang-up in twenty minutes,' yelled Gifford as Hardie arrived at his cell.

He stopped dead in his tracks as he crossed the threshold.

His normally immaculate room was a mess. It had clearly been bloody searched whilst they were in the yard.

'What the …' He took in the dishevelled bedclothes, the rearranged toiletries and extra food he had stacked. His locker had been gone through, and everything was out of place.

Hardie stomped out of his cell, his face red with anger. 'My fucking pad has been spun,' he shouted.

'Mine too,' said Mad Dog, also looking furious.

'And mine, you fucking liberty-takers,' came another voice.

Within a few minutes it became evident that the whole bloody landing had been searched.

Suddenly, Hardie's blood ran cold. His phone.

He swallowed what felt like a golf ball and, breathing heavily, he rushed back into his cell, pulled his trainers from his locker and ripped out the insole. His heart sank. It was gone.

'Fuck!' he screamed at the top of his voice.

'Hardie?' a deep voice announced from the door. He turned. A huge, muscle-bound prison officer loomed above him. His biceps stretched the fabric of his shirt.

'What?' snapped Hardie.

'I'm Mr James from prison security. We carried out a routine search during the evacuation. We found contraband in your cell in the form of a mobile phone, this is prohibited under prison rules. You're on report to the governor, do you understand?' He stared down with disdain, and it took all Hardie's resolve not to launch himself at the man.

'Fuck you,' Hardie said.

Officer James smiled, turned on his heel and left the cell.

Hardie stood there, looking at the empty shoe, fury raging inside him. He urgently needed a bloody phone. 'Fuck it. Fuck it, bastards!' he screamed. He began to kick violently and repeatedly at his plastic litter bin. 'My fucking bastard phone, you bastards.' He continued to kick at the disintegrating bin, spilling its contents all over the floor.

When Gifford appeared in the doorway, Hardie stopped his assault on the bin. He panted, leaned against the wall and glared at the prison officer.

'Mr Hardie, I had no idea that security was going to search the cells.' His voice trembled. His hair was out of place and his face was ashen.

'They took my fucking phone, Gifford,' Hardie said, his eyes blazing.

'I heard. I had no idea, I promise. There genuinely was a fire in Thompson's cell, I went with you all into the yard,' said Gifford in an almost whiney tone.

'This is your fault.' Hardie stepped towards him, finger raised. 'You get paid to see that shit like this don't happen.' Gifford took a hesitant step back, his face flinching to one side, his boots squeaking on the floor. He looked at his feet, trembling visibly.

'I know, I'm sorry,' he said, his head bowed, a schoolboy talking to the headmaster.

Hardie closed his eyes and let out a deep, soothing breath. A sudden calm seemed to descend over him. He sighed, and gave Gifford a sympathetic smile. Gifford backed away as if his kindness was even more terrifying than his anger.

'Mr Gifford,' Hardie said, his tone one of parental disappointment. 'I really need another phone.' He sat on the bed, rearranging his pillow so that it was behind his back, then settled against it.

'I'm not sure I can, Mr Hardie. We have to go through security the same as everyone else.'

Hardie picked up a paperback book from his bedside table. He opened it and began to read. Without looking from his book, he spoke again, his voice light. 'I'm sure you'll find a way. I need a phone, preferably encrypted, and I need it today, or tomorrow at the latest. Stick it up your arse when bringing it in, I don't care.'

'But—' began Gifford.

Hardie silenced him with a sigh, like a parent chiding a child over poor exam results. He lowered his paperback and turned to look at Gifford, his face relaxed and friendly, but his eyes as hard as flint. 'William, I know everything about you, I know where you live, where your kids go to school. Need I say more?'

Gifford simply nodded.

'Cut along then, I'd like to get back to this.' He returned his gaze to the page.

Gifford bowed his head, his face red with embarrassment, as he turned and left the cell.

After a few minutes, Hardie threw his paperback down on the bed and looked at the mess that had replaced his immaculate cell. He closed his eyes. He was sick to death of this shite-hole and the people who put him here. He had gone from living in a palatial home, driving a Range Rover, with a beautiful wife, and two kids that he genuinely loved. Now look at him. In a box-like cell, surrounded by junkies and low-life prisoners. Shite food, no booze and no women.

A slow smile spread across his face when he thought of the man responsible for putting him in here.

Detective Sergeant Max Craigie.

His mind turned to their final confrontation in the small cottage in the Highland coastal village. His hand went to the scar on his cheekbone.

One day, his time would come, and he would stare straight into Craigie's eyes as he ripped the bloody skin from his body and watched him squirm like a maggot on a fishing hook.

When his voice came, it was a quiet whisper, barely audible over the thumping music and blaring TVs along the hallway.

'Soon, Craigie, you bastard. Soon.'

44

BARNEY JUMPED INTO the back of an anonymous Ford van, parked in the car park of Saughton jail. He paused to flick a lit roll-up onto the tarmac, and then slid the door shut behind him. The smell of tobacco smoke followed him into the van in an acrid wave.

'Good job,' said Janie, wafting at the smoke residue. The two of them were alone inside the van. Its walls were lined with computer equipment with two swivel chairs in front of the monitors and keyboards.

'Are we working?' he said.

'Like a dream, clear as a bell, mate. Uniform suits you, by the way,' said Janie, pointing at Barney's prison service shirt and tank top combo, the front of which was spotted with flakes of ash.

'It's chuffing itchy as 'eck. This is why I couldn't be a cozzer. Daft uniform.' He grimaced as he sat in one of the chairs. His fingers flashed across the keyboard and a sudden hiss of static came from the speakers.

'Hold up, I can improve the reception a bit. Probe is secreted in the plug socket,' he said.

'Sounds pretty good, anyway.'

'Has Hardie said anything?' said Barnie, adjusting the controls.

As clear as if they were in the cell with Hardie, the sound of canned laughter could be heard. A strong Irish accent filtered through the speakers.

'*Mrs Brown's Boys*,' said Barney.

'What?'

'Hardie's clearly a fan of *Mrs Brown's Boys*,' said Barney, continuing to adjust the controls. Satisfied, he sat back, staring at the display. He pulled out his leather tobacco pouch and expertly rolled a cigarette. He gave it a cursory once-over, nodded with satisfaction and put it between his lips.

'He's not happy about losing his phone,' said Janie, 'and Gifford's got to get him a new one by tomorrow. They're planning something, and we need to get ahead of it. Hold up, I'll call Max,' said Janie, picking up her phone.

'Janie?' said Max.

'Are you getting it?'

'Yep, he's not a happy bunny, is he?'

'You think it was worth the risk taking the phone?'

'Definitely. You heard him. It means he's trading an encrypted phone for a normal one, certainly in the short term. Gives us the opportunity to intercept it, if we need to, but the probe is what we wanted. That gets us admissible evidence, which we couldn't get from any intercepts, even supposing we get one authorised. I'd say we're good to go. We recording now?'

'Yeah, he's watching *Mrs Brown's Boys*, I think.'

'No accounting for taste, is there? Right, both of you get off home. We need to be ready to go tomorrow, once he gets a new phone, so it could be a long day. We're safe to leave him overnight. It'll just be shite TV or him snoring.'

'Sure thing. Home before ten, miracles do happen.' When Max didn't respond, Janie paused. She turned away from Barney. 'You okay?' said Janie, her voice softening.

'With what?' said Max.

'Hardie. You know, after last time?'

There was a long pause at the end of the line. 'Max?' said Janie.

'Aye, sorry, I heard you. I'm fine. We just do our jobs properly, and sort this out for good, right.'

'Of course, but, come on, after what happened in Avoch, you'd be odd if you didn't have a moment or two.'

'It's all good. See you in the morning.' The triple beeps in Janie's ear told her that Max had gone.

She let out a sigh and turned to face Barney. 'We should get going,' she said. He was busy fiddling with the settings.

'Aye, you drive and I'll carry on here. I want to sort this out,' he said, his roll-up bobbling in his mouth.

'No smoking in here, right?'

'As if, love,' he said, not looking up from the screen.

She sighed as she got out of the back of the van and climbed into the driver's seat. As she started the engine and moved away, the familiar smell of cigarette smoke began to permeate from the rear. She shook her head and cracked the window a little.

Worry crept into her mind about her friend. She hoped he wasn't drinking again, even though she'd seen no sign of it. There were always his dreams, as well, but he hadn't mentioned them in ages. In fact, he'd been in good spirits since Katie came back. This was the thing with Max. He was something of a closed book, but Hardie was clearly eating at him.

She just hoped that Max never came face to face with Tam Hardie again. For both of their sakes.

45

ROSS WAS SITTING in the office scowling at the screen in front of his terminal when Barney walked in clutching his laptop.

'All good?' said Ross as Barney collapsed into a chair, yawning.

'Yeah. Feed's working okay, but could be clearer. A pal of mine is running it through an algorithm to filter out some of the lower-wave interference. Once we have the settings, we'll have the best possible sound wave quality and I can integrate it into the feed in the background.'

'Barney, your mouth is moving but you're spouting shite, man. You know my abilities in this area. Give it to me in a language a dull eight-year-old would understand,' Ross said.

Barney pointed at himself, speaking slowly. 'Clever man ... making decent-quality audio ... into better quality. He's emailing it to me soon.'

'How soon?'

'Within the hour,' said Barney, stifling a yawn with the back of his hand. 'Bugger me it's hot in 'ere,' he added.

'Aye. I've been giving Building Services shite about it. Maybe my overly brusque approach isn't working. You shoot off, man. I can sort your radiogram shite out when the email comes in. Just leave your laptop open,' said Ross.

'You sure?'

'Aye, you tell me what I have to do, and I'll wait until it comes in. I want the best-quality product available when we really go live.'

Barney frowned at him for a moment, then shrugged. 'Hardie is snoring now, but the recording we have is being enhanced. When the audio comes in there'll be a WAV file attached, just click on it and it'll auto run. Give it a listen and see what you think, then upload the email and attachments onto the shared drive and I can get straight on it in the morning. Headphones are over there. I'll integrate the updates and we're good to go.' He yawned again, his bright white teeth stark.

'Right. Piss off, you're adding extra body heat into this bastard sauna.'

'When are you leaving?'

'As soon as I've integrated your WAVVY fucking shite. Go on, sod off, I'll not be far behind you. Mrs F is expecting me to be late.'

Barney rose to his feet with a groan, and arched his back. 'Stiff as a board cramped up in that van, I'm getting too old for this.'

'You were too old for this in 1981, pal. See you in the morning.'

Barney clapped Ross on the shoulder and left.

Ross sat back in his chair and stretched out his legs in front of him, yawning deeply and sighing. He reached down and opened his bottom drawer and pulled out a bottle of Dalwhinnie single malt whisky. He poured a generous slug into his coffee cup and sipped appreciatively, relishing the warmth of the neat spirit.

He picked up his phone from the desk and quickly composed a message.

Working all night. Speak in the morning. I'm sorry, I don't want to argue anymore.

The icon next to the text turned blue indicating that his wife had read the message. He stared, his gut clenching, waiting for the reply.

The argument with his wife had been far more volatile than normal, and he was already bitterly regretting his language and tone. He loved his wife and kids dearly, and he hated these arguments, but the hours at work were just getting too much.

No reply. Fuck. She was ignoring him. He drained his whisky and poured another measure. They'd always had a fairly tempestuous relationship, underpinned by deep love and affection, but this felt different. Missing her birthday celebration seemed to have been the final straw. He sipped at his whisky again, before putting the mug down on the table.

A ping from Barney's laptop made him start. He rose from his chair, wincing at the pain in his foot, and went to the computer. He opened the email and saw a lone file. He pulled on Barney's earphones and pressed play on the WAV file. The quality was excellent, clear as a bell. He continued to listen, his eyes drifted to the ceiling and he yawned. Then he heard the sound of Hardie's voice in the cell with little or no interference.

The next words from the gangster made his blood run cold.

46

MAX YAWNED AS he let himself into the cottage. He rubbed his hand over his head, feeling the coarse stubble that was almost matched by his growing beard. His arms and legs ached, and his eyes felt sandy and scratchy. The knowledge that Hardie was active again, whilst not surprising, had affected him more than he had realised.

His overriding emotion was one of determination. He was going to stop Hardie, and those enabling him, by whatever means necessary.

His thoughts were interrupted by the blonde, curly form of Nutmeg, launching herself at him, tail thrashing wildly. He entered the living room. Katie was sitting, pyjama clad legs curled under her, her glasses perched on her nose, a book on her lap. She smiled up at him.

'Hello, stranger, I recognise you from somewhere, I just can't recall where, but please knock when you come into our house,' she said, her white teeth shining in the low light. The log stove crackled, emitting an enveloping, welcoming warmth. The warm smell of the room swept over him and he sighed, his shoulders instantly relaxing.

‘Miss me?’ said Max, leaning over and kissing his wife, smelling her warm, clean scent.

‘Miss you, I’m not sure who you are, and kissing me is highly inappropriate, as a total stranger, although you are a good kisser, I’ll grant you. If my husband returns, what would he think?’

Max chuckled. ‘Tea?’ he said, standing up and stretching.

‘I’ll make it, you’ve clearly had a long day,’ said Katie, padding across the wooden floor towards the kitchen.

Max yawned again, kicking off his trainers and collapsing into his chair. Nutmeg immediately settled next to him, resting her shaggy head on his lap. She gazed at him adoringly and yawned sympathetically.

‘How was work?’ said Katie when she returned, handing him a mug of steaming tea.

‘Busy,’ Max said, hoping he sounded convincing, but also concerned that the tone in his voice may tell a different story.

‘Everything okay?’ she asked with a frown.

‘All fine, love,’ said Max, but he knew she saw right through him.

‘Maybe if you shared? Problem shared, problem halved, right?’

‘Maybe not. Let’s talk about something else,’ said Max, a little too quickly.

‘Max?’ said Katie, her smile slipping.

‘Just a tough and very long day. How was yours?’ said Max, his nonchalant tone a little forced.

‘Dull and tedious. Property contracts, due for completion. Want to hear more?’

‘Not really,’ said Max, with a tired smile. His phone buzzed in his pocket. It was Ross.

'Sorry, I best take this,' said Max, standing up.

Katie sighed and reached for her book, with a slight shake of her head.

'Ross?' said Max as he walked towards the patio doors away from Katie.

'I checked to see if the feed was running smoothly, and I thought I'd best let you know what I heard.' Ross's voice had none of its usual levity or sarcasm. It was serious and even.

Max's stomach tightened, knowing that Ross wasn't given to panic.

'Go on,' said Max.

'I've been running the recordings through a new filter Barney got hold of to pick out voices from background noises.'

'What's your point?'

'Well, it hadn't been audible before, but I was listening to the dialogue Hardie had with Gifford, and I let it run on. I caught a bit of something we'd missed.'

'And?'

'Best I play it for you,' said Ross.

The recording hissed a little in Max's ear, a background of TV noises. Then he heard it, faint, low, almost a whisper. But it was definitely Hardie, and the words were clear enough.

'Soon, Craigie, you bastard. Soon.'

Max said nothing, his face impassive. An invisible hand suddenly took hold of his lower gut. It started squeezing, gently.

'Max, are you okay?' Ross's voice sounded very far away. 'I thought I should let you know.'

'Thanks, I'll see you tomorrow.' Max hung up, and let out a deep sigh. His hand pressed against the French doors. He stared through the glass into the inky blackness outside. His wife appeared as a reflection, but he barely noticed. His mind felt like a cog had worked loose.

He jumped a little when she put her soft hands on his shoulders, his heart pounding.

'You okay, babe?' There was concern in those soft Yorkshire tones. Kind and trusting. He made a sudden decision. He turned to face her, stared into her worried eyes.

'Katie, I want you out of here. I want you gone, tomorrow.'

Her face went from concerned to scared. 'I don't want to, what's happened?' Tears began to form and her mouth turned down at the corners.

Max stared at her in silence, taking in every line and curve of her face. Nutmeg sat at their feet, whining, clearly sensing something was not right.

Max gently brushed a spilled tear from her cheek. 'It's not safe for you here. I need to resolve something at work, and it's too dangerous for you to be at the house. I'm sorry. I love you more than I can tell you, but you can't be here.'

47

THE DREAM WAS bad.

The worst it had been for many months. It was the same as usual, but more vivid, the colours lurid, the blood almost luminous against the dark brown sand. He could still smell the copper, taste dust and sweat, as he sat up in bed, ripped from sleep, gasping for breath. The images remained after waking, burned into his retinas, like the legacy of a firework display. The flash of the IED, the deafening crump of the explosion. The stench of desiccated dirt thrown up into the stultifying heat of Helmand Province.

'Babe?' said Katie, rolling over. 'Max, Max. It's okay, honey, it's okay, just the dream.' She pulled him closer, his body sheathed in a slick sweat. He breathed heavily, the darkness beginning to subside with his wife's warm embrace. Tears ran from Max's eyes, and he choked back a sob, burying his head into Katie's shoulder.

'I'm sorry,' he said.

'Please get help with this,' she said. 'I'm begging you.'

'I will. As soon as I resolve this situation at work, I will,' said Max, knowing this was untrue.

'Leave it to someone else. You've done enough, no one could have done more than you,' she said, stroking his head.

‘I have to do this. It’s my responsibility. Hardie’ll never leave me alone, and whilst he’s still able, you’re at risk.’

‘I don’t want to go. I love being with you, and I’m scared.’ She began to sob.

‘It’s too dangerous. I have no idea what he’s planning, and I can’t protect you. Your train is at nine, and I want you on it.’

Katie opened her mouth to argue but closed it just as quickly. They had discussed this until late, and Max had told her some of what had happened and what was likely to happen over the next few days. Katie had reluctantly agreed to go to an old university friend’s place in Exeter, just for a week or two.

‘I’ll miss you,’ she said, quietly.

Max looked at the digits on the LED clock on the bedside table. It was still only five am.

He returned Katie’s embrace and they both lay there together in the dark.

48

HARDIE WAS IN association late morning the following day, playing pool with Mad Dog. He couldn't concentrate on the game, his thoughts focused on the next few days, so he was playing badly.

He scuffed another shot as Gifford strolled into the association hall and caught Hardie's eye. He said nothing, just flicked his eyes in the direction of Hardie's cell.

'Your game. I'm playing like an arse today, let some other bugger lose their super-noodles to you.'

'Aye, it's as well. I'm fucking Paul Newman today.' Mad Dog grinned.

'I'm away to my pad for a nap,' said Hardie, walking off.

He had only been in his cell for five minutes when Gifford appeared, nervously tapping on the door before entering.

'You have something for me?' Hardie said.

Gifford pushed the cell door shut, before quickly shoving his hands down the back of his trousers. He pulled out a small, cellophane-wrapped object, which he held out in front of him.

'I'm nae touching that fucker. Take off the fucking packaging.'

'Sorry,' blurted Gifford, quickly stripping the plastic from around the package. Once clear, he proudly produced the tiny mobile phone.

'What the hell is that?' said Hardie, incredulous at the size of the thing. It was only about two inches long and looked like an old-fashioned miniaturised Nokia.

'It's a Zanko T1 Tiny. Nothing smaller out there. Means you can hide it easier. Best I could do,' said Gifford, clearly pleased with himself.

'Does it access the internet?'

'No, calls only and texts if you can manage on those tiny keys. Look, I had no chance of getting anything better. Security's cracking down, and everyone goes through the checks. It was that or nothing.'

'Shit. Like being in the dark ages. How do I charge it?'

Gifford went to his wrist and fiddled underneath his watch, unwinding a short length of electrical wire. 'This end slots into the phone, you'll need to wire it into your kettle or TV plug each time you need to use it. Best I can do,' Gifford said.

'How about airtime?'

'It's all sorted. I topped it up with fifty quid. The number's on this.' Gifford handed over a scrap of paper, which Hardie immediately pocketed.

Hardie looked at the tiny phone and length of wire, with a mixture of relief and disappointment. 'It'll have to bloody do. Go on, piss off,' he said. Gifford nodded meekly and left the cell.

He powered up the tiny phone and the display flashed bright green. He needed to make the call on this primitive unencrypted handset. There was too much at stake. The importation was happening soon, and he had to be ready.

With difficulty he dialled the number from memory.

'Who is this?' The familiar voice of the contact was tinny through the speaker.

'It's me.'

'I don't recognise this number.'

'My other phone got bloody found during a fire in one of the cells. Screws used the empty wing to spin everyone.'

'How inconvenient. Is this secure?'

'Not encrypted, but it's brand new, and there's nothing to link it to me, so it's fine. I can only use it for voice calls or simple messages.'

'No messages. If the phone gets seized again, they can recover deleted messages as easily as you can delete them. This phone will be secure enough for our purposes. There's not a chance it could get intercepted in this time frame, and not without me hearing about it. Any other reason for this call?'

'No, just letting you have the number.'

'Well, I have it now. Call me back in precisely four hours. I should have news by then, but we're proceeding well. All happening in the next two days.'

'Understood,' said Hardie, but the contact had already ended the call.

Hardie dialled again.

'Yeah?'

'Scally. This is my new number.'

'What happened?'

Hardie told him.

'Bastards. Any news?'

'I'm hearing in four hours. Be ready to move, I think we're looking at the next two days.'

'I'm on it. Do we have a location?'

'Not precise, but you know the general area. Will you be on the ground with your people?'

'Yeah, certainly for this first one.'

'And the other arrangements we spoke about?'

'All in hand to go ahead after the shipment. Can't afford to have any big drama until we have the merchandise in hand. It's been paid for in advance, and it cost a shitload, so whatever happens, it's gonna happen.'

'See that it does.'

'Don't worry, it will. So, what after?'

'You're responsible for moving the product and I hand the contact's details over to you. Once this is done, as long as everything runs smoothly, my whole operation is yours.'

'I won't let you down.'

'Best you don't. They won't take failure well. There's a very large line of credit extended on this, and you'll be expected to make sure they get their money.' Hardie's voice was grave.

'I'm on it. How about the bizzies and cuzzies?'

'The contact will monitor, and he'll let you know if anyone gets too close. You'll be safe, trust me.'

'Nice one.'

'In a few days, you're going to be very rich,' said Hardie.

49

ROSS SEEMED TO be in the middle of a difficult phone call with his wife when Max and Janie came back into the office. He was sitting hunched over his desk, his voice hushed, but Max could tell from the set of his face that things were not going well. He clearly hadn't shaved again, and Max was sure that he was wearing the same shirt he'd been wearing the day before. Barney and Norma both had their eyes averted. The small room was still unrelentingly hot, but now it smelt of body odour and feet. Max and Janie took their seats and tried not to listen to the conversation.

'Aye, darling. Of course, it's difficult. I know you're lonely. I'm sorry. I know, but it's hardly my fault, is it? Mary?' He coughed as he acknowledged Max. His shoulders straightened, his chest puffed out.

His voice rose. 'Well, you don't need to talk to me like that. I'm the bloody man of the house, and what I say goes, okay? Aye, that's better,' he softened slightly. 'Of course I forgive you.' Norma rolled her eyes. Janie leaned over and transferred the call to speaker. *'Please hang up, please hang up, please hang up,'* crackled out of the handset.

'Nice work, Detective Inspector. I bet the dial tone is very intimidated,' said Janie, chuckling.

Ross's face was grim, his jaw set tight. There was a long silence as everyone waited for him to laugh, but he just stared at Janie. 'Fuck you,' he said, getting to his feet, his chair crashing to the floor. He stormed out of the office, slamming the door behind him.

'Oops,' said Barney.

They all stared at each other in turn.

'It was just a joke,' said Janie.

'I think he slept here. That's the same shirt as yesterday, and he was keen I buggered off last night. I reckon things are bad,' said Barney as he rolled a cigarette.

'Don't worry about it. Can you make a call? I'll go and see if he's okay,' said Max, rising from his chair and leaving the room.

'You okay?' said Max, catching up with Ross who was looking out of the window, over the field in front of the college.

Ross said nothing for a few seconds. He took a breath and spoke in a voice devoid of his usual sarcastic spark. 'Aye, but Mrs Fraser is being somewhat spiky, as you probably gathered. I think the hours are having an impact.' He paused for a moment and met Max's gaze. He let out a sigh. 'I slept here last night,' he said.

'We've been caning the hours.'

'Aye, but I've always done that. We all have. Maybe this is it for me. Maybe I've been doing this shit too long.'

'What shit?'

'This policing, you know. Proactive, big bad guys, guns, drugs, bent cops. Maybe I need to step back.'

'You want that?'

'Do I fuck. Return to shite day-to-day bollocks. This is all I know, but maybe I need to slow up a little.'

'Will she thaw?'

'I fucking hope so, or I'll be putting a camp bed in the office, and it's too bloody hot for that. Anyway, enough of my marital difficulties, what's going on?'

'Want to join us, so the others can contribute?'

'Not really, but come on,' said Ross, retracing his steps back to the office. He entered as if nothing had happened, picked up his chair and sat down again. He picked up the phone on the desk and dialled.

'Right then, Facilities Management, it's DI Fraser, Police Standards Reassurance in the bowels of this shite-hole. It's fucking roasting, and if I don't get someone here immediately, I'm coming down there personally, and I'm going to stage a fucking sit-in until the heating in my bastard office is sorted. Do I fucking make myself clear?' His voice was tight and hard.

He paused, red-rimmed eyes blazing as he listened to the voice on the other end of the line.

'Aye, straight away, then. Thank you.' He slammed the receiver down with such force that the computer monitors all wobbled alarmingly.

'Continue,' he said.

'Sorry,' said Janie.

'You owe me a fucking tea,' was all Ross said. Janie nodded, stood and headed to the kettle.

'I take it you heard the call from the prison?' said Max.

'Aye, can we identify the new number?'

'Not quickly enough. We'd have to do a cell mast dump, and then work through all the numbers that were hitting the mast during that time frame. Just doing the applications would take days,' said Barney from his seat in the corner of the office. His face was buried in a laptop bedecked with Grateful Dead stickers.

'Analyst's nightmare,' chipped in Norma.

'Ah well, we still have an advantage. We wait until the next call, but it sounds like whatever's happening's going down in the next couple of days.'

'Looks like it. Do we have the numbers to deal with this?' asked Max, scrolling through a copy of Norma's rapidly expanding association chart.

'Depends on what it is. We have the surveillance team ready, but if it's what we suspect it'll be then we'll need some serious extra resources, and expertise,' said Ross.

'We all just heard Hardie's reference to "the contact", right?' said Max.

No one said anything, there was no need. The only sound was Janie wrestling with the kettle.

Max broke the silence. 'He isn't just a bent cop, he's a fucking criminal. Part of the importation conspiracy, slap bang at the centre of a major law enforcement agency. We need to speak to the chief, get our ducks in a row. If we take this wide and involve all the usual players, we may as well tell Hardie and Scally the plan ourselves and cut out the middle man.'

Ross nodded, gravely. 'I'll talk to him. I just hope nothing else bad happens. We don't have the capacity to deal with anything more. I can't bloody face another problem.'

'Ross, I've bad news on that front,' said Janie, her voice

tight. They all turned to look at her. She was standing awkwardly in the kitchen, her face pale.

'What?' barked Ross, his eyes slits.

She swallowed. 'The kettle's broken.'

50

HARDIE SAT IN his cell, trying not to stare at his watch. He knew that the four hours were almost up.

He was surprised at his level of anxiety as the clock ticked in his head and he waited for the moment when he would call the contact. He had been involved in many importations, but none had made him feel like this.

All of his disposable capital was tied up in it, and it had been throughout the planning period, since before his incarceration. Even during his imprisonment, he had managed via Gifford, his lawyer and other contacts, to keep his finger on the pulse as to exactly how it was progressing. He had a simple enough way of making secure phone calls, just by using other inmates' PIN numbers, particularly if they were low-grade and unlikely to be listened into, not that the coded conversations would have meant much to anyone.

A complex web of money had been moving around the globe between shell corporations, in non-reporting territories, all handled by the money men who continued to cream off a nice profit from his endeavour.

He needed this to go well, to sort out Liz and the kids in Cyprus, but it was also something else.

Hardie had a sense of pride about his prowess as a drug importer and distributor. It would be very strange when it was no longer part of his life. He would miss the buzz, but he wouldn't miss the stress. He'd also sleep sounder at night being out of the game. There was only one end likely when you were dealing with the Colombians, and that normally ended with you being in a coffin. He wanted out now, on his terms.

He looked at his watch for the final time and dialled, the tiny phone feeling like a child's toy in his hand.

'Are you ready for the instructions?' was all that the contact said.

'Yes.'

'Loch Inchard in Sutherland. There's a small electricity substation on the road to Kinlochbervie. It's easy to find. Have your people ready there, dressed like workmen and fishermen. Scally will receive a call direct from the yacht's skipper with further instructions. He'll need two decent-sized ribs ready to go, night vision goggles and an infrared torch. Understood?'

'Yes, when?' said Hardie.

'Be in position just before midnight tomorrow. The final arrangements will be made at the last moment.'

'Understood.'

'There can be no mistakes. Your incarceration has made this more difficult, but your previous efficiency has persuaded those supplying the product that this consignment should move.'

'I should bloody hope so, it's damn well paid for,' said Hardie, puffing out his cheeks.

'Indeed, but if they had doubts, it wouldn't happen. Make sure Scally understands the consequences of failure, for all of us.'

'I will.'

The line went dead.

Hardie dialled again.

'Yeah?' Scally's Scouse drawl crackled in his ear.

'The contact has called, we're on.'

51

THE SMALL CONVOY of four trucks drew to a stop. They parked alongside an electricity substation and a decrepit-looking single-storey building. Scally got out and breathed in the fresh sea air. He coughed and lit a fag, listening to the eerie silence as the truck engines ticked and cooled. He felt the familiar buzz he always experienced when readying for a job. This was what it must feel like for soldiers getting ready to storm a building or engage in a battle. Him and his boys about to do a job, it was better than sex.

The small electricity substation sat on a twisting road that ran along the edge of Loch Inchard, a huge, tidal sea loch in Cape Wrath in the shadow of Ben Stack. Not that Scally thought much of the landscape around them. They couldn't bloody see a thing. It was an overcast and moonless night, the sort of pitch dark that only happens in this part of Scotland, far from any light pollution. Far from help, thought Scally. He chased away a shiver. They were professional criminals, drug dealers, smugglers and they could handle whatever came up.

His eyes passed over the two vehicles with trailers hitched behind, each bearing large, powerful-looking ribs.

Scally smiled, feeling a swell of pride in his broad chest.

He'd sorted this all out in just over twenty-four hours since the call from Hardie. The Colombians would be impressed, he was sure.

'Right, Tony, get the ribs in the water, sharpish, and make like fishermen,' Scally said to the small, broad man beside him.

'On it,' Tony said. He began to bark instructions at two other men, all dressed in high-visibility clothing emblazoned with the logo of the local energy provider.

Scally stubbed out his fag and went to the back of the pick-up, pulling out a set of magnetic vehicle signs, all of which bore the same logo as their jackets. He slapped them on the sides of each truck. It was enough to give them a reason to be here.

This was officially the most remote, largest and least-populated police beat in the whole of the UK. And police activity was being monitored.

Within a few minutes, the two ribs were in the loch, almost invisible in the darkness.

Their cover wasn't foolproof, but it didn't need to be. It was so quiet, particularly now, outside of tourist season, that the chances of anyone passing by were as remote as the landscape.

Scally's phone buzzed in his pocket. It was his contact from the control room that managed all the police units in the whole of Scotland.

'Yeah?'

'You're good to go. No police units anywhere near your location.'

'How sure are you?'

'Hundred per cent. All cop radios have GPS, none anywhere near you, and even if they left now, it would take them bloody ages,' she said. She was an old resource of Hardie's with an overview of activity in the whole of Scotland. Bloody goldmine, thought Scally.

'Call me straight away if it changes.' Scally hung up.

'Come round, lads,' said Scally, calling in eight members of his team. All were hard-nosed, experienced guys who Scally knew well. Only the two coxswains were recent additions, recruited for their special skills, but they came with a solid reputation, and had been thoroughly checked out. Lots of mandatory drug testing in the military over the past few years meant there were always ex-military available for work. A good payday with the promise of more to come was enough to secure their loyalty. That and the knowledge that Scally would put a bullet in the head of anyone who crossed him.

The eight men including the coxswains who were both ex-Navy, gathered around at the front of his pick-up.

'It's almost midnight, so I'll be getting a call soon. Johnny and Pablo, take the Ingrams, go a hundred metres either side of us and keep watch. Anyone at all, you have radios. No shooting unless it goes really tits-up, and only if I say so.'

Johnny and Pablo, two meaty-looking men in their forties, held stubby Ingram submachine guns. They lumbered off in opposite directions into the inky blackness.

'This is it, boys. This is the fucking payday we've been waiting for. Get this right, and it's the first of many, and we can all get proper rich.'

The five men all nodded, gravely. Scally had complete faith in them. They were soldiers going into battle, he thought, excitement gripping him, as it always did before a job. The adrenaline rush from the job was almost as good as the money. Almost, but not quite.

'Everyone check their pieces, sort out your kit and be ready to go. Shouldn't be any cops, but we're about to pick up a shitload of beak, and we have to be ready to protect it.'

Like a well-oiled machine, the men began to check their weapons, all small, compact pistols, none the same. The tension was visible in the hard faces of the team. There was a real sense of togetherness as they contemplated what they were about to do.

Scally smiled to himself. This was the big time. No more pissing about with ten or twenty kilos. After this consignment, he was going to be the boss. He was going to be the man. The daddy. The kingpin, and most importantly, he was going to be seriously fucking rich. The rough Scouse boy from a council estate was going to be a multi-millionaire. He felt his chest puff out and a prickle of excitement begin to flutter in his stomach as he considered just how far he had come.

His phone buzzed in his pocket. There was no number displayed. 'Yeah?'

'Ten minutes, then send the ribs out to the mouth of the loch, five kilometres from the shore. We'll use IR torch to guide you, so return our signal. Then come alongside vessel and wait for loading.' The voice was heavily accented with a Slavic twist.

'Understood,' said Scally. The call ended.

Within a few minutes, they were in the ribs, three in each, speeding out towards the vast Atlantic before them. The coxswains wore night vision goggles as the two powerful ribs skimmed across the millpond-flat loch. They made no attempts to be silent. Scally squinted as the salt-water spray hit his face. He was glad he'd worn shit clothes, not his usual expensive designer gear. He decided then and there that once he was satisfied his team were ready, he'd leave them to it in the future. The chief executive of a big corporation doesn't do deliveries, after all, does he? Nor does he live in a small house in a Liverpool suburb. He resolved that a big new gaff in the country was going to be top of his priority list as soon as he got back from this job. That'd keep the missus happy. His stomach lurched as the boat crashed over the sea surface, rocking him side to side. 'Fucking steady, man,' he bellowed, but the coxswain didn't hear. He swore as he wiped the salty water from his eyes. Fishing boats were common in this area, even late at night. The worst anyone would think was they were ripping off prawn creels along the coast, and that was unlikely to instigate any major activity.

As they exited the mouth of the loch, Scally shouted into his radio, 'Slow down, slow down.' The rib reduced speed to five knots, and he pulled out a pair of night vision goggles from his cavernous pocket and lifted them to his eye, scanning the horizon, lighting it up with a greenish glow.

'Twelve o'clock,' shouted the coxswain, his goggles making him look like a strange insect.

Scally swept across the horizon, and then he saw it. A rhythmic flashing of a bright green light, from a long, sleek motor yacht. It was well over thirty metres in length, its white hull shining bright in the greenish glow. Scally picked out a lone, dark figure at the stern flashing the IR torch.

Pulling out a penlight from his pocket, Scally began to flash it at the vessel. Even though no light was visible, he knew that the infrared beam would be easy to spot for anyone using night vision equipment.

'We're on, boys, let's go,' he barked into his walkie talkie.

Both rib engines roared, as they sped towards the expensive yacht.

Within moments they had been expertly guided to the stern. Ropes were thrown to the lone figure on the swim platform who quickly tied them on. The Atlantic was glassy flat, despite the time of year, with only the faintest of swells.

The yacht looked fast, most likely to ensure it could outrun any customs cutters, not that there were any within hundreds of miles of their location. The man who tied them on was leathery-faced and dressed in light trousers, deck shoes and a windcheater.

'We move quick. No other vessels nearby, I check on radar, gear is ready for you, but we need to move faster,' he said in broken English.

'Let's go,' Scally said. 'Like we practised, form a line, one bale at a time, hand to hand. For fuck's sake, don't drop any.' Scally leaped onto the platform, and within seconds, the five-kilo shrink-wrapped bricks were being passed, hand to hand, by the six men. Soon there were fifty of the white bales stacked in each rib. Scally counted them off in turn, his mind boggling at the fact that each rib now contained at least forty million pounds' worth of pure cocaine. Once cut with mannitol, or possibly benzocaine, it could be worth double. He let out an involuntary chuckle, swallowing down his nerves. He took a final glance at the yacht, wondering if something similar would be one of his future purchases.

'Nice doing business with ya, la,' said Scally as the taciturn sailor unhitched the ribs and turned towards the inside of the yacht without a backwards glance. He suppressed a rising feeling of nausea from the journey, aided by adrenaline. No way could he let the lads see him throw up.

The powerful rib engines roared into life and soon they were skimming across the surface of the loch towards their vehicles. Scally gritted his teeth in a rictus smile. Shit, he wanted off this fucking boat as quickly as possible. Last time, he resolved, no more boat trips after this. A sheet of spray slapped him across the jaw as they powered through the inky black water towards the shore.

52

TAM HARDIE WAS feeling unwell.

In fact, he was feeling awful.

He had only just woken up, and looking at his watch, he saw it was almost 1 a.m. All of a sudden, he felt boiling hot, his face flushed, his chest hot enough to fry an egg on. A huge wave of nausea swept over him, from his toes, all the way up. He shuddered, violently, a cold sweat beginning to seep from every pore.

His gut tensed like a drum, and a solid pain suddenly hit in his midriff, as if someone had a hold of his intestines. Then it washed over him. A sudden, overpowering urge to vomit.

He only just made it to his stainless-steel toilet pan before violently projectile vomiting. What remained of his corned beef hash hit the pan, but a fair bit of it went spraying across the polished concrete floor. He had never in his life felt as ill as this.

Hardie struggled to his feet, his stomach flipping, and pressed his communication bell. Then he curled up on the floor, and vomited explosively again, all over the floor this time, unable to get to the toilet pan.

The cell wicket rattled and the face of Mr Jacobs, the duty screw, appeared.

'What's up, Hardie?' When he saw the pool of red and brown vomit tinged with blood that surrounded Hardie, he scrabbled for his keys. 'Jesus,' he said, unlocking the door and reaching for his radio.

He turned Hardie onto his side, and cleared his airway, getting him into the recovery position. A fresh bout of projectile vomit sprayed from Hardie's mouth, covering the screw's trousers.

'I have a seriously ill prisoner here. We need health care now,' Jacobs barked into his radio.

He was soon joined by another guard and then the duty nurse from health care.

'What happened?' she said, just as Hardie began retching and puking again. Thin bile trickled out to join the widening puddle of blood-stained vomit that they were all kneeling in.

'He rang the bell and I found him like this. He went to health care earlier,' said Jacobs.

'I know, I saw him. He was complaining of a grumbling gut ache. Christ, this could be his appendix,' she said, reaching for her thermometer and pressing it into Hardie's ear.

'His temperature's up. This isn't good. Mr Hardie, can you hear me?' said the nurse, panic beginning to sound in her voice.

'Aye, I feel fucking awful, miss. My gut is fucking rotten. It hurts like crazy.'

'Where does it hurt?'

'All over, but worst bottom right,' he said, grimacing.

'Okay, lay on your back, I need to check you,' she said. Hardie shifted onto his back, with a gasp of pain.

Gently, the nurse began to palpate his abdomen. Hardie winced, let out a yelp of pain, and started to retch again, bile spilling from his mouth.

'We have a rigid belly, and lower right quadrant pain. Classic appendicitis,' she said, her face lined with worry.

Hardie cried out in pain again as she continued to palpate his rigid abdomen. 'Fuck,' he moaned. 'It hurts.' His face was set in a grimace and he vomited again, coughing and spluttering. Blood seeped from his mouth, his eyelids fluttered, and he lay still.

'Jesus, we have to get this man to hospital, urgently.' The nurse stood up. 'This could be peritonitis, and we can't treat him here. Get an ambulance now and someone bring up a trolley-bed from health care.'

'Where will you take him?' said the nurse as Hardie was loaded into the ambulance waiting by reception.

'This time of night, if he needs emergency surgery, it'll have to be Edinburgh Royal Infirmary,' said the paramedic. He finished tightening the straps and looked at the bank of monitors.

'What are his vitals?' she asked. Her hands gripped the lanyard around her neck, the knuckles white. Hardie was hooked up to an ECG with an oxygen SAT reader attached to his finger.

'Christ, his heart is racing. SATs are normal, temperature is up a bit, but with the extensive vomiting and rigid abdomen, we have no choice. Are we getting a police escort?' the paramedic asked.

'We've called for one, but there're no units available at the moment. Edinburgh has suddenly gone bloody mad. We only got here by being diverted from a stabbing.'

The senior prison officer rubbed his face with frustration. 'Bloody hell, we can't just take him without an escort.'

'If we don't, he'll die,' said the prison nurse.

'Right.' He let out a long sigh. 'Jacobs, you're in the back. Keep him cuffed and no one goes near him, okay?'

Jacobs stepped into the ambulance, produced a set of cuffs and secured one around Hardie's limp wrist. He attached the other to a thick leather guard on his forearm.

'We need to get going,' said the lead paramedic.

'Okay, watch him like a bloody hawk. I'll see if I can raise any other cops, at least get someone to the hospital.'

Jacobs nodded and the rear door slammed shut. Within a few minutes the ambulance was out of the prison gates, driving along Calder Road.

'How long?' asked Jacobs.

'Fifteen minutes, I'd say,' said the paramedic, monitoring the screen above the prostrate Hardie.

The ambulance hit the bypass, blue lights flashing and sirens blaring in the dark. The heavy traffic parted for them, and they made good progress, soon turning off into town on Gilmerton Station Road. They were slowing down to approach the roundabout when all of a sudden, the driver gave a shout. Jacobs looked through the front windows to see a white Ford van screech to a halt in front of them, forcing the driver to stamp on the brakes.

'Shit!' shouted the driver. Jacobs flew forward, colliding into his colleague and they all staggered, trying to keep their feet. A half-open medical backpack flew off the gurney, crashing to the floor and disgorging its contents. Hardie groaned as his bed cracked into the side.

'What the fuck!' yelled the driver. The paramedic in the rear shouted in fear, his eyes wide with shock.

Jacobs moved towards the front of the vehicle and looked out of the windscreen again. The rear doors of the van burst open, and two balaclava-clad figures, dressed in dark clothing, exited the vehicle. Jacobs stared, open mouthed, rooted to the spot. His breath caught in his chest. Without hesitation, one strode up to the vehicle and raised what looked like a pump-action shotgun to his shoulder. The gun bucked, sparks flew from the barrel, and the ambulance suddenly sagged, its tyre blown. Jacobs dropped to his knees. He sucked in a shaky breath, tried to regain control of the situation.

There was another report, and the nearside tyre crumpled.

'Oh Jesus, no,' screamed the driver, trying to bury himself in the footwell. The paramedic in the back curled into a ball with his hands over his head.

Jacobs reached for the radio clipped to his belt. His hand shook as he tried to unclip the device with fingers that felt too big for the task. His mouth was dry. Suddenly he heard a sound behind him. He paused, his radio frozen in mid-air. A shadow loomed over him, a hand flashing out and gripping his wrist.

'That's a very quick way to get yourself killed, pal,' Hardie said. 'And you're a decent sort. I wouldn't want you to get hurt.' Jacobs turned to see Hardie, standing over him, staring down, eyes blazing.

Suddenly the rear doors flew open, and a masked gunman appeared. Jacobs' eyes went to the pistol clutched in the man's gloved hand. It was levelled straight at Jacobs. His hand was stiff, yet relaxed, a hand that had held a gun many times before.

'Uncuff him, or you die,' the man barked in a flat, unaccented voice. Jacobs had not a shadow of a doubt that if he refused, he would be shot. His thoughts turned to his wife and son. Out of the corner of his eye, he saw the paramedic still crouched motionless on the floor of the ambulance, his head down, covered with his arms.

'Okay, okay, please,' he said, scrabbling at his belt for his keys. With shaking hands, he unlocked Hardie's cuff. All traces of illness had magically disappeared, Hardie now red-faced and laughing. He yanked the radio away from Jacobs' belt.

'You, here, now,' Hardie said to the paramedic crouched in a ball on the floor, his skin white with terror.

'Do as you're fucking told,' said the eerily calm gunman, switching the pistol's barrel to the paramedic.

The paramedic got to his feet and went to Hardie, who cuffed his wrist to Jacobs, shackling them together.

'We need to go, now,' the gunman said. 'Cops are busy, but it won't last.'

Hardie stepped out of the ambulance and onto the street. He sucked in a deep breath, lifted his arms into the air and yelled at the sky. Then he followed the gunman to the van. All three men dived inside, and as quickly as they had appeared, they were gone, roaring off in a cloud of exhaust fumes.

53

THE ENGINES CUT out, and the boats drifted across the last few metres of black water in silence. The sudden descent into total quiet was remarkable after the roar of the powerful outboard motors. The ribs gently buffeted against the shoreline of the loch, directly opposite the trucks.

Scally checked his watch and set an alert for thirty minutes. Nothing left to chance, it all had to run like clockwork, just as he'd planned. 'Great work, boys, smooth as bastard silk. Right, same as, no pissin' about. Let's get the gear loaded. That's twenty-five in each pick-up hide. I want us away in thirty minutes,' Scally said as they leaped off the rib.

The team began to work with practised efficiency, first unloading the mixed cargo of general junk from the load beds. They stacked five-kilo bricks of cocaine in the hides that had been constructed in false floors of the load bays in each of the four pick-ups. Once twenty-five bricks had been loaded inside each, the false floors were replaced, and the junk cargos piled on top. Any routine checks by police were unlikely to result in a search, particularly with bags of refuse, masonry, scrap metal and other detritus stacked on top of the hidden drugs.

Scally knew how bloody lazy cops were, and how they hated getting their uniforms dirty.

In just a shade under half an hour, each of the trucks was loaded. Both ribs secured on the trailers and hitched to the vehicles. They were ready to depart. Each would take a slightly different pre-planned route, which Scally had painstakingly mapped out. He'd treated it like a military operation. This was the buzz that he lived for, the feeling of it all coming together as planned. He pictured what he was going to do with his share of the profits. The fantasy place in the sun, the women, the parties, and of course plenty of coke. He always laughed when TV shows showed big dealers who never touched the gear. They all liked it as much as the next man. His boys were all saddled up in the trucks, ready to go, headlights blaring, engines growling, waiting for him. He felt like the commander of an elite team. He'd always fancied himself in the paras or marines, but his early criminal convictions put paid to that. Now he was showing them all, he laughed out loud to himself.

'Final check, and we're good to go,' said Phil.

'Right, la. Let's saddle up and roll,' said Scally, moving towards his vehicle.

Scally had thought of everything. Knowing that the intended landing point had been the west coast of Scotland, Scally had rented a spacious lockup on the outskirts of Ullapool, a small fishing village and ferry port less than two hours south. A cover story had been planned that they were setting up a rib tour business for the burgeoning tourist trade and needed storage for their craft. The owner of the lockup hadn't seemed very interested in what they were doing. He was just happy to accept a large cash deposit and three months' rent in advance.

Phil did a quick walk around, tugging at the lashing straps that securely snapped the ribs into place. The last thing they needed was one of them flying off on the journey south.

'All good, mate,' said Phil, nodding at Scally.

'Right, let's—'

All of a sudden, from the far side of the loch, there was a roar. A loud, powerful engine, gunned into life, shattering the almost mesmeric silence. The noise reverberated all around the loch and echoed off the sheer cliff face.

'What the fuck?' said Scally, staring out across the water.

'Fishing boat?' ventured Phil.

'With a fucking V8?' said Scally, reaching to the pistol in his waistband.

A dark shape was suddenly caught in the truck's headlights. It was a speeding watercraft, kicking white foam high into the air, positively flying along, bouncing across the still surface, engines roaring.

It was some kind of a rib, but it sounded powerful and didn't look like anything Scally had seen before. In total darkness, with no lights, it continued on its journey out into the open sea beyond the mouth of the loch.

'Is it the bizzies?' said Phil.

'Don't look like them. I can't see who's on it, goggles are in the truck. Let's get the fuck out of here.'

A truck door opened, and a coxswain shouted, panic in his voice. 'That's a rigid raider, Scally. It's military, probably bootnecks. We need to go.'

Scally looked at Phil to reply, but the words wouldn't come.

His mouth felt dry. He sucked in a breath and stared at the laser dot hovering in the centre of Phil's chest, quivering. His heart leaped into his mouth, and a cold fear exploded in his mind. 'What—' he began but a metallic clank pulled his attention behind them, beside the vehicles. A cylinder, the size of a can of baked beans, spun on the rough concrete, only to be followed by another.

'We're being fuck—' Scally's shout was violently interrupted by a series of devastating explosions and blinding white flashes. Percussion grenades exploded around their feet. Scally and Phil fell onto their fronts, their hands covering their ears, blinded by the violent sensory overloads from the brilliant flashes and deafening explosions.

Scally risked a glance at the trucks, only to see four balaclava-and-camouflage-clad soldiers systematically putting shotgun rounds into the tyres. The rubber shredded, each vehicle sagging to the floor. Scally knew it was over. They were screwed, and it suddenly became clear that whoever the fuck it was that was screwing them, had been there before them. He didn't reach for his pistol. He instinctively knew that to do so would result in his death. Whoever these people were, they were far too formidable.

A helicopter roared above them. Its searchlight, a night sun in the dark, illuminated them for a split second. Scally could see soldiers at the door and a large machine gun pointed down at them, as it swooped low and thundered out to sea.

'Armed police!' came the shouts, from all around them. Out of nowhere, like ghosts, there were soldiers and police officers everywhere, all brandishing submachine guns. The boys were dragged from the trucks and thrown onto their fronts, their wrists secured with zip-ties. Scally watched in a daze, wondering how they had done it. He tasted dirt as an officer knelt into his back and roughly searched him, removing his pistol.

Within one minute, it was all over. His dream of a life in the sun was gone.

Scally felt rough hands pull his shoulders up off the floor, and a torch was shone in his eyes. A balaclava-clad soldier wearing night vision goggles flipped up on his head, stared at him briefly. 'I have Scally here,' he declared in a rough Devonian accent. Scally looked at the man's uniform. He had modern camouflage clothing and a battle helmet, devoid of any rank insignia. He held a sophisticated-looking weapon in Kevlar-reinforced gloves. The fucking military, thought Scally, as he was roughly pushed face down in the concrete again, his nose connecting with the jagged surface. He swore as wet blood began to seep from his nose.

The pain barely registered above the naked fear that held him in its grasp. Not at his capture, or imprisonment, but at the fact that he had lost five hundred kilograms of cocaine. Close to a hundred million pounds' worth. The ramifications would be huge. There were a lot of interested parties, all with unthinkable amounts of money invested in this shipment. He began to shake uncontrollably.

Firm hands gripped his shoulder and rolled him onto his side. A lean-looking cop, wearing a Glock in a holster at his waist and sporting a black baseball cap smiled.

'Scally, I'm DS Craigie. You're arrested for importing class A drugs,' he read out the official caution.

'Who the fuck are these characters?' Scally said, his eyes

wide, the whites shining, his heart pounding a tattoo in his chest.

'You don't want to know, pal, trust me. You were close to being dead this evening.'

A wave of fatalism swept over Scally. 'I'm fucking dead, anyway, la,' and he let his face fall back to the concrete, his fate sealed.

54

THE PRISON TRANSPORT van pulled up next to the prostrate men, all nine of them face down on the ground. Max, Janie and Ross stood, watching over them, supported by the specialist maritime counterinsurgency team from the Special Boat Service. They were strategically positioned, covering the prisoners, assault weapons by their sides.

Within an hour of the strike, the sailor of the yacht had been brought into the loch by the SBS team on their fast rib. He was now on the floor, alongside Scally and his team.

Once Hardie had been recorded relaying the plans for the importation, things had gone pretty crazy. An intense period of planning, liaising and organisation had followed, leading to the line of prisoners all secured on that rough, single-track road.

The chief had requested military aid to the civil authority, known as MACA, because intercepting and boarding hostile vessels on the open sea was not something police firearms teams had done before. Within hours, a secret meeting between the team and the SBS had been arranged.

'I have to say,' Ross said to Janie, 'the prisoner sweatbox was a bloody genius idea to have on standby. Saved us announcing ourselves early by having a load of vans here.'

'More compliments, Inspector? Is it the baseball cap? It really suits you, by the way,' said Janie, looking at the cap, which was far too small for his enormous head.

'Aye, well, I'd say it's a stupid idea, daft bastard things,' he said, fiddling with the peak.

'I have to say, getting all this together in twenty-four hours is no mean feat,' said Max.

'Aye, they're a pretty impressive outfit. No way I'd want to get on the wrong side of those buggers,' said Ross. The team leader who had simply been identified as 'Digger', approached them, a big smile on his camouflage-cream-smeared face.

'All okay from your end?' He had a rich, northern accent.

'All fine here,' said Ross. 'Thanks so much for everything. Your boys are very impressive.'

'Easy as anything, mate. The yacht is all secured. It's being brought in here for a temporary mooring, until your lot can get to it,' he said.

'Did the captain give any trouble?'

'He didn't know what bloody hit him, when my blokes leaped from a Wildcat into the oggin and swam on board. The heavy machine gun pointing at him made him check out his personal horoscope and come to the correct decision. He was a pussycat after that.'

'Anything obvious on board?' asked Max.

'Not looked proper like, but there's a shitload more of those bricks on board. I'd say he was playing Postman Pat with Colombian marching powder.' He grinned.

'Well, these wee bastards will be taken to Inverness in the sweatbox where there are some nice cells waiting for them. We have CSIs arriving soon to process the scene. Border Force are now aware and are sending a rummage team to process the yacht, once it's here. This is going slow-time, and will take bloody days. We'll be taking a step back now. We have other fish to fry,' said Ross.

'I'm surprised there were no cuzzies here,' said Digger.

'Well, let's say that I'm a suspicious sort, and I wanted this operation to be successful,' said Ross.

'Oh, like that, is it?' Digger said, his eyebrow rising.

'Aye, something like that. Now everything's secure, we can relax and get on with the job.'

'Well, rather you than me. Can I get my guys away? We're needed back in Poole,' he said.

'ETA for backup is twenty minutes, can you wait till then?'

'No bother. I'll get the guys to get a wet on,' said Digger.

'Wet? Bloody bootnecks. Max here and I are both ex Black Watch. It's a brew, pal, not a wet,' said Ross, chuckling at the old inter-services rivalry.

Digger laughed. 'Cheers for the job, mate. It was lots of fun. We've been on counter terror standby for ages, and it's been a bit quiet.' He turned and stomped off towards his assembled team.

'Decent blokes, bearing in mind they're all marines,' said Ross.

'Are we handing this over to NCA and Serious Crime?' asked Janie, nodding at the prone forms, still lying inert and silent on the ground.

'We are. It's too big for the three of us, and we'd do nothing else for the foreseeable future. Border Force and NCA will take on the importation, MIT will pick up the remaining firearms jobs and the like. You know what we're doing, right?'

'What we always do, right?' said Max.

Ross looked at his phone. 'Shit, I have a load of missed calls.' He put the phone to his ear, and listened. His broad face cracked into a smile.

'That was Michael, the head honcho of customs, all fuming and angry that he didn't know a major importation was being busted. Got quite snarky, the snotty prick. Fuck him, he can wait. Hold up, I've a message from Barney.' His face was blank as he listened until it began to pale. He blinked, licked his lips, stared into the distance.

He lowered his phone and began to dial, frantically.

'What's up?' said Max, a feeling of dread starting to build in his gut.

'Something happened at the prison. Hardie got ill, or something. Hold up, I'll call him back.' He dialled and raised the phone to his ear again.

'It's Ross. Aye, I know, it's been chaos, eight nicked and at least half a ton seized.' He was silent for a while, his jaw clenched. 'When?'

He paused, blinked. 'How?' There was a pause as he listened to Barney. Then he simply said, 'On our way as soon as backup arrives. Keep me posted, okay?'

'Ross,' said Max.

Ross closed his eyes, almost in prayer.

'Tam Hardie has escaped,' he said.

55

HARDIE PRESSED HIS forehead against the cool glass window of the vehicle, as it cruised out of Edinburgh. He still felt ill, gripped with all-encompassing nausea and a pounding headache. It was the result of the liquid Ipecac root that he had taken prior to becoming 'ill' in his cell. The syrup had been passed to him by Gifford a few hours before, along with a single tablet of dexedrine. Despite feeling as awful as he did, elation coursed through him. It felt like he'd just done a huge line of beak. He was out. Out of that godforsaken hell-hole.

His instructions had come randomly via a fellow inmate, who Hardie had barely noticed. An innocuous guy called Daz had pulled him into a corner during association.

'At one a.m., take the drugs. It's just dexedrine and a liquid to make you hurl. You'll feel fucking awful and throw up like a bastard. You'll sweat, and your heart will feel like it's going to burst out of your chest.' He'd grinned, showing a row of broken teeth. 'Don't worry, it'll only be temporary. Once you've spewed your guts up a bit, call for a screw. Your lower gut needs to be stiff, rigid and sore as fuck to touch. This afternoon, claim you've a sore belly, okay? You'll have to put on a show so the fuckers think it's appendicitis and call an ambulance.'

The combination of the two medications had made him vomit and the dexedrine had raised his body temperature and blood pressure. Together with his stiffened muscles and protestations of abdominal agony, it was enough to fool the nurse and paramedics. From then, it was all up to the three men next to him in the large SUV.

After he'd been sprung from the ambulance, they'd driven for about ten minutes and ditched the van in a side street. Then transferred into an oldish Discovery and headed north.

His rescuers were taciturn types, with southern English accents, who didn't want to make conversation. They were tough, seasoned, not at all intimidated by his presence. Their whole attitude was one of practised efficiency.

'Where are we going?' asked Hardie.

'North,' said the man next to him in the back of the Discovery.

'What if I don't want to go north?' said Hardie, an edge creeping into his voice.

'No choice. We were told to take you north, and that's what we're going to do.'

Hardie felt his face flush. 'Listen, you don't know who the fuck I am, but I'm not known for my patience,' Hardie said in a low growl.

The lead man turned from the front seat and appraised Hardie with a baleful stare. 'Listen, mate. I don't give a toss who you are. We've been paid a shitload of cash via an intermediary to spring you and get you to a safe house. I don't know who's paid the intermediary, or why, and frankly, I don't care. Once you're there, our job will be done. You'll be given a phone, and you'll be contacted with arrangements for your extraction from the UK once things have died down. I have no bloody idea how, why or when you're being moved, and again, I couldn't give a monkey's. That's it, mate. That's our job done. But your mug is going to be all over the fucking news, so I'd keep it firmly down until you're ready to be moved, unless you want to find yourself back in jail. Now shut up and go to sleep until the drugs get out of your system.' He turned back and faced the windscreen again.

Hardie opened his mouth to argue, then decided against it. He did as they suggested, and closed his eyes, drifting off to sleep almost immediately. The combination of the drugs in his system and the stress of being sprung from jail had clearly taken their toll.

It was unlikely that he would have slept, if he had heard the news that was just being broadcast on the radio.

56

HARDIE SHOULD HAVE been deliriously happy, but he wasn't, not even a little bit.

His rescuers had driven him north for several hours before arriving just as the sun was coming up at a small, bleak cottage in the middle of nowhere, with no neighbours, and from what he could see, no shops or anything nearby. It was just an unremarkable dwelling on a single-track road in a windswept landscape. It would be impossible to find anywhere more remote in the whole country.

His rescuers continued to be as charmless as ever.

Hardie and the lead man got out of the Discovery and stood outside the house. He looked around the vast empty landscape, stretching for miles in all directions, only punctuated by sheep and a distant windfarm.

'Right, this place has been rented for two weeks. The owners live overseas and you'll have no visitors. It's a holiday let, although why anyone would want a holiday here is a mystery to me. The place is full of food and drink. There's a telly with all the channels and a basic mobile phone on the kitchen worktop on top of an envelope with a backup SIM card and the number. I don't particularly give a shit what you do, but my advice is not to use it. Stay totally dark, okay? The Old Bill hate you and they'll be turning over stones everywhere looking for you. Phone an old mate and they'll be listening, so leave the phone alone, understand?'

Hardie nodded. 'Where the hell are we?'

'Just a short hop away from Wick. Middle of bloody nowhere.'

'Okay, what's next?'

'Keep your head down for a week. After that, wait for instructions. There's an old Micra outside on the drive, keys on the hook inside the door. Drive to the location you're given, and leave the car there, keys under the seat. In the house there's a set of hair clippers, give yourself a number four crew cut, keep the beard going and use some hair dye.'

Hardie nodded, exhaustion beginning to bite.

'Right, my advice. Stay here, eat junk food, drink the lager in the house, watch telly and wank yourself stupid, but don't leave this place until that phone rings.'

'Thanks for getting me out,' Hardie said, reluctantly.

'Best of luck,' his rescuer said, turned on his heel and got back in the Discovery. With a crunch of tyres on gravel they were gone, and soon the only noises were the gentle whispers of the early morning breeze.

Hardie entered the warm cottage. It was comfortable with a well-appointed, modern kitchen and a big, cosy-looking sofa. A widescreen TV dominated the small living room, beside a log burning stove, all set for lighting.

Hardie smiled. It was certainly an improvement on his lodgings of a few hours ago, he had to admit. He went to the kitchen and opened the fridge. His eyes lit up when he saw it was crammed with ready meals and beer.

He picked up the phone on the worktop, a basic Nokia, fully charged, with a surprisingly strong signal. As described by his rescuer, the number was written on a brown envelope underneath the phone.

He sighed, feeling jittery, despite the comfortable surroundings, and the clear plan for his onward journey. This was everything. The most important time in his life, he wasn't used to feeling nervous or vulnerable.

His thoughts turned to the drug importation that should have happened by now. He looked at the mobile on the side but decided against calling Scally. That would only be a bad idea, and there was nothing he could do about it in any case. Best to do as his rescuer had said and stay off grid. He had what he really desired. He was out of that fucking shit hole of a jail, and all being well he would soon be back with his family, out of reach of the bloody authorities.

He took a can of Stella from the fridge and cracked it open. He hadn't had a drink for a long time, and the fact that it was only seven in the morning wasn't going to stop him. He took a long swig of the cold, crisp lager, and felt a smile creep across his face. He lounged on the big sofa, already feeling his eyes beginning to droop.

57

MAX STOOD IN the dusty corridor by the office at Tulliallan, his face flat and displaying none of the anger that was coursing through his system. Hardie was out, after everything he had sacrificed to get him into jail all those months ago. Max had almost been killed and his dear aunt had been held at gunpoint. He boiled internally with rage, but on the surface, he displayed none of this.

His mind shifted to Aunt Elspeth and his heart lurched at the thought of Hardie being out. He had to warn her. He picked up his phone and scrolled through WhatsApp until he hit her number. He dialled, the camera screen coming alive. She answered almost immediately, her face appearing on the screen, twinkling eyes, and a sweet, lined face. She was outside, her hair tousled by the wind, the choppy sea behind her.

'Darling. Everything okay? I'm at Chanonry Point. You should be here, the dolphins are really dancing today,' she beamed. Elspeth was deaf, but she was an expert lip-reader, hence the video call.

'Auntie, listen, a quick call. Have you seen the news about the escaped prisoner?'

'Aye, something came up on my Facebook. Why?'

'It's Tam Hardie.'

Elspeth said nothing.

'Elspeth?'

'Aye, I heard. Well, read is more accurate, I guess,' she said, her face impassive.

'Maybe you should be careful?'

'Why?'

'He's a vindictive man.'

'He doesn't scare me. At my time of life, I don't worry about things like this, and why would he come after me?'

'You sprayed him in the face with incapacitant spray,' said Max.

'Ach, fuck him. I'll lock the doors, and if he comes here, I'll go after him with my bloody poker. You take care. I think he'll want to find you, not me. Anyway, dolphins are leaping, so I'm going. I've just spotted wee "Nipper" and I've not seen him since he was a wean. Bye, darling. You take care.' And then she was gone. This was typical Elspeth, a fatalist who was not given to wasting words. He sighed as he tucked his phone away, knowing that it was futile to ask her to move somewhere else.

A cold resolve gripped him. Max knew he'd never be safe with Katie and Nutmeg while Hardie was out in the open, bearing a grudge.

He pushed the door open, bracing himself for the inevitable wave of heat, but instead, a blast of chilly air assaulted him.

'Jesus, what happened?' said Max. Every window in the office was wide open and the radiators were stone cold.

'Aye, the cheeky bastard in Facilities Management obviously took my complaints a little too literally,' said Ross, buttoning up his jacket.

Red-rimmed eyes, stifled yawns and rumpled clothing all told the story of the last forty-eight hours, as they sat around disconsolately in their coats and jackets clutching steaming mugs.

Max began to laugh and was soon joined by Norma, Janie and Barney. Only Ross sat in his chair muttering to himself.

'Why are the windows all open?' asked Max, still chuckling.

'To air the place out as it stank so much. Not sure they needed to drive screws into the frames, though,' said Janie, smiling.

'I'm gonna tear those bastards a new one. Facilities Management, my arse,' he said, reaching for the phone.

'Ross, maybe let me?' said Norma, from behind a scarf. 'I recognised one of them from my last place. Maybe a more subtle approach will do the job?'

'Subtle? I'll give them fucking subtle,' he said, although his face was softening.

'Ross, come on. You're about as subtle as dysentery. I'll make a call,' said Max, nodding at Norma who picked up the phone.

Janie, who was wearing a thick fleece, wordlessly stood and handed him a mug of dark, thick-looking coffee. 'That'll liven you up,' she said, sitting back down behind her desk.

'So how did this happen?' asked Max, zipping up his jacket before taking a sip of the strong, bitter coffee and beginning to pace on the stained carpet.

Barney filled them in on what was known about the escape.

'Shit, nothing on the probe to suggest that an escape was being planned?' Max said.

'Nowt,' said Barney.

'Hardie's cell has been thoroughly searched. No trace of a phone, and nothing else of value. So, he either ditched the phone in the prison, or has it with him,' said Ross, reading a report on his computer.

The team had travelled from Kinlochbervie to Tulliallan, once all the prisoners had departed for Inverness. They had briefed the CSIs, Border Force and Serious Crime teams, before setting off, not arriving until early afternoon, red-eyed and exhausted.

'Did Scally have a phone with him?' said Max as he paced up and down the room.

'Aye, it's already been downloaded and shared with me. A brand-new SIM with just one inbound call from the skipper of the yacht. Looks like they were practising good tradecraft.'

'Still no idea what number Hardie was using in jail?' said Janie, stifling a yawn.

'Nope. They've been careful, I'm betting Hardie will ditch the prison phone, if he hasn't already,' said Barney.

'Shit,' repeated Max.

'You know what I think we should do?' said Ross, wiping his damp, sweaty brow with an off-white handkerchief.

'I'm imagining you saying go home, have a rest, run a bath?' said Janie with a laugh.

'Actually, you're correct. We're knackered, and we're doing no good in this state sat in this fucking Baltic shite-hole office. If you'd heard what Mrs Fraser just said to me, you'd understand my rationale. We need to make clear-headed decisions, and we can't do that when we're down on two nights' sleep. The team at Inverness are dealing with Scally, and they're keen that we stay out of it to protect us for the future.'

'And Hardie?' asked Max, his voice level, but his fists

clenched as he continued to pace the office. As Ross checked his computer for updates, Max stopped at the far end of the room where a whiteboard hung from the wall. An A4 picture of Tam Hardie was attached with brightly coloured magnets. Max stood and stared at those piercing, cruel eyes and contemptuous smile. He took a small crumb of comfort from the bruises and cuts across the face in the photo, injuries that he had caused during their last confrontation in Elspeth's home. Fatigue washed over him, his limbs suddenly feeling leaden. He leaned against the thickly painted concrete wall and looked out of the open window, almost enjoying the cool breeze.

'Another team has been formed to recapture Hardie,' Ross said, looking up from his screen. 'We'll assist as necessary, but no leads right now.' His face was impassive, but Max could sense his boss's frustration.

'We know the loss of all that coke is going to have massive ramifications,' said Max. 'We know what we're looking for. We should be at least doing the background work on this. We heard the probes. He has the contact on his side, and unless they box clever, Hardie will know about anything they do. We can look at our own angles, right?'

'Of course, but the boss was clear. We aren't focusing on Hardie. Others are prioritising that,' said Ross.

'They have no phone for him, no idea where he's gone. They don't know the car, and from what I've read, he was sprung by a professional team. Maybe I can poke about a bit, at least on the basis that the contact will be as keen to see Hardie gone as we are to capture him,' said Max.

'I take it we're no nearer to a number for the contact?' asked Janie.

'Nope. I was hoping Hardie's prison phone would help, but he didn't leave it. I can start looking at a cell mast dump and try and tie it in with the exact timing of the calls, but bugger me, it'll be some undertaking,' said Barney.

'We can try,' Norma said. 'I can run it all through i2, and you never know your luck. I've worked cell tower dumps before.'

'Successfully?' asked Max.

'Yes and no, we found the number, but it took three weeks of analysis,' Norma said, a touch of embarrassment colouring her cheeks.

'Well, let's at least get the data. You never know, may throw something up. Can you get started?' asked Ross.

'Like a coiled spring, Ross-Boss,' said Norma, spinning her chair and beginning to attack her keyboard.

'Ross-Boss? Jesus, Norma, I'm already regretting recruiting you,' said Ross.

'You'll change your mind, I've just worked my magic on Zander in Facilities. He's promised to sort the windows and heating,' said Norma, her eyes bright.

'He fucking better,' said Ross, but with no conviction.

Max ignored the exchange between Ross and Norma, with a shake of the head. 'We get that number for the contact, then we have something to go on. Even if it's an encrypted handset, it still uses cell sites.'

'On it like a car bonnet,' said Norma in a faux cockney accent.

'Can you send me the data?' asked Max.

Norma laughed. She thumped the desk. 'What, you? So you can fuck the whole thing up and spill cranberry juice all over your laptop again?' she said.

'I'd like a look.'

'Yeah, what are you going to do, stare at it until the contact's number appears?' said Janie.

'Just a wee lookie, that's all,' he said.

'Aye well, enough of this. I'm bloody knackered. I crave the company of my children, something you wouldn't know about, eh?' said Ross, standing and stretching, revealing dark sweat circles under his armpits. He brushed egg sandwich crumbs from his shirt and Janie's eyes looked away in disgust.

'Your kids are both in their late twenties,' said Max. 'They'll be at bloody work.'

'Piss off, both of you. We all need sleep. See you in the morning. Norma, Barney, call me if anything comes up. I'll be in early, unless Mrs F murders me, in which case avenge my death.' Ross began to move towards the door.

Norma stared at Ross. 'Come here,' she barked, her voice sharp.

'What, me?' said Ross, looking confused.

'Aye, you. Bring your credit card.' She beckoned him over with a finger. When she swivelled her monitor around, it was open on a floral delivery service web page.

'What are you going on about, woman? I know you're good at your spreadsheet shite, but I'm not buying you flowers.'

'Not me, Mrs Fraser. I've a pal at this shop who's going to deliver a beautiful floral spray to your dear wife. If you put your credit card details in here a bouquet will wing over to Mrs F and arrive later today. Now dust off your wallet. I suggest this one.' She pointed to an elaborate display of white and pink roses.

'Now my eyesight isn't what it was, but that seems to be

saying forty-five quid.' Ross leaned in closer with a frown. 'For a few fucking blooms. I can call at the garage and get something for a fiver,' he said, but he had lost his bluster, his hand already reaching for his wallet.

'I imagine if you arrive with garage flowers, you'll need to get them surgically removed. No arguments. We're sick of you moaning about Mrs F. Now buy these.'

Ross sheepishly handed over a bank card. Norma tapped away for a few seconds before smiling, widely.

'Done,' she announced, proudly handing back the card.

'Aye, I bloody well have been done, too,' he said, tucking his card away, his head bowed.

'You'll thank me later.'

'We'll see. Right, I'm pissing off to save my marriage,' he said and left the office.

'You're brutal,' Max said to Norma.

'You want a lift home, Max?' asked Janie.

'Aye go on, then, makes no sense to have a job car at home if you're passing, but promise me one thing?'

'Of course.'

'No bloody music.'

'Philistine.'

'You two okay if we go?' said Max.

'Yeah, you heard the boss, piss off. Me and Barney can work through this shite. Get some kip and we'll see you fresh tomorrow. Just remember my bloody donut,' Norma said, not looking up from her screen.

58

'HOW DOES YOUR wee doggy always know when you're arriving home?' said Janie as they pulled to a stop on Max's drive. The small shaggy form of Nutmeg hopped up and down on the lawn, her tail thrashing wildly.

'Sixth sense. She's always here, if she's not, it's like an early warning to me. Coffee?' Max said, opening the door and stepping out of the big Volvo.

As always, Nutmeg launched herself at Max, delirious with glee at his return, covering his face with wet and slobbery licks.

'Aye, quick one before I go,' said Janie as they walked towards the front door. She stopped and turned to face the way they had come. 'I love where you live,' she said, looking at the sweeping vista stretching down to the Forth. It was cold, but bright, and the sun was low in the sky, casting long, inky shadows.

Nutmeg leaped from Max's arms and then turned her attention to Janie, her tail thumping against her legs.

They went inside, Max picking up a small pile of post from the floor. He crossed the open plan space to the kitchen and switched on the coffee machine.

Whilst he was waiting for it to heat up, he went to a small

box next to his Wi-Fi router, and powered it on, inserting an SD card.

'What's that?' asked Janie, flopping down on Max's leather sofa with a sigh.

'Remember I put the hidden cameras up when all the shenanigans were going on with Hardie last time?' he said, pulling out his phone and fiddling with the screen.

'Aye.'

'They're still fitted, but I haven't been using them. Makes sense with Hardie out, to have a bit of extra security,' he said, turning the phone around to show the sharp image. Janie waved at the smoke alarm in the ceiling above her head that housed the covert camera. Other cameras were covering both doors, all accessible from Max's phone.

Satisfied, Max returned to the sleek, chrome coffee machine, and within seconds two steaming cups of black coffee were on the worktop. The rich aroma filled the room. Max wasn't a drinker, but he loved good coffee.

'This smells awesome, man,' said Janie, accepting her cup.

'I use a specialist roastery in town. No shite in this house.'

'You okay?'

'I'm fine.'

'Katie not about?'

'Visiting a pal,' he said, sipping his coffee.

'Any reason?'

'You heard the tape. Hardie blames me for everything. I wanted her away until it's sorted.' Max sat heavily on the sofa next to Janie, yawning. Nutmeg immediately jumped up in between them, deciding who to snuggle against. She chose Janie, her head immediately falling across her lap with a deep, contented sigh.

'I'm not sure he'll risk coming after you. His face is everywhere, and he needs to get out of the country. If he can get to Cyprus, we'll struggle to get him back.'

'It's unlikely, but who knows.' Even as Max said the words, he knew that there was no way Hardie would let this go. The faint, static words from the probe came back to him.

'Soon, Craigie, you bastard. Soon.'

'Anyway, I can't sit around shooting the breeze with you. My presence is required elsewhere. Excuse me, Nutty,' said Janie, shifting Nutmeg from her knee and draining the last of her coffee.

'Anyone nice?' said Max.

'Aye. Very nice. In fact, I like this one a lot,' said Janie, her face softening. He and Janie were good friends and colleagues, but he had no idea about her personal life. She wasn't one for sharing, and Max wasn't usually one for prying. Maybe it was his level of fatigue that made him say what he said next.

'What's his name?' he asked, feeling his eyes begin to droop, just a little.

'Melissa,' said Janie, her eyes glinting with mischief.

Max's eyes opened wide, his face colouring. 'Oh, sorry, I didn't mean to pry. I've never asked and maybe I shouldn't have assumed.' Max stumbled over his words, his stomach churning with embarrassment.

'Stop it, ya big Jessie. It's no big deal. I never share much about my life outside work. The last one was called Dave, so you had no reason to think anything at all, mate, but I'm happy.' Janie smiled.

'Well, that's great,' said Max, relief replacing his burning embarrassment.

'I'll pick you up in the morning,' she said, tossing the car keys and catching them.

'Thanks, come a bit early and I'll make you some breakfast.'

'Sounds perfect, see you in the morning. Be careful, yeah?'

Janie headed towards the door. Nutmeg followed closely but halted on the porch as Janie exited. She whined, softly. She'd been doing this a lot since Katie left, staring out of the door, looking, waiting, her face sad. She missed her. Max did too. He looked at the photo of her on the fire surround, her glinting eyes, choppy hair and warm smile. He shook his head, took a breath.

He sat back, his mind still whirring, caffeine mixing with fatigue, unable to shake thoughts of Hardie. He was out there, somewhere, and they just needed a break. They just needed a starter for ten.

The phone he had used in prison was key to this. It would give them the numbers he had called, maybe the contact and Scally, who seemed to change SIM cards like he changed his underwear. He just needed someone with the skills or connections, and the motivation to be able to cut through the cell site. Many thousands, possibly hundreds of thousands of phones would have been connected to that specific cell mast at exactly the same time.

A name suddenly flashed into his mind. Someone who ticked all of those boxes and above all wanted to find Hardie.

Quickly, Max reached for his phone and dialled a number from the contacts list that was just marked 'BF'.

'Max Craigie? I was waiting for your call,' said the firm voice, with a distant Caithness accent.

'Hello, Bruce,' said Max.

'I heard that our mutual friend had escaped from prison. How?'

Max told him. Bruce Ferguson was a man of mystery. Ex-British Special Forces, and current head of security for a Russian billionaire. He was also the brother of Duncan Ferguson and cousin of Willie Leitch, both of whom were murdered on Tam Hardie's say so, during the last major operation. He was a man with resources at his fingertips, and a deep, unbridled loathing of Tam Hardie.

'I suspect that Hardie will be keen to keep a low profile after his consortium lost a hundred million pounds of cocaine, am I right?'

'How did you hear about that?' said Max, knowing full well how Bruce knew.

'I get about, plus I had a couple of pals on the SBS team you used. I've also made it my business to keep abreast of Mr Hardie, and his activities, over the last few months. What do you need from me?'

'Hardie had help from a corrupt law-enforcement officer somewhere and he also had a phone in the prison, which he used to call him. We need to know the number. If we get that, we can trace it.'

'What data do you have?'

'Exact timings of the calls, and a cell mast dump of all the phones using the mast.'

'Is that all?'

'Afraid so,' said Max, regretfully.

'Okay. Ping it over. Usual email address. I'll have someone take a look. They may have access to some resources you don't,' said Bruce.

'Thanks,' said Max.

'I'll call you if we find anything.' There was a click as he hung up.

Max forwarded the message from Norma, containing the raw cell data and a flow chart of Hardie's calls. He suspected it was a longshot, but Bruce's boss owned a number of telecommunications companies, and had many contacts in the intelligence world, so it was a risk worth taking.

He stretched and yawned. He needed a shower, something to eat, and a good night's sleep.

Max's phone buzzed on the coffee table. He picked it up, frowning. It was Bruce. He opened the message.

This is the number. It was easy to find. Best of luck. BF.

Max looked at the number in the message. It had taken him precisely three minutes to find what his team were struggling to identify. He shook his head in admiration and dialled Norma.

'Why aren't you in bed you daft twat?' she said.

'Don't ask how I got it, but I need you to run this number urgently: call data, billing, top-up information and cell sites. I'm confident it's the phone that Hardie was using in Saughton jail.' Max read out the number to her.

'Max?' Norma blew out a stream of air.

'I said no questions. I'll come up with a plan, depending on what you find, but for now, we'll call it an anonymous tip-off.'

'On it. I'll leave you to explain things like attribution, proportionality and necessity of doing this check when the chief asks for it, right?'

'Absolutely.'

Norma hung up.

59

HARDIE WOKE UP with a start, slumped on the sofa, a half-drunk can of Stella still in his hand. He groaned and wiped beer from his rookie prison joggers. His head pounded. It felt like an angry small man was stomping around in his skull, systematically attacking it with a pickaxe.

His hands went to his forehead, trying to massage the pain away. Ipeca root, mixed with dexedrine and Stella, without water, was not a cocktail he would be trying again in a hurry. Add to that a serious vomiting bout, and a resultant dehydration headache was almost guaranteed.

He went to the kitchen, found a pint glass, filled it with water and downed it in one go, quickly followed by half of another. He rooted through the cupboards, grabbed a first aid kit, and rummaged around inside. He let out a sigh when his hand closed around a packet of paracetamol. He downed two, with some more water, and suddenly realised that he was absolutely starving. He hadn't eaten anything since 4 p.m. yesterday, and he had thrown up all of that.

Looking in the well-stocked fridge, he selected a microwave curry, jammed it in the microwave and set it to cook, massaging his temples as he did.

The microwave pinged and he tipped the contents onto a plate, found some utensils, and carried his meal into the lounge with the water, his stomach rumbling.

He located the TV remote and flicked it to the news, unable to resist seeing whether his escape was being featured.

There was a story on the news about some nonsense that a government minister had been getting up to with his mistress. Tam barely noticed, as he shovelled spicy curry into his mouth with relish.

The story ended to be replaced with a picture of a remote Scottish loch. A lone reporter stood in front of the camera, microphone in hand, talking animatedly.

'Police confirm that nine men were arrested in a joint police and military operation. The suspects were apparently caught red-handed unloading a significant quantity of material believed to be cocaine that had been brought ashore on fast speedboats. A military helicopter and, what I'm being told were special forces, intercepted the luxury yacht just outside Loch Inchard. No shots were fired, and all those involved in the importation are in custody at an unnamed Scottish police station.'

Hardie stopped chewing, his fork hovering in mid-air. He didn't taste the curry anymore. His hunger had suddenly deserted him. He felt his cheeks begin to flush, and a cold, icy sensation rise in his gut.

He stood and went to the phone on the worktop. He had no choice. He had to speak to the contact.

He dialled the number from memory, and it was answered immediately.

'Yes,' the familiar voice said.

'It's me,' said Hardie.

'Are you on a clean line?'

'Brand new phone.'

'How the hell did you manage to escape, and why didn't I know it was happening?'

'Scally arranged it as my fee for handing over the operation to him. I didn't know any of the details, but I faked appendicitis and they busted me out of the ambulance.'

'Efficient,' was all that the contact said.

'I'm in a safe house. The phone is brand new, but I've just seen the news. What the hell happened?'

'It's a nightmare. The Colombians will go mad.'

'Who got nicked?'

'All of them. Scally's whole crew and the yacht captain. They've seized a massive amount. I'm getting reports about it all from my sources in the police and the Border Force rummage team that are taking the boat to pieces. It was your old friend Max Craigie and his team, sanctioned by the Chief Constable and kept away from the normal teams. They didn't even use police firearms; they used the bloody SBS.'

'Max Craigie,' said Hardie, his hand gripping the phone. 'That bastard.' The name tasted bitter in his mouth.

'Are you out of sight?'

'I have to stay here until I'm called to move after a week, and I'll be smuggled out of the country.'

'Well, stick with it then. I think I can keep myself out of the shit with this, but Scally's going to get a hard time. Get out of the country as soon as you can. Where are you?'

'Middle of bloody nowhere in a safe house near Wick.'

'Right, leave it with me, but for God's sake keep out of

sight. The world and its wife are looking for you. Go bloody anywhere and you'll be spotted, understand?'

'Aye,' said Hardie, his thoughts on Craigie.

'Right, keep your head down, and keep this phone on. I'm going to see what else I can find out, but there are a lot of very angry people who have lost a great deal of money.'

'I'm one of them. I've lost a bastard shit-ton of money.' His voice cracked. He took a deep breath and stared out of the window.

'I know, but it's about damage limitation and persuading the Colombians that we aren't to blame. We need to shift it onto Scally. He's screwed, anyway, the wrath of the cartel won't make things any worse.'

Hardie said nothing. He couldn't focus, his grip tightened around the phone, knuckles whitening.

'Aye,' was all he could muster.

'Stay out of sight. I'll be in touch.' The phone went silent.

Hardie placed it down gently on the coffee table. His jaw tightened. A name flashed in his mind in hot, iridescent letters.

Hardie's eyes swivelled to the kitchen and the knife block on the counter, his head pounding. He slowly crossed the room and went to the longest of the black handles, gripped it in his hand and withdrew it. The blade was long, at least eight inches of glittering steel. He thumbed the blade. There was a sharpening steel at the top of the block which he took and began to draw along the rough surface of the blade, just as he always did before a family roast. He worked at it for a few minutes, his palms sweaty, the rhythmic scraping of metal on metal almost hypnotic, his eyes flitting from the knife to the car, then to the road.

60

MAX RAN. HE ran hard.

The dream had torn him from sleep, gasping for breath. It had ended at the same point as always. Dippy's eyes glazing over, the pain slipping away, to be replaced by a momentary look of confusion, then nothing. Nutmeg had whined in concern, nuzzling his cheek with her cold nose, trying her best to make him feel better. It worked a little, as it always did.

At 6 a.m., he'd grabbed his trainers, shorts and a hoodie, and then run hard with Nutmeg for an hour in Fife's winding country lanes.

He was downing a pint of water when his phone buzzed in his pocket. It was Norma.

'You up?'

'Aye, just back from a run,' said Max, still mildly out of breath.

'I hope you are, or I'd be worried about you getting a bit breathy, there, mate,' said Norma.

'To what do I owe this pleasure?' said Max.

'The number for Hardie. Cell sites are back.'

'And?'

'He's a busy boy. The phone was switched off until a few

hours after the escape, when it came on in Inverness. It's been on ever since, moving quickly.' Her voice was excited but tinged with fatigue.

'Any calls?'

'Nothing. It just bounced between masts going south and now it's static, hitting a cell site in London.'

'Whereabouts?'

'Holborn or so. It's been there for a good while now. I'm trying to tie it down. From what I can see, it's somewhere between one and two clicks south-east of the Angel, Islington. We've alerted the local cops, but without any intel, there isn't much they can do. Ross is going for an urgent intercept, but it's a very quiet phone. No calls in or out since he broke out of the jail.'

'That's a bit odd, right?' said Max, taking another long swig of his water.

'Why?' said Norma.

'He's the most wanted man in the country. Why keep a phone on?'

'He doesn't know we know about it.'

'Perhaps, but he must know about the drugs bust. Why hasn't he made a call? And if he isn't using the phone, why keep it on? Hardie's nobody's fool. It doesn't make sense.'

'It's odd, I grant you.'

'Tell you what, can you plot the cell sites on a map, and send it to me? I'll have a look. I need to visualise it.'

'On its way, mate, I've plotted it already. Are you gracing us with your presence, today?'

'At some point. Janie's picking me up in a wee while.'

'Okay, it's in your inbox.'

'You're ace,' said Max.

'Correct, and where the bloody hell is my donut, you tight-arse? I've been waiting for it for days.'

'Next time I see you, I promise,' said Max, opening his laptop as he hung up. He moved over to the kitchen and switched on the coffee machine, suddenly desperate for a strong cup. He ground some Arabica beans and scooped the granules into the portafilter. He locked it into place and pressed the button, his thoughts wandering, as the machine buzzed and the heady smell of fresh coffee pervaded the room. He wondered what Hardie would do now, where he would go, what he would be thinking. His gaze went to the kitchen window and out to the garden beyond. He blinked.

He thought he saw movement out there at the back of the garden. A shape travelling along the hedgerow. He gripped his coffee mug, leaned closer to the glass, but as he watched, he saw a bird emerge from the bushes. It took off, blown sideways by the stiff wind, and whipped across the fields. Max let out a sigh. He was getting jumpy. Where the hell was Hardie, and why would he run to London? With all its CCTV, facial recognition and ANPR, it was the worst place to go. Or maybe not? Hiding in plain sight, in one of the busiest cities on the planet.

As promised, the email from Norma was waiting for him when he opened his email application. He clicked on the attachment, and a map appeared with arrows and speech boxes pointing to cell locations and activation timings.

Max traced the route south, through the Highlands, over the Cairngorms, along the A9. Past Perth, bisecting Edinburgh and Glasgow, before heading further south via Manchester, until it arrived in London some eleven hours later, just a few hours ago.

Max frowned at the map again, something scratching at his subconscious. The route and timings were familiar.

He opened a Google window and quickly performed a search, sure of what he was going to find. He stared at the webpage, his heart sinking, and then compared it with the map, and the current location of the activation, two kilometres south of Angel. He sighed, frustration flooding over him.

He picked up his phone and dialled again.

'What do you know?' said Norma.

'The phone was on the mail train. It's now at the Mount Pleasant sorting office in Farringdon. The bastard posted it south from Inverness. Bloody clever, when you think about it,' said Max.

There was a pause and the sound of tapping computer keys.

'Shit. I'll tell Ross to call off the intercept application. No point bothering the First Minister now, is there?'

'We need to think of something else. Anything on the calls made from the prison phone?'

'Just single calls to burners. The one to Scally is obviously off, and so is the one to the contact.'

'Where did they cell site?'

'Scally's close to his place in Liverpool, and the contact was in London.'

'London? Whereabouts?'

'Hitting a cell tower on the Thames by Lambeth Bridge. Have a guess which azimuth?'

'How could I possibly know that?'

'It's firing out west. In the signal's path is MI5 headquarters, the NCA offices at Old Queen Street and, even worse, 2 Marsham Street, HQ of the entire Home Office.'

'Shit.'

'Aye, it fits. Someone with access to high level intelligence has been leaking it to Hardie. I reckon the Home Office, NCA or MI5 have that intel.'

'But it doesn't narrow it down. There are loads of spooks in MI5, agents in NCA, or whatever they call themselves, and the Home Office is full of Border Force, Immigration, cops, the lot.'

'Well, they'll make a mistake soon. I gotta go, Ross wants an update. See ya, and don't forget my bloody donut.' Norma hung up.

Max sipped his coffee, feeling the dark thoughts rising as he considered their options. Hardie was gone and could be anywhere. The one bit of intelligence they had was a dead end. Hardie out of jail, enabled by a corrupt bastard, and the trail running colder by the minute.

Max jumped to his feet, and began to pace the floor, Nutmeg watching with a concerned expression. She followed him with her eyes as he walked, his jaw tight and brow furrowed. The little dog whined, and her tail sank between her legs.

The sight of her fear snapped Max out of it. He needed to release a valve in his brain, or he was going to be no use to anyone. He knew exactly what to do. He checked his watch. He had enough time before Janie arrived. He drained his coffee, went out to his garage, Nutmeg at his heels, and lifted the up-and-over door. He flicked on the light.

His garage had a dual purpose. It was for storing his beloved KTM motorcycle, and a tower unit of drawers that housed his tools. But it was also his gym. A squat rack, bench and racks of weights took up half of the space, and a punch bag was suspended from the ceiling to one side. Max pulled on a pair of sparring gloves and began to work at the bag. Moving, punching, jabbing. He went hard, almost zen-like, his body moving through the familiar routine. Max had been a boxer most of his life, and whilst he rarely fought anymore, he often used the bag for exercise and sometimes therapy. A doctor may have prescribed anti-depressant medication to deal with Max's occasional mood issues, but he found that a run with Nutmeg and a bit of bag work brought the same feeling of catharsis, without the accompanying side effects.

Despite the early morning chill, a sweat began to prick Max's skin. He jabbed, crossed, uppercut, ducked and punched, left and right, grunting with each blow as he circumnavigated the bag. His feet were never still, his head weaving, as if the leather could return his punches. He felt the pent-up aggression beginning to fade, his breath coming out in gasps, his jaw loosening, his eyes slits of concentration.

Nutmeg watched with her usual expression, a mix of confusion and interest at what her master was doing. She sat on one of the floor mats at the rear wall of the garage, her tail twitching.

Max finished the session with a colossal right straight punch, letting out a bellow as his gloved fist rocked the heavy bag back, its chains clanking and creaking in protest.

Max stood there, facing Nutmeg, his breath escaping in rasps, his sweat steaming from his shaved head and dripping onto the cold garage floor. He gripped the bag in both hands, steadying it, taking deep breaths. He immediately felt better, a calmness replacing the darkness. Nutmeg whined again, standing and moving forward, her eyes looking at something beyond Max. She let out a little bark, just a small, fearful yip.

Max turned, dread rising in his chest.

61

TAM HARDIE STOOD in the entrance. His hair was cropped short, dyed dark brown, and he had a beard. But it was Hardie, of that there was no doubt.

In his right hand he clutched a large silver kitchen knife. The steel blade glittered under the strip lighting.

'Hardie—' began Max, but as the words left his mouth, Hardie screamed, an animal howl of pure, unmitigated fury. In what almost seemed like slow motion, Hardie rushed forward, still bellowing, the knife being drawn back, low in his hand, ready to stab, aiming for Max's middle. Hardie's eyes were alive with loathing as the blade swished through the air. At the last millisecond, Max dived to his right, shoving the punchbag into Hardie's path. The knife bit into the leather, slicing a large gash, spilling wadding across the floor.

Nutmeg let forth a torrent of terrified barking, her tail low as she backed away to the corner of the garage.

Hardie paused, reset himself, blocking Max's escape. He switched the knife from hand to hand, his eyes never leaving Max.

'This is it. You cost me everything, took away my family.' He pulled back his hand, in an underslung arc, firing the knife out with terrible force, aiming low. Max stepped back, parrying Hardie's forearm as it swung past his midriff, the blade slicing through his hoodie. He felt a jolt of pain as the knife bit into flesh, the wickedly sharp metal grazing his skin. His stomach suddenly felt warm and wet as blood began to flow. He knew this was now a fight for his life. Hardie had over-extended himself, and he stumbled slightly, his balance momentarily lost. As Max stepped backwards, his hand fell upon a plastic-coated five-kilo weight. In a single movement, and without pausing, he threw it at Hardie. It connected with a dull thump, a glancing blow against the side of his head, and ricocheted off, smashing into the timber to the side of the door with a sharp crack. Blood flowed. Hardie lifted his hand to his ear, touching the trickle of red that ran from the side of his head. He smiled and licked blood from his fingers.

'Best you've got? That's fuck all, man.' He laughed, a throaty cackle, and his eyes shone with madness. He switched the knife from hand to hand again, still blocking Max's exit from the garage.

Hardie feinted to the left with the knife, but Max didn't move. He just stood there in a fighting stance, legs planted firm, fists ready. His eyes never left the blade.

Suddenly, Hardie raised the knife, and swung, a vicious, sweeping overhead blow aiming at Max's head. But it was too slow, too predictable and Max could easily follow its trajectory, moving his whole body to the side, feeling disturbed air as the knife whistled past, inches from his face. Instinctively, Max stepped right and delivered a short, sharp punch to Hardie's head, just beneath the ear. Hardie dropped to the floor in a heap to the side of the door. Leaping backwards, Max moved to the rear of the garage, his fists up again, ready to engage, breathing heavily, but focused and set.

Nutmeg suddenly let forth a further torrent of barks, terrified of the man attacking her owner. Out of nowhere, Janie appeared at the door, mouth open and eyes wide in shock at the sight of Max, his midriff soaked in blood.

'Janie, watch out—' Max began but before he could finish, Hardie's knife swept forward. From his semi-prone position on the floor, Janie was an easy target. The knife flashed towards her in a backhanded arc, the blow aimed at her gut. Janie's instinct was too slow to catch up with what was happening. The knife hummed through the air and tore into the top of her leg. Janie reacted instantly, kicking out her foot and connecting with Hardie's chest, the force propelling him onto his back. Janie's foot instinctively returned into the fighting stance, secure and ready to deliver another blow, but something terrible was happening. A sudden forceful jet of dark blood erupted from the top of her thigh, her elevated heart rate propelling liquid from what looked like a severed femoral artery. She screamed in sudden agony, as her brain caught up with what was happening, and she fell backwards over the threshold of the garage door, landing on the drive outside. Another jet of blood spurted. Her hand went to the wound, the blood bursting through her splayed fingers.

Hardie sprang back to his feet and Max roared in blind fury. He exploded off the ground, hitting him with immense force, his shoulder connecting in a classic front-on rugby tackle, driving him through the door, past the prone Janie and onto the rough gravel drive outside the garage. The breath exploded from Hardie in a whoosh, as they hit the floor. Max attacked, immediately grabbing the arm that clutched the knife, and driving his spare elbow into the gangster's face, crushing his nose. Hardie howled, releasing the knife, Max grabbed it and threw it away from them, Max knew he was more than a match for Hardie, so he just wanted rid of the knife. He didn't want to stab Hardie, he was a cop. He wanted him back where he belonged. In jail.

There was a terrible scream from the front of the house; Max's neighbour, Lynne, was standing on the lawn, watching the scene before her with horror.

'Max!' Janie screamed, terror in her eyes, tears streaming down her cheeks. 'He's done my artery. Shit, help, help me.' Her hands pressed into the wound, her jeans now black.

Max looked across at Janie, the blood still pulsating from her thigh. It suddenly hit him. His friend would die if she didn't get help right now.

'Lynne, call police, call an ambulance, now. My friend has been stabbed in the leg. Get in the house and lock the doors,' Max screamed. Lynne stared in shock for a moment, then she reached into her pocket, produced a phone and dialled.

Hardie wriggled underneath him, his nose destroyed. He was physically beaten, but the hate still smouldered in those cruel eyes, along with a dawning realisation.

'Your friend is going to die,' he hissed. 'She's only got a few minutes left. How long will she survive?' Max hit him again, thunked his head back against the hard surface. He coughed, grinned. 'Her artery is done, it won't be long now. How many minutes has she got left? You've a choice. Arrest me, and let her die, or you can let me go, and help her.' He chuckled again, a nasty, throaty sound, laced with darkness.

'Shut up,' Max shouted, moving his forearm until it was jammed against Hardie's windpipe. 'Shut up!' He pressed down. Hardie's eyes immediately bulged, and a strangled cry came from his lips, as his lungs fought for air. Max had a sudden, terrible urge. Just a few more seconds. Hardie deserved to die. Thirty seconds more and he'd be dead. Gone. No longer a problem. Katie could come home. He pushed harder, and Hardie blinked in terror, his struggles becoming weaker. Darkness began to creep across Max's vision, as he stared into Hardie's eyes.

'Max!' screamed Janie. 'You can't. Don't kill him, not like this. Help me,' she wailed, her legs and midriff now almost black with blood.

Max gritted his teeth as he stared down, eyes blazing at Hardie, but he knew she was right. His desire to help her was greater than his desire to capture Hardie.

He released the pressure from the gangster's neck, and Hardie took a deep, rasping breath. 'Police station is close,' Max said. 'I reckon you have five or ten minutes to get away. I'd take it if I were you.'

Max stood, and Hardie groggily got to his feet. Without a backwards glance, he staggered away, still holding his throat. He picked up speed, reaching an unsteady jog as he disappeared into the trees at the side of the driveway.

Max tore off his hoodie and T-shirt, ignoring the sharp stab of pain from the shallow wound in his midriff, and rushed over to Janie. She was on her side, her hands clutching her upper thigh.

'I'm here now, I'm here,' said Max, balling up the T-shirt, and pushing it against the wound. 'Hold it in place.'

Janie's hand clasped over the wound, the flow of blood immediately saturating the garment.

'I don't want to die,' she mumbled. 'I don't, I really don't.' Tears carved furrows down her blood-flecked cheeks.

'You're not going to die. Just look at me, okay? Keep looking at me. I'm going to stand on your leg, yeah? You know the drill. It's going to hurt, but it'll stop the blood loss.'

Janie nodded. She knew as well as any cop how to treat an arterial bleed. Indirect pressure between the wound and the heart. Stop the flow, stop the catastrophic haemorrhaging.

Max placed his trainer-clad foot on the upper part of her thigh right by the groin and put down all his weight. The blood flow stopped as suddenly as a garden hose with a kink in it. What seemed to be gallons of deep red blood began to flow down the incline through the gravel like a bloody, ebbing tide. Max turned away from the gruesome sight and fixed Janie with a stare. Her eyes were fading.

'Oh shit, Max. I've lost so much fucking blood.'

'It's stopped. Look at me, Janie. Don't look at the blood, you've plenty left in you despite being a skinny wee gadge.'

'You're an arse for dragging me into this shit,' she said, a trace of a smile visible through the pain. Her face was deathly pale, her lips a blueish hue. Not again, thought Max, a flicker of the memory of Dippy appearing in his mind. He wiped a tear from his face. He forced himself to stay calm, but Janie's face was growing ever paler and more ashen. No, no, not Janie, not now. He tried to slow his breathing, to stem the rising tide of panic that was surging in his chest.

'You love working with me.'

'Get tae fuck, you Teuchter bastard,' she said, beginning to sob.

'Back at yerself, ya bloody Sassenach,' Max countered, not taking his eyes from his friend. Nutmeg, cautiously approached from where she'd been cowering in the corner. Her tail was low, but twitching, and she lay down tight into Janie's side away from the blood pool. Her tongue flicked out, licking Janie's hand. Janie rested her palm on the dog's head. A smear of blood from Janie's hand darkened her blonde curls.

The three of them remained like that, together on the gravel drive outside the garage on that chilly Scottish morning.

'Max, I'm cold,' said Janie, the tears streaming down her face, shivering.

'Hold on pal, look at me, yeah?' said Max.

'I'm tired, I want to sleep.'

'Janie, no. Keep looking at me,' said Max, his vision blurred with tears.

'Max,' Janie said, her voice fading.

Max watched her pale face, as the sound of sirens grew nearer, a sick feeling of dread in his stomach.

62

MAX SAT IN the waiting room at Forth Valley Accident and Emergency Hospital, looking at, but not seeing, the words in an old *Top Gear* magazine. He had felt almost sick with relief when the paramedics had arrived. They had immediately begun to stabilise Janie with IV fluids.

'She's gonna live, pal,' was all that the grizzled, tattooed paramedic had said. It had been enough.

Janie had been whisked into resuscitation as soon as they had arrived at the hospital. She had lost a lot of blood, but the paramedics had immediately got an IV into her and applied an oxygen mask. Max had sat and held her hand as they worked, his stomach churning. Not again, he kept thinking over and over.

Ross appeared in the waiting room and limped over to Max. He looked worse than normal, his suit crumpled, his shirt grey, the collar frayed. A dark rash of stubble covered his face.

'You okay, pal?' he said, taking in Max's blood-soaked clothing.

'Aye, I'm fine, just a wee scratch. Anything on Hardie?'

'Someone matching his description was seen diving into a shitty little Micra, parked on the adjacent track to yours.

He must have snuck through the trees at the back to get to you. Looks like it's false plated, but there've been no sightings. Every bugger in the country is looking for it, and it's flagged to ANPR. What state was Hardie in?'

'I smashed his nose to pieces, and I actively considered killing the bastard, but he'll live. Have they found the knife he used?'

'Aye, it was in a flowerbed. You made the right decision,' Ross said.

'What do you mean?'

'You saved Janie, rather than keeping hold of Hardie. I'm saying that was a brave thing to do. Janie's going to be fine. She's lost a lot of blood, and it's a nasty injury, but if you'd held on to Hardie, I'm not sure she'd have survived. You get respect from me for that,' he said.

'Aye, but he's still out there, and so is that corrupt bastard. Maybe I should have killed him.'

'You had a choice at that particular moment, and you made it. You made the right decision.'

'Maybe.'

'No. You made the *right* fucking choice. Never forget that.' Ross's eyes blazed.

A nurse in a blue uniform came over to them.

'Your pal wants to see you, guys,' she said with a wide smile.

'Is she okay?' asked Max.

'She's lost more blood than we'd like. She'll need surgery to properly repair the artery, but she'll be fine. You saved her life. Another minute and it would have been too late.'

A long silence enveloped the three of them in that busy waiting room.

Max was suddenly overwhelmingly weary, but despite this, he felt a surge of determination. He had more reasons than ever to help recapture Hardie.

'Come on,' said the nurse.

Max and Ross followed her into the ward to one of the booths. Janie was propped up in a bed, monitors attached to every part of her. Her eyes were closed, and she looked pale and tired.

'Janie, your pals are here,' said the nurse.

Janie's glazed eyes fluttered open. She took a moment to focus on Ross and Max, her pupils like pinpricks. Her lips twitched upwards at the corners in an approximation of a smile.

'Max, you said she was fucking hurt,' said Ross. 'I've done worse shaving, man.'

A smile played across Max's face.

Janie's eyes brightened. 'Shave your inner thighs often?' she croaked.

'Never you mind, DC Calder,' said Ross, reaching out and touching her hand.

'How did Mrs F like her flowers?'

'A great deal. She even smiled. First time I've seen her do that in a long time. I owe Norma a donut.'

'Me too,' said Max.

'What about Hardie?' Janie asked.

'No sightings, false-plated car,' said Max.

'Bastard.' She closed her eyes.

'Aye,' said Max.

'Any leads?' Her voice was growing weaker.

'Not at the moment, but we're doing everything possible.'

'I know. Now stop buggering around with me. I'm fine, if a little sore. Go and find that bastard,' she said.

'You'll be back with us soon. We need you even if it's just to keep the office tidy,' said Max.

Janie nodded, her eyes half-closing. 'Aye, give me a day or two. I'm flying like a kite, ripped to the tits on morphine. It's bloody great.'

The nurse gave them a look that could only have been interpreted one way. She wanted them gone.

'Will you get any visitors?' said Max.

'I hope so, she's been on the phone,' Janie said, yawning, her eyes beginning to close.

'I'll see you tomorrow,' said Max.

'Max?' said Janie, her voice laced with fatigue. 'Thank you. You saved my life.' Tears pricked at her eyes, and she reached out to touch Max's cheek.

He touched her hand. 'No, if you hadn't shown up, Hardie would have killed me, so I should be saying thanks.'

'I'm glad you didn't do it. Things like that can change you forever. Hardie's time will come.'

'Right, that's enough, some of us have work to do. Now that DC Calder is skiving,' said Ross with his usual false bluster. But Max could see that there was an unusual amount of water in their boss's eyes.

'Inspector?' Janie said, her voice fading into sleep.

'Janie?'

'Piss off.'

Janie's eyes closed, and she slept.

63

TAM HARDIE TURNED into a small farm track just outside Dunblane and pulled over.

He lowered the sun visor and looked at the state of his nose in the vanity mirror. It had been squashed almost flat, but after clearing up the blood with a rag and some water from a plastic bottle it didn't look too bad. He raised his hand and gently touched the surface, wincing as the all-pervading ache throbbed, spreading quickly into his head. One thing was for sure, he was going to have some huge black eyes. In his boxing days, even a light blow to his nose always resulted in vivid bruising. He really needed to get out of the country soon, before the contusions all over his face made him even easier to find.

He realised now that going after Craigie had been bloody stupid. He should have stayed up at Wick with his head firmly down, should have paid a professional to do the job. A bloody daft mistake, but he had always been hot-blooded. Seeing his whole operation at Torridon go up in flames on the news had tipped him over the edge.

He jumped out and quickly unscrewed the number plates that he had earlier stolen from another car before making the journey. Once done, he tossed the plates into the field and reattached the originals. He was going to have to get back to Wick.

He would never get even with Craigie now. He would be too aware, too well guarded, it just wasn't worth the risk. He cursed his stupidity, but then vigorously shook his head. Craigie could wait for another day.

The drug bust had cost him a large amount of money, but he still had enough to live on, particularly in Cyprus.

He got back into the car and took a swig of the mineral water. His Nokia rang in his pocket, making him jump.

'Yes?'

'What the hell are you up to? I've just heard that you tried to take Max bloody Craigie out, in broad daylight, at his fucking house. And you stabbed a cop? Please tell me it isn't true ...'

'I can't do that.'

'Christ, what the hell did you think you were doing?'

'I know. I lost my rag, I wanted to kill him myself.'

'This is not how professionals operate, and certainly not now, after a major drug bust that has pretty much finished us all off. Where the hell are you?'

'Dunblane.'

'Did you drive the car left for you?'

'Aye, but I changed plates. I can get back up to Wick without ANPR pinging me,' Hardie said.

'Right, this is what you're going to do. Firstly, switch this bloody phone off, and don't switch it on again for twenty-four hours, then get yourself back to Wick, and sort yourself out. Don't go above the speed limit, don't stop anywhere, and if you need fuel, get it early from a small place with no CCTV, and pay cash. Don't leave the safe house until you hear from me, okay? I'll update you at this time tomorrow. I'm going to accelerate your exit. I want you out of this country, urgently, understand?'

'Plans are being made already,' said Hardie.

'Not anymore. I can't trust you. I'll make the arrangements now, just get your head down and keep it there. You can't be caught. If you get caught the Colombians won't let either of us live. They're like that.'

'Aye, but don't talk to me like I'm a bloody child,' Hardie said, his face flushing with anger, his voice deepening an octave.

'You lost my respect when you went after Craigie in some stupid bloody vendetta. You need to stop behaving like an idiot, or you're going to find yourself back in custody with all the terrorists. The Chief Constable of Police Scotland is going mental and throwing every resource at you. Don't fuck this up.' The phone beeped in Hardie's ear.

He sighed, his rage giving way to a sudden desperate urge to be safe, with his wife and kids. He'd be fine in Cyprus. He had lots of friends in positions of power who could help them stay out of reach.

He looked at the phone again. He longed to speak to his wife, but he couldn't call the house phone or her regular mobile in case they were watching. His Cypriot house wasn't well known to the authorities in the UK, and they couldn't touch it anyway. He wondered if Julie had her burner with her, the one she kept for exactly this type of situation. They had spoken on it in the past, when he was inside, using phones loaned to him by other cons.

It was worth a try, he figured. The number wasn't known

to the authorities, as he had never dialled it from the prison phones, where you were obliged to get authority to call only approved numbers. Julie would have seen the news and would be mad with worry, wondering what was happening. She was a bright woman, and accepted Tam for who he was.

He held his breath and dialled. It went to voicemail.

'Julie love, it's me. I'm safe, and I'll be home soon.'

He put the phone down on the seat and smiled to himself. He'd be safe, with his beautiful wife and kids. Scotland, and the whole of the UK could fuck off.

He started the Micra and drove north.

64

MAX AND ROSS went to the pub.

It seemed a slightly strange thing to do, bearing in mind what had happened, but they needed to step away from the investigation for a moment, and take a little time to reflect.

'Hardie must hate you, pal,' said Ross, sipping his pint in the lounge bar at the Crown, a short walk from the hospital.

'Feeling's mutual,' said Max, eyeing his glass of cranberry juice on the table in front of them.

'You think Janie'll be okay?' said Ross.

'She's a tough cookie, and she's smart. If I know her, she'll be back at work soon.'

'How about you?' Ross looked straight at Max, his blue eyes sympathetic.

'Mixed feelings.'

'Meaning?'

'I'm glad Janie's okay, but I'm also hating myself for letting him go. Who knows what he'll do now? I should have choked the fucking life out of him.' Max's jaw clenched.

Ross sighed, reached for the packet of pork scratchings on the table, opened it and shoved a handful into his mouth.

'He deserved it,' Max continued. 'A man like that. I should

have bloody done it. Whilst he's still breathing, I'll never be safe at home. Wherever he is, he can still reach me, even if he doesn't do it himself.' He paused to sip his juice. He noticed a tremor in his hand as he brought the glass to his lips. As he tasted the cold, crisp liquid, he imagined it was an old, expensive whisky. He exhaled, scratching his shaved head. He knew what he needed to do.

'I'm going home. I need to check that Lynne and Nutmeg are okay.' He stood, grabbing his coat, his jaw tight.

Ross swallowed a mouthful. 'Be careful, man. Don't do anything daft, eh? We'll sort this. There's a big team looking for Hardie. Miles Wakefield is as good a detective as I've worked with. They'll catch the bastard. There's a full Gold Group meeting tomorrow, and the chief wants answers.'

'And how about the bent bastard that allowed all this to happen?'

'That's our job. We'll do it, and we'll do it well. The clock is ticking, and he or she will slip up. Come on, I'll run you home.'

Ross necked the rest of his pint and pocketed the remaining pork scratchings. They walked out of the pub and over to the car. As they reached the vehicle, a small, wiry man appeared. He was lean and whippet-like with a shaved head and piercing eyes.

'DI Fraser?' he said.

'Aye?' Ross answered, suspiciously.

'Shuggie Gibson. I'm a freelance journo. What can you tell me about the events of today?'

'Precisely fuck all, I'm afraid. Who d'you work for?'

'Freelance. I've a blog with lots of followers. Is the officer okay?'

'She's sore but fine. I'd appreciate you leaving her alone. You understand me?'

'Of course. Is it linked to Tam Hardie's escape from Saughton?'

'Nothing to say on that. It's ongoing and being handled.'

'Are you on top of it? The public are concerned about a dangerous criminal being on the run,' he said, his voice calm.

'You got a card?' asked Ross.

'Aye,' he handed over a plain business card.

'Keep this under your hat for a while, and maybe I'll give you an exclusive.'

'I can't promise, but I'll listen,' he said.

'Don't release anything about where it happened, and don't mention any officers' names. This was at a cop's home, and the last thing we need is more reporters around the place. I've heard of you, of course, and I'm told you're not a scumbag. I'd rather work with you, okay?'

The journalist looked hard at Ross for a long moment, before his jaw relaxed. It was replaced by a smile that was not without charm.

'I'll wait for your call, Inspector.'

Max and Ross got in the car and shut the door. Once the journalist had walked away, Max turned to his boss. 'You sure about that?'

'I've heard about Shuggie. He's like a bloody terrier but will cooperate if you play fair with him. I'd rather not have him against us right now. He's relentless if he gets a sniff of corruption. Could be a valuable resource.'

'Fair enough.'

'Come on, let's get you back home.'

*

For once, Max wasn't surprised when Nutmeg didn't greet him. Ross pulled up outside the house on the empty driveway. He was fairly certain that she would be at John and Lynne's after the traumatic events of a few hours ago. A low, damp mist had settled in Culross and the usual spectacular view was nowhere to be seen. The dank weather settled over them like a shroud. Max yawned, deeply.

'Sure you're okay?' said Ross, looking at him with concern as they sat motionless.

'I'll be fine. I need a run, and a decent meal, then I'll be good to go tomorrow,' said Max, already opening the door.

'Don't do anything daft,' said Ross, fixing him with a steely gaze.

'I won't. Is Mrs F okay?'

'Aye, we'll be grand. I've agreed that I'll spend at least a couple of evenings during the week at home and protect weekends as much as I can. She's up for it, I think, although she'll still bloody moan, I have no doubt.' He shrugged, but his eyes glinted mischievously.

'See you tomorrow,' said Max, avoiding eye contact, slamming the door and turning away.

He walked up to John and Lynne's, conscious all the time of Ross sitting motionless in his car, watching him. The door opened as he came close, and Lynne dashed out to meet him, throwing her arms around his neck and hugging him tight. Only then did Ross start the engine and drive away.

'I'm so glad you're okay, but how's your friend? The poor wee thing,' she sobbed into his shoulder. Max held her tight in return.

Max told her about Janie and Hardie's visit.

'Och, that's horrible. What a terrible man. Will he be caught?'

'Aye, don't worry, we'll get him. Is Nutmeg okay?'

'She was scared, but she's out the back with the dogs. I'll call her.' Almost on cue, Nutmeg trotted around the corner of the house, accompanied by Tess, the much older golden Labradoodle. Nutmeg yipped in joy and rocketed up to Max, her tail thrashing, leaping high in excitement. Max scooped her into his arms, and she began to slobber at his face, joyously.

The far more sedate and dignified Tess just sniffed Max, with a serene expression, her tail swishing gently.

'Are you okay?' Lynne said again. 'It looked horrible. You're lucky to be alive.'

'I'm fine. Just stay aware of things, yeah?'

She touched his face with her hand. 'Of course, I'm so glad you're all right.'

'Is John all right?'

'He's grand, off to the market, looking for a goat of all things.' She shook her head, smiling.

'Aye, well, it's not a smallholding without a goat.' Max laughed. John was a frustrated farmer, always disappearing off to market and returning with ducks, or chickens for their few acres.

She smiled. 'You know my husband.'

Max laughed, put Nutmeg on the floor, and they both walked back to Max's house, unlocking the door and going inside. He had a strange sensation in his stomach, which he couldn't quite pin down. Then it hit him.

He was hungry. He couldn't remember the last time he ate.

Max went to his fridge and looked inside. Finding some

eggs, he busied himself mixing them together, adding butter and milk and in a few minutes, he had a large plate of scrambled eggs on toast. The kettle whistled on the hob and he grabbed two mugs with which to make tea. He stopped, staring at both mugs in his hands. Muscle memory. Two cups, one for him, one for Katie. He sighed. His wife's face seemed to follow him around the house, staring out at him from pictures, items of clothing, furniture. Nutmeg whined, her tail twitching, looking between Max and the door.

'I know, Nuts. We both miss her.' The little shaggy dog's tail went from a twitch to a wag, and Max bent down and tickled her ears.

He flicked on the TV and watched the BBC news channel, which was running the Hardie story. Thankfully, the incident outside his house seemed to have been successfully repressed.

An image of Hardie filled the screen, the cruel eyes, the silver hair, the contemptuous mouth. Max blinked, a forkful of eggs held in front of him, his mouth half open. His hand shook as he put the fork down again, his hunger replaced by cold fury.

His phone buzzed on the counter top.

It was an email, not from a recognisable address, but from a series of numbers and icons. He'd seen a similar email address in the past.

Bruce Ferguson was very well connected, but he was shy, and the email address would be completely untraceable, of that Max was sure.

The body of the email simply contained two phone numbers, one a UK mobile phone number and the second a longer number with a country code of ++597.

Max enabled his phone's speaker then clicked on the audio

attachment. The sound quality was clear enough, and there was no doubt who was speaking.

'Julie love, it's me. I'm safe, and I'll be home soon.'

Tam Hardie's voice was flat and emotionless.

Max scribbled down both numbers on an envelope and dialled.

'Max?' said Norma.

'I'm going to give you two numbers from an anonymous tip I've just received. Can you work them all up? The full package, subscribers, billing, cell sites. One is foreign, and I suspect will be in North Cyprus.' Max read out both numbers.

'How urgent? I was about to go home.'

'You know the answer to that question, mate, sorry,' said Max.

'You're a pain in the arse, but I'm on it. I may be asked about where it's come from, especially as one of them is a foreign number. You were right, North Cyprus, according to Google. That always slows stuff down,' she said.

'Anonymous tip is as good as I can come up with right now, but I'm sure it's reliable. Any issues with the telephone unit, let me know,' said Max.

'They'll be fine. I'm surprising myself with how assertive I've become with bureaucracy, particularly since working with you.'

'Nice one, thanks.' Max hung up, and began to eat his eggs again, his appetite returning.

The net was closing.

65

EARLY THE FOLLOWING morning, Max sat in the office with Norma, both staring at her screen, frowning at the complicated i2 chart. The temperature in the office was pleasant, and the windows were not only shut, but had been cleaned.

The door burst open, and Ross swept in, beaming. He looked tidier than normal, his unruly hair tamed, his suit clean, and in his hand, he clutched a box of Krispy Kreme donuts.

'Look out, here comes lover boy,' said Norma.

'Someone got lucky last night,' said Max.

'I take it the flowers have had a positive effect?' said Norma.

'Aye. Shall we say a thawing of the previous frosty relationship with Mrs F has occurred. Mostly down to my sparkling personality, although I'll admit that the flowers had a contributory effect. I also can see that the bottle of whisky you made me pay for helped with Facilities Management, thank Christ. It's almost temperate and pleasant in here,' said Ross, peeling off his jacket and loosening his tie.

'Well, Ross-Boss, maybe this is a lesson that shouting oaths at people doesn't always get things done. Glad to hear about Mrs F. You should maybe employ me as your relationship counsellor.'

'You can fuck right off. Now, we don't have long as the Gold Group is meeting soon, the chief is getting very impatient, so we're going to have to dazzle him with our progress. What do we have?' said Ross, taking a donut for himself.

'All the phone work is back.' She paused to chew. 'I'm in the process of analysing it, but, if I'm honest, there isn't a lot of data. Very few calls were made,' she said, her cheeks bulging.

'Okay, start at the beginning.'

'The prison phone we know about is a burner, with forty-seven quid's worth of credit remaining on it. It made the calls we already knew about, to Scally and the contact, both of which we recorded. There were no other calls made or received. Anyone want to guess how it was topped up?'

'Just tell us,' said Ross, taking a bite of his donut.

'Using cash at a newsagent right outside the prison. We have the exact time and date, so an inquiry there might give us some CCTV.'

'Nice, but not urgent,' said Ross, popping the last of the donut in his mouth then making a note.

'How about the contact's number, anything on that?' asked Max.

'Very few calls made. Mostly to Hardie. It's switched off a lot of the time, and only turns on to make or receive a call. Good tradecraft all round.'

'Any top-up data?' asked Max.

'Nothing I can find.'

'Cell sites?'

'Close to Gartcosh, or near Lambeth Bridge in London, close to MI5 and the Home Office building.'

'I understand you received an "anonymous tip",' Ross said, miming quotation marks with his fingers.

'Just two numbers that someone believes are attributable to Hardie, or people close to him.' Max read the numbers out.

'Okay, now ignoring the suspicious and shady nature of this intelligence, have we learned anything from it?' Ross said.

'Well, the Turkish Cypriot number is unknown on any system, and we can't access the subscriber detail, but it's hitting cell sites in Lapta, on the northern coast. The British number is an untraceable burner.' Norma paused theatrically to sip her tea.

'I'm required at a meeting, where I'll be by far the most junior officer present, so hurry bloody up,' said Ross.

Norma chuckled, tapping at her keys and bringing up a map. A route traced a line between highlighted cell sites. 'The phone was first activated a couple of days ago, somewhere near Wick. Yesterday morning it moves south, hitting all the usual masts, until we can safely assume it arrives at your place, Max. It then moves away, becoming briefly stationary just outside Dunblane, a short while after the attack in your garage. With me so far?' Norma said.

'Quicker,' said Ross, his fingers tapping on the table.

'This is the good bit. Our man receives a ninety-second phone call from the mysterious contact, after which the phone is switched off for the first time since it went live,' said Norma.

'So, we have a current and live phone for Hardie, and the contact?' asked Max.

'It seems so. I'm really good, aren't I?' said Norma.

Max breathed a heavy sigh of relief. 'Major result, this, guys. Puts us in the driving seat.'

'Interesting that Hardie's phone gets switched off right after that call.'

'Well, not exactly. First, he calls the Cypriot number and leaves a voicemail,' said Norma.

'How about the contact's phone, is it switched on?' said Max.

'No, it went off right after making that call.'

'Where was it?'

'Same place as before,' said Norma, her face impassive.

'Dirty corrupt wee bastard. I need some suggestions. I have to be in Gartcosh in two hours,' said Ross, standing up and pulling on his suit jacket, tucking in a stray flap of shirt tail.

'Why Gartcosh?' said Max.

'Chief was there for something else, and as everyone else works from there, he thought it would be handy. Not for bloody me, though,' he said, straightening his tie.

Max stood up suddenly. He looked at each of them in turn. 'We need to create an initiating incident.' He began to pace the floor.

'What are you getting at?'

'Think the chief can get some authorities in place quickly. Like really quickly?' said Max.

'You know the chief. He doesn't piss about. Are you going to get to the point?'

'We need to throw a nice little rock into a pond at this meeting, then we sit about and watch the ripples.'

'I'm up for it. I bloody love upsetting senior officers. What do you need?'

66

THE LARGE CONFERENCE room at the crime campus was a hive of activity. It was awash with senior officers from NCA, Border Force, PIRC and from the drug bust inquiry team, as well as representatives from MIT.

Ross looked at the raft of senior officers around the table with a mix of anticipation and distaste. He stifled a smile at what was about to happen. This is why he did this job, he thought to himself. First, he had to get through this event, listen to everyone trying to argue that their leadership was having the desired impact. No one wanted to be accused of not bringing something to the party, such was the rivalry, one-upmanship and self-interest of high-level law-enforcement leadership. Ross often had thought that the naked and rampant ambition of many of those in very senior positions caused most of the problems facing law-enforcement. Self-advancement always seemed to trump what was actually the right thing to do. He knew that his promotion days were probably gone, so he fully intended to enjoy the next few hours. He stifled a grin once again.

'Okay, can we crack on?' said Chief Constable Chris Macdonald, dressed in a smart suit at the head of the long conference table.

The hubbub of conversation stopped and was replaced with a hushed silence. Eyes shifted from side to side, suspicion hanging over the room like an aura. The past few days had seen law-enforcement shaken to its foundations. Multiple murders, NCA officers killed, Hardie's escape, the attack on DC Janie Calder. Things had happened that weren't supposed to happen.

'Firstly, I'd like to thank everyone for attending and taking time away from your respective organisations and investigations to ensure that our collaborative working is coordinated. Firstly, can we do a quick round of introductions and roles? There are a couple of new faces.' Macdonald nodded at Miles Wakefield who began, followed by each of the attendees.

'Miles Wakefield, head of Serious Crime, currently handling the murders attributed to these conspiracies.'

'David O'Neill, Police Investigations Review Commission. I'm monitoring this meeting for the commissioner.'

'Louise Ellis, NCA Scotland.'

'DCI Sue Brown, Serious Organised Crime, in charge of the manhunt for Tam Hardie.'

'Michael Jones, Border Force, overseeing the response to the importation.'

'Mark Macleod, Governor of HMP Saughton.'

'DI Ross Fraser, Police Standards Reassurance,' Ross said, looking down at his phone, wearing a frown.

'Thanks, everyone. Ross, I understand, you're currently managing some real-time intelligence on Hardie that is being evaluated as I speak,' said Macdonald.

A buzz rippled around the room. Glances were exchanged and eyebrows raised.

'Can I ask what?' said Sue Brown, an efficient-looking woman smartly dressed in a business suit.

'It's developing literally now, Sue, hopefully Ross will give a fuller picture. Ross, I see you're multi-tasking with your phone here. Anything coming in?'

'Yes, sir. Reliable intelligence, literally hot off the press, suggests that Hardie is currently hiding in Wick. A witness has seen him in the area in a vehicle similar to the one seen leaving the scene of the DC Janie Calder attack. This is also supported by certain sensitive intelligence, which I can't talk about in this room.'

There were a few muffled gasps, a shuffling in seats. No one spoke. They all knew what this meant. Sensitive intelligence only meant one of two things, human intelligence or communications interceptions. Neither could be openly spoken about.

'Okay, my apologies, we should break for a few moments whilst I discuss this with Ross and Sue. We obviously have to act quickly here, and we need to make sure we have sufficient resources. I'm sure we can all acknowledge Hardie's recapture is paramount. Shall we say twenty minutes?'

The room soon cleared, leaving just Macdonald, Ross and Sue Brown. They looked at each other, silently, until the last person had left, and the door had closed.

'Are we ready?' said Macdonald.

'We are,' said Ross.

'Us too,' said Sue Brown.

'Okay, twenty minutes.'

67

SOMETHING BAD WAS happening. The contact pushed through a door and walked along the corridor, his shoes clicking on the shiny marble, as he tried to slow himself down, keep himself in check. His stomach churned, it felt like the wagons were circling around him, but he looked at his phone screen, nonchalantly as he walked. That bloody fool Hardie had screwed up again. There was no other explanation. He must have been seen, must have made a call which had been intercepted. He looked at his watch, hoping to God that Hardie had switched his bloody phone on by now. The arrangements to get Hardie out of the UK had been made with short notice and at great expense. Now time was running out. The police could be ready to smash in doors at any moment, and then it was all over. There was no telling what Hardie would say if he thought it could benefit him, and that included selling the contact down the river.

He left the building and walked quickly to his car, trying not to break into a jog. Spots of rain were beginning to fall from a leaden sky that promised more to come. He cursed himself for leaving his jacket on the chair inside. It was too late to go back for it now. A soaked shirt was the last thing he needed. He got to his car, a classic Jaguar XJS that was parked in the far reaches of the car park. He'd paid forty grand for it last year, and it was his pride and joy, but right now, he had other priorities. He inserted the key with a shaking hand and unlocked the door, jumping into the passenger seat. He slammed the door and glanced back the way he had come, making sure he hadn't been followed. He let out a sigh, closed his eyes and slowed his breathing. He checked his watch. He was running out of time. He reached into the glove box and pulled out his burner phone, fumbling to power it up, feeling like his fingers had trebled in size.

He dialled a number from memory, but it took several attempts to go through, because of his shaking hands. It was answered immediately.

'Yes?'

'Elrick, it's me. Are you ready to move?'

'I can be in an hour. This is earlier than I expected.' His accent was soft and Scandinavian.

'Get ready to go. Things are accelerating.'

'Okay, no problem.'

'Stay by the phone,' said the contact. He ended the call and dialled again. 'Come on, come on, come on,' he said, his hands shaking.

It took him three attempts to type in the number correctly.

He looked at his watch again. Just three minutes to go before Hardie would switch on his phone. Drops of rain pattered against the windscreen.

It went to voicemail. 'Fuck,' he hissed, his breathing accelerating and his heart pounding as the automated voice spoke in his ear.

He hung up and dialled again.

Voicemail again. The contact scratched a non-existent itch on his cheek, trying to stem rising panic. He breathed deeply, closing his eyes. Calm yourself, man, he thought.

He stared through the window, his mind reeling. Cops could be swarming on Hardie right now. He cursed himself for getting involved with Tam Hardie after his father had died. He could have easily broken from him at that point and moved on with his life. Tam Hardie senior was old school and could always be trusted. He was a vicious, evil man, but he had a code, and not grassing was written in stone at the top of it.

The contact sucked in a lungful of air and dialled again, looking at his watch. It had been ten minutes already and he had to be back in the meeting soon. Bearing in mind it would take at least five or six minutes to get there, he was cutting it fine.

The phone rang and was answered almost immediately.

'Yeah,' Hardie's cultured voice sounded imposing.

'It's me, are you at the safe house?'

'Of course, where else would I be?'

'You're not safe there. The cops somehow know you're in Wick. They're making a plan to come and get you. You need to get out, fast.'

'How the hell do they know where I am?'

'I've no idea, maybe an informant or intercepted calls. They can't know either of our numbers. Please tell me you haven't called anyone else?'

The hesitation told him everything he needed to know.

'Oh, Jesus. You called someone.'

'I called my wife, to let her know I was coming home. It

was to her burner in Cyprus. I can't see how they'd intercept that,' Hardie said, his voice quiet.

'You idiot, you bloody idiot. They could be monitoring calls to Cyprus with keywords, they'll know that's where you're going. You need to get out, and ditch the SIM. Do you have another one?'

'Aye, they left one in the safe house,' said Hardie.

'Number?'

Hardie told him, and he scrawled it down on his hand.

'I'll call you on the new number when I can. No calls to anyone, understand? You wait for me to call.'

'Yes. Where do I go?'

'Take the car right now, get out of the house and find somewhere to hole up for an hour, then make your way to Wick Harbour, far side of the marina, opposite all the pleasure yachts. You'll see a yellow and blue seiner,' the contact said, brusquely.

'What the bloody hell is a seiner?'

'Fishing boat, about thirty metres long and bearing the name *Odin*. It'll be flying a Norwegian flag. Once you're on board, switch on your phone again, in case there are any developments. The captain is called Elrick, and he's expecting you, so get straight on board and for Christ's sake do as you're told. You'll be taken over to Stavanger and met by someone there who'll organise the rest of your journey. He'll have your papers.'

'Cyprus from Norway, Jesus,' Hardie muttered down the phone.

'The plans that were in place for you are now no use, thanks to your bloody actions. Your face will be seen by every cop,

NCA and customs agent. Think yourself lucky that Scally only paid for you to get busted out of jail, and wasn't aware of where you were being taken, or your onward travel plans. He'd be grassing right now, with the amount of shit he's in. If they were intercepting our calls, then they can link us to that fucking importation, even if it can't be used in court. This is the only way we can be sure of getting you clear. Listen, I have to go now, I'm supposed to be in a meeting. Get out of there now.'

The contact hung up. He looked at his watch and swore. Only six minutes left. He quickly opened the back of his burner, took out the SIM and bent it in half, ditching it under his seat. He removed a new SIM from the glove box, slotted it in and put the handset back in the glove box, thankful for this foresight of having multiple cards available.

He jumped out of the car into the drizzle and jogged across the car park, towards reception, fear gripping his insides.

68

MAX SAT IN the Volvo in the car park, looking at the screen on his tablet, a smile stretching across his face. He picked up his phone and dialled.

'Please tell me it went well,' said Ross.

'Hopefully, but it'll take a couple of hours or so to be sure,' said Max.

'Okay, the meeting is about to reconvene. Everyone is rushing back in, looking as important as they can. Text me as soon as you know. I suspect it'll go on for some time. You know what senior officers are like.'

'Rather you than me, pal,' said Max.

'Soon as you know, yes?'

'Have I ever let you down?'

'Frequently. Now bugger off.' The phone clicked.

Max immediately dialled another number.

'Max?' Norma said.

'Anything on the phones?'

'Aye, the contact called Hardie straight away. Hitting the same cell site as before, putting him squarely here at Gartcosh. Hardie's cell site puts him in Wick. Still too big an area to tie him down, though.'

'Are the phones still on?'

'No, both went straight off again.'

Max paused for a moment. If they were being careful, would they ditch the phones altogether, or switch SIM cards.

'Can you do handset searches with the phone unit? If they've switched SIM cards, I'd like to know about it.' He hoped they wouldn't go as far as changing devices, and a simple search using the handset's unique number would be enough.

'Sure thing, I've an open line with the phone unit, and the chief has pre-authorised all the checks. Wish it was always like this,' she said. Max could hear the tapping of computer keys in the background.

'Cool, let me know. We're making headway,' said Max.

'Brilliant, now bugger off.' The line went dead.

Max dialled again, this time using WhatsApp's video-calling feature.

'Darling, to what do I owe the pleasure of this call?' A kind, lined face with sparkling eyes stared out at him. 'What a lovely surprise.'

Making sure that his mouth was fully visible in the video clip Max spoke, enunciating his words carefully. 'Hello, Auntie Elspeth, I need a favour.'

69

TAM HARDIE PULLED up in a small side street in the centre of Wick, close to the Telford pub. He yanked the handbrake, and withdrew the ignition key, dropping it under the seat as instructed.

He sighed as he flicked down the vanity mirror and took in his damaged features. His nose was swollen, and bruises were forming beneath his eyes. He slipped on a pair of clear spectacles, which he had found in the cottage, to obscure some of the injuries. His head pounded with a thumping headache that had hardly shifted since his escape. He was tired, grubby and hungry, and he wasn't looking forward to the long sea journey.

He cursed his stupidity at travelling down to Craigie's place. There would have been plenty of opportunities to take the bastard out in the months, or years to come. His thoughts turned again to his father. He had been a cruel and sadistic man, often meting out terrible punishments to those who crossed him, but he could bide his time. Craigie would pay. One day, Hardie would take everything the bastard had, including his wife, and that little shite of a dog. There were always people he could pay to do it, and modern technology meant he could have a ringside seat. But right now, he had to get out of this hell-hole of a country. Almost on cue, the rain picked up, a solid sheet of water battering against the car and the surrounding grey buildings.

Hardie flipped up his coat collar and pulled a waxed cap low over his eyes. Not that people would be looking in this terrible weather. Any fools out on the almost deserted streets would have their heads firmly down.

Hardie tucked the phone into his pocket, new SIM already inserted, opened the door, and stepped out into the deluge. He had nothing with him, aside of the Nokia. A new life waited for him with his family in Cyprus. He smiled at the thought of the spacious villa, close to the sea, with wonderful views. His smile grew wider as the rain whipped across his cheeks. Litter swirled in the gutters at his feet, the drains clogged with debris. Fuck the lot of them.

He jammed his hands into his coat pockets and set off towards the harbour, just a couple of roads away.

Rain hammered down on the deserted streets. Peat smoke hung in the air, making it difficult to see, the acrid smell everywhere. It took only a couple of minutes for him to emerge by the sea front, next to the marina. Mountainous waves rolled towards him across the water, smashing into the harbour walls. Spray exploded upwards into the air, before being whipped away in the wind, mixing with the rain. Hardie groaned, his stomach already beginning to lurch at the prospect of getting on a boat in this.

He walked past the drab buildings, net repair huts, industrial units and shipping containers, his head down. His feet were already wet, his trousers sodden. He was thankful for the Barbour jacket and the cap, which he had found at the cottage and were keeping the worst of the weather away. With any luck the fishing boat would have some amenities, even if it was just a dry place to get his head down.

As he walked, he squinted through the driving water, just about making out a blue and yellow fishing boat. It was rocking gently on the far side of the harbour, opposite all the pleasure craft moored in the marina. He upped his pace and was soon alongside the vessel. It was a good thirty metres in length and seemed to be in decent order. He looked along the hull, until his eyes fell on the boat's name plate.

Odin.

He saw the blue cross on a red background of the Norwegian flag dancing in the stiff breeze. This was it.

Hardie stepped onto the gangway and took a few steps onto the rising and falling vessel. The slippery deck rolled under his feet, and he reached for the handrail, walking towards the wheelhouse at the rear.

As he approached, the door swung open, and a vast man stepped out onto the deck. He wore a yellow oilskin with his hood up. Hardie looked at the man, took in his Slavic features. He was well over six feet tall and almost as wide.

'Mr Hardie?' he said in a deep, heavily accented voice.

'Aye, are you Elrick?'

'I'm Piotr. Elrick is in cabin. You join us for trip to Stavanger?'

'Aye, how long will it take?'

'Depend wind. Two day, maybe three. I show your quarters. Please follow.' The big man returned to the bridge and pointed to a small hatch. He opened it and they descended a narrow set of stairs. Soon Hardie was in a warm, tiny but functional cabin, with a small bunk and sink.

'This'll do just fine. When will we depart?'

'Soon, maybe hour. The tide will be slack by then, making it easier for us. You're safe here.'

'Thanks, Piotr.'

'Elrick come and see you soon, yes?' The big man turned and left Hardie alone.

Hardie removed his jacket and hung it on the back of the door, then he pulled out the mobile, powered it on and placed it on the tiny table.

He closed his eyes as the reality finally dawned on him. Just a few days ago he was in a high-security prison, surrounded by the stench of other prisoners, and now he was about to embark on a journey home, to his family.

70

ROSS COULDN'T BELIEVE that the meeting had been going on for almost two hours, now. So much toadying bullshit spouted from the very senior officers who liked to call themselves 'leaders' rather than what they bloody well were. Faceless politicians, all completely uninterested in anything that did not advance their careers. It hit Ross, as it always did at meetings like this, that the ability to spout vacuous shite was almost in the job description of anyone above superintendent.

His phone buzzed in his pocket, and he surreptitiously checked it under the table. It was Max.

H heading for a fishing boat at Wick Harbour, ready to depart soon. Need to scramble a team.

'Excuse me, may I interrupt for a second?' asked Ross, cutting across the faceless moron from PIRC.

'Ross?' Macdonald said, eyebrows raised.

'I've a message just come in from Max. Some new, live intelligence, something about Hardie. He's heading to a fishing boat somewhere, leaving the country imminently,' said Ross, standing up.

'Get on with it,' Chris said. 'Scramble whatever resources

you need. We'll finish off here, and then you can brief me later. Sue, best you join him.'

Sue and Ross both rose from the table and left the room.

'Sorry, David, carry on with what you were saying, something about a thematic review of Police Scotland's internal affairs?' he smiled.

71

MAX WAITED FOR Ross and Sue in the corridor. He began walking as they approached, heading for the exit. Ross and Sue fell in step alongside him as they walked into the wide-open space of the lobby. When they reached a bench at the end, they sat down together, whispering conspiratorially.

'Where?' was all that Ross said.

'Wick Harbour, a seiner boat called *Odin*. Captain's name is Elrick and they're heading for Norway, imminently.'

'How old is this intel?' asked Sue, producing her phone.

'Ninety minutes.'

Sue spoke on the phone in a hushed whisper.

'Shame we couldn't get it faster,' said Ross.

'Aye, but we've done well, bearing in mind what we had to work with. They bloody switched SIM cards, as well.'

'Bastards.'

'We have this,' said Max, holding up his iPad.

'How confident can she be?'

'She's sure it's Wick, and that the boat is *Odin*, but the rest is a bit of guesswork.'

'Good work.'

Sue put her phone down, her brow creased with frustration.

'My team is still an hour away. We're scrambling from Inverness, because we didn't know where he would poke his head up. I had to split resources.'

'That's too long,' said Max.

'I'll get uniform, at least see if the bloody thing's still there,' said Ross, yanking out his phone.

'I'll check with Norma,' said Max, dialling.

'New numbers in Hardie's handset,' Norma said. 'In central Wick. The contact's phone hasn't been switched on yet, so we won't know if it has a new SIM until he powers it on and it handshakes with the network. As soon as it does, I'll call.'

'Great, thanks.'

'Pleasure.'

Max hung up and told Ross and Sue the news.

'Right,' said Ross, finishing his call. 'The closest cop car in Wick is thirty minutes away. They're blue-lighting it now.'

Ross stood up and began to pace. His shirt had come untucked again, his shoe lace untied. 'If they get away,' he muttered, 'we're buggered. The whole bloody thing is fucked. No police boats, no coast guard, nothing. Shit,' he swore again.

'What do we do?' said Sue.

'We wait.' Ross stopped pacing. 'We try and get Hardie, and then we bring in the corrupt, scheming bastard currently sitting in there.' He pointed towards the conference room.

'Why not bring him in now?' said Sue.

'No, let's give him a little more rope to hang himself with,' said Max.

'Aye, good call, you got a plan for that?' said Ross.

'Of course.'

72

HARDIE WAS SLEEPING in his cabin when the door was pulled open. Piotr's massive frame totally dominated the space.

'We need go, now. Come on deck and speak Captain Elrick.' He turned and disappeared.

Hardie shook the sleep from his head and followed the huge Russian up the companionway and into the wheelhouse. A short, wiry man was starting the boat's engine, running checks and preparing for departure. He had an engaging smile, and icy-blue eyes. He was in his forties with the lined skin of a man who spent much of his life outdoors.

'Mr Hardie, my apologies for not being around when you came on board, I had matters I really needed to attend to. We're ready to depart. I've received word that the authorities are on their way and will be here imminently.' His diction was perfect English with a trace of Scandinavian.

'Christ, we need to get going.'

'No need for concern. We're casting off now. If you would, Piotr?' He nodded at the big Russian.

'Can we be followed?'

'No chance. No customs cutters nearby, no coast guard, and the police have no way of tracking us. We'll switch off our geolocator and we'll be all but invisible in a minute or two, particularly with this weather. It may make for an unpleasant trip if you're prone to seasickness.'

'I've no idea, pal. My seafaring experience is limited to a pedalo in the Mediterranean when I was pished.'

The radio crackled on the control panel as Piotr radioed in from out on deck to confirm that he was casting off. The engine note increased as the throttle engaged. The boat gathered speed and was soon gliding out of the marina and into open water. It began to pitch and roll as it met the dark breakers and the impenetrable, driving rain of the open North Sea.

The radio crackled again. Piotr's voice confirmed they were clear. A few moments later Piotr opened the wheelhouse door. Water ran down his yellow oilskin and pooled on the floor. 'Police come,' he said with a grin.

'Fortunate timing,' said the captain. 'You may as well go down below again. The journey is a solid two days, and in these seas, it might be challenging,' he said.

'I want to go on deck and watch Scotland disappear,' said Hardie, looking out the window, back the way they had come.

'Take care, it's rough out there and the deck will be slippery,' said Elrick with a smile.

It was already hard to see the harbour, such was the ferocity of the downpour, but he could just make out the strobing blue light of a police car. A solitary, blue-uniformed figure stood beside it, looking out to sea.

73

MAX COULD TELL from Ross's expression that the news wasn't good. Ross wandered towards them across the marble floor of the reception area. He looked lost. His normally beetroot-red face had paled and there was a faraway look in his eyes. It wasn't anger. More like desolation. A solitary receptionist was sitting behind the counter and a lone cleaner mopped the floor, headphones attached to his head, whistling tunelessly.

'Oh, Christ,' said Sue when she saw Ross. She was sitting on a bench beside Max.

'He's gone,' Ross said. 'Patrol car arrived, just as the boat left the harbour. It's already out of sight because of the hateful weather up there. Fuck,' he hissed through gritted teeth.

'Is there any way to follow him? Coast guard, helicopter, anything?' said Sue.

'Weather's so bad that no one'll go, and there're no government vessels out there. We can put Norway on standby to be ready for them, but their coastline is too big. Can't guarantee he'll stay on the same craft either.'

'So, we've lost him?'

'For now, maybe the Norwegians will get lucky,' said Ross.

'They'll not find him. This was too well planned. But we

still have a chance, right. Are we ready to get him in?' said Max, his voice flat and emotionless.

'Aye, let's go. We've an opportunity.'

'Opportunity?' said Sue.

'Aye, the corrupt bastard has been in that spirit-crushing meeting for bloody ages, without looking at his phone. He doesn't know Hardie's heading into the North Sea,' said Ross.

'How do we capitalise on it?'

'I'm going to interrupt the meeting now with some news, and we see what our corrupt little friend does. Is Norma watching the phones?'

'Like a hawk,' said Max. He wasn't looking at them, instead focusing on a stack of boxes of photocopy paper that had just been delivered. It was being loaded onto a trolley, and the plastic wrapping straps that had been securing the boxes together lay strewn across the floor.

'Right, I'm going to do it now,' said Ross. 'Sue, get your folks ready.'

'On it,' she said, walking away, taking out her phone.

'Max, you watch the car. Be ready for the bastard, yeah?'

'I can do better than that,' said Max walking off. On his way out he squatted by the stack of boxes and picked up a plastic wrapping strip. As he left reception, he folded it and continued towards the car park.

He called Norma as he reached the fresh, chilly air.

'Max, what gives?'

'Shit is about to go down, mate. Watch the phones. Watch them like a bloody hawk.'

74

CHIEF CONSTABLE CHRIS Macdonald was just getting ready to wrap up the Gold Group meeting. David O'Neill had finished with a nauseating diatribe about all having to 'work together collaboratively in a multilateral fashion to ensure accountability to customers'.

Chris had wanted to laugh out loud at the pretentious prick, but just about managed to keep a straight face. Customers? What bloody customers? In policing there were criminals and victims, but no bloody customers. Macdonald was slowly beginning to realise that his time in the police was probably drawing to an end.

But he nodded and grinned at the PIRC manager. 'Thanks, David, very helpful, and also a little inspiring.' He widened his smile. 'Okay, folks, I think that's us, so—'

At that moment, the door to the conference room flew open and Ross appeared, his face flushed, his hair unruly. He waved a piece of paper triumphantly above his head.

'We have him. He's on a fishing boat at Wick, preparing to sail at any second.' Ross was breathing heavily, his eyes shining.

'Good news. Do we have units close?' said Macdonald.

'Aye, closing fast. Should be there in fifteen minutes.'

'Okay, folks, let's cut and run. Looks like we'll be meeting on this again soon. Can you all stay nearby until we have a resolution? We may need some assistance. Ross, can you update me fully, please?' said Macdonald, standing and moving to the far end of the conference room. The other attendees all began to gather their things.

75

THE CONTACT'S HEART pounded as he hurried along, trying not to break into a jog. He passed through reception and out into the car park, turning up his collar against the now heavy rain, looking about him as he did so. Nobody seemed to be paying him any undue attention.

He felt far too exposed making the second phone call in as many hours to Hardie, but he had to warn him. He had no choice. If Hardie got caught, particularly with that handset, it could be game over. His hands were all over the accelerated plot to get him out of the UK. Whilst he was fairly sure he'd been careful, he had enough experience in law enforcement to know that a big team of officers could always find the one thing that would lead back to him. But if Hardie escaped, he was home free.

He approached the classic Jaguar, his key already out of his pocket. It had cost him a bloody fortune on the respray a few months ago, but it looked stunning. He shook his head as he slid the key into the door lock and twisted, feeling the clunky mechanism move. The thought that he had spent too much money in general recently flashed through his mind as he settled into the leather interior. The rain beat a tattoo against the roof. He looked through the window, as rivulets of water carved trails down the glass. His spending was his Achilles heel, he had to admit, but he promised himself that if he got away with this, he would be more careful. He opened the polished walnut-finished glove box and withdrew the burner phone, powering it up. His expensive lifestyle, funded by Colombian cocaine importation, would be hard to explain away. The big house, the classic car, the expensive holidays, all beyond the reaches of his colleagues.

He willed the phone to hurry up and get a signal. 'Come on, you bastard thing,' he muttered under his breath, his eyes glued to the small screen. He exhaled with relief as the signal indicator hit full strength. He dialled the number that was roughly scrawled on his hand.

The phone began to ring.

One ring, two, three, four, five, six, seven. It hit voicemail.

'Shit, shit, shit,' he gabbled, redialling, his hands beginning to shake, his throat dry.

The phone started to ring again.

'Yeah?' Hardie's voice boomed down the line, barely audible above a rushing and whooshing sound.

'Hardie?'

'I can hardly ...'

'Hardie?'

'Hold up ...'

'Hardie?' The contact's voice rose an octave. A vein pulsed in his temple and a small drop of spit flew from his mouth.

Then suddenly the line cleared. 'Sorry, I was outside. It's blowing a bloody hoolie out there, man,' said Hardie.

'You need to move now. The police know where you are and there's a car just ten minutes away,' blurted the contact.

'What?' said Hardie.

'The cops know what vessel you're on. They're coming. You need to go now,' he said.

There was a moment of silence. 'We've gone already,' Hardie laughed. 'We're bloody pitching around in the North Sea, have been for the past half an hour. I saw the cop car pull up, but we were well gone. They've missed us.'

There was a long pause. The contact's brow furrowed. He held his breath, gripped the phone, tried to compute what was going on. What the hell had Fraser been going on about?

'How long ago did you say you left?' said the contact.

'Half an hour, why?'

'Shit, Hardie, ditch the phone,' he blurted and hung up. He held it in his hand and let out a long sigh. His eyes closed.

'Oh, dear. Michael, what have you done?' a voice from the back of the car said.

Michael Jones, the Director of Crime and Financial Investigations, United Kingdom Border Force, jumped in his seat and let out a yelp of alarm. Looking over his shoulder, he saw DS Max Craigie lying down, in the soft leather of the back seats. There was an amused expression written across his features. There was something else about him that Michael noticed too. Something in those cold, flat eyes.

76

'JESUS, YOU SCARED the life out of me. What the bloody hell do you think you're doing in my car? This is going to cost you your job.'

Max said nothing.

'How did you get into my bloody car?'

Craigie held up a strip of plastic packing tape in his hand.

'Thing is, this is a truly lovely old car, but the problem with old cars is security. Just a mechanical lock, nothing this little piece of plastic can't bypass. A car thief in London showed me how to do it years ago. He was a talented man who could get into any car. Pretty amazing, bearing in mind how secure modern cars are. Fortunately for me, you drive this lovely old classic. Almost beautiful in its simplicity. Comfy back here too. I even locked myself in again. Who were you on the phone to, by the way?'

'None of your fucking business. I'm the Director of Crime, and you've no right to be here. I hope you have a fucking warrant. This is my private space.'

Craigie didn't speak, just held up his hand, silencing Jones. He put his phone to his ear.

'Norma?'

A cloying silence filled the car as Craigie listened to what was being said on the phone.

'Thanks,' said Craigie, returning his phone to his pocket.

'Okay, I'll tell you who you were calling. You were calling one of the most wanted men in the UK, a man responsible for multiple murders, who tried to murder my elderly aunt and who, just yesterday, tried to kill me in my own home.'

'You've got nothing. You've got nothing, because I was doing nothing. You're not even recording this, are you? What an amateur operation you and Fraser are running, what a joke.'

'Nope. No need, I'm just here to make a totally legal arrest.'

'You weren't even recording or intercepting the phone call, were you?'

'Nope.'

'Then my solicitor will soon have this all sorted out. I was phoning a covert contact, not Hardie. I've never spoken to Hardie, never met him. You won't find his phone, and there's nothing to find on my phone. You have no evidence against me whatsoever, and if Hardie's fled, you've even less than you think. Now, get out of my car.' Jones reached for the handle and opened the car door, his jaw fixed with a smug grin. Rain poured in, pattering against the leather seats.

Craigie yawned. He stretched and began to chuckle.

'Didn't you hear me? Get the fuck out of my car, or I'll call the police.'

'Go on. Call them. I'll wait, I'm very comfortable in here.' Craigie's grin widened.

Suddenly, the other car door flew open and Jones was

grabbed by his lapels. DI Ross Fraser pulled him forcefully out of the car, expertly spun him around, and slammed him onto the bonnet. His hands were painfully wrenched behind his back, handcuffs snapped into place.

Ross Fraser's mouth was right by Jones's ear. 'As my cockney friend Max would say, you're fucking nicked, my old son.'

77

MICHAEL JONES SAT next to his solicitor, a lean man wearing a well-cut suit, and a sombre tie. He was tapping at a laptop computer as Max Craigie inserted two DVDs into the recording machine.

'This interview is digitally recorded. I am DS Craigie, also present is?'

'DI Fraser,' muttered Ross. He was sitting next to Max, a paper cup of tea in front of him together with a packet of biscuits.

'I'm interviewing, can you introduce yourself, please?'

'Michael Jones, Director of Crime, UK Border Force,' Jones said, his voice low, his eyes fixed on the Formica-topped desk.

'You are also legally represented by?' Max paused, looking at the solicitor.

'Daniel McLennan, from McLennan and Smith Associates,' he said in a cultured Edinburgh accent.

'Okay, Mr Jones, I'm going to interview you about the offences you've been arrested for. You're not obliged to answer, but if you do, your answers will be tape-recorded and noted and may be given in evidence. Understand?'

Jones nodded.

'For the recording please,' said Max.

'Understood.'

'Mr Jones, you were arrested today for assisting an offender, conspiracy to murder and conspiracy to import a class A drug. I'd like to give you the opportunity to explain to me your role in this conspiracy.' Max looked up from his legal pad, and fixed Jones with a baleful stare.

McLennan cleared his throat. 'I would like to read a prepared statement on behalf of my client, on the basis that this is a highly complex and serious allegation, and I do not believe that sufficient disclosure has been served upon me, limiting my ability to advise my client. *I, Michael Jones, deny any allegations of collusion with the escaped prisoner Tam Hardie. I have never met, nor spoken to or, indeed, had any contact with Hardie. I went to my vehicle today during the Gold Group meeting to speak to a covert contact in relation to my role as Director of Crime. At no time did I have any dealings with Hardie. I have no connection to the importation of controlled drugs into Loch Inchard, nor leaking information that resulted in the deaths of the two NCA agents, Callum Mackintosh and David Hamilton. I believe I have been corruptly targeted by Police Scotland, and no evidence has been disclosed to me that justifies my public and violent arrest. I will make no further comment.*'

McLennan passed a handwritten document across the table to Max, who read it slowly before setting it down. Max stared at Jones, but he wouldn't meet his gaze.

'Thank you for this. Most helpful. I'd now like to play a piece of authorised surveillance footage that was shot by an operative, today, of the first visit you made to your car. To remind ourselves, this was after the first disclosure by DI Fraser at the Gold Group meeting, at which you were an attendee, that Hardie was believed to be hiding in Wick.'

McLennan interjected, an irritated tone in his voice. 'I've not had disclosure of this.'

'I know. Why not watch, eh?'

'I will require a consultation after it has been played.'

'Fine,' said Max.

He opened an iPad and pressed the screen. A pin-sharp piece of video began to play, clearly shot from within another vehicle. Michael Jones jogged across the car park and climbed inside the Jaguar. He rummaged around for a moment, then waited, before eventually raising a phone to his ear. The camera zoomed in on Michael Jones as he made a phone call, his mouth moving rapidly, his brow furrowed. The sky was steel grey, the rain only just starting to fall, and the depiction of Jones's face was clear.

'Sorry, what are we looking at, here?' said McLennan.

'We'll let it play through,' said Max.

The phone call ended, and then it seemed that a further call was made. That soon finished and Jones got back out of the car and jogged across the car park and out of sight.

'Who was that call to? Mr Hardie?'

'No comment.'

'What did you say during that call?'

'No comment.'

'Ross, anything you want to add?' said Max.

Ross shook his head. 'Nah,' he said simply and took a sip of his coffee, his eyes fixed on Jones, hard as steel.

Max produced a piece of paper and read from it. 'I have

a phone record here which shows that the phone you had in your possession when you were arrested made a call into a handset which we believe was used by Hardie. This handset was earlier used to make a call to a Turkish Cypriot registered number that was cell sited very close to an area where, we have evidence to suggest, Tam Hardie's family are currently living. We suggest that you called Tam Hardie.'

'No comment.'

'Did you call Tam Hardie?'

'No comment.'

'Officer, if this is all you have, then I'm afraid you have miscalculated. There's no evidence that my client was calling Hardie. You are unable to prove what my client said during that phone call. My instructions are that he was talking to a covert contact, which he is unable to share with you, as it's classified information. So, do you have any further evidence?'

There was a long pause, as Max sorted through a sheaf of papers. Ross unwrapped the pack of biscuits, the plastic rustling loudly in the tense silence, and selected one, inspecting it with relish. He dunked it deeply in his drink. Jones and his solicitor seemed almost mesmerised as he pulled the biscuit out and raised it to his lips, slurping as he popped it in. He chewed noisily, a look of satisfaction on his meaty features. The solicitor screwed up his face in distaste.

Max found the piece of paper he had apparently been looking for. 'We have a record of another call into another number that we believe was used by Hardie, following a SIM switch between handsets. You do realise, Mr Jones, that we can tell each and every SIM card that has been in a particular handset?'

'No comment.'

'It was the same number presently scrawled on your hand right now, which we have also photographed. We have all this evidenced, Mr Jones. All of it. You were calling Hardie, weren't you?'

'No comment.' Jones's eyes were drawn to the smudged and barely legible number on his hand.

Max smiled, slowly, and handed over another piece of paper, which McLennan accepted. 'This is a witness statement from Elspeth Marchbank, a registered forensic lip reader. She has fully transcribed that telephone conversation here for you to read. Of course, you'll be able to have your own expert view this footage to confirm Mrs Marchbank's conclusions.' Max sat back, his eyes never leaving Jones.

McLennan looked briefly at the statement. He swallowed, adjusted his tie.

'I'd like the interview suspended. I need to consult with my client,' he said, quietly.

'Ross, anything?'

'Nah,' Ross said, his gaze still fixed on Jones.

'Fine, take all the time you need. Interview suspended.' Max switched off the machine and ejected the two DVDs, which he quickly sealed. He offered them to Jones, who scrawled on both.

Max and Ross stood and left the room, leaving Jones and McLennan alone.

The solicitor turned and faced Jones.

'You're screwed. It's all over.'

78

HARDIE SLEPT HEAVILY, despite the constant pitching and rolling of the seiner. He woke to a loud banging on his door. Groaning, he rolled over to see Piotr standing in the entrance, clutching a large mug of tea. His huge, Slavic features split in a wide grin.

'Tea, Mr Hardie. Captain like to see you. We are good progress, and the sea has calmed down.' He handed the steaming mug to Hardie.

'How long have I been out?'

'Eight hours or so. You tired, no?'

'Aye, cream-crackered, pal.'

A confused furrow stretched over the Russian's brow.

'I mean, yes very tired.' Hardie sipped the strong tea.

'I go back up. You come soon, yes?'

'Aye, pal, five minutes.'

The Russian left the tiny cabin.

Hardie yawned, and sipped his tea again, thankful that the boat was now far more stable. He was surprised that he hadn't succumbed to seasickness on the rough passage and felt a ridiculous sense of pride at the sea legs he seemed to possess.

Hardie left the bunk and crossed the minuscule corridor, through a door which led to an equally tiny bathroom. He yawned again as he used the toilet, making a note to ask if there were any toiletries available. His mouth tasted like the bottom of a parrot's cage, his skin itchy with sweat and grime. He was sure that he didn't smell too good either.

He climbed up the small companionway, and was soon back in the wheelhouse. Elrick smiled at his arrival, his hand on the wheel, looking ahead at the large expanse of open sea.

'You slept well, Mr Hardie?' said Elrick. His eyes twinkled with amusement. It suddenly occurred to Hardie that the man's face was somehow familiar. He frowned at the lean-looking seafarer.

'Very well, thanks,' said Hardie. 'Have we met before?'

'I don't think so,' replied Elrick, turning his attention to the instruments in front of him.

'How long?' said Hardie, staring out of the wheelhouse window.

'Long as it takes. The sea is being kind, but things can change at a moment's notice.'

There was something in Elrick's voice that Hardie didn't like. The English accent with just a trace of Scandinavian had changed slightly, become a touch rougher, almost Scottish. It was odd, but maybe he was imagining things. Hardie's face darkened, as he watched the man, searching for a tell, sifting through his memory. The seaman stared at the open sea ahead of him. There was an uncomfortable feeling in the small wheelhouse, and Hardie suddenly felt claustrophobic.

'I'm going outside for some air,' he said.

'Take care, the deck will still be slippery,' Elrick said, with a strangely pointed tone.

A prickling sensation began to niggle at Hardie as he

stepped out on deck. He sucked in a lungful of icy wind and spray. The boat cut through the frigid waters of the North Sea, its bow rising and falling, inky black ocean for miles beneath them. He couldn't put his finger on it, but something wasn't right, and he had survived this long by paying attention to those feelings.

He breathed deeply, drinking in the smell of the sea, trying to organise his thoughts.

He looked towards the stern of the small vessel and stopped in his tracks. Shock hit him like a smack to the face. He reached out and gripped the railing.

Land.

There was land behind them, just a few miles away. Land he recognised. He took in the cluster of buildings and the three massive oil rigs.

A mixture of fear and anger gripped him when he realised where they were. They should have been eight hours closer to Norway, in the middle of a vast expanse of sea by now.

They were about four or five miles off the coast of Cromarty on the Black Isle. He had recognised it almost immediately, because they had travelled up here only last year, visiting some family in Fortrose. He had taken the kids on a dolphin-spotting sea trip from Cromarty Harbour, and he had seen this exact view from the rib.

He suddenly realised that he was no longer alone on deck. Elrick and Piotr had emerged silently behind him. They stood and stared at him, their faces unreadable. His normal reaction would have been one of violence, but he was way outside his comfort zone. He had no chance against the two tough-looking sailors, and there was nowhere for him to run.

'Don't hand me over to the cops, please,' said Hardie, his voice low. 'I can pay you both. I can make you very rich, just take me somewhere safe. I just want to rejoin my family.'

Neither man spoke.

'Please—'

'Don't waste your breath. We don't want your money,' said Elrick. Even as fear took hold of him, Hardie realised that Elrick's accent was now completely a soft Caithness one.

'Who the hell are you?' he said.

'Bruce Ferguson. You may remember me from a few months ago. You had my brother and my cousin murdered, and you tried to kill me. Ring any bells?'

Then he remembered. He had seen the man before, even if it was just his face in some crude video footage, and a grainy photograph. His insides turned cold, realising they were not planning on returning him to Scotland and into the hands of the authorities. Money wouldn't save him now.

With almost breathtaking speed Piotr's arm shot out and grabbed the loose fabric of Hardie's jacket. He pulled him close and wrapped a bear-like arm around his body, trapping him in a vice grip. Hardie struggled but could barely move. The man's other arm closed around his neck, trapping him like a rodent in the grip of a constrictor snake. Hardie tried to struggle, but the more he moved, the tighter the hold became. He felt his lungs fight for air.

'Please?' he gasped.

'Now isn't the time to plead. You didn't give my brother and cousin the opportunity to plead, did you? You tried to kill Max Craigie, a man I respect immensely, and held his elderly aunt at gunpoint. In short, I think the world will be a better place without you.'

'Please?' he tried again, but only a hoarse whisper escaped his lips.

'"The Deil's awa wi' the Exciseman",' said Ferguson.

Hardie's brow furrowed at the mention of the Burns poem, which he had heard just months ago after his father's murder.

'The feud ends here. My ancestor killed your ancestor because he was a bastard corrupt exciseman. No more feuds, no more murders. Yours will be the last.'

Ferguson stepped forward, fixing something around Hardie's ankles, snapping it into place. The deck of the boat pitched and bucked with the waves, and the ozone smell of the sea was almost overpowering. Hardie always knew this moment would come. He knew he'd never make old bones, but he hadn't imagined he'd go out like this.

Ferguson picked up a heavy anchor from the corner of the rib and hefted it to the side. Without hesitation, he lifted it and dropped it overboard, into the heaving, pitching sea. It rattled as it fell away from the boat, sinking into darkness, the weighty chain snaking down after it, leaving a trail of bubbles in its wake. Time seemed to slow down as Hardie watched the metal anchor disappear, listened to the chain clank against the guard rail like fingernails against a chalkboard. He felt a sharp tug as the chain played out and stopped with a jerk, the weight trying to pull him after it. Only the immense strength of Piotr stopped him from being dragged over into the impenetrable grey water. The weight of the anchor and its chain tore at his legs, and it felt like his bones were going to snap. Piotr grunted with the effort of holding him still. The boat pitched and groaned, and a sudden gust of wind threw spray onto the deck drenching them in icy, salty water. Hardie gasped.

'Please …' But nothing else would come. His chest was too tight, his throat too constricted.

Ferguson produced a mobile phone and pointed it at Hardie, nodding at Piotr. Hardie's vision started to blur. Piotr, as easily as if he were tossing a large fish, threw Hardie off the boat. He gasped in a huge lungful of air as he hit the icy water. Panic exploded in his chest. He tried to fight the weight of the anchor, swirling around in the sea. Freezing, salty water filled his mouth and washed over his tonsils. He coughed, bobbed up for one last time and sucked in a final breath. Spluttering in panic, he felt the heavy steel chain tighten and he sank below the surface again. Hardie lifted his arms and looked up at the light above him as he plummeted. The anchor continued its descent, dragging him with it, down into the black abyss.

79

MAX ARRIVED BACK home, exhaustion descending on him like a weighted blanket. He unlocked the door, Nutmeg deliriously gambolling around his legs, and walked into the house, switching on all the lights.

He went straight to the kettle, desperate for a proper coffee, after what seemed like days of drinking instant. He ground the beans and scooped the aromatic powder into the portafilter, slotted it into place and powered up the machine.

It seemed like he had been at work forever. There had been further interviews with Michael Jones, who had made limited admissions once he'd realised the strength of the evidence against him. He had been charged just a few hours ago. There would be mountains of paperwork and liaison with the Procurator Fiscal, but they were already suggesting guilty pleas and looking for reduced charges.

Michael Jones was finished. His career over and a long jail sentence coming his way. A massive importation of pure cocaine had been seized which would cause ripples in the drug smuggling community for many years. Scally and his crew were all remanded, and the case looked like a slam dunk, even though no one had pleaded guilty. The wheels of the criminal justice system kept on turning, albeit slowly.

Gifford, the corrupt prison officer had been arrested, the evidence overwhelming, and suspended pending further inquiries. He'd lose his job, and almost certainly was staring at a prison sentence.

Lenny Farquharson was now fully on board with the prosecution, trying to lessen his sentence by offering evidence against anyone he could think of. He was locked away in a secure location. Someone else's problem now.

But Max felt none of his team's elation. There was nothing to celebrate. Hardie was gone. Escaped. Free.

'Fuck it!' Max yelled in the empty room, making Nutmeg cower.

'Sorry,' he said, calling her over and sitting on the floor, stroking her shaggy ears. Max's phone buzzed in his pocket. It was Norma.

'Don't you ever go home?'

'I was just tidying the phone data. I ran Hardie's phone again, and some funny shit has been happening.'

'And?' said Max, not in the mood for Norma's mystery games.

'Well, when he fled, his phone was still on. It then dropped off the network, presumably when he got too far away to hit a cell mast, right?'

'Yeah, so?'

'Well, it came on again.'

'What?'

'About four hours ago, it hit a cell tower in Cromarty on the Black Isle. You know it, right?'

Max suddenly felt cold. The Black Isle. His thoughts turned to Elspeth, but how? Why would he come back? His mind reeled.

'Well, it was only on for a few minutes, then it disappeared off the network. I don't think it was powered down, and neither does the telephone unit.'

'What does this mean?'

'His phone was near enough that cell tower to hit a mast. That's all I can say.'

Max digested this.

'Thanks, anything else?'

'No, mate. I'm going home.'

'Good idea, see you tomorrow,' said Max.

His phone rang again immediately. This time it was Sue Brown.

'Yeah,' said Max.

'I'm not sure what this means, but *Odin* was discovered several miles off the coast of Cromarty by the coast guard. No one on board, just drifting.'

'What?'

'I know. Want to know something else?'

'I'm not sure,' said Max, his head swimming.

'The real crew of the *Odin* was discovered by Wick cops, handcuffed inside a boatshed, just a few hours ago. They said that a couple of scary buggers grabbed hold of them, secured them and pissed off in their boat. They're both dodgy bastards, so aren't cooperating, but it doesn't make sense.'

'Jesus, can this case get any madder?' said Max.

'We're looking into it. The boat is being searched and forensically processed now, but no bugger has a clue what happened.

They could have got onto a new craft to muddy the waters, but I doubt it somehow.'

'Why?'

'The boat owners are believed to be smuggling drugs and also people trafficking. They aren't cooperating, but we think that they're the ones employed to get Hardie out.'

'So, what happened?'

'God knows. We're all going to the pub. You coming?' said Sue.

'I'm good. I'm bushed.'

'Okay, mate. Good work. Chief is delighted. We're watching North Cyprus to see if he turns up, but there's certainly something funny going on.'

'Okay, cheers.' Max ended the call. He stared down at Nutmeg, who returned his gaze, her tail thrashing wildly, delighted that he was home.

Max's phone buzzed once again, an email this time. The familiar series of numbers, characters and letters were in the address box of the message. Max swallowed. He opened the email and his stomach leaped at the poem written there.

The deil's awa the deil's awa,
The deil's awa wi' the Exciseman,
He's danc'd awa he's danc'd awa
He's danc'd awa wi' the Exciseman.

Max sighed when he saw that there was a video clip attached. He opened it, his heart in his mouth.

The clip was brief but it told Max everything he needed to know. Hardie was being restrained against the handrail of a boat by an enormous man, whose face was pixelated. Hardie wasn't small, but he looked like a child in the giant's grasp. He was struggling, gasping for breath. A heavy chain was secured around his ankles, pulled taut, the other end disappearing over the side of the boat. In a flash, the big man tossed Hardie into the sea. The camera moved to the side of the boat and pointed at the water. Hardie's pale face could be seen, a white spot growing smaller and smaller by the second, as he plummeted down, swallowed up by the darkness. Max closed the email and it immediately disappeared from his inbox. He checked his trash bin, but it wasn't there, either. He had no doubt, whatsoever, that there would be no evidence on his phone, or his server, that the email had ever existed. It was as untraceable as Tam Hardie, former head of the Hardie crime family, now little more than a pile of bones on the bed of the frigid North Sea.

Max sat on his sofa, sipping coffee. He closed his eyes, relishing the smooth, rich smell. A smile spread across his face. It was finally over.

He had one last phone call to make, then he was going to bed, to sleep for a month.

Max dialled, his eyes beginning to close, exhaustion sweeping over him.

'Max, babe, are you okay?' the voice of his beautiful, caring, wonderful wife.

'Hi, Katie.'

'Max?'

'Yeah?'

'Is everything okay?'

'Everything's okay. Will you come home?'

'I would love to. Is it over?'

'Yes, it's finally over.'

Acknowledgements

AS ALWAYS, HERE we are having written 'The End' at the conclusion of writing about ninety thousand words, that I hope you all enjoyed as a right old ripper of a story.

Whilst I've plugged away on my own to get this tale out of me and onto the page, making it into a book that you the reader can enjoy takes a much bigger effort.

Huge thanks, therefore, go to a number of people who really helped all this happen.

My agent, Robbie Guillory, who has kept my feet on the ground, encouraged me, thrown ideas up the flagpole and taken a bird's eye view to make this story as good as it can be. I'm glad you're on my side in navigating this treacherous old business which is publishing.

To everyone at HQ who has taken this from the semi-legible ramblings of an ageing ex-cop through to a proper book. My editor, Finn Cotton, is a master at his job, despite being annoyingly young. His editorial insight is absolutely vital to the process, and without it, this book wouldn't be anything like the finished product that I hope it is.

To Sian and Jo for getting this book out into the big wide

world so that people will hear about it, and hopefully part with their cash for it.

Colin Scott. For the shits and giggles, sage advice and inspiration. I genuinely wouldn't be doing this without you.

Huge thanks also go to Marian McNally, consultant anaesthetist at Raigmore Hospital on helping me to be accurate on anything medical. I'm glad that your family all appreciate a local crime writer asking questions that may otherwise seem a bit odd.

To my big, crazy, raucous family for all the laughs and encouragement. Knowing how proud you all are makes this worthwhile.

To Clare. Just for being you. Love you always.

Alec, Richard and Ollie. This book is for you, dudes. You rock.

To all the booksellers, book bloggers, bookstagrammers, buyers, festival organisers and those who write about books and writers. You are the guys who get the books out there and into the hands of readers.

To all my brothers and sisters wearing the blue serge. I'm six years away from policing, but my admiration for you knows no bounds.

And last but definitely not least. You, dear reader. Without you, what is this? A book is nothing without a reader apart from some paper glued together with a bit of ink. You're the ones that matter.

Neil

If you loved *The Blood Tide,* don't miss this exclusive early sneak peak from Book 3 in the Max Craigie series…

MAX CRAIGIE 3

Title and cover coming soon!

Remain silent.

A lawyer vanishes one morning on a lonely cliff top at Dunnet Head on the northernmost tip of Scotland. It was supposed to be his honeymoon, but now his wife will never see him again.

Do not resist arrest.

The case is linked to several mysterious deaths, including the execution of a gangster who was recently acquitted of murder. DS Max Craigie knows this can only mean one thing: they have a vigilante serial killer on their hands.

Do not try to escape.

But this time the killer isn't on the run; he's on the investigation team. And the rules are different when the murderer is this close to home. He knows their weaknesses, knows how to stay hidden, and he thinks he's above the law…

1

SCOTT PATTERSON YAWNED as he left the dark streets of Edinburgh and drove towards the leafier suburb of Ravelston. It was pitch black, dry and cloudy, and the city was deserted this early in the morning.

His head felt heavy after spending the evening with some pals in a nice pub in the centre of town. He'd drank champagne, smoked a joint, and snorted a line of Charlie, so whilst he probably shouldn't have been driving, he was hardly drunk. He was, however, knackered after a whirlwind of emotions and celebrations. A few days ago, he'd been given a 'not proven' verdict at the High Court. He'd gone from facing a life sentence in Saughton Jail to freedom, and it was all a little hard to take in. He settled with pleasure into the soft leather seat of the BMW X5, and yawned again. Time to go home and continue getting reacquainted with the wife.

His phone buzzed on the seat next to him. He picked it up and looked at the screen, his eyes widening as he saw the name of the caller. Jackie McLennan. *The* Jackie McLennan. A man to be feared and revered in equal measure.

'Jackie, my man,' he said.

'Scotty, I just heard. You're out of Saughton and dinnae tell me, eh?' a rough Edinburgh accent barked in his ear.

Jackie was a serious face from the Edinburgh underworld with fingers in all sorts of pies. Scott hadn't seen him for a while, but then he hadn't seen anyone after almost a year on remand in Saughton Jail, awaiting trial for a rather nasty murder.

'Ach, you know. Been busy, catching up with my lady and my boys.'

'Aye, I guess. So, a not proven then. You jammy bastard, how'd you pull that off, eh?'

'Innocent as a wee lamb. The cop in charge got fucked by my lawyer, and the rest is history. What a shame, eh?' he guffawed.

'Fucking Teflon-boy, you are. Rumours were, you were bang-to-rights for a life stretch.'

Patterson opened his mouth to retort, but paused, distracted by movement in his rear-view mirror. A big, dark car suddenly pulled out of a side street. It was accelerating hard to catch up with him. Within seconds, it closed the distance until it was only a few feet from his bumper. Its bright halogen headlamps pierced the darkness, flooding his car with blinding, white light. Scott was a man of the world, and a car that close, with its lights on full beam, meant only one thing.

Trouble.

Either a cop car, or worse, a rival gang. The cops didn't bother him too much. He had a gram of coke in his pocket, and a small knife in the door of the car, but he could either ditch those before the cops pulled him, or just brazen it out. Worst case, if it was a lone cop, he would intimidate the life out of the bastard. Scott was used to doing that. At well over six feet tall and close to eighteen stone of solid muscle, it wasn't hard. A tooled-up rival gang was a different matter altogether. He'd made plenty of enemies in his years as a gang enforcer for hire, and he was always ready for trouble. His hand gripped the phone, his eyes dropped to the door pocket where he was reassured to see the glint of the lock knife.

His jaw set tight, and he growled softly, under his breath. No one fucked with Scott Patterson. Not the cops, and certainly not some wee gadgies wanting to make a name for themselves.

'I'm gonna have to go, Jackie. I've got company.'

'You okay?'

'Aye, someone on my tail. I'll call you later.' He hung up without waiting for a reply, hoping Jackie wouldn't be offended.

Then it happened. He watched in the review mirror as an arm came out of the pursuing car's window. It clamped an oscillating blue light on the roof.

Fuck. Cops. Even worse, not regular cops, but a covert specialist unit by the look of the car, a decent-sized SUV with a covert light. They probably had him under surveillance, but he was sure he hadn't seen anyone. Only been out a few days and the bastards were already trying to fuck him over. Anger flared in his chest like sudden indigestion.

Patterson floored the powerful BMW and roared off, gathering speed along the long straight road. The cop car accelerated too, but Scott was making good ground. Seeing the junction ahead he swiftly turned right onto Strachan Road, heading towards Ravelston. He mashed his foot to the floor again. The BMW screamed as it sped along, tyres protesting. Soon the streetlights ended, and he found himself on Ravelston Dyke Road. It was a dark and lonely stretch, lined with woodland on either side. The cop car briefly disappeared, so he quickly lowered the passenger window. Reaching into the door pocket, he tossed the lock-knife out over the low wall and into the woodland, closely followed by the small wrap of cocaine. He checked his rear-view mirror, to see the pursuing cop car screech back into view in hot pursuit, blue lights strobing and flickering through the surrounding trees.

He smiled to himself, his confidence rising now the contraband was gone, and he was certain they couldn't have seen him ditch it. If they were CID officers, they'd never have a breath machine with them and they'd certainly never have a field drug test kit. If he made enough of a fuss, they'd probably leave him alone. Police manpower in this bit of Edinburgh was shite, and they'd have no desire to wait for ages with an angry Scott Patterson. They were almost universally fucking cowards.

As quickly as he'd accelerated to get away from the pursuing police car, he stamped on the brakes and pulled to the side of the road, just past the entrance of the empty car park of Ravelston Golf Club. He sighed, totally relaxed now. He chuckled to himself, his eyes glued to the rear-view mirror.

The cop car stopped close behind him, almost touching his rear bumper, headlights on full beam, the pulsing blue light blinding him.

'Jesus suffering fuck,' he said to himself, flipping the mirror up to avert the beams of light. Turning to the wing mirror, he saw the cop car door open, and a shadowy form step out. Through the glare he could just see the cop's Hi-Viz ballistic vest as it began to move towards him. Cheeky bastard, he thought. He was going to make his life a misery.

He'd only seen one person get out of the car. Whoever it was had made a big mistake.

Paterson decided that he was going to stay put. The fucker could come to him. He turned the music up and began to scroll through Facebook on his phone. The photos from his celebration a few days ago were there, and he grinned at the pissed carnage that had ensued that night.

A full minute had passed before he looked up again. The lights were still burning into the back of his car, but there was no sight of the cop. He killed the music and squinted, trying to see what the hell the pig was playing at. Was he trying to freak him out?

He looked down at his phone again, but he couldn't concentrate. Something tickled at his subconscious. He'd been stopped by cops a million times, and they always approached the car. They were usually all over him like a cheap suit. Suddenly, the cop car's headlamps and blue flashing light died, and the BMW was plunged into darkness.

'What the fuck?' he murmured, wishing that he hadn't tossed his blade.

He looked at the car behind him. It was quiet and inert in the gloom, as shadowy and ominous as the night itself. He leaned out of his open window and strained to hear, but his engine was too loud. He pressed the ignition button, and the BMW fell silent. Everything was suddenly shrouded in darkness. The only sound was the engine ticking as it cooled, and the soft breeze whispering through the trees. The silence was almost physical in its intensity. He flinched at a rustling noise from the edge of the woods beside his car. He swivelled his head towards it, his eyes wide, but could see nothing through the deep, impenetrable blackness.

'Fuck this for a game of soldiers,' he said, opening the door and stepping out, pulling himself up to his full height, muscles tensed, massive shoulders squared. 'What the fuck is going on?' he bellowed towards the car. Nothing. He felt a prickle along his spine as he waited. There were no other cars, no one else on the street. At that moment, the full moon broke through fast-moving clouds and a shaft of light hit the car, bathing him momentarily in a pale glow. Long shadows crept across the road and then vanished into the trees as the moon disappeared.

'I'll have my fucking lawyer on you bastards?' he shouted, his voice loud, but without the furious anger of before. He walked up to the silent cop car that was black enough to melt into the night. There was no sign of a blue light on the roof, and nothing on the dash. What the hell was going on? Despite the cool autumnal air, a bead of sweat ran down his spine. His heart thudded. He swallowed and turned towards his car.

As he strode back, he glanced around once again. Nothing. He tried to stay calm as he peered through the still-open door of his vehicle. The interior light was on, illuminating everything in a soft glow. It would be fine. He would just drive home and forget this ever happened. But he couldn't escape the feeling that he was missing something.

Then he saw it.

His car key had gone. It was no longer in the slot next to the steering wheel.

Paterson groped around in the footwell, hoping it had fallen onto the floor, but after a moment, he stopped. He stood up, blinked, balled his hands into tight fists. His nails dug into his palms as he took a ragged breath and his insides turned to ice.

'Where the fuck are you?' he yelled, but he sounded scared.

His words were quickly swallowed up by the surrounding trees and the deep, velvety night.

There was a faint cackle of laughter behind him. The snap of a twig under a boot. Patterson froze. He turned slowly, looking into the undergrowth for the source of the noise. Something moved, came out of the dense trees, a slow-moving shadow, only just visible. He gasped, sucked in a lung-full of air.

The shape approached, one arm outstretched, clutching something.

Scott Paterson cried out in terror and turned to sprint into the darkness.

He ran for his life.